A LADY on the CHASE

WYCLIFFE
FAMILY
BOOK 3

JESSICA SCARLETT

REDWING PUBLISHING

OTHER TITLES IN THE WYCLIFFE
FAMILY SERIES:

A Lily in Disguise
A Lord of Many Masks
Managing Mary

Dedicated to the readers who loved Matthew from the beginning.

And to Matthew Wycliffe. Don't tell Peter and William, but you've always been my favorite.

Swoons

CHAPTER 1

Sussex, England
1818

THERE WAS NOTHING QUITE AS TAXING AS BEING THE CENTER OF everyone's attention. Especially when I was noticed for the wrong reasons—which tended to happen frequently, much to the chagrin of my family.

Haughty sneers and greedy gazes decorated a room whenever I entered it, tracking my movements with a religious obsession. *There goes Lady Alicia, the bane of England, the breaker of convention and the embarrassment of her father. Whatever will she do next?* Sometimes I wished I'd been born into more obscurity, if only to get a moment's peace.

And what I wouldn't give for one right now.

"Lady Alicia, how well you dance," said Lord Hawthorne as he led me off his ballroom floor, his light brown hair bouncing every time he shook his head at me in adoration. A harp plucked lilting notes while couples moved to the packed sidelines and new ones replaced us, lining up for the next set. The air smelled of sweat, starch, and something cloyingly sweet; like decomposing roses. "I don't know that I've danced with anyone so light on her feet. I imagine you dance much like how a swan would."

While I was not ungraceful, I was not an exceptional dancer, either, and I hardly warranted his comparison. Despite this, I'd been whisked onto the floor time and again since walking into the great, marbled hall, never once having an opportunity to occupy my seat.

All night, I'd smiled and twirled and refrained from doing anything that would draw more attention to myself—something like stomping on my partner's toes, dashing toward the window for a breath of fresh air, and then scouring the crowd for the one person I actually came here to dance with.

So far, I'd refrained. But acting rashly grew more tempting by the minute.

Stealing a peek at my reflection in a gilded mirror hanging on the wall, I loosened one of my blond ringlets. "So you have partnered with a swan before, my lord?" I said dryly. "What an adventure that must've been."

"Yes, it was—er—no, it wasn't. That is, I've never danced with swans—that would be ridiculous! But at any rate, you are, of a certainty, the best dancer in the room."

"The best? I should hardly think so. There are at least three others better, I am sure." I said the words with mild interest, but the truth was, I'd already tuned Lord Hawthorne out. The man hadn't stopped paying me compliments since the evening began. And while flattery was nice to hear, it bordered on vexing when you only received it because your favor, fortune, or hand in marriage was being sought.

Lord Hawthorne continued to babble as we wove through the crowd, passing under pillars that extended up into a balcony before branching out like decorative, golden trees. His hand pinched his cravat, bringing to mind the memory of how he'd fiddled with it all through our minuet. It was an ostentatious little thing; pale orange silk, and embroidered with white flowers that I only noticed because he wouldn't stop fingering them.

"I did spend an entire afternoon one summer observing the swans on the lake of my estate. They did a strange maneuver with their wings—" He reared his arms back to show me, which twisted my elbow since it was still linked in his. His other hand smacked a lady's coiffure, making a few of her beads plink and scatter around the floor. Those closest to us gasped. "Oh, I beg your pardon," he said to the woman, whose eyes were wide. His hand hovered around her hair for a few moments as if to pat it, but then he seemed to think better of it and steered me in the opposite direction, steps quick. Clearing his throat, he said, "Anyway, the birds were very beautiful. But somehow threatening, too."

"Much like how a lady dances." I gave a subtle tug on my arm in an attempt to claim it back, in case he tried to wield it again.

Missing my unironic tone or choosing to ignore it, his grip tightened in excitement, preventing my escape. "Quite so! A woman stepping so close creates alarm of the highest proportions! And a pity it is too dark, or I would take you outside and show you the swan's exact movement. There is insufficient space to do it within the crowd, just now. But yes, your dancing does remind me of them."

Ahead of us I glimpsed my seat, where my aunt, a mass of gentlemen, and a well-earned reprieve from Lord Hawthorne's rambling currently waited for me. I breathed a sigh of relief. "Well, my lord, it has been a pleasure—"

"In fact," the man went on, "your grace is so unparalleled that I would like to solicit you for a second set. I simply must experience the enjoyment of being your partner again."

Oh, no. I was certain I could not endure another dance with him chattering on and toying with the orange silk around his neck. Throughout the night, I'd dropped as many clues as I dared that I wasn't interested in his attentions. I was exhausted from my hints being ignored—particularly since I received more than my share of his company when he called on me at home.

When I didn't immediately respond, his hand reached for his cravat yet again, fluttering around it like a swarm of moths. Perhaps he'd thought to impress me with the expensive fabric, but at this point my only thoughts toward his cravat involved a pair of scissors and a large bonfire.

"But, if you are too tired to continue, my lady, I should much rather spend the *entirety* of the evening in your radiant company. Seated beside you, I'll not encounter a dull moment! Perhaps we could even continue our discussion on swans—"

"Another dance would be splendid." I quickly stepped in front of him, making him halt. "But Lord Hawthorne, I do believe there is something amiss with your cravat!" If subtle hints wouldn't drive him away, perhaps something bolder would. And he *did* just reveal how alarming it was to be so close to a woman. Before he could respond I reached up and inspected the knot with my hands, making certain to brush my fingers against his neck.

His mouth fell open and for the first time tonight, he was silent.

I grinned. "Ah yes, there is a smudge right here. No wonder you have been fussing over it! Do let me fix it for you." Without asking permission, I retrieved a handkerchief from my reticule and began dabbing at the imaginary stain. Taken aback at my sudden proximity, he made no move to stop me, even though more eyes were noticing our scandalous behavior and a few gentlemen had appeared at our side.

Drat, this was drawing all the wrong kind of attention. Again.

But I had tried to be patient, hadn't I? And at this point, the opportunity to rid myself of the man before me was worth the price.

"As I was saying," I went on, scrubbing harder and ignoring the murmurs passing half a dozen lips, "standing up with you again would be a great honor. Oh, but my feet feel rather sore just now. Perhaps in a few hours they shall feel better. But then your ball is likely to be over, so that does put us in an unfortunate predicament."

Noting the way he watched me with complete rapture, I took my time smoothing the cloth down and adjusting until it was back in its place. Stepping back, I smiled admiringly at my handiwork. "There, sir. Now that is a sparkling cravat, if I do say so."

He blinked in a daze. Then he opened his mouth to speak, but only a light, wheezing sound came out. He tried to swallow, then reached up to loosen the knot.

Before he could, I sandwiched his hand between my own and turned to one of the gentlemen that had congregated around me before I'd even made it to my seat. "You, sir, do you not agree? Isn't Lord Hawthorne's cravat so becoming on him?"

The gentleman, a fellow with a square jaw and a shadow of a mustache, smiled, pleased with the attention I'd paid him. "I quite agree, my lady."

"I say, Lady Alicia, how did you notice a stain like that?" another man said, a lazy smile spreading across his handsome features. I couldn't recall his name, but remembered that he was known around the *ton* to be a rake. "Weren't you looking at the man's eyes?"

He thought himself clever, but I only smirked back at him. "It isn't my fault, sir, that cravats happen to be at my eye level. It is unfortunate I was not born shorter—then instead of being doomed to notice a man's neckcloth, I might've had the pleasure of noticing his shoulders." Chuckles spread through the group.

"Then perhaps you might be persuaded to dance with me," the rake went on, tilting his head suggestively, "and tell me which of *my* features you notice first."

I cocked an eyebrow. *If it would send the lot of you away, I would.*

By now Lord Hawthorne had finally managed to give his knot a bit more slack, and while tugging at the fabric he said, "Here now! Lady Alicia had just expressed to me how sore her feet were—we should find her a chair, not force her to stand here and notice things."

At this, two of the men scrambled away in search of a proper seat. I raised my chin and folded my arms, aware of the covetous looks shooting at me from a dozen female eyes. While the men were often *too* friendly, I preferred their company over the women's. Experience had taught me that jealousy was often an insurmountable barrier in a friendship, and I had more than one scar on my heart to show for it.

I fingered the beaded bronze lace trimming the seams of my cream evening gown—probably one of the reasons I'd received so many introductions tonight. Dressed as elegantly as I was, I knew I smelled of money, and even in the countryside there were plenty of fortune-seekers.

I scoured the mass of bodies for the one person who could grant me my escape. Not seeing him, I returned my focus to the dozen men around me who were arguing over who would dance with me next. They were a sorry lot indeed. Often childish and trite.

Most of them were younger sons—men who'd been produced as a spare in case their elder brothers died, and now served no purpose but to drink and gamble and hope to marry a woman whose dowry would pay for it. They were desperate enough for money that they were willing to overlook my scandals. Some were tall, some were short; some were handsome, most were not. Some had traveled all the way from the northern coast, and some lived only a few miles away in Brighton. But even with such a wide assortment of men, there was one trait which they all shared:

They were all equally forgettable.

None of them desired a true connection. They were here to flirt, smile, and shower me in compliments until I swooned at their feet and begged to be their bride. Then once they finally got their prize, they would return to maligning me, or ignoring me, or finding every opportunity to leave. Eventually, they would realize that they never cared about me to begin with. Not in the way that truly mattered.

Surrounded by a sea of people, I felt more alone than ever.

Lord Hawthorne—who was *not* a younger son—turned to me, beaming. "Lady Alicia, I plan to call on your father in the near future. Perhaps you would tell me your favorite flowers so I might bring them when I visit?"

I bit my tongue. Apparently my flirtation earlier hadn't completely appalled him—probably because he got more than enough support from my father, whenever he called at Lawry Park.

Hoping he would take the hint, I sidled up to the nearest gentleman. Knowing the handsome rake wouldn't take my compliments seriously, I linked our arms and stared lovingly up at him. "Cornflowers are my favorite, Lord Hawthorne—for they are the exact shade of Sir Hasting's eyes. Oh, but I could drown in them!"

Lord Hawthorne's hopeful expression dampened, and the other men began voicing their protests.

"But Lady Alicia, have you not seen my eyes? They are twice as handsome at least!" "Cornflowers cannot be your favorite—"

"Sir Hastings does not even have blue eyes!"

A flash of blond hair stole my focus, his familiar gait steady and unobtrusive. He came from across the room, a soft message in his gaze that I would've inquired after, had we been alone. Voices all around continued to caress me, but they were drowned out by him winding his way through the crowd, unnoticed, until he was close enough to slip me a small piece of paper and then disappear from sight.

Henry.

Heart beating fast, I glanced around, pretending to be interested in what one man was saying, and then another, nodding and smiling at the appropriate times until I found the opportunity to quickly read what was in my hand.

Meet me on the balcony at eleven.

I inhaled and tucked the piece of paper into my evening glove before anyone noticed. My eyes shot up, scanning the direction he'd gone until I found the back of him, moving across the floor unseen by all but me.

And, thronged in by grinning gentlemen, I watched the only gentleman I actually cared about retreat to the balcony overlooking the ballroom, wishing the clock's hands would move faster.

CHAPTER 2

I WAS LATE.

Now, after having finally found the opportunity to slip away, I lifted my skirts and scurried up the stairs, my excitement mounting with each step.

To pass me a note amid a throng of admirers was a romantic gesture—one which I'd been expecting from Henry for the last three years. I'd never said as much, and neither had he, but there was a certain level of expectation that came with sharing jokes, smiles, trinkets, and looks across a ballroom—to say nothing of an entire childhood together.

Oh, I had so many hopes. My hands were shaking.

When I reached the landing, I glanced down the hall to find him leaning against the railing, smiling softly at me. I approached.

He was the perfect man. Thoughtful, gentle, impossibly good. I'd never heard him utter a cross word in his life. He'd seen me through the hardest days of my life, and I wanted him to be there for the rest of them, too.

"Well, Henry," I said, stopping before him and forming a teasing smile, "I hope you did not summon me here to show me swan-like maneuvers."

His white teeth gleamed in the candlelight when he chuckled. "I see Lord Hawthorne insisted on gracing you with his charm again."

"Yes, I daresay he twisted my arm." Quite literally. "I was glad to receive your note, as it promised me a respite." I cocked my head and glanced up at him through my lashes. "But that isn't the only reason you asked me up here. Is it?" I couldn't help the hopeful note that entered my tone.

Henry shifted. "I did notice your need for rescue, but you are right. It was not the only reason." He rubbed the back of his neck, smile receding and eyes darting between me and the floor.

I sucked in my lips, trying to tame the giddy butterflies whirling around in my stomach.

I'd spent the last few years dreaming of the day I'd hear my childhood friend, Henry Crawley, utter the four words that would launch my happily ever after. And on this night, on a balcony over-looking a glittering ballroom, the next four words that passed Henry's lips made my heart stop, and then trill a nervous beat. They made my childhood flash before my eyes, and my future press in with dizzying expectancy.

"I've joined the military."

Every hope, every carefully laid plan I'd ever made ripped out from under me. I let the nervous fist scrunching the scalloped gauze overlay of my dress fall to my side. Head swimming and limbs weightless, I blinked at him. "You've what?"

Perhaps I heard him wrong. I *must've* heard him wrong. Below, couples swirled around the dance floor and reveled in their refreshments, oblivious to the mortification I was experiencing a floor above.

Grasping my wrist, Henry led me behind one of the pillars of the balcony that lined the ballroom, shielding us from wandering eyes. He clasped his hands behind his back. "My brother purchased me a commission in the Regulars, and I've just received my orders.

I'm to report for duty on the twenty-second, after which they will ship me off to India."

India? Father had recently passed legislation in the House of Lords that approved a whole regiment of soldiers to be sent to the country; something about an anti-war effort. Was Henry part of that regiment, then? Quickly, I did the math. Nineteen days. Nineteen days until he would embark on a journey which would lead him halfway across the globe.

I shook my head, mind still trying to process the overwhelming news. This couldn't be happening. This night couldn't be going so horribly awry. Henry was not a military man! He was too genuine, too good. Too soft on all accounts. The picture of him in uniform was so subtly . . . wrong. Like a tickle in my ear, or the feel of wearing two left shoes.

When Henry had passed me the note, I'd assumed it was because I looked radiant, and he'd finally woken up to the fact that he was in love with me. That I was in love with him too. I'd assumed he meant to offer himself, and that I would leave Lord Hawthorne's ball an engaged woman.

I'd already had three Seasons. Any more, and I was in danger of being labelled a spinster—and Henry, still bafflingly blind to my feelings, had joined the Regulars?

I shook my head, searching for words—any words. Why was he only telling me now? When had this happened? Was he happy about this sudden development? Could I change his mind? No? Yes. Yes, I had to make him change his mind.

"I know what you're thinking," he said.

My eyes snapped back to him.

"You have your scheming face on. You wish me not to go and are thinking of ways to keep me here."

A lifelong friendship granted him the ability to read my expressions—a talent few possessed. I swapped my "scheming face" with one more penitent, trying to conceal the fact that he'd guessed me correctly. "But Henry, think of your future! What of your prospects, and relations? What of England being your home? What about—what about finding a wife and settling down?"

"I shall miss this place dearly. And I admit, finding a proper wife will be devilishly hard once I'm out of the country."

I sighed. "There now! You see? You must stay."

"But even if I did, no one would have me. I'm only a baron's penniless second son."

Is that truly how Henry saw himself? Worthless? Beneath my notice? I took in his straight blond hair, grey eyes, and fine figure. No woman on earth could say he was unattractive. And while his clothing was modest, he bore them with great regality.

He shook his head. "I'm not like you, Alicia. No one cares if I marry well."

A new thought struck me, filling me with dread. If he saw himself as far beneath me, then had the thought of marrying me—a duke's daughter and heiress to a considerable fortune—never even occurred to him? Had it been so far out of reach that he'd never considered it? My pulse raced with panic. Here I'd been all these years, stupidly waiting for something that hadn't even entered his head.

The match would be lopsided, to be sure, but not unsuitable. And even if it were, hang it all! Being a duke's daughter had some benefits, and one of them *ought* to be marrying the man I'd loved all my life.

"I care." I clasped his hand. "I care a great deal." With timid movements, I interlocked our fingers. "And I happen to know of one high-born lady in particular who would not be averse to you courting her . . ."

He smiled wanly, reclaiming his hand. "Miss Hayfield does not count."

I frowned. I inhaled but he went on before I could declare myself like an unconventional, besotted fool.

"I know it's not what you were expecting, but the military will suit me well." Chin lowering to his chest, he added, "It is a fitting profession, for someone of my station."

Of his station? For the last time, who had put this silly notion into his head?

My thoughts ground to a halt. Of course. Father or Aunt Beth must've spoken to him and warned him away. Nothing else could explain this sudden shift. I went rigid, ready to insist they were wrong, to tell Henry it didn't matter what my family said, that he was my equal in every way—but faltered when I saw the look on his face.

His eyes were tinged with regret, and the grim line of his lips told me he meant to leave, regardless of what I said about the matter. In this, he would not be persuaded. I'd never seen him so set on anything.

A feeling of helplessness clawed at my stomach, carving out a gloomy cave where I would live alone for a thousand years, with only the sound of my dripping tears to keep me company. "But . . ." I said in a small voice, ". . . but what of me?"

Henry set his hands on my shoulders and looked deep into my eyes. "You, Alicia Kendall," he said softly. "You, I shall miss most of all."

I hated the tenderness in his voice, and how it felt like a goodbye. Shaking my head, I fought down the tears. I didn't want to accept it. I couldn't. "You shan't leave. Not without me."

Henry's lips parted and he blinked in quick succession, perhaps in an effort to push down tears of his own. I was not making this easy for him—but I didn't care. All I cared about was getting him to stay.

"You cannot come with me, Alicia."

"Why not?"

"Hang it all." He laughed under his breath, hands sliding down to rest on the top of my arms. "I know you and I wouldn't put it past you to actually try. Fine then, let us wager on it."

We always wagered on things. It was something we'd done since finding that seashell on the beach when we were nine. We'd done it so many times, I'd lost count of who had won the greater amount. But to wager on this—this felt too real, and the stakes were too high.

"If I go to India alone as planned," Henry went on, a sad twist to his mouth, "you shall have to give me your left glove."

That was the other thing about our wagers—the prizes were never monetary; they were only ever random, innocuous items. A yellow ribbon, hair powder, a gold chain, a single horse hair from Cressida's tail, a teaspoon of snuff, an empty spool, watches, wild-flowers, hand bells, and candles—all of them had been risked at some point. There were too many to list. And if Henry were to really ship away, wagering with him was a tradition I'd have to forgo, probably forever. The knowledge made my heart twist.

I folded my arms. "And if *I* manage to slip onto the boat, we shall force the captain to turn around, and you shall move back to England. For good."

Henry sighed and dropped his arms to his sides. "Alicia—"

"You *cannot* go!"

"I shall still be here another three weeks—"

"And that should console me? We might as well say our good-byes now!"

Henry fell back a step, expression wounded. "You cannot mean that."

I didn't. I swallowed. "I do. If you're really going to leave, then I have no wish to see you." It was pure pride that made the words slip off my tongue—that, and a stupid, blind hope that he would change his mind if I only made him feel guilty enough.

Taut silence stretched across the next few moments. Henry's eyebrows sloped upward. He took another step back, then another. At last, he nodded and murmured, "As you wish," before turning and retreating down the hall of the balcony. When he disappeared, I spun around and watched him slowly descend the stairs, and, ultimately, exit the ballroom.

I gritted my teeth against the remorse, determined to quash the urge bouncing in my feet to run after him. The power to attach himself to me—forever—was completely in his hands. If he wanted to propose, he was free to do so.

And why didn't he? I was fully aware of how he looked at me, and of how many times he'd reached out to touch me only to hesitate and pull away at the last moment.

Why did he always pull away?

With one hand I rubbed away some of the pressure building in my temples, sighing. For now, I should return to the ball and fulfill my promise to stand up with Lord Hawthorne again. Though his cheery company was an ordeal, it was far better to get the dance over with than spend the evening living in dread.

After glancing around to ensure no one else had witnessed mine and Henry's spectacle, I breathed a sigh of relief at the deserted balcony.

Wait, no . . .

Down the hall, there stood a man leaning over the balcony, forearms resting on the railing, hands clutching a book. Only a small part of his face was visible in the candlelight, but I didn't recognize him. He was oblivious to the gaiety below, more absorbed in his hard-back book. Maybe he hadn't overhead mine and Henry's conversation? But no. We had been much too loud.

Father would berate me for being involved in yet another scandal if this man were to go spreading rumors about me. Whether or not they were true. Drat it all, I'd have to grovel and beg for his discretion.

I cleared my throat, subtly trying to get his attention. The man didn't look over. I sucked in my cheeks and cleared my throat louder, but his eyes never strayed from his book, his face obscured in the shadows.

Surely he heard me? I looked around, debating what to do. I walked forward. "Sir?" I said to his profile.

Still, there was no response, and yet I stood only a few feet away. Why wasn't he answering me? "Sir?" I repeated louder. "*Sir?*"

"Yes, I heard you." His voice surprised me. Soft, deep, and . . . thoroughly disinterested.

"Excuse me?"

"I said, 'Yes, I heard you,' though since you need me to repeat myself, it appears it is not my hearing you should be questioning, now is it?"

My lashes batted in disbelief and my mouth dropped open, a bit of breath escaping in my shock. I tilted my head to the side, trying to get a better look at his face, but it remained hidden. "You heard me? Then why did you not react, sir?"

He looked up at the ceiling. "By all England, must I spell it out for you?" Returning his gaze to his book, his voice took on an annoyed quality. "One would have to be either deaf or stupid to miss the conversation you and that Crawley fellow were having, and since I am neither of those, well, we can assume that *yes, I heard you.* And since it was a rather embarrassing exchange, what with you practically throwing yourself at the man, I should think you'd desire anyone who had overheard it to ignore you. I—out of the benevolence of my heart—was most willing to do just that, yet now you are forcing me to do otherwise. If I were being completely honest, it's somewhat aggravating that you would rather be here disturbing my peace and demanding my attention when half the men downstairs are stampeding over themselves to dance with you. And while I am presently much more stimulatingly preoccupied."

My mouth dropped further and I scoffed, eyes widening. How dare he dismiss me so rudely. And he was reading as he did so! All thoughts of groveling before this man flew out the nearest window. "I *beg* your pardon?" I said. "Nerve? Demanding your attention?"

"Ah, here we go." He licked his thumb and turned a page in his book. "Here is the part where you call me all sorts of names. 'Arrogant' seems to be a favorite, but it's redundant and a tad cliché at this point so I'd suggest something else. Something more demeaning like 'pontifical' would do nicely. And then, once you've exhausted your vocabulary—which usually happens relatively quickly, for your type—you shall stomp your foot and storm away, muttering angrily along your way. Then if you happen to see me in the future, you shall turn and gossip to your friends, saying, 'That was the man who wounded my pride, when all he wanted in the first place was to be left alone.'" He heaved a long-suffering sigh. "This pattern is getting rather tiresome. Let's hang tradition and skip this part, shall we?"

I scoffed again, eyebrows plunging. "How dare you?" I cried.

"I guess we're not skipping it, then."

"How dare you, sir? You cannot dismiss me at the wave of your hand—"

"To be fair, I did not wave my hand."

"It does not matter if you waved it or not!"

"On the contrary, to say that I did implies a boorishness with which I have not yet treated you. It inadvertently draws a parallel between me and tyrants like Caligula and Robespierre—which, admittedly, is a bit extreme, don't you think?"

"Yes—no—!" Oh, he was mixing me up! My face scrunched, stare hardening. Who was this strange, rude man, and why was he attempting to teach me a lesson in philosophy? "Who are you?" I demanded.

"As I said—you really ought to pay more attention—I am a man whose only wish is to be left alone."

"*Who are you?*"

He closed his eyes and let out another long, heavy sigh. Then he opened them and at last turned his face away from the shadows, toward me fully. My frown deepened.

He was handsome.

No, not just handsome. He was *beautiful*.

From beneath a wavy, dark head of hair looked rigid blue eyes and perfectly full lips unused to smiling. Maintaining eye contact only amplified his suffocating air of assertion and condescension.

He was very tall—perhaps even taller than Henry—with a lean physique, though not without muscle. He took me in as well, eyebrows raising a fraction, unimpressed. "I am a man you should not underestimate," he said at length. "Far too many do."

Unsatisfied with his answer, I lifted my chin. "Well, I will forgive your insolence this once, as you obviously do not know who I am—"

"Lady Alicia Kendall. Daughter of the Duke of Cabourne and heiress to a considerable fortune."

I rocked back. "You know of me?"

"Unfortunately."

Working my jaw, I stepped up to him. "Then you know my father is powerful, and I pity the man who spurns his family and incurs his wrath. Now what is your—"

"I don't understand this fascination with my name." He snapped his book shut and straightened. "And you could have only one of two motives for discovering it. The first is that you wish to report me to your father as you have threatened, starting malicious rumors about me and further scorning me from society. The other possibility is that you are completely enamored of me and are contemplating a pursuit. If the first, then you already know society cannot possibly scorn me more than I have scorned it, but why the devil would I assist you in the endeavor? And if the second . . ." He paused, looking me up and down again. "Well, I decline."

Conceited man!

What a shame such a face belonged to this reprehensible character. One who was despicable and patronizing and contemptible and arrogant and—! My mind halted, angry at myself for falling into his trap. He'd predicted I would call him names, and now I did.

"Nay, I decline," I said.

His face remained immovable. "You misunderstood me entirely. I never offered."

That did it.

"I did not mistake you, but merely wanted to put you at ease that such was never—and never would be—my aim. Mr. Crawley and I disturbed your peace a moment ago—and I can pretend to summon some sympathy for you, if you wish, as I can see you are *deeply* wounded—but that is no reason to dismiss me, yes, *with a wave of your hand.* And I hadn't the slightest inclination to bring my father into this. I only wanted to know who on earth could justify themselves behaving in such a way toward a lady."

One of his brows twitched, almost with a hint of curiosity. But the rest of him remained frozen, making me question whether I saw it there or not.

My eyes narrowed. "Now for the last time, who are you? I demand to know your name, sir."

I expected something else in his face to change—and it did, slightly—but contrary to what I was accustomed to seeing after such a speech, it was not repentant. It was determined.

He watched me for a silent moment, then stepped toward me, leaning forward so far I heard my breath catch and my head had to inch back against the railing to keep him in focus. He was so uncomfortably tall, and he was close enough now that I could smell something on his clothes. Pine.

His head cocked to the side, expression still infuriatingly lifeless and indifferent. "By all means, my lady . . ." he whispered, almost tauntingly, ". . . demand away."

Then he turned and again leaned on the balcony, reopening his book. "Now if you'll excuse me, I have better things to do with my time than chatting with an offended debutante."

My blood boiled, face red with embarrassment and anger. I glanced around, huffing. And when it was clear I was to get nothing more out of him, I stomped my foot and stormed away, muttering angry words along my way and not caring that I had just proved the hateful man to be right.

CHAPTER 3

AN HOUR LATER FOUND ME SITTING IN MY CHAIR, ALONE WITH my aunt and still fuming at the encounter.

For the moment, the horde of men had dissipated. Under my skirts, I rolled my ankles, trying to relieve my feet from the soreness that had been building with each exhausting dance.

"How did your meeting with Henry go, dear?" Aunt Beth asked disdainfully from the chair beside me, not quite covering her smirk with her fan. The jewels of her gaudy necklace twinkled under the chandelier, making me squint when she turned my direction. She'd obviously seen Henry slip me the note, and had deduced the rest.

"Atrociously." I folded my arms. "Why send a letter telling me to meet him in secret tonight if it did not involve anything romantic?"

"So he told you his plans, did he?"

My eyes narrowed as I studied my aunt. "You knew he had joined the military."

She sniffed. "Of course. I know everything there is to know about everyone."

I stamped my foot. Luckily for me, the dance in the center of the floor was a lively quadrille and disguised the sound. "Aunt! You should've told me, for you could've saved me a world of embarrassment."

Her fanning sped up. "While I would never go out of my way to sabotage your relationship, I can do with my information as I see fit. Henry is beneath you, and he is wise to scamper off. Shows he knows his place."

My mouth—for the third time this night—hung open. So I'd been right. Aunt Beth had warned him away. "Henry is a gentleman, and the son of a baron. I daresay he is ten times the man of other characters I've met this evening."

That caught Aunt Beth's interest. She snapped her fan closed. "Oh? And who has earned your wrath this time?"

I bit my tongue on the memory, choosing to ignore my aunt's patronizing tone. "He refused to tell me his name. Gentleman indeed!"

"Point him out to me, dear. I'm sure I could tell you his identity."

It was rude to point, but after the way the man had treated me, I had a hard time summoning manners of any kind. My eyes strayed to the balcony, and sure enough he was still there, leaning on the ledge and reading his confounded book.

"Up there," I said. "On the balcony."

Aunt Beth followed my gaze. She squinted at him for a long moment before her face cleared in recognition. "Ahhh." The word climbed a mountain and sledded down, as if now Aunt Beth understood my foul mood completely.

I leaned forward in my seat. "Well? Who is he?"

She didn't answer right away, a smug smile crawling onto her lips. "That, girl, is Mr. Matthew Wycliffe."

An obnoxious name for an obnoxious man. How fitting.

The sound of his name seemed to reverberate through the air. A few pairs of eyes darted toward us before darting away. Noticing it, I glanced back up at the brooding man on the balcony, re-weighing him. Something tickled the edge of my memory. "Wycliffe? You mean—"

"Yes," Aunt Beth said, "he is the younger brother to Lord Wycliffe."

Younger brother. Not half as important as he pretended to be, then. "It is a wonder he should go around acting so pretentious. Surely the brother to a viscount doesn't earn enough of a salary to do naught but read books all day."

Aunt Beth leaned over and whispered behind her fan. "On the contrary, my dear. When the late viscount died, he left Mr. Wycliffe a small sum and an estate here in Sussex, where Mr. Wycliffe currently resides. It is my understanding that his family—especially his late mother—wanted him to go into the church, or the military. To which he quite infamously stated that the church was too boring, and the military too much *effort*."

She scoffed. "However, he has quite a head for business—used his inheritance to embark on several ventures and investments. Each of them has been wildly successful. Men of society watch him closely, and if Matthew Wycliffe invests in something, the rest of the *ton* scramble to snatch up the shares. Without fail, they profit. The man *is* a genius. Perhaps it is from his extensive knowledge of the market—or of everything, for that matter—but in truth, no one knows how he does it. His success has been so enormous, in fact, that in regards to fortune, his wealth has greatly surpassed that of even his brother's."

So. Handsome *and* wealthy. My dislike of Mr. Wycliffe doubled.

Aunt Beth continued. "He is what you might call, 'New Money.' Yet, with his titled relations and noble blood, one cannot quite lump him in with all the other insolent social climbers. Quite the opposite, in fact. He's somewhat of a novelty."

"I cannot imagine why." My lips screwed up. "Did you know that throughout my whole encounter with him, not once did he show any sign of being human? As stone-faced as a statue he was, even while he insulted my attributes."

"I wasn't aware you had any." Aunt Beth cocked an eyebrow.

Though I was sure my aunt was half serious, I chose to ignore the jab altogether. I was used to such comments—from without my family, and from within. Venom filled my mouth, eking out in my voice when I said, "If gossip can send poor Henry scampering off to the Regulars, why hasn't Mr. Wycliffe received his share of censure for his manners? Surely I am not his only victim."

"Certainly not. As you can imagine, his wealth has made him a target for eager young ladies. But I daresay they are wasting their time, for he is notorious for snubbing his admirers. And one must continue to overlook his unpolished manners because he is, after all, rich as Midas."

I huffed. "What is the world coming to, when not even *good manners* can be expected of a gentleman? Nay, not a gentleman, but a cad—and so I suppose good manners *cannot* be expected."

Aunt Beth's fan lowered. "Bite your tongue, girl. He is looking this way."

My eyes shot up to the balcony, where Mr. Wycliffe's gaze pinned me to my spot. Though there was no way he heard me, I flushed in the knowledge that somehow he knew what I had said. Our eyes met, and it surprised me when he did not immediately look away. When at last he did, it was not in embarrassment, or smugness, or *anything*—only that he'd had his fill and had grown bored.

I folded my arms across my chest. "If he is going to while away his time in a secluded corner, why bother coming to a ball at all?"

"He attends perhaps only three or four functions a year. The man's a staunch recluse. No one knows when he'll venture from his house and deign to make an appearance, or why. But if he *does*, it is a compliment of the highest order and you can wager his presence will send shockwaves through society. Why, tonight I've heard talk of little else since he stepped through the door. Like it or not, Mr. Wycliffe's opinion carries great weight in higher circles.

"Regardless of the function, he is always invited. And of course there are dozens of young women who want his fortune, and must have their opportunity to chase him."

I gave a derisive chuckle. "I cannot imagine why anyone on earth would voluntarily resign themselves to his company for one night—let alone a lifetime." A maid passed by, offering a tray of punch in glass chalices. I accepted one eagerly, parched from all the dancing I'd done.

Aunt Beth shrugged. "His fortune is *enormous*. If his being the most well-connected man in society and his excellent breeding are not compelling enough factors, he is unquestionably one of the handsomest men in England. His recommendations are so impressive, in fact, that even your father would be hard-pressed to find fault in him, if you were to secure him."

I choked on my punch, barely managing to keep it from sloshing onto my dress and staining my shimmering cream ball gown with purple splotches. "Aunt, how could you suggest such a match? I would not marry that man if he were the Dauphin himself! He is brash, rude, and nothing like Henry. Just let him *try* and woo me."

CHAPTER 4

I LOOKED AROUND, UNFAMILIAR WITH THE CRAGGY STRETCH OF bluffs that I stood upon. The light was dim; neither sun nor moon shone in the sky. Down the cliff, a woman stood on the precipice, skirts billowing in the wind, blonde hair strung about her face. I couldn't make out her features, but I knew she was hauntingly beautiful, looking at me with the knowledge of eternity. I wanted to call out to her, but the intense, wind-filled quiet tied my tongue.

She was not here for me.

A blackness, thick like fog, crept in on the edges of my vision, crawling up over the cliffs. It slunk across the ground, devouring everything in its path. Trees, grass, flowers, rock. Nothing was exempt.

The shadows veered, swarming toward the woman. They were going to consume her—there was nothing I could do but watch in horror.

I opened my mouth to scream. "Mo—!"

MY EYES FLEW OPEN AND I SAT UP IN BED, CHEEK DAMP FROM some drool that must've slipped out while I slept. Using the sleeve of my nightgown, I wiped it off, wishing I could as easily wipe away the dark images of the nightmare that had plagued me for years. Blinking, I looked around my room, wondering what had woken me so suddenly. No knock had sounded on my door and no maid had entered.

Then I heard it again: my father's laugh, drifting faintly upstairs from the breakfast room. After a week-long excursion, he'd apparently returned to Lawry Park.

I threw off my covers and jumped out of bed to ring for a servant. After dressing me, the abigail took my hair out of its rolls and pinned it in a high chignon, and I barely restrained myself from wringing my hands through the whole routine. Father's stiff chuckle came again, this time accompanied by Aunt Beth's voice. I silently urged the girl to hurry.

My father was never home, and my father never laughed. And good news for my father was never good news for me.

Once she finished, I grabbed the shawl draped over the great chair in my room and dashed down the stairs. As I entered the breakfast room at a brisk walk, my father said, "Ah, Alicia. We were just talking of you."

We?

From behind my expectant father stepped a young gentleman, all spiky brown hair, broad teeth, and shiny buckles. I repressed a groan. Bad news indeed.

"Good morning, Lady Alicia," Lord Hawthorne said with a massive smile.

I looked to Aunt Beth, who lounged at the table. She wore a garish yellow silk and an amused twitch upon her wrinkly lips. One of her silver slippers tapped against the shiny lacquered hemlock floor, waiting for my response.

When would they ever stop scheming?

I turned back to the man. "Good morning, Lord Hawthorne. How fortunate we are to have your company. Again. For the fifth time this week."

"My mother always says I ought to be more neighborly," Lord Hawthorne said. Then, seemingly for my father's benefit, he turned to him and added, "She's devoutly religious, you know."

Yes, she certainly was. Lady Hawthorne often refused to talk of anything else. And having such a spiritual benefactor in his life was one of Lord Hawthorne's many "amiable qualities," or so my father kept telling me.

Since Father had no sons, when he died, his title as the Duke of Cabourne would pass to the closest male relative—which happened to be Hawthorne. Hawthorne's great-great grandfather was a Kendall, and so he would inherit Lawry Park.

To marry him would not only be advantageous, but infinitely convenient, since I would be mistress of my childhood home and Father would pass all his wealth along to his family instead of some backward stranger. Because of these facts, Aunt Beth and Father kept inviting Lord Hawthorne over, in the hopes that an attachment might blossom between us.

The agony.

My circumstances could certainly be worse—he could be a rake, or a drunkard. Though his smile was overused, he was charming enough, and not bad-looking. But he was also ridiculous, and only pursued me because someone had put the idea into his head that ours was a match destined to be made.

Because of it, I could never seem to get a moment's reprieve from the man. He was everywhere I turned.

From behind his back, Lord Hawthorne produced a bouquet of purple-blue flowers and held them out to me. "I hunted the north field for these cornflowers, my lady, as you said they are your favorite. Do you like them?"

He waited for me to take the bouquet, bouncing on his toes. Father and Aunt Beth's faces looked on with approval. I frowned and chewed the tip of my tongue, not wanting to encourage the man any more than I had to. Finally, I took the fragrant flowers and sniffed, before announcing, "I like them, my lord."

He smiled and breathed a sigh of relief.

I handed them back to him. "But not nearly as much as I would've liked daisies."

His smile dropped. Father's lips pinched, but before he could comment, I plowed on.

"*Daisies* are actually my favorite flowers. But of course, I only tell that to my close acquaintances, so it is understandable you did not know."

Hawthorne's eyebrows sloped upward. He glanced at the flowers in his hand, like they had betrayed him. "Oh . . . my apologies. I had thought—that is, *last* time you said your favorites were—"

I waved my hand. "It changes regularly, my lord. So regularly, that if you were to leave in search of daisies this very moment, by the time you returned it would have changed to kingcups! So you see, it is likely you shall never bring my favorites. Best to do away with bringing flowers altogether."

His expression plummeted.

In the sudden, taut silence, I studied my father and Aunt Beth in turn. The gray and white that peppered Father's otherwise dark hair, his dark eyes. Aunt Beth's mouse-brown locks and shrewd countenance. My father's stern face, drawn in a perpetual scowl, and Aunt Beth's sharp eyes and ever-smirking mouth.

I knew they were disappointed in me even without the tell-tale signs—but what was I to do? It was far crueler to encourage Hawthorne—do as they wished—when I'd never accept his proposal.

Father snapped his fingers angrily and one of the footmen took the bouquet to find a vase. In an attempt to rescue the conversation, Father smoothed his features and cleared his throat. "Hawthorne just stopped by to show me some sketches his man made for new tenant houses." He resumed a hopeful expression.

At the sight of it, I grimaced. It was unseemly the amount he smiled around Hawthorne—all approval and enthusiasm for what-ever the man said.

Lord Hawthorne saw my grimace, mistaking its cause. "Do you not approve, my lady? The new homes would provide better accom-modations for the tenants."

I sauntered to the sideboard, helping myself to a piping hot cup of tea, and a buttery roll coated in apricot jam. "Oh, sir! I am a woman and therefore know nothing of such matters. But for the sake of conversation, what will these designs of yours improve?"

Out of the corner of my eye, I saw my father tense.

Lord Hawthorne seemed taken aback, but he recovered. "The fences, particularly."

I took a thoughtful bite of the roll, still chewing when I said, "I hardly think new fences would help much when they live in such squalor. Don't you think greater access to soap and water would better suit? I'm happy to say my father's renters aren't in such a state, but some lord's tenants are practically living in their own excrement."

My father's jaw clenched. And it was not in anger over the treat-ment of some tenants.

Aunt Beth's hand flew to her mouth, admonishing me for more than just my comment; that I would justify crudeness in order to dissuade Lord Hawthorne. "What a revolting thing to say, girl," she chided. "Care you nothing for propriety?"

"Not in the least," I lied, sliding into a chair halfway down the long table. "Nor care I much for the poor, apparently. I suppose for that reason alone, I could never marry a vicar. Or any man whose mother is devoutly religious, come to think of it." Ignoring my father's red face, I took another delicate bite of my roll.

Lord Hawthorne's smile faltered. He fidgeted with his topper and cleared his throat a few times. "Well, I have a few more errands to run, so perhaps I should take my leave. It was wonderful to see you again, Lady Alicia." He bowed to each of us in turn.

"Give my best to your mother."

Lord Hawthorne turned back to see me blink innocently. He fidgeted some more before nodding and finally disappearing through the double glass doors.

"Alicia, why can you not hold your tongue?" Father fumed once he'd gone. "Headstrong. Foolish!"

"Don't lose your temper, Rupert." Aunt Beth stood, gathering up her shawl.

Father sputtered. "What she needs is a good whipping!"

I continued to sip my tea. Father always got into these raging fits of empty threats, but they usually subsided after a few minutes with no harm done. Aunt Beth poured her own cup before settling in a dining chair farther from me.

Father dropped into the head seat and picked up the newspaper resting on the gleaming silver tray before him. He brooded in silence for a few moments before twisting the paper into a stick and slamming it on the table.

Overlooking Father's outburst, my aunt said, "Have some perspective, brother. Alicia will have little motive not to cooperate soon, since you-know-who is leaving."

I slapped my cup on its saucer. "Aunt!"

Aunt Beth gave my father a meaningful look, and at the sight of it, some of Father's steam dissipated. Nothing else could've cooled him down so quickly as the thought that even if I didn't marry Lord Hawthorne, at least I would not marry Henry.

Five days had passed since the ball. I kept waiting for Henry to come crawling back to me, but every day there was no post, and every day he did not visit. Doubt had begun to creep in; a fear that this time, unlike all other times, I could not sway him.

Henry had been by my side since we were children, stealing the turkey legs from the platter when no one was looking and slipping under the table to devour them in between our giggles. The memory brought a panicky feeling to my stomach. I wouldn't know what to do without him.

I took a deep breath, reminding myself that nothing was

settled until the final approval of recruits at Brighton, in two weeks. If it hadn't been for Mr. Wycliffe, I might've gone after Henry at the ball and convinced him to see reason. In fact, if it weren't for Mr. Wycliffe, I'd have spent this last week devising an adequate strategy, instead of brooding over the encounter on the balcony.

I swatted the annoying thought away. "I don't wish to talk of Henry," I announced, nudging my plate forward. "Neither of you have ever given him a chance." Ignoring the way my second sentence nulled the first, I instead fixed them both with a hard glare.

Aunt Beth laughed. "Why would we ever give the second son of a baron a *chance?* And where it concerns you, Henry has already shown his *stripes.*"

The pun was not lost on me, and I scowled. Blast the Regulars and Henry's ghastly determination to be one of them! "Henry is confused," I said, standing. "But whether you like it or not, I am going to be his wife."

Expecting them to voice their usual, adamant disapproval, I sucked in my cheeks. Instead, both Father and Aunt Beth held their peace. They exchanged a look that made my insides squirm like a can of worms.

I glanced between them. "What?"

A servant entered with a vase for the cornflowers and set them on the sideboard before opening one of the big windows. Cool morning air swirled at my feet. Father sat and threaded his hands on the table. "Lord Hawthorne has, this morning, solicited me for your hand in marriage."

My knees buckled and I collapsed back into my chair. Through the open window, birds twittered a cheerful song, mocking me. The servant left.

"Marriage."

"You've given me little choice, Alicia. You know the position I am in, in parliament. It was my proposal they passed to send troops to India to prevent war. But the Peerage can hardly take me seriously when I have a daughter upending society left and right.

"My plans to send those troops aid in autumn is quickly losing support because word has spread through the House of Lords that I cannot even control my own daughter. And I've a mind to believe they're right."

Father leaned forward onto the table, eyes were heavy with defeat and disappointment. As usual, I gave no sign of seeing it—and ignored the sting I felt whenever I saw it there. Which was altogether too frequent.

I cast my head down. At the very least, I took some comfort in the knowledge that none of my scandals involved intimacy with a man. Such a scandal was the pinnacle of humiliation. It would break both my father and society in one fell stroke.

"Lord Hawthorne's mother harbors deep objections to the match," Father went on, "and justified objections, with the way you carry on. Three Seasons with nothing to show for them but a series of embarrassments. Yet, despite his mother's stern disapproval, the man is unaccountably, hopelessly smitten. He could have his pick of the Peerage daughters, and he has chosen you."

I stared blankly at my plate of food, appetite gone. "And I am to feel flattered by this?"

"Indeed you should. The marriage contract has already been drafted."

Already drafted? Without consulting me at all? "He has no need of my money or status, and there is no emotional connection between us—which means that he only wishes to marry me because he finds me prettier than everyone else."

"And a good thing you are, or he might not have you."

My jaw set and I gripped the napkin in my lap. "I would rather die an old maid, sir."

"You will marry him if I order you to!"

I may have inherited my fair looks from my mother, but I got my dark moods from my father—and when his voice rose, mine rose along with it. "He's completely dull! He can scarce string two interesting words together, and every one of them is uttered in his mother's shadow. Force me to marry him, you may, but if I die of tedium in the first week, it shall be on your head!"

Aunt Beth rearranged the shawl about her shoulders, flicking its thin tassels at me. "Henry leaves for India in a fortnight, does he not?"

I stilled, disliking the sudden change in subject and the cunning gleam that entered her eye. How did she know *when* he would leave? Unable to guess what she was playing at, I finally nodded.

"If he loves you, as you claim, a fortnight should be ample time to secure a proposal from him. Don't you agree?"

My brow furrowed. A long-strangled hope inside me gasped in a little breath. ". . . You're not saying . . . You do not mean—"

"I do, my dear. You are convinced our displeasure at the boy is the only thing keeping you two apart—but there are far greater hurdles in your path, I assure you. And meanwhile, your obsession with him causes you to disgrace the Kendall name every other week. In one way or another, this circus *must* end. Henry, Henry, Henry. Well, if it's Henry you want, then pursue him. For two weeks, you shall have my blessing."

Father shot up, knocking his chair over. Aunt Beth held up a hand to mollify him, before going on. "Catch him, and you may keep him. You'll not hear another naysaying word from me." She stood, a foreboding, calculated look overtaking her features. "But if, after two weeks, Henry has not proposed, he will leave and you will put away this childish nonsense once and for all. You will create no more scandals, act in a manner that befits your birth, and cease tarnishing your father's name. *And* you will marry Hawthorne."

I fell back against my chair.

Aunt Beth looked between me and Father, who grumbled something unintelligible. "What say you, Rupert? Are you in support of this plan?"

Father tapped the table with the knuckles of his fist. "Devil take

it—I don't suppose there's any other way she'll let go of the boy."
After another moment, he gave a curt nod.

Satisfied, Aunt Beth turned to me, waiting for my agreement.

Aunt Beth was not a liar; if she said she and Father would let me
marry Henry, it was as good as done. I never dreamed they would
put their misgivings against Henry aside—for any length of time.
And two weeks was certainly enough time if I played my cards
right. Yet, even in my confidence, I faltered.

Aunt Beth was cunning, and I'd never known her to strike a
bargain with someone unless she was getting the better end of it.
How was she so certain I would fail? What were these greater
hurdles she spoke of?

Then again, I'd known Henry my whole life. I'd seen for myself
his secret longing glances, felt his soft, restrained touches. If something stood in the way of our marriage, it wasn't a shallowness of
feeling.

Having Hawthorne for a husband was a steep price to pay if I
were unsuccessful. I held little affection for the man, and even less
for his mother. But without a doubt, any risk—even one as
distasteful as a marriage to Hawthorne—was a risk worth taking, if
it meant I could have Henry.

Three years now I'd been waiting for an official proposal from
him. Now I just had to make it happen sometime in the next two
weeks.

The weight of what I was about to agree to hung over me like
an ominous sky, threatening the most terrifying thunderstorm if I
failed. This wasn't going to be like a steady stroll through the park.
It was going to be a grueling chase. A chase for my future, my freedom, my happiness. My Henry.

That settled it.

I nodded. "We have an agreement."

CHAPTER 5

THE FUNNY THING ABOUT GARDEN PARTIES IS, THEY AREN'T really parties.

On Lady Bentley's lawn, mounds of scones stood as tall as cottages, trays overflowed with jellies, and a river of tea poured from the spouts of a dozen teapots—and if a garden party only consisted of these things, it would indeed be a party of the most heavenly sort. But alas, food was only one rung in the chain of an enjoyable afternoon. The other, much more important element, was the company.

And that was where a garden party tended to turn into a hellish chore.

"I say, Alicia, is that the same dress you wore to Lady Iris's soiree last season?" Bethany Hayfield sat next to me, chattering with an enthusiasm that rivaled jaybirds. Our table was one of many adorning the expansive lawn. Two or three of them sat within earshot, and their occupants lacked subtlety in the way they leaned out of their chairs with ears extended, eager to catch the next juicy morsel from Bethany's lips.

"How out of date it is!" Bethany continued. "The color is

becoming, but not particularly with your complexion, if you do forgive me for saying so. Oh, but I do think you wore it to Lady Iris's—yes, I recall it quite clearly. And I daresay who wouldn't remember? What with that fit of temper you threw over the seating arrangement. How red your face was!"

The periwinkle sky was peppered with great, bubbling clouds, and though the early summer air was crisp, the sun provided ample warmth. I stared at a knot of gentlemen playing bowls and pins near the house, giving a show of indifference toward my past scandals. As embarrassing as it was to listen to Miss Hayfield, it was far better than staying home in an empty house, as I took no pleasure in solitude. Since Aunt Beth thrived on social outings, she attended every one she was invited to, so staying home only served as a reminder of Father's constant absence.

It had taken Bethany nearly ten minutes to arrive at my most recent scandal, the one with Lord Hawthorne's cravat. I'd been very, *very* close to the man, touching him with unabashed forwardness—and in plain view of the entire room, no less!

There was the time I'd offended Lady Prima by ordering her not to laugh so abundantly. I'd refused to stand up with Lord Morley, then stood up with another man not two sets later. I let dogs loose through Hyde Park, forgot to wear mourning when Aunt Beth's husband died, sang a vulgar country song when called upon to perform . . .

The list went on.

Now Bethany brought up Lady Iris who had insulted the rank of my birth by purposely placing me near the bottom of the table. I wouldn't have cared at all where I was seated—the *ton's* fixation with rank was never something I'd shared—but then she'd seated Henry beside her and continued to fawn over him and shoot me smug smiles in between courses. She'd separated us on purpose; because she knew I loved him. What else was I to feel but anger? And then, somehow, it had blown into a scandal.

My feet pressed into the grass as my patience wore thin.

It's not as if the stories weren't true. But there were plausible reasons behind every one of my actions, and it was unquestionably rude to mention the instances in my presence.

". . . and then you switched the place cards when Lady Iris wasn't looking! Why I was certain she was going to order you to leave, if her glare was any indication! But no, she eventually let you have your way, as is customary. For you must *always* have your way, Alicia."

That was certainly the last straw.

I turned to her. "If you recall, Bethany, Lady Iris arranged the seats with the express desire to vex me."

"And vex you she did, I daresay," she chortled.

I returned her fake smile. "Yes. 'Twould vex anyone to be seated next to—not one—but two blathering idiots." Down the lawn, a rolling bowl collided into a cluster of pins, causing joyous cries to ring out when every one of them fell. Nervous hope fluttered to life in my chest when I saw Henry among the group.

"But dear Alicia," Bethany put a hand on my arm and bringing my attention back, "your memory is skewed. For *I* sat next to you at Lady Iris's soiree."

I stood, froomping open my parasol and letting it rest on my shoulder. "Yes, I remember. Indeed, how could I *forget*."

Bethany gave a small gasp. I flashed her my most winning smile before strolling away with a sway to my walk, twirling my parasol as I passed the other tables. Mouths hung agape. Snippets of whispers met my ears. *Uncouth. Shocking. Would be mortified to have her for a—*

I quickened my pace, having no wish to overhear any more. I already knew what people said about me.

As it happened, this *was* the dress I wore to Lady Iris's soiree. But Bethany was mistaken when she said it did not become me—I knew that for certain. It was a soft, pear-green muslin, with a white gauze overlay and lace at the hems. Ornate flowers stitched with darker thread decorated the bodice. The green brought out my eyes and complemented my golden curls when it shimmered in the sun.

The dress was stunning, and I'd worn it for the special purpose of garnering Henry's notice. Nothing would help my cause more than reminding Henry that, though I was his friend, I was also a woman. A very marriageable woman. With only two weeks to secure a proposal, every moment counted.

To my right, Lady Bentley's dark head of hair caught my notice. As she was the hostess of the party, I knew I should seek her out and pay my respects. It had been kind of her to invite me and I hadn't seen her since she'd helped me during my first Season. But as it was a large party, she was surrounded by dozens of other guests, each one making demands on her attention. I didn't know how long Henry was planning on staying and couldn't risk letting him slip away from the party before I'd had a chance to talk to him. Because of this, I knew Eliza Bentley would understand my decision to forgo greeting her, just as I knew my aunt would pay my respects for me.

The long grass swished beneath my boots as I trekked down the lawn. When at last I neared the house, I pinched my cheeks, adjusted my shawl, and sidled up to my friend.

Henry turned, eyes lighting. "Alicia." Then he fell back a step as he took in my dress. After studying me for a long moment, he uttered my name again, softer, and even more surprised than the first time.

I smiled—the first genuine one in days. "Good day, Mr. Crawley. It is fine weather we are having, do you not think?"

He opened his mouth to say something, but then stopped himself when I snuck a piece of paper into his hand. "Fine weather indeed." His eyes darted all around; down my dress, to my face, toward the men who laughed, bowled, and drank their lemonade as if they weren't listening to every word of our conversation.

I could see him debating whether or not to ask me about the note. Though it was common knowledge we were acquainted, Henry's station would be elevated if society knew the level of our familiarity—just as my station would certainly be reduced. Any other man would think to profit himself from the connection, but not Henry. He only ever wanted what was best for me. My heart swelled.

He was best for me.

At last he cleared his throat and repeated, "Indeed."

Dipping my head in farewell, I smiled and ambled away.

There. In one hour, Henry would meet me in the gardens and we would have the conversation we'd been avoiding for the past five days. I would at last convince him of his folly. He would propose to me then and there, and our lives would be as I'd always planned them.

One hour.

Nothing could possibly go wrong before then.

THE GARDEN WAS BURSTING WITH POCKETS OF YELLOW AND PINK flowers, attended to by thrumming bees. Fronds of green shoots and new buds crawled out of their beds and onto the path, giving the garden a rugged, wild feel, much unlike my own manicured gardens at Lawry Park.

I arrived a few minutes early to prepare. My plan, as it currently stood, was flimsy. I knew the quickest way to a proposal was by elevating Henry's position in society somehow—but I failed to see how such a thing was possible, let alone attainable. Instead, I'd worn my best dress and concocted a few arguments.

I would tell him how terribly far away and foreign India was. I'd remind him of our growing up in Sussex, of the blackberry patches near the river. Of all the memories that would fade away. All the connections he'd made—and would lose. And if none of that worked, I would tell him how much I cared for him, and that I couldn't bear to lose him. If Henry would not confess his love, then I would be the first to lay my heart on the line.

The plan as a whole was simple, but I was fairly certain it would be effective.

Behind me, the sound of boots crunching on gravel grew louder. I smiled in relief. I waited until I knew Henry stood just behind me. Then I turned around and—

Ow!

I collided into a wall of muscle. He grabbed me to keep me from losing my balance, and the book in his hands tumbled to the ground.

"I'm sorry, Henry, I—"

I cut off as my eyes snagged on the blue cover of the book in the drive. A book. Henry didn't read. He *loathed* reading. Why on earth did he have a book at Lady Bentley's garden party? My head snapped up.

Of all the faces I might have expected to see here in the gardens, clutching my arms, it certainly wasn't Matthew Wycliffe's. In a flash of surprise, I was struck again by how handsome he was, making me blink dumbly up at him. I quickly smothered my response with the memory of his horrible treatment of me.

What was he doing here? Surely a garden party couldn't be of much interest to a recluse like him.

He realized my identity at the same moment, for his lips quirked into a disgusted frown. He retrieved his tome from the path. Dusting it off, he straightened and muttered, "Blast. This was my good copy."

Though the memory of his horrible treatment of me was still vivid, I should at least try and be civil. Perhaps he was typically polite, but I'd happened upon him when he was having a terrible evening; I knew all too well the effects of someone forming a judgement based on my worst moments, and it felt unfair to do the same to someone else. Summoning every ounce of good breeding and manners, I dipped my head. "I beg your pardon, sir."

"No need to beg," he said, eyes cutting to where the group of party-goers thronged around the corner of the house. "Considering your conversation with Mr. Crawley on the balcony, you have enough groveling in your future as it is."

My brow furrowed. He wasn't insinuating . . . He couldn't know I'd given Henry a note—telling him to meet me here—with the express purpose of garnering a proposal . . . Could he?

Mr. Wycliffe attempted to brush past me, but of its own volition my hand shot out and grabbed his arm, stopping him. "I was determined to be amiable, sir, despite your undeserving self—yet it would seem your pride is still wounded from the ball."

He went taut and his brows pulled down, gaze travelling to my hand on his arm and burning holes into my skin until I dropped it away. To touch a gentleman—anywhere—was a bold move for a young lady, but most men didn't mind my touch. Mr. Wycliffe seemed more discomfited by the gesture than the situation warranted; as if no one ever touched him, and he preferred it that way.

Hm. Interesting.

"If I recall correctly," he said, "and I always do, it was *your* pride that was wounded that night, madam, not mine. In fact, I had quite forgotten the encounter until just now."

The fact that I had stewed over this hateful man for a week, and fumed whenever I remembered our meeting, and repeatedly envisioned how cleverly I might put him in his place if ever we met again, made me hate him even more with the revelation that he'd not thought of me at all. I felt an overwhelming urge to stamp my foot. Not even a smidge? I knew I hadn't left a favorable impression, but surely our meeting had, in the very least, been *memorable*.

I rolled my shoulders back. "I did not think of you once these past five days either," I lied. "And in fact, when we part ways now, I shall not think of you again."

His expression turned bland. "You speak rather brazenly to a mere acquaintance, Lady Alicia."

"The hypocrisy in that statement is most unbecoming, sir. And we are not even acquaintances, as you refused to tell me your name!" I craned my neck back, annoyed that he towered over me. It gave him an edge in the conversation. As though he always had the higher ground, regardless of my argument.

He tipped his head to the side. "There is no need. You have already deduced it on your own."

What? How could he possibly know that? I blinked nonchalantly, but my teeth were gritted. "Why would you assume so?"

"Because if my identity were still a mystery to you, you would have demanded to know it by now."

It unnerved me that he was so astute. That he could predict me. No one had ever been able to predict my actions—it was one of the few things I prided myself on. Even if they were terrible, and Father scolded me, and Aunt Beth tsked at me for weeks because of them, no one could ever say I was predictable. Hasty and unorthodox, yes, but predictable? Never. Half the *ton* held their breaths in anticipation of what I would do next.

Mr. Wycliffe obviously did not. And I didn't know why, but it bothered me.

"You are correct, Mr. Wycliffe. And may I say that I do not intend to throw myself at you the way every other female in the *ton* is intent upon doing."

The corner of his lip turned downward. "I see also that you have given ear to the nonsensical gossip surrounding me. You should not judge a book by its cover."

"Then let us review the contents, shall we?" I folded my arms across my chest. "First you insulted me, then my father, then you nearly topple me to the gravel just now—"

"As much as I would enjoy hearing such an undersized list of my faults," he said with a long-suffering sigh, reopening his book and fiddling with its pages, "I really haven't the time at the present moment. Content yourself in the knowledge that the rumors surrounding me are half true—a high percentage, but still unreliable at best. And as for throwing yourself at me," he glanced back up, "believe me, my lady, when I say I would not wish you to. I have found catching collapsing women to be a most tiring business."

He spun away.

I would *not* let him have the last word again. Snagging his arm, I twisted him back. "A *moment*, sir!"

He shook me off, quite vehemently. "When you said you had no intention of throwing yourself at me, this is not what I envisioned."

My face heated. "I do not throw myself at you, sir, I—!" I caught his sleeve. Finally! A good hold he couldn't just pry himself out of. "Ha!"

"What the devil—"

He snapped his arm back, pulling me into him. Hard. He lost his balance—and I, being the fool who still held his sleeve and would never in a hundred years let go because that would mean moral defeat, lost it with him. We crashed onto the gravel pathway, sprawled together in a heap.

I wheezed in a breath, coughing on some dust. After a moment, Matthew looked at me. Strangely. He did not seem angry or embarrassed. Instead, his gaze roamed my face with a confused, re-evaluating look, as if he had pegged me wrong and was only now discovering it.

"Matthew!"

Both our heads whipped over to see a man near the corner of the house staring at us with wide-eyed shock. He so greatly resembled Mr. Wycliffe that I could only assume he was his elder brother, the viscount.

This was bad.

It was so very bad, but I couldn't move from my incriminating position, doomed to watch the nightmare play out in a daze of horror.

The viscount glanced behind him toward something hidden from view, before hissing, "Compose yourselves!"

Mr. Wycliffe shoved me off him and stood with impressive speed, a blush creeping up his neck. Spell broken, I caught myself with my palms, hissing when they stung on the sharp pebbles of the pathway.

At that moment, a group of guests strolled around the corner of the house, gasping and halting when they came upon us. I froze, mind reeling. No one besides Mr. Wycliffe's brother had witnessed the scandalous position, but the signs were still there for anyone suspicious enough to look; the cloud of dust, the dirt on Mr. Wycliffe's trousers, the fact that I was still sitting on my rump in the path.

Swiftly, Lord Wycliffe offered me his hand. I took it and he helped me up, giving me a good view of the shocked crowd before me. "There you are madam," he said. "Are you quite all right? What an unfortunate thing to lose your balance like that. I shall see to it that all protruding rocks are removed from the trail, straight away. We wouldn't want any other young ladies accidentally taking a tumble like you did."

My head was still spinning, but somehow I managed a nod, grateful for Lord Wycliffe's quick thinking.

This was the part I despised most. The raised eyebrows, the haughty, sometimes pitying once-overs, before the whispers. I could already hear them, sharp and taunting. *Lady Alicia and that handsome Mr. Wycliffe! In the gardens with only Lord Wycliffe for a chaperone. What-ever could it mean? What a spectacle that Kendall girl is. And her poor father! Oh, what shall he ever do with her?*

Well, I knew what he was going to do with me—chain me to the wall for a month, feed me bread and water, and scold me half his waking hours for the rest of his life. Which might not be very long, after he heard this news.

My stomach sickened and the world tilted.

Lord Wycliffe turned to the crowd, who had already begun to bare their teeth in feverish conversation like a pack of wolves lusting after their dinner, spinning questions and speculation. "Let us all return to the party. I believe Lady Bentley was just about to begin a rollicking game of blind man's bluff."

The crowd dissipated, no doubt eager to spread the juicy news, but instead of following after them, Lord Wycliffe indicated for both Matthew and I to stay. Soon I was again alone in the gardens with the two men. Awkward silence followed, all of us hesitant to confront it.

Well, there was nothing to be done. I'd never be able to show my face to society again, not unless—

No, I could never. I swallowed the lump in my throat and straightened the lace that had wrinkled at my waist. I may not have liked society and its standards, but that didn't mean I was ignorant of them. There were certain standards that remained unshakeable; certain lines that could never be crossed if you wanted to live among the *ton.* And I had just crossed one. Ignoring the hard ball of lead in my stomach, I dusted off my dress with shaky hands, trying to keep the panic at bay. I pivoted to locate Aunt Beth.

"Just a moment, madam," the viscount called. I turned back, noticing the look he gave his brother that was anything but subtle. "Matthew?" He knocked his head in my direction.

Matthew Wycliffe glanced at me, then back at his brother. "What?"

He was play-acting at being obtuse, and we all knew it—which only made it worse.

The brother raised his eyebrows. "You must offer for her."

Heat flooded my face.

Matthew looked at me again, this time with a frown. "An engagement isn't necessary, Peter. No one saw the worst of it, and the incident will be forgotten by weeks' end. I shan't be forced to suffer for something I neither initiated nor encouraged."

Peter huffed. "You are such a cad sometimes."

Matthew stepped closer. He was not quite as broad as his older brother, but he was an inch or so taller. They didn't look enough alike to be twins, but it was very close. "I seem to recall you telling me of a similar 'accident' happening to you, but you were not roped into an engagement for it."

"Because there were no witnesses. And I ended up marrying the girl anyway, now didn't I? You cannot know that no one saw you two, so you must do right by this woman and marry her."

This wasn't going anywhere. There was no way on earth Matthew Wycliffe—the man I hated above all others—was going to offer me his hand in marriage. And indeed even if he did, my pride would never allow me to accept him.

"I appreciate the sentiment, Lord Wycliffe," I said, "but I do not want your pity." They both turned to me. I gathered up my skirts, lifting my chin and salvaging what little dignity I still possessed. "I would not expect a man to sacrifice his entire future based on a few moments. And neither would I expect a man who isn't a gentleman to be willing to."

I turned on my heel, quite pleased with my closing line. *Now* that lout would think of me; stew over me as I had him. Insufferable, arrogant, ill-mannered little—

"Lady Alicia."

I halted at the sound of Matthew Wycliffe's voice, but did not turn around.

Boots plodded with his approach. A pause. He sighed like it cost him the last of his will to do so. Then, "Will you accept my hand in marriage?"

His voice was as flat as a pond's surface. No desperation, adoration, or even anger. How could someone be so devoid of emotion or passion of any kind? How could I contemplate tying myself to such a man?

I wouldn't. I had Henry to think about, and my bargain with Aunt Beth. It was absolutely out of the question. The answer was no. Unequivocally no.

Although, my reputation . . . I bit my lip.

I had survived a few bad scrapes before, but this was the cream of the crop, the straw that was sure to break society's back. Even the barest whisper from someone who *thought* they might've seen us tangled together, was enough to destroy my virtue. The cold ball in my stomach hardened. The *ton* had overlooked my past scrapes, but if the truth were to get out, they would not forgive me for this. I knew it in my bones. I was to die an outcast, ostracized and forever summoning shame upon my family name.

And Father. Father would bear the brunt of it. I would be viewed as damaged goods—and how would having a daughter with tarnished virtue affect his plans in parliament? He would be exiled from polite society altogether, and unable to send the troops in India the aid they needed. Because of me.

Oh bother!

Whether to Hawthorne or to Henry, I was already promised—my deal with Father guaranteed that. In two weeks, my fate would be sealed, and no amount of scandal could change it.

But, in the meantime, an engagement to Mr. Wycliffe might put from people's minds what had really happened in this garden—or from speculating on far worse things. Barring the agony of being around the man, there were only good things to be gained from the brief engagement. It would spare my Father's name from being dragged in the mud. It might drive Lord Hawthorne's interest else-where, and force Henry to wake up to his feelings for me.

While true that more gossip would crop up when I called it off in two weeks, I would wager my best pair of slippers it would be mild compared to the backlash I would've received had I *not* produced a fiancé. An engaged woman, in any situation, was much better off than an unengaged one.

And I wouldn't have to marry the brute anyway, so why not? Matthew Wycliffe would never have to know I'd only ever intended it to be temporary. I wasn't going to feel one shred of guilt for using him as a buffer against the rumors.

Mouth working, I twisted around and met Mr. Wycliffe's blank stare. "May I ask why you are doing this, sir?" I couldn't understand why he was offering me marriage if he cared so little of what society thought of him.

"It is wise to maintain a certain level of respectability."

"So you do this in self-interest?"

"I do nothing outside of it."

I scoffed, sarcasm dripping when I said, "What a surprise indeed!"

"There is no one alive that doesn't wish to satisfy their own ends. The only difference between me and other men is that I make no pretense at chivalry first."

Behind him, Peter Wycliffe planted his head in his palm and groaned. Though Matthew did not look at his brother, his eyes darted to one corner before returning to me.

It could've been a trick of the ear, but his voice sounded a tad softer when he added, "What I mean to say is, I've never had any aspirations toward marriage, so it is not as if you will be taking someone's place."

My eyes strayed to Peter, standing beyond him and looking apologetic. Perhaps Matthew did not care for society's opinion, but his brother's.

Which wouldn't make sense at all.

"Very well, Mr. Wycliffe!" I said and extended my hand to him. "I accept your proposal."

There was a long moment of silence, during which Mr. Wycliffe's gaze flitted from my hand to my face, still maddeningly blank. The expectation for him to kiss it was obvious, and yet instead of taking it he turned to his brother and said, "Mark my words, this will not end well." Then he strolled down the pathway and out of sight.

My hand fisted and fell to my side, itching to claw at something. Or some*one*.

Aunt Beth appeared around the corner and gestured urgently to me that it was time to leave. She'd already heard the gossip, then. After hesitating a moment, she glanced the way Mr. Wycliffe had gone and strode after him.

"I'm terribly sorry about all that, Lady Alicia," said Lord

Wycliffe, approaching me. "Matthew has always been . . . rather hard to get along with."

"Always?"

His answer was a pained look. "But trust me, he's a good fellow. He will come around." Lord Wycliffe grasped my limp hand and kissed it in his brother's stead, gracing me with a hopeful smile. "And may I be the first to offer my sincere congratulations." He left.

There I was, alone in the gardens as I had been only a quarter of an hour before, only now the course of my two weeks was completely altered. Henry had never come, and I was affianced to someone I despised more than Hawthorne. A crazed laugh burst out of me. I couldn't help it.

Congratulations?

I laughed harder. Father was going to have my head. It was unclear what he would be most upset about: that I had toppled a man, that people had witnessed the aftermath, or that I had come away engaged to someone other than the two men we'd agreed upon.

CHAPTER 6

"You're *what*?"

I held my hand out as if trying to soothe a wild stallion. "Calm down, Father—"

"Do not tell me to calm down, girl!" He slapped the dining room table with his palm. Everyone in the room flinched—even the footmen, who were making a mighty effort to keep their expressions stoic. Father shook his arm out, muttering something. "If this is some silly prank, if you only concocted this to make me furious, I'll —I'll—"

"Heavens, Rupert," Aunt Beth said from the other end of the table, "you're scaring the help. How they will gossip after dinner."

"Let them gossip! Apparently they have good reason to. My only daughter has been off dallying with fops and cads, promising herself left and right, and sees fit to tell me of it in the same sentence she asks me to pass the French beans!"

Oh, bother. This was going even worse than I'd feared.

Father stabbed a finger in my direction. "You mean to say that in the space of *three hours* you met a man, toppled into him, and walked away engaged?"

"Of course not, don't be silly. It was not our first meeting." I took a sip of wine. Against the glass I mumbled, "And it only took *one* hour."

Father clumped his dark hair in one hand.

Aunt Beth's eyes cut to me. "This isn't what we had in mind when we gave you free rein. But I can't say as I object to the match. You couldn't have picked a better substitute."

"She's made a coarse spectacle of herself, more like!"

I took a bite of my sliced duck and took my time chewing it. The food had a difficult time sliding down my throat.

Pointing her butter knife at Father, Aunt Beth said, "All the better she shall be married off soon, don't you think?"

"I did! Do! Married to Hawthorne, not—not—" He turned to me. "Who did you say the man was?"

This was the part I'd dreaded most. Using my napkin to pat my mouth, I said, "I have not yet said."

Father whipped his napkin against his plate, sending his silver clattering. "Then tell me, plague take it! Who is the man? Is it Morley? Or that peacock fellow, whatever his name is?" His face lost some of its hardness as he blanched. "It's not Henry, is it?"

At the mention of his name, I felt a prick behind my eyes, but I stamped down the emotion rising to the surface. I couldn't give a show of caring. Not now, in front of Father's penetrating gaze. "No," I said quietly.

Father sat back in his chair, breathing a sigh of relief. "Thank heavens for that, at least." He took a long draught of wine, finishing it off before planting it on the table. A fortification against the news. "Well?" he demanded. "Who is he?"

As I'd revealed everything to Aunt Beth during the ride back from the garden party, she already knew his identity. I looked at her now, hoping she would spare me from uttering his name, but she remained tight-lipped. I set my napkin on the table, patting it down gently, meticulously. Returning my hands to my lap, I raised my head and looked my father square in the eyes.

Matthew had been right. This was not going to end well.

"I am engaged to Mr. Matthew Wycliffe."

Aunt Beth grinned wickedly, the corners of her mouth sharp enough to slice me open. If she liked his money so much, why didn't *she* marry him?

I sighed in frustration. "Pray tell, what else should I have done under the circumstances? People will gossip if I am not engaged, and they will gossip if I am—but at least this way they will mitigate their whispers and show a scrap of deference."

I lowered my head and chewed the inside of my cheek, tone softening when I added, "Believe me, I had no intention of falling upon the man. And I am sorry for the position I have put you in, Father. Forming an engagement was the only thing I could think to do to remedy the situation."

"Remedy?" he said, voice like ice. I glanced up to find him shaking his head, lips pressed in a stern line. In his eyes, I had still done the wrong thing. "There is no remedy for this. The damage is already done, or it soon will be." He rubbed his mouth with a frustrated, open palm. "Matthew Wycliffe! I do not even know the man."

Aunt Beth huffed. "Of course you do not. He is a recluse, just like you."

Father harrumphed. "Not a Peer."

"He is the son of the late Lord of Ambleside. The second son."

"Second son to a viscount?" He grimaced. "Gads, he is barely a step up from Henry."

"Actually, Rupert," Aunt Beth practically gushed, "not in regards to fortune, or importance. In fact, I daresay he greatly exceeds even Hawthorne."

A thousand scoffs of indignation rose in my throat.

Father gave a thoughtful grunt and turned to me. "Have you given no thought to the rise of rumors when you call off the engagement, as you inevitably must?"

I faltered. "Of course it crossed my mind—"

"I very much doubt that." Aunt Beth signaled to the footmen. They stepped forward and swapped out our plates of sliced duck in bitter orange sauce for braised celery.

"The deal is still on," Father said. "You cannot break it—will not. In fact, the only thing you shall be breaking is Mr. Wycliffe's heart, a fortnight hence."

Imagining a certain man beneath my knife, I rigorously cut my celery, muttering, "That would require he *have* a heart."

Father's voice took on a soldier-like quality—a habit from his years in the service that only emerged when he was dead set on something—making me halt my motions. "Because of the unfortunate predicament we find ourselves in, we will pretend your engagement to Mr. Wycliffe is a love match."

My knife clanked onto my plate. "I couldn't. I couldn't even if I *tried.*"

His hand on the table rubbed itself in a fist. "If people see you have not formed an engagement out of love, they will draw their own conclusions—and most assuredly, they will assume the worst." Father levelled me with a stern, meaningful look. I gulped, a blush rising to my cheeks. "We need to salvage what few shreds of your reputation that remain. Control the damage, before it has a chance to spread to parliament—and Lord Hawthorne, for that matter. Far better for everyone to believe you in love, and then flighty when you change your mind, than to view you as a prime article."

But a *love* match? To Matthew Wycliffe? My brows plunged. "I cannot!"

"Then we will forgo all this nonsense and I will tell Hawthorne you accept him."

I was trapped. Dash it all, why'd everything have to get so muddled up? Lips folding into a line, I contemplated this new turn of events. Though even the thought of pretending to love Matthew made me feel like I'd inhaled an acre of oily, black smog . . . for Henry, I could do it. Still, there was something else.

"If I am forced to act like I love Mr. Wycliffe, how am I to win Henry? How would he even know to offer himself?"

Aunt Beth cleared her throat. "That, dear, is *your* problem. Not ours."

My nostrils flared. "It's egregiously unfair."

"You might've thought of that before you accepted the man— better yet, before you toppled into him. How you must wish you'd heeded my counsel at the ball and snatched him up in a more dignified fashion."

Before I could formulate a retort to that ridiculous suggestion, our butler swept into the room with a bow. "Mr. Crawley for Lady Alicia, Your Grace," he said. "I put him in the study."

A spark of hope lit my stomach.

Henry.

"What the devil can he want?" Chairs scraped against the floor as Father and I stood in unison.

Aunt Beth sniffed. "An ungodly hour for him to pay a visit. Most indecent—and when we are at supper! Alicia, you must turn him away."

But I was already hurrying toward the exit. "I shall send him away immediately!" I said over my shoulder. Behind me, she heaved a hefty sigh. She knew I would do no such thing.

PROFILED PAINTINGS AND BUST SCULPTURES ABUTTED BROCADED wallpaper in my father's study. Henry sat on the window seat, looking out onto the drive. In his hand he held one of Father's soldier figurines, stolen from the shelf. His outline stood stark against the light from the window, but I could still make out his thick blond hair, his square jawline, and the hairline scar on his temple I'd given to him when we were children. A soft smile came to my lips.

I cleared my throat.

Henry spun around to find me standing on the threshold. "Alicia."

Even though he came specifically to see me, he still seemed surprised to find me standing there, just as he had earlier at the garden party. Maybe he thought I was still angry with him. Or that I'd actually meant it when I said I no longer wished to see him.

He stood. "I know the hour is unusual, but I wanted to see you."

My heart did a little flip.

"That is, I-I wanted to ask you . . ." He glanced down. "Is . . . Is it true that you are engaged?" He didn't look at me while he asked the question, instead fiddling with the figurine soldier, thumbing over its etched glass features.

I blinked. Of course. Henry would have heard the rumors already, but I didn't expect to have to confront him about it so soon. I didn't even know what to tell him.

Why not the truth?

Father said I must pretend to be in love with Mr. Wycliffe, but that didn't bind me to utter secrecy. Having Henry know wouldn't compromise the situation. In the end, it might help him propose.

I nodded. "It is true. I am engaged."

Henry's frame sagged, head lowering.

"But it is a sham. A hoax, until the rumors blow over."

He glanced up.

"Oh Henry, I have gotten myself into hot water again. With society . . . with Father. I didn't know what else to do. For now, at least until things settle down, I must remain engaged to Mr. Wycliffe."

Now it was Henry's turn to blink at me. "I see," he said slowly. He returned the toy statue to its place on the shelf amid two dozen identical soldiers, but his hand never left it.

I walked forward until my nose nearly touched his shoulder. He smelled warm and earthy. Like amber and tree sap. "If someone else were to offer for me instead . . ." I said quietly. Hesitantly, I covered his hand on the shelf with my own. This time, he didn't pull away. ". . . you should know I would accept him."

Finally, his eyes darted over to me, expression conflicted. He pulled out of my grasp. "And you should know he could never offer. Even if he wanted to."

He moved away, dragging with him the answers to all the questions I wanted to ask. Wandering to the other side of Father's stately desk, he half-sat on it, folding his hands in his lap. "Everyone holds their breath when we are together. Don't you see it? You must've noticed by now, how afraid they are that I shall seek to rise above my station."

I shook my head, throwing away all hypotheticals. "I don't care about that."

"You should." He sighed. "Perhaps if things were different . . . if society held me in higher regard. Perhaps if my father's will had actually been found and he'd left his fortune to me, instead of my brother. Graham was verbally disinherited—we all heard my father say it, even you. So even though he died suddenly, I was expecting . . ."

He blew another sigh, combing a hand through his hair. "I was expecting things to be different. But you see, they aren't." Standing, he walked to the window, choosing to keep his back to me. "I have no money to my name, so I've joined the military. And frankly, I'm glad I shall be shipping away, so that I won't have to watch you—" He turned his head to the side for a moment, letting me glimpse his profile, before lowering it again.

Quieter, he said, "What did you wish to speak to me about, at the garden party?"

My heart sank a little. Our conversation. I'd prepared arguments to convince Henry to stay, but the things he'd just revealed rendered them irrelevant.

"Oh, I . . . I only wanted to apologize for how I acted at the ball." I swallowed. "I did not mean it. I always wish to see you."

He glanced over his shoulder, a sad slant to his eyebrows. "I am sorry, too," he said. I got the sense that he wasn't just speaking of the ball.

If he left, all my hopes and dreams would never come to fruition. What would I do without him? Whose shoulder would I cry on? How could I marry any man but the one I was in love with?

Henry's stark shadow moved along the rug, eclipsing me when he drew near. I stared into his eyes, at his hair that seemed to shine like a halo.

He swept my cheek with the back of his hand. I relaxed at the touch. "We shall see each other plenty before I go. Graham is throwing a party at the castle next Wednesday, to see me off. Your whole family's invited, including your—well, your fiancé."

A pit cut in my stomach. *Henry* was supposed to be my fiancé; this wonderful, thoughtful man who, as it turned out actually wanted to marry me. Unlike Matthew Wycliffe. It wasn't fair. It was *not* fair.

"And then there is the week of celebrations in Brighton, before I ship off," Henry continued. "Plenty of opportunity to spend time together. Come." He indicated my expression with a tilt of his head. "No more sadness. You are so independent, I am certain you won't even notice my absence." A half-smile lifted the corner of his lips.

My vision clouded, but I blinked away the tears before they fell. How could I not notice the absence of my only friend? The only person who cared for me?

He gave my arms a squeeze before stepping around me and heading for the door. Pausing in the doorway, he sent me one more hopeful glance before slipping out of sight.

Alone in the musty, sunlit room, stubbornness burned in my gut, as hard as a ball of lead. I leaned back against Father's desk, folding my arms. All these years of waiting and planning and dreaming, all for naught? All because of Father and his campaign and society's silly rules? I couldn't accept it.

And if I were to ever see him again, it would be years in the future, for only a few days at a time. He'd be deep in the jungles of India, facing danger every day—in large part thanks to the very issues my father was pushing in parliament. The thought frightened me.

Henry may be an unparalleled swordsman, but he was too soft for the military. He had a tenderness and sincerity about him that others liked to exploit. Besides the jeers from peers he'd surely receive, Henry had neither the stomach nor disposition for bloodshed, valuing decency and humanity where other men failed to.

He was like that soldier figurine on the shelf: tough, stoic, seemingly battle-ready. And his eyes may have been hopeful, but his paint was chipped—and one little bump from his place on the shelf would send him spinning to the ground where he'd shatter to pieces.

I'd been going about this all wrong. I didn't need to change his mind at all. Henry wasn't leaving because he wished to. He was leaving because—in his eyes—he had no reason to stay. All I needed to do was forge a different path, and he would follow it.

If society held me in higher regard . . .

If only I had a fortune . . .

I kicked my slipper against the rug. While the obstacles in front of Henry were enormous, surely it was not impossible to move them. There had to be a way to give him the wealth and recognition he needed to propose. Even *with* my being already engaged.

My mind came to a crunching halt as a new thought entered my head, quiet at first, but it grew louder by the second. I straightened, arms unfolding, a smile spreading over my mouth. I rushed upstairs to fetch a cloak and bonnet.

It was time to pay a visit to the only man whose importance in society was as over-inflated as his ego.

CHAPTER 7

I MADE A MAD DASH DOWN THE STAIRS, TUGGING ON MY GLOVES as I went. The hour was indecent, but such trivial things had never stopped me before. Matthew believed our engagement to be legitimate. For him, it was not a nightmare to be endured for two weeks —it was a nightmare that, save for a miracle, would last a lifetime. How happy he'd be when I dropped that miracle into his lap.

I crossed the spacious marble entryway, heading for the front door.

"Where are you running off to?"

I halted at the sound of Aunt Beth's voice drifting from the wide dining room doorway, sharp with suspicion. Pasting on my most innocent smile, I twisted around. "Oh, nowhere." A quick glance behind her told me Father's chair at the table was empty. With any luck, he'd already retired.

Her face took on a shrewd grin as she glided nearer. "I wasn't aware you needed travelling clothes to go 'nowhere.'"

I made a show of brushing off my cloak and gloves, to avoid eye contact. "As a matter of fact, I thought I'd take an evening drive.

The sun has not yet set, and the country is so vibrant this time of year. I hear it is quite good for the disposition."

"Mm," she said, looking me over from head to toe. "What a sudden interest you have in your disposition, Alicia, when all your life you've been sourer than a basket of lemons."

"A basket I am determined to turn into lemonade." I spun on my heel and clutched the brass doorknob.

"Where do you go?" Her voice was like iron, trapping me in a cell until I gave her an answer.

My hand on the doorknob faltered. I spun back to find Aunt Beth's all-knowing gaze boring into me. There was no point in lying if she would discover the truth soon anyway. Clearing my throat, I said, "I go to Mr. Wycliffe's."

"Are you that lovesick for him?"

How low.

"Yes!" I said with mockery, putting a hand to my brow. "I am head over heels for the man and cannot go another hour bereft of his presence. My heart! It yearns to be with its other half. Cruel miser, do not deny me this meeting of kindred souls!"

Aunt Beth watched my theatrics with narrowed eyes. After a moment she said, "I will give you a word of caution, Alicia, though I know you will not heed it: Do not spend these two weeks diving headlong into folly. Curb these reckless choices—if not for our sake, then your own."

Slowly, I felt my expression sober at the unflinching seriousness in my aunt's gaze.

"Mr. Wycliffe may not have a heart," she went on, "but you, my dear, do. A cold and bitter heart, perhaps, but I would wager it still beats. And if you do not take care, you will lose it before the end—regardless of which man you marry."

A chill crept up my spine. I frowned, perturbed that Aunt Beth had managed to get under my skin. With a swish of her skirt, she ambled away.

"You are not going to stop me?" I called after her.

She kept a steady pace up the stairs, calling over her shoulder, "I have been stopping you all your life. Now it is time to open the cage and let you experience the consequences of your rash decisions. I fear anything less, and you would not learn your lesson."

When she disappeared on the landing, leaving me alone in the spacious foyer, I huffed. Somehow, her giving me this freedom was worse than if she'd forbidden me to go. The echoes of her warning lingered on the walls, dripping down like wax.

I shook it off. Nothing bad would come of all this. Aunt Beth would see. I was about to save my future and she couldn't stop me. Securing my gloves, I slipped out of the house and headed toward the carriage I'd summoned, waiting in the drive.

MATTHEW WYCLIFFE LIVED IN THE SMALLEST OF HOUSES.

To either side of the green door sat pairs of tall, rectangular windows—matching the five lining the second story. Three chimney flues jutted from the roof, giving some dimension to the otherwise squat, square, and bricked building. The house itself was small enough that ten of them would've fit into the grandeur of Lawry Park. I took it in with a wrinkled brow. It wasn't at all where I imagined one of the wealthiest men in England to reside.

I stepped out of the carriage and moved up the walkway leading to the door.

To say that the house was symmetrical would be an understatement. Every hedge, every stone in the pathway, every blade of grass was perfectly trimmed and arranged to match the one next to it. Despite the smallness of the abode, the immaculate appearance gave everything an intimidating air.

And despite myself, I was intimidated.

I rolled my shoulders back before giving three hasty raps with the knocker. A butler opened the door.

"Excuse me, is Mr. Wycliffe at home?" I said.

He swung the door wider. "Ah, Lady Alicia. He is expecting you."

My eyebrows raised. Expecting me? How could Mr. Wycliffe know to expect me? The butler escorted me into the foyer and led me down a hallway. An extension branched off at the back of the house, unseen from a frontal view, giving the house more square footage than it appeared to have.

After sliding open a pair of double French doors, the butler ushered me into the room beyond. As a pungent mixture of wood and glue met my nose, I fell back a step.

Books. Books everywhere. Shelves upon shelves upon rows upon rows. Tall ones, leather ones, thin ones, thick ones, deepest black to lightest blue; each one in an orderly, categorized place, each one in pristine condition. I didn't know this many books even *existed*.

Inlaid bookcases stretched from floor to ceiling. More of them protruded in from the sides, like a giant's fingers lifting the room up. A long rug spanned the length of the middle walkway, leading to a cluster of chairs and tables.

I couldn't believe my eyes. The library took up most of the house; and there was little enough of it to begin with!

The butler bowed, before closing the doors behind him. Near the enormous alcove window, reclined Matthew Wycliffe in a stuffed wingback chair. Squinting, I saw what Matthew stared at—a little table with assembled chess pieces.

Out of pure habit, I scanned the board and discovered a winning move, before peeking behind the last bookcase to find Matthew's opponent nestled in a chair of his own. He was a servant, if his simple attire was any indication. The setting sun cast an orange glow around Matthew as he moved one of his pawns. "Checkmate, Prescott."

Prescott shook his head. "Didn't last more than two minutes, this time. I don't know why you enjoy playing me, sir."

"I don't," Matthew said flatly, gathering up the pieces and

stowing them in a box. "But you're the best among the servants, and I must play someone. You may go."

I frowned at the scene. The words themselves were brusque, but Matthew delivered them with an air of familiarity . . . to a servant . . .

Hm. Interesting.

Prescott tucked in his chair before offering me a bow and breezing past. I waited for Matthew to finally turn and notice me, but instead, he selected a book from a nearby shelf and sank back into his chair.

Flipping through the pages, he said, "I knew you would come." He propped his legs up on the table before him and dove into his book. He still didn't look at me.

This was going to be drudgery.

I crossed my arms. "One might wonder *how* you knew I would come."

"Mm, one might," he agreed, "but it would surprise me. People don't usually care how I'm right—only that I am."

How utterly arrogant. I stifled my scoff. "So? How did you?"

He turned a page. "There is still much about our engagement to be discussed, and the setting prevented us from pursuing the topic. The matter requires discretion, and therefore privacy. And it needs to be discussed soon, in order to form a proper plan before all and sundry hear of it. Tomorrow would suit, but you strike me as a hasty sort of girl—a girl who can't abide waiting for anything she wants—and so I knew it would be tonight. And of course you would come here, because you wish to keep our meeting a secret from your father."

I blinked. Matthew put it so logically—as if it would be more surprising to learn he *hadn't* been expecting me, than if he had. But most people didn't have that kind of logical foresight, the ability to predict others—much less the unflinching faith in that ability to make arrangements for the outcome. It was unsettling, to say the least.

"Not to mention," he added, "that I have too much dignity to hasten to your side like an obedient hound simply because you bid it. Unlike that Crawley fellow."

My lips bottled up a torrent of defenses that rose to my tongue. I didn't come here to argue over Henry—and I didn't need to prove his worth to the likes of Matthew Wycliffe. Besides, the more I lashed out at Matthew, the less amenable he'd be to helping me.

And I desperately needed his help.

"As it happens," he went on, setting his open book back against his stomach and glancing up, "I'm glad you came. Once you left the garden party, Peter pulled me aside—and after giving me the scolding of a lifetime, made me promise him something." Matthew's face took on a pained grimace. "He wants us to pretend ours is a love match."

My head knocked back, brows raising. I knew why *I* needed to pretend to be smitten, but I could see no reason why Matthew would. "But why?"

He rubbed his eyes with his thumb and forefinger. "The whole lot of it is stupid rubbish. Despite my protests, and because no one in my family *ever* listens to me, my sister and sister-in-law have entertained fanciful notions about my future marriage. Simply put, they want to see me in love. They'd be more heartbroken over my loveless marriage than I'd ever be. Peter wants to spare them that. And, unsurprisingly, he insists that if we pretend long enough, eventually, it will come true."

The distaste written on Matthew's face showed he hoped that would never happen. Luckily for him, I knew for a certainty it wouldn't.

"Very well," I said with a shrug, not letting on to the fact that I was already going to put on a charade anyway. "If you're sure you can manage it."

"I have never known myself to be incapable of anything."

Conceit flowed from his lips like a river. "We shall have to conjure a story," I said, "to get our facts straight."

"I shall leave that part up to you." He looked at me sharply. "If you're sure you can manage it."

A growl scratched at the base of my throat. I forced myself to sound polite. "I can."

"Good. Oh, and expect a dinner party invitation from Peter tomorrow. Don't blame me, it was his idea." Matthew plunged into his book anew, an unmistakable hint that he wished me to leave. If only.

"Actually, I came here to enlist your help," I announced.

Matthew's eyes stopped scanning the page. After a pause, he clucked his tongue. "I sincerely hope you do not mean that, madam."

"Most earnestly."

"Then you shall be disappointed. I do not 'help' people, willingly or otherwise. All it ever does is waste precious time."

"Not even if it will release you from our engagement?"

Without moving his head, he glanced up, eyes alight with curiosity.

I smiled. Finally, I'd caught his interest. I let it ripen before going on. "Henry was supposed to propose to me, that night at the ball—not tell me he's shipping out of the country. But you see, this evening, he came to me and said he *would* offer me marriage if not for two things."

This was the crucial part. I needed to make Matthew believe he needed me as much as I needed him.

Stepping behind one of the wingback chairs, I rested my forearm on its back. "Neither of us wants this match. I want to marry Henry, and you want to, well—to read books all day, or whatever it is you do. It is in both of our best interests to remove the obstacles blocking mine and Henry's path. And, once they are removed and I have Henry's proposal, we can break our engagement and carry on as we were always meant to. Separately."

Matthew's forefinger tapped the book where he gripped it, before he set it on the table before him. His eyes narrowed.

"What are these two obstacles, and how easily are they to be overcome?"

I gnawed the inside of my cheek. "That bit rather depends on you."

Flecks of dust floated in the waning shafts of sunlight, beaming through the large window. They were the only thing that moved as Matthew waited for me to go on.

"You see, the first of Henry's objections is fortune—or rather, lack of it. I could come up with a way to find him one, or earn him one, but that could take resources, and time—something which we don't have much of, since Henry leaves in a fortnight—"

"*Or?*" Matthew prodded, drumming his fingers on his leg.

"Or . . . you could give him one."

His fingers froze mid-air. Then they gripped his chair as he stood, slowly. "*Give* him a fortune? Of what sum?"

Not expecting to get this far, I hadn't premeditated an amount. To buy time, I examined a tortoiseshell snuffbox sitting by itself on the table, thoughts racing. Henry's father hadn't been extraordinarily wealthy, but he'd definitely been rich. I could only guess at the amount he would've bequeathed Henry upon his death.

"Thirty thousand pounds," I said at last.

Matthew's eyebrows shot up. "Ha!" An empty, smile-less laugh escaped his lips. Then without a word, he strode to the other side of the room and consulted a row of books. It was another calculated move, meant to dismiss me, just as he'd clearly dismissed my proposal.

Undeterred, I followed him. "You have money enough."

"That is entirely beside the point. Deuces—the cheek of you, my lady, is beyond fathom." He extracted a brown leather book, read its title, and replaced it.

I leaned a shoulder against the bookcase, batting my lashes. "Surely that amount is a paltry pittance in exchange for the agony you would endure, being tethered to me for the rest of your life."

He blinked over to me. "To be sure." His finger slid down the spines of books. "But do you hear yourself? You, a lady, are asking me, a gentleman—"

"A debatable term."

He selected another book. "—to give *thirty thousand pounds* to another man—not as a loan, but as a gift—simply because I had the misfortune of crashing into you—"

"Unfortunately for us both."

He opened the book and flapped through several pages. "—and I am to give this money to this man—a man who is, by all accounts, not your fiancé, as that *honor* is currently held by me—so that you may marry him."

"Which is what we both want."

Matthew glanced up. "Yes. What we both want," he agreed. "But is still quite out of the question." He snapped the book shut in my face, making me flinch, and returned it to its place.

My hands went to my hips. "Why?"

Matthew found the book he was looking for and stalked away. Again, I followed him.

"Because," he said, settling into his chair, "if Mr. Crawley is any kind of man, he would never accept charity, especially so large a sum. And if he *would* accept it . . . well, then he isn't any kind of man, so why would you want to marry him in the first place?"

I wanted to marry Henry regardless of any wealth or lack thereof.

"Give it up," Matthew said. "No man is worth thirty thousand pounds."

Henry was. Yet, though I didn't want to admit it, Matthew made a fair point. Henry would refuse the money—adamantly.

Drat. So much for the easy route. On to plan two.

"Fine then. For now, I will meditate on how else to get him a fortune. But one way or another I will—and I *will* do it in a fortnight."

"I'd very much appreciate it," he said like I was already destined to fail. "And what is the other obstacle?"

I picked up the green stuffed pillow resting on the wingback chair and hugged it to my chest. "Societal recognition. Henry needs to be accepted in higher circles before he will consider marrying me."

He sucked in a breath. "Conundrum."

"Not so, sir, as *you* happen to be in the highest of circles." I was as well, but society didn't exactly respect me the way they respected Matthew. "A ball is being held in his honor, next Wednesday. Attend it, and everyone shall be viewing him with different eyes. Be friendly to him, and you might even cause a few fainting spells." I was half-joking—but in reality, wasn't far off the mark. Why Matthew's opinion mattered so much I should never know, but since it did, and since I was forced to be engaged to the man, I might as well use it to my advantage.

"You want me to go out in public?" He grimaced. "I would rather give you thirty thousand pounds."

"Does being in polite company pain you that much?"

"Yes. The only reason I go out at all is because my dearly departed mother wished me to make an effort."

I squeezed the pillow tighter, taken aback at his openness, and the way he didn't seem to regret it. This was another subtle suggestion that though he didn't have a heart, he at least cared for his family and their good opinion. Another contradiction.

Picking at a loose thread on the pillow, I said nonchalantly, "One appearance, one little interaction—that is all I am asking of you. We may not succeed, but it is your only chance to wash your hands of me. Will you really see it slip through your fingers, just to spare a little pride?"

Matthew looked me up and down slowly, evaluating. Mouth working. "And what of the fortune?"

"Leave that bit to me."

He shook his head. "I cannot believe I am saying this, but . . . fine. This one thing I shall do. But understand that I do not do it for you."

My insides leapt in celebration, but I kept my expression only mildly interested. "Yes, so you shan't have to marry me."

"No—so I shan't have to marry at all."

I blinked, remembering what he'd said in the garden. Matthew hunched down further in his chair, hiking the book up to cover his face. Another dismissal. Setting the pillow down, I opened my mouth and—

"I'd rather not be quizzed at the present moment, so please, spare me your questions." His voice was muffled from the book. "You are curious about that comment, and my mother, and why I agreed to help you, tempting incentive aside. But I shall give you no more answers today."

Oh, for all the—

"*How* do you do that?" I threw at him.

"Do what?"

"Predict that I would come? Know what I'm going to say before I say it?"

He shrugged one shoulder. "Human nature. People are people, and they always have been. Once you've studied ten, you know the thought patterns of a thousand."

I sucked in my cheeks, a glare darkening my forehead. What an odd, presumptuous thing to say. And he was still hidden behind his book, ignoring me. My posture went rigid. "Yes, but how do you know what *I* will do?"

"You are a woman," he said, as if that explained everything. He turned a page. "Oh come now, do not get so defensive. I did not intend it in the way you think."

I scoffed. "And how did you intend it?"

With a drawn-out sigh, he closed his book. "Has no one ever taught you it is impolite to disturb someone when they are reading?"

"It is also impolite to insult me—which you have done, and continue to do at every opportunity. Now what did you mean by that, sir?"

After uncrossing his legs, he drew them in, tossing the book in front of him. "Firstly, calling my comments 'insults' implies I spoke intentionally to aggravate you, which I have never done. I have only ever spoken fact. However, being the stubborn, temperamental girl that you are—*that* one I intended as an insult—you have been all too eager to take offense, if only for the reason that moments after you met me, you decided you didn't like me."

I took a big breath, but he plunged on before I could retort.

"As for your question: I have found that, in general, women tend to value love above all else. When it is offered, compromised, or taken away, it evokes patterns of behavior in females that are, in a word, predictable."

My chin jutted. "And you think it is weak to value something so emotional as love."

"On the contrary," he muttered, "I think it is a great strength."

My head reared back slightly, surprised again at his honesty. I sat in silence, some of my anger dissipating. But not all. "And do I fall into this category of predictable women?"

Matthew's lifeless eyes locked onto mine. There was something different about them. A subtle squint to them that indicated . . . amusement? Interest? Disdain? Why was he so blasted difficult to read?

"You, Lady Alicia, are the most predictable woman I have ever met."

I ground my teeth. Now *that* was an insult. And just when I thought he might actually possess a soul! He did not know my thoughts, or my heart. He didn't know my dreams, or aspirations, or the memories that shaped my life.

"How *dare* you imagine—"

"That I know your heart and every important event that has shaped your life?"

My mouth clamped shut. Then, after restarting a few rage-filled sentences, I finally managed, "That's not what—"

"Not what you were going to say? Not what was going through

your mind just now? Ah, but your wide eyes and tightened fists would beg to differ."

I immediately relaxed my fists. "You couldn't possibly—"

"Know what you'd been about to say. I have no way of *ever* proving that I'm right, so I should give up predicting what you'll say altogether." He clucked his tongue at me. "You shall have to do much better than that, my lady. Better to remain silent and be thought a fool, than to speak and remove all doubt."

I emitted a growl unfit for polite company. Fiend seize it! *How* was he doing that? If it was the last thing I did, I would show Matthew Wycliffe that he did not know everything.

That he did not know everything about *me*.

I needed to do something unpredictable. If I could, right in this moment, it would usurp him from his throne and humble him until he was beaten into dust. My mind flashed to the image of my hand on his arm in the garden. A hot burst of loathing propelled me forward, bolstering me into doing what at any other time would be absolutely unthinkable. The only thing that I knew disarmed him.

He stood as if to leave.

In one giant step, I'd closed the gap between us, making Matthew jerk and fall back into his chair. For once, I wasn't dwarfed by his imposing figure, and I relished the sense of power it granted. Before he could recover, I pinned his shoulder in place.

For perhaps the first time, Matthew's expression gave him away. His head inched back, his brows sloped slightly up, his breath became a little less stable. Subtle signs on any other man—but where Matthew was concerned, astronomical.

My aunt's warning rang in my ears. *Do not dive headlong into folly .*
. .

Smirking, I raked my other hand through his rich, dark hair. It was so soft. So cool and silky. I allowed my fingers to linger, my anger morphing into satisfaction. This was retribution—a rare opportunity to unsettle him the way he constantly unsettled me. And it felt marvelous.

When I leaned in, his lips opened, his gaze darting between my eyes. "There now, sir," I whispered in his ear, watching my breath tousle his hair, cocking one brow in triumph. "Did you predict that?"

I inhaled his scent—a little too deeply, but I couldn't help it. Being so near him gave me a heady feeling, like I never wanted to pull away.

His hand shot up and clamped around my wrist, mouth pulling into a frown. Slowly, he pushed my hand away from his hair until I was forced to back up as he stood. I licked my lips and attempted to calm my heart, still pounding from the surprise of what I'd just done.

After fishing out his book which had fallen into the crack in the chair, he straightened, his knuckles white around its spine. A muscle in his jaw ticked. He stared at me for another beat before his eyebrows did a little bob. "No, my lady. I did not."

He turned and left, steps neither slow nor hurried, posture neither bolstered nor sagging. For one fleeting moment I had managed to startle him. One moment, and then he had bounced back, completely collected, never to be surprised by me again.

But still I smiled, considering it a victory—for I had discovered a secret that no one else knew: Matthew Wycliffe was human, after all.

And, as he had so thoroughly explained, humans could be predicted.

CHAPTER 8

Two days later, in the throes of a jostling carriage ride, I remembered the secret passageways.

When we were children, Lord Crawley used to take Henry and me on each knee and captivate us with stories of dead nobles who roamed the secret tunnels hidden in the castle. I remember his hands, gesturing against the backdrop of a roaring fire, his voice haunting as he described the medieval ghosts in vivid detail.

And I remembered one night best—the one where Henry fell asleep on his father's shoulder, and Nicholas Crawley whispered to me where the entrance to the secret tunnel was. The next day, keeping as unseen as one of the ghosts from his stories, I slipped into Lord Crawley's study and searched for it high and low. Alone. I didn't tell Henry because I wanted to find it for myself. But when an afternoon passed and no secret passageways were revealed, I quickly lost interest. Lord Crawley never mentioned it again, and I never told another soul.

I smiled as I watched the hills blur by outside the carriage window. It was the only explanation which made sense. Upon Lord Crawley's sudden death, there had been a mad scramble to find his will. Everyone knew his solicitor had drafted one, and there was the looming question of which son he'd left his fortune to. Inch by painstaking inch, the castle had been searched, five times over—in vain. No will, no fortune for Henry.

But, since Nicholas Crawley had likely disinherited his elder son in his will—a son who was apt to burn the document if he ever laid hands on it—I suspected the old baron had hidden it somewhere it *couldn't* be found. Somewhere it would be kept safe, and no one would think to look.

No one, except perhaps me.

It was so perfect, I couldn't believe I hadn't thought of it before.

"What are you smiling about?"

I turned to Aunt Beth who was leaning back against the blood-red cushions of the carriage walls, studying me. Father sat beside her, both hands on his silver-knobbed cane. Fiddling with the teardrop beads adorning the inside cut of my purple muslin, I schooled my features and leaned back, opting not to answer her.

That turned out to be the wrong idea, because an amused gleam entered her eye and she said, "Eager to see Mr. Wycliffe again, I hope."

Slathering my voice in as much fervor as I could manage, I said, "The *eager-est*, aunt! Though I fear Father will find Mr. Wycliffe sorely lacking in his qualifications—if he is able to sniff at someone as golden as Henry."

Father exclaimed something unintelligible as Aunt Beth waggled a finger at me. "My dear girl," she said, not missing my sarcasm, "you should make the most of this dinner party by using that pretty face of yours to win him over, as that is obviously what heaven intended you to do with it. I daresay it's not good for much else."

I'd heard variants of the sentiment often enough from my aunt's lips, but it still needled each time.

Instead of reacting, I crossed my arms and turned back toward the window. This evening, I knew, was going to test all my limits. If

I emerged without imagining what Matthew's chest would look like with a dagger in it, I planned to call the night a success.

Father tapped his cane with one finger, his tall frame hunched uncomfortably in the small carriage. "I don't understand why we have to suffer a devilish long carriage ride to attend a supper party when we could've just had dinner at home."

Aunt Beth's shoulder bumped into his in the swaying carriage. "Because Lord Wycliffe specially invited us for the purpose of introducing us to his family. If we are to pretend this engagement is legitimate, we must attend."

A sinking feeling settled in my stomach. In the gardens, Lord Wycliffe had kissed my hand and congratulated me. Despite the less than ideal circumstances, he'd seemed genuinely pleased I was engaged to his brother. Now I was to fool him into thinking the engagement would actually lead to marriage—on top of fooling the rest of the family into thinking we were in love.

And I'd told myself I wouldn't feel a drop of guilt for Matthew, but that was proving to be difficult, as well. Though I didn't feel particularly sorry for him, I realized that none of this mess was his fault; that it was *I* who was wreaking havoc on *his* life, not the other way around. And now, even though Mr. Wycliffe hadn't orchestrated the dinner party, I was being invited into his close family circle. The least I could do was try to get along with him.

"And," Aunt Beth continued, "as you haven't even met Mr. Wycliffe, Rupert, you really ought to act more interested."

Father scowled. "Of course I'm interested—I want to wring the little man's neck! But I'd rather do it in the comfort of my own home, plague take it." Muttering, he added, "Dashed presumptuous, this invitation. Haven't even been introduced."

"Yes, and we had better take advantage of his presumptuousness if Alicia is to secure his fortune." Aunt Beth wrapped her shawl tighter around her shoulders. "Lord Wycliffe is known to be a gracious host, unlike his younger brother. But then, the brother has other qualities which make up for it."

At that moment, Lord Wycliffe's residence came into view.

A grand, sprawling estate that rivaled Lawry Park, Ambleside stood in a little valley ensconced in the gilt rays of a setting sun. Lit torches lined the drive, leading us to the entrance. After helping Aunt Beth and I down, Father took in the measure of the estate with a shrewd purse to his lips. He would not be easily impressed.

I took in the scene as well, trying to imagine Matthew as a young boy, growing up here. It was hard to picture, but if the mansion contained any sort of library, I'm sure he had a very easy, very secluded childhood. The thought brought a smile to my lips.

Father gave a harrumph before striding up the steps and into the entrance. Aunt Beth followed him eagerly. Whether or not I was prepared for this nightmare, it was about to unfold. To save my reputation, spare my father from ridicule, and thereby open the possibility for my marrying Henry, I had to convince the entire party I loved Matthew. Failure meant never seeing my friend again and living out my days with Hawthorne as a husband.

How did everything get so complicated?

I squared my shoulders. *I'm in love*, I drilled with each step up the stairs. *I must convince them I'm in love.* Another speech quickly treaded on its heels: *And whatever happens, I shall be civil to Matthew Wycliffe.*

Lord Wycliffe stood in the foyer, greeting his guests. Spotting me, he bowed as I curtsied. "Lady Alicia! It is good of you to come on such short notice. Might I introduce my wife, Lady Lillian Wycliffe." He gestured to a stunning woman with sparkling eyes standing at his side.

She stepped forward with a smile and a curtsy. "It's so good to finally make your acquaintance. I was surprised to hear of Matthew's engagement, as he's never been inclined toward romance, but it is also like him to keep monumental secrets to himself." In a softer voice, she added, "I hope we may be friends."

I stared into her eyes, taken aback by the sincerity I found there. I'd never been friends with anyone besides Henry—through no choice of my own. Anyone I'd tried to befriend had either attempted to use me for my station or turned green with jealousy, eventually stabbing me in the back. I'd long given up trying to form real connections with women.

I knew all about cutthroat social calls and barbarous balls—but someone wanting to be my friend, not for prestige, but simply for companionship? That was foreign.

And here I was, planning to betray the lot of them in a fortnight.

The guilt stroking my insides grew claws. Finally, I managed with a dip of my head, "I-I hope so, too." She gave me another wide smile. Turning to Father and Aunt Beth, I finished the introductions. Father retained an aloof but evaluating expression, obviously still forming his opinion on the Wycliffes. I felt a strange flutter in my stomach, anxious for him to like them, although I didn't know why.

"Where is he?" I asked, craning my eyes to look behind them. It took me a moment to realize I should clarify. "That is, where is Mr. Wycliffe?"

"He's, erm . . ." Lord Wycliffe looked at his wife with inquiring eyes. "Lily?"

"I haven't seen him all day," she said quietly.

Lord Wycliffe turned back, expression a mixture of embarrassment and vexation. "It appears we do not know where he is. Please, you must forgive him—it is not your company he wishes to avoid."

I highly doubted that.

"I am sure Matthew is somewhere lurking about the library," he went on with obliged enthusiasm, "and time has simply got away from him. Again. Only give me a moment and I shall fetch him." Lord Wycliffe bowed and slipped away.

We moved into a drawing room adjacent to the hall, passing a dozen milling guests and greeting them as we went. Aunt Beth made a few introductions, eliciting raised eyebrows and forced, polite smiles from a handful of them when she mentioned my name. My reputation preceded me, it seemed. Face feeling suddenly warm, I rubbed it with the back of my fingers and made my way toward the other end of the room.

"Can't be bothered to make an appearance—not even for his fiancée," Father said under his breath as he sank onto a sofa, joining me near the fireplace. Aunt Beth sat next to him, and I took a seat in the blue velvet chair opposite them.

Aunt Beth looked around, ensuring no one was near enough to eavesdrop. "We are interested in more than his social skills."

I smirked. "If staying away is a high offense, Father, I shudder to think what your opinion of the man will be once you actually meet him." Just the picture of it was a sight to behold: Matthew, the swift-tongued offender meeting Father, the traditional, hot-tempered duke.

I could already see the sparks flying.

"Why do you say that?" Father asked.

I leaned forward, resting my elbows on the arms of the chair. "Only because I wish to prepare you. Mr. Wycliffe is not some shy fellow incapable of forming a sentence. Don't let his books deceive you—he is tediously clever and quite simply the horridest man to ever walk the earth."

"Quite."

I shot up at the sound of his hollow voice above my head, and spun around to find him in a burgundy tailcoat that complemented his smooth complexion. Drat it all. He was still annoyingly handsome. Remembering my commitment to be civil, I sidled up to him. "Why, Mr. Wycliffe!" I said, for the benefit of those who had turned their heads to watch us. "How good of you to finally show your face."

Matthew's eyes went to my hand around his arm, and he scowled. "Yes. Just in time for you to caricaturize it."

Lord Wycliffe appeared and clapped Matthew on the back. "Found him. In the library just as I suspected. Your Grace, Lady Beth, might I introduce my brother, Matthew Wycliffe."

Father analyzed Matthew as he gave a stiff bow, and I knew what he must be thinking. I could practically hear the words resounding off the walls. *Tall. Too lean—one of those uppity types who can't tell one end of a musket from the other. Shifty character. His movements are too fluid. Too graceful to be unpracticed. Shallow. Not much of a man at all.*

Aunt Beth, on the other hand, grew an approving smile until it was a full-fledged grin. She saw something entirely different.

Using his cane, Father stood with squinted eyes. "I have heard much about you, sir."

Matthew's eyebrows lifted the tiniest fraction. "And I you."

"Good things, I hope?"

"Not all, Your Grace."

Father frowned. I smiled wider. Perhaps the evening would prove entertaining after all.

Matthew bowed again, expression still blank. "If you'll excuse me." He pulled away to the other side of the room, eliciting a scowl from Aunt Beth and a string of mutterings from Father.

Lady Wycliffe approached, and a throng of chatting guests with her. "I hope you find our home to your liking," she said to me after a moment.

Taking in the swirly, embossed ceiling, the mint-green walls with golden mirrors, and the French-styled chairs, I said, "I do indeed. It is very elegant." The room made it clear to everyone that its master was incredibly wealthy, and yet the atmosphere wasn't stuffy or pretentious. Quite the opposite. If this was how rich Lord Wycliffe was, I couldn't imagine the magnitude of Matthew's wealth. It supposedly greatly exceeded Peter's, but one would never guess so by comparing their houses.

I was beginning to understand that Matthew was a simple man. A confusing, complicatedly simple man.

Lady Wycliffe beamed at my answer. "I thought so too, my first day here. But enough about me—I want to know all about your engagement. Matthew's been predictably tight-lipped about the whole affair and refuses to answer any of my questions."

"Does he." I glanced at Matthew, who reclined against the far wall, reading. He didn't appear to be eavesdropping, but as I'd learned with him, looks could be deceiving.

"What was it about Matthew that first drew your eye?"

Quieting their various conversations, everyone in the group turned to hear my answer. At the back, Father gave me a stern stare. *You're in love. You must convince them you're in love.*

The blood rushed to my face as my thoughts raced. What did I like about Matthew? Nothing. Absolutely nothing. He was arrogant and dismissive, condescending and brash, perceptive and—

I hoped he wasn't listening. Oh, how I hoped he wasn't listening.

"He is the handsomest man I've ever seen," I blurted.

The group chuckled. I studied Lady Wycliffe for any suspicion or disappointment, but she laughed along. In fact, her smile was broader than anyone else's.

But the words lingered and soured in my mouth. Not because they were a lie, but because they weren't. Matthew Wycliffe *was* the handsomest man I'd ever seen. And I hated it. I hated that he outshone Henry in every measurable way.

"Even more so than Peter?" Lady Wycliffe asked, eyes twinkling. "Many have made the same statement about my husband."

I swallowed, uncomfortable, but gave the question some thought.

The Wycliffe brothers could easily be mistaken for each other, but side by side there were subtle differences which set them apart. Matthew's cheekbones were higher, his chin sharper, his gaze more cutting. In general, Peter's features were softer, and because of it, I had no doubt most women would say he was the more attractive one, as well.

But Matthew was more striking. More memorable. He had a face that haunted dreams; one that made you wonder if you'd rather watch a candle burn through the night, or slip into sleep and never wake up again.

When Peter looked at you, you melted. But when Matthew looked at you, you trembled. From fear, or attraction, or anticipation—whatever it was, it was terrifying. And though Lord Wycliffe was indeed incredibly handsome, he didn't have that kind of effect on me.

He didn't terrify me.

I cleared my throat before turning to Lord Wycliffe. "Forgive me, sir, but yes, I would say he is even handsomer than you."

Instead of being offended, Lord Wycliffe laughed. His wife gave me a conspiratorial smile. And through the crowd, not moving an inch from his huddled position over his book, Matthew locked eyes with me.

Fear. Attraction. Anticipation. They hit me one after the other like a masterful pianist building a crescendo.

He looked away. One little glance that told me he had been listening, after all. I gritted my teeth against the blush rising to my cheeks, turning away before anyone saw it.

"Shall we adjourn to the dining hall?" Lord Wycliffe gestured to his left. The party began migrating through the double doors and seating themselves around a large table. Father offered his arm to Aunt Beth and left me alone with Matthew, who snapped his book shut, tucked it into an unseen pocket in his tailcoat, and pushed himself off the wall.

"I cannot hide my disappointment that you didn't say I was the most *intelligent* man you'd ever seen." He neared, stopping just inches away. Though he did not smile, I got the sense that he found my confession amusing. Or . . . sincere? Satisfying? "Beauty is nothing."

Remembering my earlier determination to be charitable, I swallowed the temptation to be angry at him for making me feel embarrassed. From what I could tell, he didn't appear to be teasing me. "Is that what you believe?"

"It is an illusion—one that fades all too quickly."

"I disagree with you, sir. Beauty takes many forms, and though it may not be very useful it is certainly not nothing."

"Perhaps." His gaze shot down to my feet, then back up.

My thoughts ground to a halt. *Wait.* Had he just—

"In the least," he continued, "I suppose I should be grateful you don't find me all terrible."

"No, I don't," I agreed, and I wasn't just talking of his appearance. A truly terrible man wouldn't have concerned himself with my reputation enough to offer me marriage. We quarreled and he got under my skin, but that didn't mean he didn't possess any good qualities. "It might surprise you to learn, Mr. Wycliffe, that I am not all terrible either."

"I am not surprised."

I was spared a reply to that confusing comment by the sound of a throat clearing. Both our heads turned to find Lord Wycliffe in the doorway, motioning for Matthew to escort me in. After Lord Wycliffe had disappeared again, Matthew glanced at me. His eyebrows bobbed once. Then he skirted around me and strode in the dining room.

Without me.

On *purpose.*

Of all the obnoxious things! And just when I thought we had begun to call a truce! Mouth in a firm line, I scurried up and forcibly took his arm, all thoughts of being friendly to him now dead and buried in the earth where they belonged. Though he made no audible protest, he frowned at the touch. "I thought you said you were capable of anything," I whispered through the side of my mouth so as to not draw any attention. "I am coming to doubt that, Mr. Wycliffe, as you do not make a very convincing fiancé."

"Neither do you."

"And now we must pretend to be in love, even though I'd rather gnaw off my arm with my own teeth."

"An opinion we share." He glanced at me from the corner of

his eye. "And do hurry, my lady—for then I shall be spared the trouble of escorting you. No arm, no way to lead you into dining rooms."

Matthew cut off my retort by letting go and tugging my chair out. Lifting my chin, I moved past him with a hard, pointed bump to his shoulder. As I sat, Matthew pushed my chair in—a little too far. My stomach hit the table, making me grunt in pain.

He'd done that on purpose.

Matthew sat opposite me, flung his napkin from its shape, and tucked it in over his cravat, all while staring at me with the same cold stare.

I stared right back, showing him I would not be cowed. That trick of his might work on a lesser woman—and indeed, might've worked on me a week ago—but not anymore. If his game was intimidation, I knew how to play.

Servants entered with our first course, dishes of chilled soup and roasted beets.

"Lady Alicia," Lady Wycliffe called from the end of the table, "perhaps I might persuade you to tell me how you met Matthew. As he is a difficult man to pry information out of, I still do not know enough details!"

Now was my chance to get back at the conceited man sitting across from me, and I wasn't going to let the opportunity pass me by. "Certainly." I blinked innocently. "We met at the Pantheon, during my last Season."

The collective, surprised swallows of soup were nearly audible. Matthew's lips angled into a disapproving slant while mine did the exact opposite.

Public masques were notoriously rollicking and disreputable. Anyone wishing to keep their standing intact wouldn't be caught dead at one. Many of the young Peers still attended, believing their masks would hide their identities while exercising their bravado and rebellion.

To my left, Father turned every shade of red, face pinched in anger. I would deal with him later. Now, vengeance was more pressing.

"Matthew?" Lily said, brow furrowed. "At a masquerade? I can scarce imagine it."

"Upon better acquaintance, I can scarcely imagine it myself." My gaze settled on Matthew, who looked annoyed. I simpered at him. "But he was there, at the Pantheon. And if you can believe it, he was dressed as a—"

"A Spaniard," he cut in, voice clipped.

Drat it, I was about to say something much more denigrating.

"And Lady Alicia," he went on, "was dressed as a *milkmaid*."

My hands fell out of my lap and gripped my chair. A milkmaid! He couldn't have picked a more humiliating costume. Matthew blinked at me in victory, that intense, stubborn gleam in his eye absolutely insufferable.

I leaned over my bowl. "Yes, I remember. A milkmaid. And you found me *so* desirable dressed thusly that you asked me for three dances."

The table erupted with light chuckles and murmurs, and finally something entered Matthew's expression. Anger. At the Pantheon or not, three dances with one partner was shocking and indecent. His cheeks pinked.

"So, *so* desirable," he muttered through clenched teeth. He was keeping his tongue in check—and it must've taken a lot of effort, especially for someone for whom snappish rebuttals came easy. How he longed to put me in my place with a rapid retort. But he couldn't. And that made it all the sweeter.

"He saw me through the crowd," I said, "and he thought, 'That's her. The girl—'"

"—who threw her handkerchief into my path," Matthew finished.

My fingernails dug into the grainy wood. "'And I must return it to her, else she will miss it.' So Matthew quickly came to my side, and when he saw me up close, and beheld how extremely beautiful I was, he said—"

"—'Shouldn't you be at home with your cows?'"

I shoved my foot into his under the table. "To which I replied, 'Indeed! For they have *much* better manners!' But of course, all this was after he praised my golden tresses and—"

"—remarked on how their color resembled Mr. Cunningham's teeth." He kicked my foot right back.

"The poor Mr. Wycliffe was obviously at a loss for words! So incapable of expressing his admiration, he resorted to awkward similes! I had to accept the dances—what else was I to do with him groveling at my feet?"

Matthew winced as if I'd kicked him again. "It could hardly be defined as groveling." He didn't like being depicted as a helpless, besotted man—didn't want to be at my mercy in any way, fictionally or otherwise—and it probably ate him away inside.

How utterly wonderful.

"It couldn't be defined as anything less," I said, mouth twisted into a wicked smile. "You groveled and groveled."

A muscle jumped in his temple. Rage trembled in his eyes. And revenge.

"What a peculiar tale," Lily said. Everyone's gazes had volleyed between the two of us while we verbally sparred, but now Lady Wycliffe tapped one knuckle against her chin, eyes thinned and shining in amusement.

Oh, dear. I hadn't tried to make it believable. Neither of us had.

"Peculiar indeed," Peter chimed in from the other end, looking at his wife. "Just like Matthew himself."

Mr. Goodrich and his two young daughters had wrinkled foreheads, but thanks to Lord Wycliffe, everyone else returned to their soup with a chuckle and without suspicion. Matthew must have a past just like me —one that caused his acquaintances to always expect the unexpected.

Perhaps this fact alone had salvaged the illusion that we were in love. I breathed a sigh of relief. Perhaps our back-and-forth could be interpreted as passion. And it certainly was that—but for a completely different reason than everyone thought.

"I say, Mr. Wycliffe, what are your politics?" Father cut Matthew a calculating gaze. It was the same look he'd been giving him all evening, and I was sure Matthew had noticed it by now.

Aunt Beth tsked. "For heaven's sake, what a depressing subject! You're likely to frighten him away."

"If you please, madam," Matthew said, taking a swallow of his drink then thumbing over the carved crystal once he'd returned it to the table, "such topics will sooner put me at ease than frighten me."

Lord Wycliffe cleared his throat loudly, and the look he gave his brother could only be interpreted as a warning. But Matthew didn't even glance in Peter's direction. He was obviously practiced in the art of ignoring his brother.

"I have no politics, Your Grace," Matthew said.

Father scoffed. "None?"

The response surprised me as well.

"I will admit, out of the two parties, I have more cause to rally under the Tory banner—but I have serious qualms with them."

Father's face took on a thoughtful frown. He was a Whig, through and through.

"In general," Matthew continued, "I find the separation and formation of parties to be barbaric and ultimately frightfully dull."

"Dull?"

"Certainly." Matthew reclined in his seat. Why did he always look so languid? So careless? "Why can't a man stand on his own principles, instead of conforming to what any one party says? And why should I let one rallying cause define my identity, when the minutiae of my opinions are too complex to paint them with a broad brush? I am a man with principles—and I will stand on them, be they on one side of the aisle or the other. The formation of parties prompts the spouting of pre-determined rhetoric for the sake of loyalty. They are tantrums thrown by toddlers—yes, barbaric and dull—and those are the conversations I find to be most tedious." He glanced at me, sending me a double message.

You are just as tedious as I, I retorted mutely.

Father sat back, and though he still frowned, there was an impressed glint to his eye. Matthew knew his own mind—a trait Father liked in any man, whether Father shared his views or not.

"What are your thoughts on Waterloo?"

Lily laughed from the other end of the table, though it sounded forced. "Such topics are several years old. I'm afraid they've already been hashed and rehashed—"

"A massacre." Matthew ignored his sister-in-law's attempts for peace.

Father's face screwed up. Being a strategy enthusiast, he prided himself on determining the best military course in any situation. In his mind, Waterloo had been a smashing success. "How so, sir?"

Matthew set his spoon down. "Waterloo appealed to the public, but it wasn't actually necessary."

"Wasn't necessary!"

"No, Your Grace. Napoleon should have been defeated long before Waterloo."

Father puffed. "Young man, they all tried! Several times. No one saw Little Boney coming, or predicted his ruthless tenacity, nor his ever-rallying support—"

"I did."

The room grew silent.

If any other man had uttered such an outrageous statement, I would have discarded it immediately. But I had witnessed Matthew's genius and mysterious gift of foresight firsthand. Judging by the way Lily bit her lip and Peter rubbed his eyes with his fingers, I had the suspicion that it was true. They'd probably been forced to listen to Matthew's rants on the subject long before Napoleon's surrender.

"You did, sir?" Father looked unsure what to make of the declaration.

"Yes. I did." Matthew rolled his head over to look at Peter. "But no one *ever* listens to me, *do* they?"

"Just as no one is ever going to let the matter rest," Peter muttered, giving Matthew a pointed glare.

Lily cleared her throat. "Pray, let us not quarrel. I hear the season is to be a fruitful one, good for crops, and replenishing our . . ."

Everyone around the table settled back into their different conversations. But Father wasn't quite finished with his interrogation—and Matthew met it head on, without the slightest hint of the uncertainty or intimidation Father usually inspired in his victims.

"Do you hunt, Mr. Wycliffe?"

"No. I despise guns."

"Then do you ride?"

"Not if I can help it."

Father leaned forward. "What do you think of Brummel?"

"A fop."

"Byron?"

"The same, but with actual taste."

"Voltaire?"

"Brilliant."

"Shakespeare?"

"Overrated."

"Me?"

Matthew's eyes narrowed slightly. "I think, Your Grace, you form your opinions quickly, and once made, they cannot be unmade. I think you do not want to be here, and never did, and believe me I share the sentiment. I think you enjoy terrifying others with your wealth and title, so you are disappointed that neither have any effect on me. And I would apologize for your disappointment, Your Grace, except for the impossible fact that I am not sorry."

Father sat in shocked silence. Matthew had done it now. Father was sure to be furious. He was sure to—

My thoughts cut short at the sound of Father laughing—actually laughing, just as he did with Hawthorne. Just as he never did with Henry. I exchanged a glance with Aunt Beth, who seemed just as perplexed as I.

"You are correct, sir," Father said at last. "Correct on all three counts. Mr. Wycliffe, you have greatly surprised me."

Matthew's brows raised. "Sentences I hear often."

That made Father laugh again, and the sound felt like a punch to the gut. My fingers pinched the neck of my spoon. I didn't know which was worse: Father hating Matthew, or actually *liking* him—and never in my wildest dreams had I imagined the latter would be true.

At last, Matthew finally looked at me—the opportunity I'd been searching for to send him my glower. But his face lacked any expression. He just blinked at me. Slowly. Bored, as he raised his glass to his lips and swallowed.

Oh, how I hated him.

CHAPTER 9

DINNER HAD BEEN A DISASTER.

The men had already drunk their after-supper port and several card games were in motion around the drawing room. Currently, Matthew was surrounded by guests congratulating him on the news of his upcoming nuptials, and he received each well-wisher with a nod and a look of supreme discomfort.

Tapping my foot against the rug, I watched Matthew anxiously, waiting for an opportunity to catch him alone. I was so busy studying him that I didn't see Father approach until he stood at my side.

"What an amiable family." He fiddled with his cufflinks, gaze sweeping across the room. "Quite genteel. Good heads on their shoulders. And Mr. Wycliffe! Very amiable indeed."

I frowned at Matthew. "Indeed."

Lowering his voice, he said, "It is a pity your marriage contract to Hawthorne has already been written up. I highly approve of Mr. Wycliffe—second son though he may be." Father took in a breath and turned to me. "But it is for the best, I suppose. Hawthorne is still the better catch."

"You forget, Father, I may not marry Hawthorne."

"You will if there are any more scenes like the one at dinner." He pulled out a chair from an empty table and sat. After extricating his silver snuffbox, he spooned some snuff onto the side of his hand and inhaled deeply. He snapped the box shut and tucked it back into his coat. "If you cannot be convincing, Alicia, if rumors start to circulate that you are not attached to Mr. Wycliffe out of love . . . you will have broken our deal."

I chewed on the inside of my cheek, knowing what a broken deal would mean—that I would be the next Duchess of Cabourne, not the next Mrs. Crawley. "I understand, Father."

"Good." He used his cane to stand, grunting, then strolled over to Lord Wycliffe and engaged him in conversation.

I crossed my arms, stewing over his words before my mind drifted to the realization I'd had in the carriage ride here, remembering the secret whispers about hidden passageways. My gaze flickered over to Matthew again, finding him now secluded in his own corner. He reclined against the wall with one shoulder, one leg crossed behind the other, looking for all the world bored with life as he read.

I was about to make his life much less boring.

Not wanting to arouse any suspicion, I waited until everyone else in the room was otherwise engaged before brushing past him and muttering, "Meet me in the hall." I didn't look to see if he followed.

Out in the hall, I studied some paintings underneath an alcove. After several minutes had passed and Matthew still didn't appear, I started to wonder if he'd been too absorbed in his book to hear me. Or if he'd heard me and ignored it. That reason was more likely. Ready to forcibly drag him if I had to, I turned, then stopped short at the sight of him appearing at the mouth of the alcove.

"What can you possibly have to say," he sighed, leaning against the corner, "that must be said in secret?"

I released my dress, which now bore creases from where I'd

crumpled it. The poor thing was always ending up in my fists. "You mean you don't *know* already? You must be losing your touch."

"Oh, I already know. But it is much more entertaining to hear you say it."

I huffed, folding my arms across my chest. He couldn't possibly know my plan—I hadn't even told him about the missing will. Still, he'd proven me wrong before.

Drat it all. He was getting inside my head.

I plunged in. "Everyone knows Nicholas Crawley loved Henry better than his firstborn—but, upon his death, his will was never found. If it was, it is sure to bequeath everything currently in Graham's possession, to Henry. Servants and relatives alike searched Crawley Castle for months afterward, scouring every known crevice, but no one ever found it. They gave up. Everyone surmised that the old baron's will simply must not exist. *But* . . . if, by chance, it does . . ."

Matthew waited for me to continue, unimpressed.

". . . Then it means I wouldn't have to earn Henry a fortune after all—he already has one. And all I have to do is find it."

A wary glint entered Matthew's eye. "You mean to say that not only do you not have this will, but such a document might not even exist."

"Yes, it might not."

His lips pulled down into a frown. "Then why don't you speak to Mr. Crawley? The two of you can search for it together and leave me out of this."

I put my hands on my hips. "No, you see, that is what I cannot do."

Matthew was under no obligation to help me beyond attending the ball and paying Henry his respects, but there were many reasons why I needed his help in the secret tunnels. For one, though it pained me to admit, Matthew was highly intelligent and good at thinking on his feet. There were any number of obstacles we could run into, and he could prove useful.

Secondly, Graham and I weren't on the best of terms. If I were to be caught rifling through his den, I'd be able to explain my presence with Matthew there. The situation would be more damaging, but we were already engaged, so what did it matter?

And last of all, Matthew was the only one I had power over. The only one I might be able to convince to help me by flexing that power and making him yield. Nothing better than the prospect of me as his wife to force him into a wild chase.

He was by no means my first choice for a partner in crime, but he was all I had.

Matthew's face grew bland. He drew a pocket watch from his coat and consulted it. Tucking it back in, he said, "So you will search for this will in secret. Sneaking into Mr. Crawley's castle uninvited would be an impossible feat, and, if caught, even more impossible to explain—so you will wait until he has extended an invitation. Preferably to a function where he can be entertained by someone other than you, allowing you to slip away. Ah, but you cannot wait long, for he will be shipping away—so you will do it at the ball his brother is hosting next Wednesday, committing a heinous crime in the cloak of darkness while society enjoys their dances. Have I left anything out?"

I pursed my lips, trying not to be unnerved that he had surmised everything. "Well, you have yet to guess the color my gown shall be."

"Blue. And there is one thing you have not thought of. What makes you believe you could find the document in the course of one evening when Mr. Crawley has been unable to unearth it in the months since his father's demise?"

Because no one knew of the secret tunnels—Lord Crawley had been inebriated when he'd revealed their existence, so far gone I doubt he even realized I was there, overhearing him. But if I told Matthew the "secret passageways" part of the plan, I was certain he wouldn't go along with it. It was proving difficult enough to convince him to tag along without throwing hidden levers and ghost stories into the mix.

"Because," I said, "as it happens, I have one advantage that Henry does not."

He said nothing as he waited for my earth-shattering revelation. I was talking about knowledge of the entrance to the tunnel, but Matthew couldn't know that. I opted for something much less impressive.

"You," I said.

Silence reigned in the hallway. A little twitch of one eyebrow. That was all that changed about his face. "I have never in my life heard a more absurd notion." He turned away.

I snagged his sleeve. "With two pairs of eyes, we will cover twice as much ground."

He shook me off and spun back. "Not only do I have no desire to be anywhere near you, my lady—let alone together in the dark in such an intimate situation—what you speak of is a *crime*."

"No, it isn't!" I said, even though it most certainly was. "It is only Crawley Castle, and it's not as if we are going to steal anything. Only look around a bit."

With jerky movements he attempted to straighten his tailcoat, but only skewed it. "*We* shan't be doing anything of the kind. You may tangle yourself in a criminal web if you wish, but I shall not assist you—"

"You are just as embroiled in this as I!" I stamped my foot. "If you can conjure something better, then be my guest—but unless I find Henry's fortune and gain a proposal, you are stuck with me."

Or so he thought.

He scoffed. "This idea is preposterous. Ludicrous. Debasing."

"Even so, it is our best bet. Now, are you going to help me, or not?"

Matthew studied me for a long moment, his jaw tightening a little. I could feel his desire to be rid of me rolling off him in waves. It had the smell of burning wood, the feeling of hot wax dripping onto raw fingers. Something changed in his eyes. His jaw relaxed. He was going to help me.

"Not."

And then he marched back down the hallway. After a few frozen moments, I spurted forward and caught up to him, matching his strides.

"You are really not going to help me?" I panted. My, he had long legs.

"I once accused you of being hard of hearing, madam, but I never took you for a simpleton. Foolish, yes; brazen, perhaps—but never simple. You are proving me otherwise. Oh deuces, I hate it when I'm wrong."

A surge of anger burned in my chest. Yes, so it was a crime, but only a little one. I may not have to marry Matthew, and this mess may have been my entire fault in the first place, but he had been so dismissive, demeaning, and difficult at every turn that I *refused* to let him get off so easily.

Mr. Goodrich's two young girls tittered into the hallway. They stopped when they saw us, fixing on our red faces and Matthew's skewed tailcoat. A stroke of luck, if ever I saw one.

Snagging his lapels, I pushed him sideways into the wall.

"What the devil—!" He grunted upon impact.

"Oh, Matthew," I cried, "forgive me! I am sorry I was late to our tryst—but I was afraid. I cannot give you what you ask. No, sir, you mustn't kiss me yet—it is far too soon!"

Matthew gripped my wrists, brows slanting down at a fierce angle. "Why are you—?"

"How impassioned your note was, darling. And I feel the same! But we must refrain, for my father would never condone such bold behavior."

He attempted to shove me away. "I don't care a whit about your father! Now stop talking and let me—"

One of the girls watching gasped, covering her smile with her fingers. Matthew's head whipped over and froze, noticing them for the first time; realizing how our situation must look. They whispered to each other and giggled. A blush, red as crimson, crept up his neck. The girls backed away to give us some privacy, but the damage was already done. A smug smile danced on my mouth as they left.

Matthew's face swiveled back and stopped with precision. The unchecked loathing in his eyes made my smile falter. Made me want to hide in the nearest hole.

"My lady, have you *completely* lost your mind?" he enunciated. His hands, still around my wrists, tightened.

I stood taller. "I wouldn't rule out the possibility. But should I fail, we will be forced into a marriage neither of us wants—and you shall be forced to kiss me every day for the rest of your life. Is that what you want for yourself, Mr. Wycliffe? Because if not, I would recommend reconsidering your decision to help me."

His expression didn't change, but he seemed to be internally battling something. His eyes twitched; flashed down my face, once. At last, slowly, he released me. Straightened his waistcoat. Composed his features until they once more resembled condescending disdain.

"I shall see you Wednesday." He left, taking all the charged energy in the air with him.

I smiled. I suppose that meant yes.

CHAPTER 10

"LADY ALICIA, YOU ARE THE MOST BEAUTIFUL CREATURE IN THE world."

I stared at Hawthorne's broad white teeth, wishing he would put them away for even a moment. The sight of them flashing was giving me a headache.

The gloomy stone walls of the castle were made merry by garlands and six-hour candles. A sea of white and pink dresses weaved through the middle of the floor to the sound of violins dueling, accompanied by their black-coated partners. Father had predictably stayed home from the ball, and, being the matchmaking woman she was, Aunt Beth had left us unchaperoned the moment Hawthorne materialized.

I fanned my face. No matter what I did, Hawthorne seemed intent upon sticking to my side. The stifling, humid air of the ballroom made it difficult to breathe as it was, without adding to the mix the man's intrusion of personal space. Every word from his lips was an effort to seek favor, and every word bored me out of my skull.

"Am I, my lord?" I said absently, watching Henry across the

room and secretly vowing that if Hawthorne made one more remark on my ravishing appearance I would retrieve a glass of punch for the sole purpose of dumping it over his head.

I'd assumed that once Hawthorne learned of my engagement, I would be spared his constant company. But, the man had spent so much time at Lawry Park the last few days, apparently the news hadn't reached him yet. After all, my family talked of my scandals far less than the rest of the *ton* did.

"But of course!" he went on. "And rightly so, the way your eyes sparkle like emeralds."

Emeralds. How original. That did it. Where was the punch?

"Every other woman pales in comparison—like the paltry flame of a candle standing next to a blazing inferno."

This called for some outfoxing. "And what about Miss Jennings there?"

He stared at me for a moment, not comprehending. "Oh . . ." Glancing at Miss Jennings who was laughing and twirling the feather in her hair, he said, "To be sure, she is pretty—"

"I believe her five times prettier than me. Wouldn't you agree, my lord?"

He gave me a confused look. "No, you are far prettier—"

"Not so, sir! Just look at her delicate brow and slim figure. Anyone with two eyes can see that Miss Jennings is the handsomer. I can then only assume that the reason you compliment me is either because *you* are blind, or because you believe me to be. Which is it, my lord?"

"No! Lady Alicia, I—" He swept up one of my hands, giving it a squeeze. "Please, you mustn't think that. I—" He puffed out a smile, eyes softening like a puppy's. "—I adore you. I would do anything for you."

I slipped my hand out of his warm grasp.

There exactly was the problem. I didn't want someone who adored me. I wanted someone who loved me, yes, but said it through—not his words—but his actions. Words were meaningless. Compliments were meaningless.

My gaze again strayed to Henry underneath an archway, greeting guests with his brother, Graham. Almost mindlessly, my hand brushed my left glove. Henry had already proven his love. He'd been the only one to stand beside me through the years, everyone else turning cold.

And while Lord Hawthorne had been constant so far, he didn't strike me as someone who would defend my honor if confronted with my string of scandals. I could picture him clearly. He would cower and stammer and solicit his mother for a reply.

And I could never seek companionship with someone who didn't defend me.

The lull of conversation dampened. The music quieted until only an errant string or two creaked underneath a bow. Heads turned. Whispers traveled. And I knew what caused the sudden shift in the air even before I turned around.

Matthew was here.

It was about blasted time. Another moment and I might've had to fetch that glass of punch after all.

I glanced toward the entrance. Matthew descended the stairs as he sized up the room, its occupants ogling him in awe. When his line of sight landed on me, his leg on the step froze. And there, while everyone watched him, his head lolled to the side and he grimaced at me, somehow managing to look dignified as he did it.

Anyone else would be discomfited by the attention of the entire room, or puffed up; but Matthew couldn't care less. All he cared about was that he was forced to be at this silly ball, when what he wanted was an evening of solitude.

When Matthew's feet hit the ground level, lively music started up again and the crowd resumed their conversations, doing a better job at concealing their intense interest. Scraps of whispers met my ears.

Wycliffe . . . why did he . . . here tonight . . . engaged . . . could it be—

Dressed in snow-white gloves, a knotted cravat, and an ocean-blue tailcoat that matched his eyes, he approached me. Bodies parted the way to make a path. His wavy dark hair curled at his temples, over his ears, and at the nape of his neck. His appearance matched his personality: meticulous and sensible, with the slightest hint of swagger. No jewelry, no suggestion of gold or silver. He didn't need the help of anything flashy to cut a fine figure. And I hated myself for noticing.

He stopped before me.

Hawthorne spoke first, smiling wide. "Ah, Wycliffe, it is good of you to come. Didn't think I'd see you again for a few months—especially after you turned down my offer to buy up your tobacco shares! Lady Alicia, might I introduce you to Mr. Wy—"

"We've met." He hadn't taken his eyes off me since he entered the room. If he were any other man, I'd think he found my appearance captivating, that he was beginning a flirtation. But not Matthew. Far more likely this was another measured move meant to intimidate me and to simultaneously voice his displeasure at being here. So I was surprised when he added softly, "You look very well this evening, Lady Alicia."

My blinking stuttered, lips parting. And I didn't know why, but unlike moments before when Hawthorne had complimented me, I felt something thaw inside me. "As do you, Mr. Wycliffe."

Hawthorne's eyebrows pulled together. "Ah—Oh . . ." He looked between us, no doubt sensing that *something*. If Hawthorne had thought us unacquainted, then I couldn't have asked for a better opportunity to discourage his suit.

I turned to him. "Indeed. Mr. Wycliffe and I know each other quite intimately—for we are engaged."

Hawthorne's eyes widened. A pouty look overtook his face, like a child who'd been promised candied pineapple only to have it snatched out of his hands before he'd even smelled it properly. "To . . . To be married?"

"Yes, and we couldn't be more thrilled!" Slinking to Matthew's side, I clasped his arm. "Do give my best to your mother." I pulled Matthew away before Hawthorne could sputter out any more questions through his gaping mouth. "Nice of you to finally arrive," I murmured to Matthew once we had passed out of earshot.

"It is, isn't it? Seeing as how I'm doing this out of the benevolence of my heart."

No one approached us. Eyes peeped at us from behind shoulders and fans. Being the daughter of a duke and the cause of many scandals, I was accustomed to curious glances—but not like this. Not with their eyes shining in eager respect; and it was all due to the fact that my arm was linked in Matthew's.

I didn't let the fact annoy me, as it was why I had asked Matthew along in the first place. If he conversed with Henry, that same respect would transfer over to him too, and the first obstacle would be out of the way.

As for the second obstacle . . .

I tightened my hold on Matthew's arm, whispering, "We don't need to remain at each other's side all evening—just until you've paid your compliments to Henry. Then when the time is right, I'll catch your attention and we'll begin our search for the will."

He sighed. "Yes, yes, like the anarchic interposer you are. Let's just get this over with, shall we? Where is your Mr. Crawley?"

I led Matthew toward the other side of the room, where Henry still stood underneath an archway with his brother. Aunt Beth joined us as we arrived, muttering something to me about how she still needed to pay her respects.

Graham Crawley was a flinty figure. With jet-black hair and pale skin, he looked nothing like Henry. Henry had always had more of their mother's coloring, whereas Graham looked like their father. Unlike the Wycliffe brothers, if you were to see the Crawleys side by side, you wouldn't even guess they were related.

While Graham was preoccupied with another guest, I beamed at Henry. "I see your celebrity has drawn many guests," I whispered.

Though my arm was linked in Matthew's, he was turned the other way, allowing me and Henry a moment of privacy.

Henry chuckled, one shoulder lifting halfheartedly. "They are not here for me. I am sure half the room is confused as to whose ball they are actually attending."

My eyes darted to Matthew before returning. "I wager my fan for your cufflinks that will change within the hour."

Henry's face crumpled in confused amusement. "Done," he said, obviously certain of his victory. "And I should add that in addition to your fan, I am looking forward to claiming your left glove as well."

My limbs sagged. Our wager on whether he would leave for India without me.

At that moment, Graham finished conversing with his guest, prompting Aunt Beth to step forward and cut off whatever response I'd been about to give. "Lord Crawley," she said, "it is so good to see you again. Rupert sends his regrets."

"Yes." Graham said, looking beyond her shoulder at me. "I see he sent all of them."

I bit down on my tongue.

Henry's lips parted. "Graham . . ."

Matthew's arm tensed under my touch, but his face was still blank, silently watching the exchange.

The only thing I would accomplish by lashing out was a squabble—and then Graham was sure to glare at me all night, watching me like a hawk and preventing me from sneaking into his den. Not that he didn't always watch me like that already. I decided to not cause a scene.

Reminding myself of what a lady ought to do—be more cordial, even in the face of provocation—I bobbed a curtsy, using every ounce of willpower to smile politely. "Good evening, Lord Crawley."

Graham didn't react to my greeting, turning his attention to Matthew. "You must be the fiancé I've heard so much about. Mr. Wycliffe."

For one fleeting moment, I envisioned Matthew joining Graham in his derision, forming a friendship where they were unified in their mutual hatred of me.

Instead, Matthew remained upright, refusing to bow. A calculated and highly offensive snub, since Graham technically outranked him. "Yes," he said. "Lady Alicia's fiancé. And you are a brave man indeed, Lord Crawley, to insult her in my presence."

My gaze whipped to Matthew, shocked that those words had fallen from his lips. I searched his face for signs of sarcasm, but there were none. He had claimed me and issued a hidden challenge in the process. No teasing, no added insults, only him defending my honor.

Graham chuckled nervously, but when he caught Matthew's serious expression, he stopped. He cleared his throat. "Of course, Mr. Wycliffe, I meant no disrespect. Alicia and I are old friends. She knows I jest."

"In future, best ensure I know it, too." The reply was soft but threatening, even as Matthew blandly blinked away, dismissing him. I watched the interaction with confusion. How did he do that? Possess so much arrogant dignity, so much superiority but expectancy—that even a titled man like Graham Crawley felt compelled to accommodate? It was beyond comprehension.

Remembering my place, I spurted to the side and indicated Henry. "Mr. Wycliffe, might I introduce to you Mr. Henry Crawley." At his cue, Henry bowed.

I subtly nudged Matthew with my elbow, and his eyes flitted to me in annoyance. But when Henry straightened, Matthew curled forward, deep and low, a respect reserved for royalty. Shocked tones rippled through those standing near. They'd given a show of not paying attention, but of course they were. I'd learned long ago that they always were.

Henry flushed, his eyes darting around. Graham glowered.

Straightening, Matthew said, "I am honored to make your acquaintance, Mr. Crawley." More whispers met my ears. I nudged

Matthew again, making his lips purse. "Lady Alicia has told me much about you, and I have the highest respect for you, sir."

"I-I thank you, Mr. Wycliffe. And I you." Henry's eyebrows scrunched, but all I saw were the many heads turning his direction, looking at him in wonderment. Word of tonight would spread, and by week's end, the penniless second son of a baron would be viewed in a completely different light.

I smiled. On to the second obstacle.

THE BALL RAGED ON.

Matthew had long left my side in search of some quiet corner he could hide in. I danced and laughed and answered question after question about my sudden engagement, disappointing every rake who'd ever flirted with me and doing my best to act like a besotted bride-to-be. All the while, I kept a steady eye on Henry.

While the ball was being held in his honor, most of the attendees had no doubt accepted the invitation out of respect to Graham. But now, a constant swarm hovered around Henry, everyone curious as to why the revered Mr. Wycliffe had paid him special attention.

At last, I found a moment alone to myself and collapsed against a wall, fanning myself with one hand. Across the room, young girls flashed Henry coy smiles. Instead of feeling a prick of jealousy, the sight warmed me. Henry had always had great merit. It was high time everyone else noticed.

I tucked my hands behind my back, feeling the rough stone graze my palms. These stones encapsulated so many memories—memories of ringing laughter in the corridor, shapes of hand shadows, the sound of clanging armor while Henry and I pretended to fence. This old castle felt more like home than my stiff, solemn Lawry Park.

Perhaps one day it *could* be home . . . although a lot needed to be accomplished if that were ever to come to pass. Now was as good a time as any to begin.

I scoured the crowd for Matthew, finally spotting him tucked in a little alcove adjacent to the massive, cold fireplace. There he was, reading in a corner again. Did he travel with books in his tailcoat, to be whipped out at the first sign of dull company? How many did he have in there?

Matthew's eyes darted up, focusing on something before they went back to his page, jaded. A few moments later, he did it again, quickly. Subtly. As if he didn't wish to be caught. I followed his line of sight until it met Graham, near an open window. I watched them for another moment.

Matthew's hand moved along the page of his book. At first, I thought it was marking his reading pace, until I noticed the tip of a pencil the size of my littlest finger as he stashed it away in his coat. He'd been writing something about Graham.

My gaze honed in on the little green book, suddenly intensely interested in its contents, especially given the way Matthew had defended me. What had he written? Who else had he written about? And why did he do it so secretively?

An overwhelming urge to know propelled my feet forward. Once I reached him, I arched onto my tiptoes, hoping to catch a glimpse over his shoulder. "What did you write?"

Matthew jerked away and snapped the book shut. An irritated look overtook his features. "Couldn't save all your prying for later, could you?"

I chose to ignore the jab. "What is in the book?"

He scoffed and pushed himself off the wall. "Wouldn't you like to know."

"Yes, I would."

Tucking the book into an inside pocket, he said, "The day you read this book, I vow I shall follow through with this blasted scheme and marry you."

I shrugged one shoulder. "Perhaps that is a price I am willing to pay."

"Perhaps. But I am not." He turned toward the doorway.

I folded my arms. "Who's to say I won't sneak into your library to take a peek? I am an *anarchic interposer*, after all." I smiled at his back.

His frame halted, and he spun around. He wasn't smiling—did he ever smile? I'd certainly never seen it—but his eyes were lit with begrudging amusement. "I doubt you would get the chance. I would hear your thoughts a mile away and burn it long before you ever arrived."

You, Lady Alicia, are the most predictable woman I have ever met.

He was gloating—flaunting his ability to predict me—but without the charming smirk, or strut to his walk, or any of the other signature characteristics of a conceited man. He said it with the straightest of faces—like it was universal fact, like I would be the inanest of idiots to contradict him. Which made it all the more infuriating.

I dug my nails into my palms, trying to keep my anger in check. We hadn't even begun searching for the will yet, and already we were at odds.

No matter.

If only to spite him, I would find out what was in that book, even if it took me a hundred years. And contrary to his claims, I would ensure that he never saw it coming.

I forced my hands to relax and shrugged my shoulders again. "For you to hear my thoughts, it would require that I think before I act, Mr. Wycliffe. We both know that I do not."

He gave a humorless laugh. "Indeed."

"And on that note, perhaps we ought to get to it." That was all I said before brushing past him.

He followed me into the hallway. Candles flickered near red and blue tapestries, and a few milling guests studied paintings of the ancestral Crawley line. "I cannot believe I am doing this," Matthew said under his breath, gaze darting to the other people in the hallway.

"It will be over before you know it."

We made our way back toward the castle entrance. When there were no ball attendees to witness it, I retrieved a candle from the drawer of the entry table and quickly lit it. Henry's father had always kept candles there, and I was relieved to see that hadn't changed upon his death. I led Matthew to the west wing toward the den, where we slipped inside.

Mounds of loose paper piled the tables and floor; some wadded, some crumpled, some even burnt. The few books that occupied the barren shelves were toppled and disorganized. Quill shavings and blots of ink scattered the desk. Henry's father had never been a tidy person, and it seemed Graham had inherited the trait. The accounts were sure to be a horrid mess. I set to searching while Matthew stood in indecision, out of his element in more ways than one.

"I still wonder at how, exactly, we are supposed to find this will." He folded his arms. "No doubt the Crawleys have already searched high and low. And it will take us years to sort through this mess."

Luckily, we weren't here to go through the accounts. I glanced down the row of books, searching for anything out of place. Now that I'd brought him this far, I'd have to tell him about the secret passageways sooner or later. "I'm sure old Lord Crawley had planned on telling someone where his will was located—most of all Henry. However, he died quite suddenly, shortly after his solicitor said the record was drafted. The mystery of its whereabouts has sparked several wild goose chases around the castle. But, as he likely wanted to hide his will from Graham, I suspect he wouldn't have kept it in any ordinary spot."

"Wonderful."

I set the candle on the mantle and tugged at the stones of the fireplace, seeing if any came loose.

After a moment of watching me, Matthew said, "What *are* you doing?"

I heaved a frustrated sigh. "What does it look like? I'm trying to—"

"Budge the fireplace?" He clucked his tongue. "I have some sorry news for you."

I ran one hand along the dusty mantle. "Henry's father once told me of a network of passages in his castle—the entrance to which was in his den. If such a thing existed, Henry's father would've stored his will somewhere in the tunnels. I am sure of it."

I didn't have to turn and look to gauge Matthew's reaction. I knew by his silence his face was incredulous, with a dash of horror.

At length, he said, slowly, "Please tell me you have not dragged me down here for this mad scheme on so little a hunch."

He was going to be disappointed.

I found a handhold on the mantle, and after giving it a yank, to no success, I replied. "It would explain why no one's managed to find the will. And as I said, two heads are better than one."

"Not when the other one is yours."

I retrieved the candle and spun around to face him. "*Must* you insult me so?"

"According to you, I know how to do little else. Oh yes, except for searching for documents that may or may not exist, and finding secret passageways that are a figment of a girl's imagination. Apparently I am top notch at that." Matthew braced his arm against the edge of a large painting and lost his balance when it scraped open to reveal an empty square of black behind it.

I gave a triumphant cry. Matthew righted himself, muttering something indecipherable.

The musty air from the open passageway seeped into the den. I held the candle up to the encroaching dark before turning to him and saying with a sly smile, "Top notch indeed."

He shook his head. "I am not going in there."

"You must. You promised you would help search."

"You said nothing of travelling through dirty tunnels in that endeavor."

I thinned my eyes at him. He didn't strike me as a dandy. A perfectionist who didn't like to be inconvenienced, perhaps, but not someone who valued clothing over his chance to be rid of me. There was something else at play.

He huffed. "The situation is highly irregular—not to mention outrageously scandalous. Improper. I . . ." He swallowed. "I-I do not think it wise."

Since when was he concerned with propriety? I looked back to the tunnel. "There is room enough to stand. I can then only assume it is the dark you are afraid of, sir." I gave him an innocent look. "Unless . . . unless it is *me* you are afraid of . . ."

He blinked at me.

"Or perhaps *yourself* when in my company. Alone. In a tunnel."

He swallowed again.

I grinned. "You fear we might accidentally brush hands. Or worse—brush lips! Oh, the horror! So close to me," I took a step toward him, "out of sight from the rest of the world," he inched backward, "just you, me . . . and the dark. My, my, my. Perhaps it *is* the dark you fear after all—"

He growled and strode past me into the passageway. He swept his arm forward, an invitation for me to lead the way. My grin widened before I entered and swung the painting back in place.

CHAPTER 11

THE STUDY HAD BEEN DIM, BUT THIS DARKNESS WAS ALL-encompassing. Thick; tangible. Gulping, I clutched the brass chamberstick tighter, grateful for the candle more than ever.

As we started down the tunnel the air grew chillier, smelling like rain and the potato skins cook used to leave near the stables. The walls of the tunnel, coarse, cold, and sometimes damp, scraped my skin and snagged at my dress when I ventured too close. Every so often we passed rusty metal sconces, bereft of their torches.

"Why did Lord Crawley speak to you so?" Matthew's voice echoed down the passageway, the only noise to fill the silence besides the scuff of our feet on the stone.

A chuckle bubbled in my throat. "*Now* who is prying? And indeed, I am surprised you have not come to the answer on your own, as you pretend to know everything about me." In the close confines of the tunnel, I could hear him thinking; something he did far too often.

Unable to help myself, I spun around, and he almost bumped into me. The light from the candle flashed on his face in red and orange tones. "Why do you want to know?"

Eyebrows rising slightly, he said, "I can better defend your character if I know the truth."

I studied him, brow furrowing. No one had ever stood up for me the way Matthew had, though there had been plenty of occasion to. Perhaps I'd mistaken his character that night on the balcony. Perhaps he had more good qualities than bad ones. "And how do you know my character is worth defending?"

He said nothing to that, only stared at me. Slowly, almost imperceptibly, I felt a connection of common ground start to form between us, a bridge that joined our two, lonely cliffs. Unable to discern if that was a good sign, I resumed leading us down the tunnel.

After a moment of walking, he prompted, "Well?"

This was not a conversation I wished to have, especially with Matthew, of all people. But there was little else to do as we wound through the dimness. And who knew? Perhaps I would discover a soul buried beneath that stone exterior.

I sighed. "Graham Crawley . . . once made me an offer of marriage."

"What?"

This was a bad idea. And as with all other bad ideas of mine, I ignored the beacon of caution flashing in my mind and forged ahead. "Though it may be difficult for you to believe, it was of his own volition, too. It happened three years ago, during my first Season. No one knows about it. Not my father, nor even Henry."

"How could they not?"

"Because I didn't tell them, and neither did Graham. I cannot fathom why, but it has always been an unspoken agreement between us."

Matthew grew silent, allowing me to hear our shuffling feet and the sound of something dripping nearby. I sidestepped a few puddles that had congregated in the cracks in the stone. At length Matthew said, "And he talks about you in that way because you turned him down."

My heart squeezed a little at the memory. "Yes," I said past the lump in my throat. "Growing up, Graham liked to shove me into walls, yank my hair, slap my cheek. He only liked to hurt me because he knew it made Henry angry. So years later when he proposed, I knew it was only out of spite for his brother, and had no trouble rejecting him."

My voice quieted, and our steps with it. "I can still see his face —all affronted and full of rage. I can still feel the sting of his hand."

Matthew remained silent, and I dared not glance back to try and gauge his expression. I'd rather just imagine him aloof to this conversation, or better yet, oblivious. Anything more would actually mean something.

"All these years with Graham as an older brother, Henry never stood up for himself. So I've done it for him." Watching Graham's constant mistreatment was one reason why I was so protective, why Henry and I had gotten so close. Why the thought of him leaving cut me to the core. Not wanting to dwell on the past any longer, I shrugged the gloomy memories away and said, "Now it is my turn, to ask a question. What did you write in your book?"

"I will not tell you." Matthew's tone was definitive. "Ask me something else."

"Why not? Is it horrendous?" I gasped dramatically, sweeping cobwebs away from my face. "Are you a writer? Blending fact and fiction together. Oh, and Graham is the inspiration for your villain!"

"No—how did you know I wrote about Lord Crawley?"

"Like you, I'm rather good at observing—perhaps better than you, since you didn't notice I was." I glanced over my shoulder, noting the annoyed shakes of his head. "Or you are a clandestine artist! You have pictures of the woman you're secretly in love with, and are afraid of anyone discovering her identity."

Matthew scoffed. "Do not be absurd."

"Then what? Why are you afraid to tell me?"

"The book is mine, and mine alone; no one is to ever know its contents. You may ask me anything but that."

I mulled that over. If he didn't want anyone knowing about it, why did he carry it with him all the time? "Fine," I said, deciding to not push the matter. There were plenty of other things I was curious about. "Why did you defend me earlier? I thought you and Graham would be best of friends, the way you both enjoy insulting me."

"I don't enjoy it."

What utter nonsense. Of course he did. Just as I did him.

A draft blew by, and I shielded the candle's flame with one hand. "That still does not answer my question," I said.

Matthew's reply didn't come for another minute. ". . . I may not like it, but you are my intended. And though I may 'insult you' as you call it, I mean to ensure that no one else does. At least not in my presence."

I rolled my eyes. "Because you have an image to uphold?"

Matthew's feet stopped. I turned to look at him, the candle illuminating his face again. "No," he said, forehead wrinkled, confused as to how I'd arrived at that conclusion. He sounded offended. "Because it is the right thing to do."

The reply made me laugh. "Are you confessing to *gallantry*, sir?"

"I am confessing to the fact that I always look after what is mine. As we are engaged, you are mine now, too."

My face relaxed out of its smile, cheeks warming. Our engagement may have been a sham, but no one had ever claimed me so boldly. Without hesitation or regret. And Matthew's phrasing made it seem like . . .

He walked up close. Extracting the candle from my grip and sending a thrill shooting up my arm, he looked down into my eyes. "For the time being," he murmured, then brushed past me.

Faint music filtered through the stone. The tunnel must be leading us back toward the ballroom. I rubbed my still-warm cheeks and we pushed on.

The passageway angled down and branched out into a chamber. To the left, the tunnel continued down into darkness, but to the right sat furniture covered in white sheets, like imposing ghosts. Matthew pulled the sheets off and coughed on the thick layer of dust he unsettled. A squat table bore various trinkets and a rusty sword, and old chests stacked each other against the wall.

Matthew discarded the wads of sheets. "More dirt. Wonderful."

"That tunnel probably reemerges in the forest somewhere," I said, pointing. I fiddled with the leather buckles of some of the smaller chests and scraped them open. "Spare candles, wine stashes, extra blankets. Lord Crawley must have spent a considerable amount of time here, when he was alive. If he had a will, he would surely have stored it here, in this chamber."

"At least it is more organized than the den."

I took the candle from him and moved to the table. "You start over there, and we'll meet in the middle."

Reluctantly, Matthew set to searching his end of the room, while I scoured the table. Setting the candle down, I fingered the hilt of the rusty sword, remembering mine and Henry's pretend-sparring sessions; the ringing of laughter and metal. He'd always let me win, though he was a master of the blade even then.

I lovingly gripped the sword with both hands, then gave it a few test swipes.

"I can't see a blasted thing," Matthew said from his corner. "How am I supposed to find a will when you have the candle?"

I moved my feet slowly, the footing Henry taught me returning in bits and pieces. It had been a while since we last fenced. "Improvise," I said.

Matthew retrieved a candle from a chest and came to the table, dipping the wick in the flame. "You are surprisingly adept with that," he said, not looking up.

I dropped my arm which held the sword. "Adept enough to run you through."

He scoffed. "I should like to see that."

As he straightened, I arched the sword toward his neck and

stopped. It hovered only an inch away. He froze. I grinned. "As would I."

His gaze stuttered over to meet mine.

Fear. Attraction. Anticipation. Only this time, instead of it shining in my eyes, it shone in his.

I blinked, and the image was gone. *Must've been a trick of the candlelight.* I threw the sword away and it clattered to the stone floor. "Another night perhaps," I said flippantly. "People are sure to ask questions if you don't return to the ball."

Matthew relaxed. "I disappear from balls more often than you'd think." He resumed searching with his newly acquired candle.

Glancing over the contents of the table, I quickly discerned that there wasn't really anything useful. But my interest caught on a gold filigree pocket watch. I held it to my ear. Still ticking. Inset in the gold, opposite the clock face, was a likeness of Henry's mother, Rachel. I set the watch down.

Just as I turned away, my eyes snagged on the corner of a letter, tucked underneath a book. I tugged it out and noticed its creases, dull from being bent and re-bent dozens of times . . . as though Henry's father had agonized over its contents, up until his death.

I squinted and read.

Lord Crawley,

I apologize for the shock my previous letter must've been to you. Please understand that my purpose in writing of your wife's infidelity was not to defame her memory, but because I haven't the means to care for the boy on my own.

For the sake of Rachel's family, you must promise me this secret will never be brought to light. And you must promise me Lenny will never know the truth about his father.

I humbly await your assistance.

- C. M.

My brow knotted. I stared at the note, unseeing. The letters on the parchment jumbled together, rearranging to form a single sentence:

Henry has another brother.

My stomach sickened. But how? How could something so monumental still be a secret? How had no one noticed? I wracked my memory until it stumbled across something Aunt Beth had mentioned once—something about a summer where Lady Rachel Crawley had disappeared, only to come back with pale skin and haunted eyes. She'd remained that way until she'd died, five years ago.

I picked up the letter and examined the corners, flipping it over. No date. My mouth ran dry. How old was the boy? Sixteen? Ten? Eight? . . . Five? I examined the letter closer, noting the frayed edges and yellow color. It appeared to be old, but that might've been more due to the paper's quality than its age. There was simply no way to tell. It had to be at least five years old.

If Lord Crawley had known about this boy, did Henry and Graham know, as well? Or was it a secret Lord and Lady Crawley had taken to their graves?

. . . Was it a secret I should keep too?

"What is the matter?"

I looked up to find Matthew's stare upon me and the letter I clutched in my hand. Without any words I held it out for him. He took it and read.

"A third son," Matthew said after a moment. He handed the letter back, unfazed. "Perhaps this 'Lenny' will be mentioned in the will."

I nodded, but part of me doubted it. Why would Nicholas Crawley leave any money to a boy who wasn't even his son? Who only served as a reminder of his wife's unfaithfulness? He'd been good-natured, but such would be a trial for even the most amiable of men.

But . . . if this letter had plagued him, perhaps it was because he'd never lifted a finger to help this boy, and regretted it. Perhaps he wanted to make restitution.

Nothing could be certain until the will was found. I doubled my efforts and sorted through a few of the chests. Bottles of wine clinked together as I checked the seams of a chest for hidden compartments.

"Here," Matthew said at last.

I brought my candle over to where he hunched over an open trunk, reading a piece of paper. His lips moved as he read. I skimmed the top of the page. *The Last Will and Testament of Nicholas Crawley* . . . An exultant, relieved feeling rushed through me. I snatched the will from Matthew's hands, reading it over for myself.

"He recognizes Henry as his only son," Matthew provided. "A small sum and the castle is meant to go to Graham, but essentially, Henry was supposed to inherit everything else."

Just as I suspected. But after skimming the rest of the will and then rereading it, slower, I discovered it said nothing of any 'Lenny.'

The edges of my vision blackened as I lost myself in my thoughts. I should be overjoyed. I'd found the will, and Henry finally had his fortune. If he proposed, nothing stood in the way of our marriage.

But instead, I couldn't stop thinking about this poor boy, estranged from his mother and brothers. Who was he? Where did he live? Did he have a caretaker or was he all alone, after being abandoned on the side of the road?

And most of all . . . should I tell Henry about him?

If such a person existed, I would want to know I had a brother —but I wasn't so sure Henry would. He'd idolized his parents, so to know a flaw like this would shatter him. Not to mention that the letter from the mysterious "C. M." had requested that the boy's parentage remain a secret.

Matthew doused his candle and returned it to the box. "How do you intend to explain to the man you're in love with that you came by his father's will in a secret chamber, inside a secret passageway, after poking around in his older brother's sanctum at the ball held in his honor—unchaperoned, and aided by your unwilling fiancé with whom you will now break all ties?"

I folded the will back up. "I'm not sure. But definitely not like that."

The chamber was gloomier with only the single candle again. I eyed the letter on the table, then snatched it up and tucked it away with the will. "I can scarce believe it. By some miracle, we managed to remove both obstacles in one night."

"Suits me. And just in time, as my sister is planning on paying me a visit tomorrow. The fewer of my family that meet you, the better." Matthew took in the miserable room one last time, before sighing and turning to me. "I take it you want me to carry the will."

I chuckled. "I don't want you anywhere near this document."

"Why?"

I tapped his nose with the paper, making him rear back and frown. "I know how madly you love me. You're sure to sabotage this will for the sole purpose of keeping me at your side."

Matthew gave a compulsory snort.

"Besides," I went on, dropping my sarcastic tone, "I wouldn't want it getting mixed up with all the books hiding in your coat."

"All the . . . What books?"

"I know you have a stash of them hidden."

"What? I don't know what you're talking about."

I put the back of my wrist on my hip. "You're always reading, wherever you go. Different books each time, sometimes within minutes of each other. That wouldn't be possible unless you carried them in your coat."

"Drivel, the lot of it."

"How many are there in there?"

"You couldn't possibly—"

"How many?"

"Six! Now would you leave off!"

I smiled in victory, pleased at the pink, exasperated tinge to his cheeks. It was a most becoming look on him—especially when it meant I had placed it there.

"If you must take something," I said, "take the candle." I shoved the chamberstick toward him—but the lingering victorious feeling swirling in my veins made me clumsy, and I shoved it too quickly. He hissed and pulled back when hot wax splotched onto his hand. The candle tumbled to the ground and rolled into a puddle filling the cracks in the stone, where it sputtered out.

Darkness closed in from every direction.

We both held completely still. After a stretched moment, Matthew exhaled, long and heavy. "Wonderful."

I waved a hand in front of my face, but couldn't see anything. Throat convulsing in panic, my ears throbbed in the sudden silence. In the all-encompassing dark, a memory racked my mind . . .

CHAPTER 12

"SHE'S MY MOTHER!" I ARGUED.

Father set his hands on my shoulders, gently backing me against the second-story wall. "A birth is no place for a child. You are simply too young—"

I rolled my eyes. "That is what you always say. And yet no matter how old I grow, it is never old enough."

"And in this case, it is especially true."

Through the open bedroom door to my right came the soft moaning of my mother, and the soothing lilt of the maid attending to her. Father turned at the sound, a sense of urgency lighting in his eyes. He bent onto one knee and cupped my chin. "I shall fetch you the moment the babe is born. I promise."

I shook my head. In this moment, Father's promises weren't good enough. I could smell in the air that something was wrong—like dried blood and diluted alcohol. I could see it in the worried glances between the servants. Hear it in the undertones of Father's voice.

I needed to be there.

A hand clamped onto my arm, pulling me away from my father, who stood. Away from my mother, who needed me at her side. I yanked my arm back. "Please, Papa, let me come."

"I shall keep her occupied," came my aunt's voice above me, grave.

My vision prickled with hot tears. "Please. I can help. I shall not be in the way, I promise."

Father looked between me and his sister, hesitation etched in his brow. But then my mother's cry came again and he snapped to a decision. "Thank you, Beth," he said, before turning into the bedroom and shutting the door.

I flinched. Then my aunt dragged me down the stairs, saying something about getting me a plate of food. I knew what she was trying to do. She was trying to distract me from what was most important—my mother—and I wouldn't have any of it.

"Let me go!" I wiggled out of her grasp and dashed away.

"Alicia!"

I didn't turn back. Running at full speed, I fled down the hallway and twisted into the parlor, wiping frantically at the curls that kept sticking to my wet cheeks. I didn't want to be distracted or listen to Aunt Beth's empty assurances that everything would be fine. Right now, all I wanted was my parents. And if I couldn't have them, I wanted to be alone.

I darted into the dining room, eyeing under the table. No, she would look there. My gaze caught on an open cupboard at the far wall, where the servants stored spare dishes and extra bottles of brandy. I rushed over and inspected it. Between the bottles and platters was a space just big enough for a seven year old girl to wedge herself in.

After climbing inside, I situated myself until I was comfortably leaning against the wall. Then, creaking the cupboard closed until only a thin panel of light shone through, I held my breath, knowing Aunt Beth was close behind.

I didn't have to wait long.

Clacking footsteps echoed through the hall and turned into the dining room. I squeezed my legs into a tighter ball and froze. The steps passed the cupboard, then stopped, before coming back, slower.

I clenched my jaw, anticipating the door squeaking open. Aunt Beth might've found me, but I wasn't going to come out. Not unless I could see my mother.

"Why is this open?" a masculine voice muttered, before the wood slid

shut and the quiet grinding of a lock clicked into place. The dark closed in, wrapping me in an embrace. The footsteps retreated.

I let out my breath and rested my chin on my knees, not caring that I was locked in. If they found my starved corpse a month from now, it would serve Father right. I hoped the guilt ate him away. My death would be worth it. If I had just let Alicia be there, *he would think,* this wouldn't have happened. I should have listened to her. I should have let her stay at her mother's side, and not consigned her to Aunt Beth's miserable company. I should have—

It wasn't fair.

I kicked my leg in frustration. It smashed into a bottle, bursting its contents onto the floor of the cupboard. The fiery, fruity odor of brandy filled my nostrils. I pulled my leg back, scraping broken glass across the wood.

Then I buried my face in my hands and cried until I fell asleep.

Hurried footsteps and urgent voices in the hall woke me. I blinked my eyes open, but I still couldn't see anything. The darkness in the cupboard was absolute. Straining my ears, I picked up a few snippets.

". . . doctor says . . . is fading fast . . . asked for her daughter . . ." It was Aunt Beth's voice. ". . . need to find Alicia. We need to find her before—" The words broke off on a sob.

A new voice came, one of the servants. "You, search the nursery. Hettie and I will check the grounds. We can circle back and comb through the rest of the house, and if we still haven't found her—"

"By then, it will be too late."

Too late?

"In here!" I called, then paused to see if anyone heard me.

The voices came again, more distant this time. ". . . we'll find her."

"—deserves to see her mother one last time—"

Panic gripped my chest as I realized what was happening. "I'm in here!" I pounded at the cupboard door. But no one heard me. No footsteps came.

The panic grew, the darkness closing around my throat with invisible hands, stealing the air from my lungs. I fought back, taking in a huge, tearful breath. I choked on the sharp taste of brandy.

No. No, no, no.

I got to my knees, hissing when they slipped on the glass. A warm wetness dribbled onto my palms. I shook the door until it rattled on its hinges. "Help me! I'm in here! Father!" But the door held fast.

Tears streamed freely down my face, and still I cried harder. An age passed, a lifetime. I screamed until my throat was hoarse. No one heard.

Then, finally, footfalls thumped down the stairs, and these ones sounded slower, weightier. Awful. Like someone breaking the neck of a rabbit. Like the deepest beat of a drum. They left the house, and somehow I knew it was the doctor.

I quieted, inhaling shaky, hiccupping breaths as I listened for the dreadful news. But it never came. All I heard was the sound of my father's crying filtering down the stairs and echoing through the halls. My stomach turned over at the cloying smell of blood and brandy. The darkness took on shape, twisting into a monster whose clutches I couldn't escape.

"Help me!" I screamed, throat closing up. I hit the door over and over until splinters dug into my already bleeding palm. "I want to see my mother!" I collapsed, against the wood, sobbing. ". . . I want to see my mother . . ."

The sound of a key sliding into the lock made me bolt up. The door opened, revealing a surprised Henry. He looked me over, taking in my tear-streaked face, the blood, the glass, the purplish liquid oozing onto the dining room floor.

His eyes widened like he was scared. "Alicia, where have you been?"

I climbed out of the cupboard and threw my arms around him, breathing the air like I'd been suffocated. He'd saved me. Henry had saved me from the dark. I swiped at my tears and pulled back. "What's happened to her?"

Instead of answering, he swept my hair out of my face, murmuring, "You're going to be all right."

A few moments later, Aunt Beth and a few servants rushed into the room, faces distraught. Most of them looked like they'd been crying—but I didn't care about that. I left Henry's embrace, and with a bloody hand, clutched my aunt's dress. "What's happened to her?"

Aunt Beth whisked me out of the room and led me up the stairs. At the end of the hall, the door to my parent's bedroom opened. Father emerged as white as a ghost, and the look on his face made me stop in my tracks.

Aunt Beth let me go and charged past my father into the bedroom. She left the door ajar, and through the slit in the door I saw a body on the bed, a mass of blond curls. Mother.

"What's happened to her?" I asked for the third time, voice shaking. My body trembled.

Father drew near. He put one hand on my shoulder—only his touch didn't feel strong and sure like it usually did. It felt weak, defeated, ready to fall apart.

"I'm sorry, Alicia," he choked out. Then, walking like it cost him the last of his strength, he left.

The world around me tipped and spun, growing cold. Growing dark again. I collapsed to my knees, burrowing my face into my injured hands, not caring about the blood, or my heart ripping in half and shredding into pieces. Not caring about anything but my mother.

There, on the floor outside my mother's bedroom, I rocked back and forth, hugging myself, since no one else ever would.

No one had answered me.

No one needed to.

I already knew.

CHAPTER 13

I COULD NOT HAVE CONJURED A WORSE NIGHTMARE.

"I told you this was a terrible idea," Matthew said in the dark. "And did you listen? No. Of course not. No one ever listens to me—why should you?"

My clammy hands clung to my dress. "I . . . ." I tried to swallow, but my throat hit a lump. The awful memory wouldn't wash away, growing larger by the second. ". . . I do not perform well, in the dark." My voice quivered.

A pause. Then, "*Now* you tell me?"

Moisture flooded my eyes. Though I knew no bottle had been opened, my nostrils inhaled the scent of brandy, making my stomach turn over.

"You might've mentioned that before you dove headlong into a pitch-black tunnel," Matthew said.

I crammed down the terror welling up in my gut. "I had to find the will, and we had a candle! I didn't think it would matter. And now, I-I don't know which direction to go. If we accidentally head toward the exit instead of the entrance, there could be a whole labyrinth of circles and dead ends. No one will know to come looking for us, and we'll never get out of here! We're trapped—locked in—!"

Matthew's hands settled on my shoulders, cutting off my babble. "All right, calm down. Take deep breaths."

I shook my head and clutched the fabric at his forearms. I was back inside a closet, scratching at the wood until my fingers bled, listening to the sounds of my mother dying. The deep shadows tightened a rope around my neck, strangling the air from my lungs. Crowding in, closing in . . . My breaths shallowed, coming faster and faster.

Matthew shook me. "Alicia, listen to me. Listen to my voice. Concentrate on that, and nothing else."

His voice was deep as it echoed through the chamber; soothing, just like Henry's had been that day. A tear trailed down my cheek. My name. He'd said my name. I tucked my head down, resting my forehead against Matthew's chest. I took deep breaths. I relaxed my grip, hands moving to rest on the lapels of his jacket.

I hated this. I hated that he was witnessing my vulnerability and there was nothing I could do to stop it. But even though I hated it, I would let Matthew hold this over my head for the rest of my life, if only I survived it.

"Please don't leave me," I whispered. I heard the smallness in my own voice. The voice of a seven-year-old girl locked in a cupboard. "Don't leave me trapped in here alone."

"I would never leave you." One of his hands circled around my waist while the other splayed the back of my head. "We're going to get out of here, do you hear me? We'll find our way back—but you must calm down first."

His embrace was gentle but firm; loose enough to let me breathe but tight enough to hold me together.

I nodded against him, inhaling deeply through my nose. Not thinking about the dark. Not thinking about how I could keep my nose burrowed in his coat for ages and never tire of the scent. Not thinking about his rapid heartbeat pounding against my cheek, faster and faster the more I melted into him.

"Now, let us think about this and not make any rash decisions. Was there any flint in the trunk with the candles?"

I shook my head.

"Any matches?"

"None."

"Are you certain?"

"I'm sure of it."

He squeezed my arm. "Then we'll have to venture back in the dark. Right before we entered the chamber, the path sloped downward. If we start on a path and it inclines, we'll know we are going in the right direction."

I licked my lips and nodded, straightening. His hand fell away. I shivered at the sudden loss of contact, but even though the foolish part of me wanted to stay tucked away in his arms, my pride wouldn't let me.

I squared my shoulders. As annoying as his level-headedness had been before, I was grateful to have it now.

"May I take your hand?" he said softly.

The air rushed out of my lungs again, but this time for a different reason. I was glad I couldn't see his face. And that he couldn't see mine.

"I do not wish you to fall behind, or become lost," he added when I didn't say anything. "It would be prudent, given the circumstances."

". . . Yes, that—that would probably be best . . ."

Slowly, with the lightest of touches, Matthew's hand trailed down my arm, leaving a stream of tingles in its wake, before closing over my own. I gulped.

This *had* been a terrible idea.

Matthew tugged me forward. I held my other hand in front of me in case we were about to run into any walls, and we made slow progress across the chamber. I knew we entered the tunnel when my fingers connected with a wall, and our echoing footsteps became louder. The path slanted upward, making me breathe a sigh of relief. We picked up speed as we went along, and I was able to anticipate turns by the curvature of the wall.

Despite not being able to see where we were going, we retraced our steps much faster than before. My pulse rushed feverishly under my skin. I told myself it was because of the increased pace, and not because of Matthew's warm hand around my own.

Without the ability to see, all other sensations heightened. I heard the scuff of our steps, Matthew's quiet breathing. I felt his hand, warm and strong; surprisingly gentle as he led me through the darkness.

What would it be like to hold his hand in the daylight? To stand at his side while the world looked on with envy? To have caught the uncatchable Mr. Wycliffe in earnest?

I cut the thought off immediately, afraid that Matthew— through some unknown, cosmic power—had heard it. How he would glower if he knew! Besides, it wouldn't do to imagine such a scenario since Henry was the man I was going to spend the rest of my life with.

After fifteen minutes of wandering through the dark, my hand hit something solid and we stopped. It wouldn't budge. We felt around the edges of the doorway before Matthew finally found a lever and pulled it. The painting creaked open, revealing gray, triangular light.

A weight lifted off my shoulders as we stepped through the opening and into the den, making breathing a little easier. Sweat coated Matthew's forehead, his hands shaky as he swung the painting back in place. I couldn't help but wonder if his reaction was due more to the darkness of the tunnel, or his proximity to me for such a long period of time.

Now that we were free, it wasn't hard to re-imagine the last few minutes, filling in faces where before there had been only black. My mind replayed every touch, every little twitch of every finger as we traveled through the dark. Suddenly, unlike before, being alone with Mr. Wycliffe felt far too intimate. I cleared my throat in an effort to stamp down the color I knew was rising to my cheeks.

"Thank you," I said softly, somewhat surprised that I actually meant it.

Matthew's attention shifted from the painting to me, but he otherwise didn't acknowledge my thanks. His breathing was steadier now, too, I noticed. Because we were no longer touching? He swallowed, eyes travelling to the open door, obviously ready to exit the den and put this whole night behind him.

My thoughts ground to a halt, gaze honing in on the door. We'd left it closed. Why was it open?

A voice echoed down the chamber outside the den, growing louder by the moment. I clutched the paper in my hand. Beside me, Matthew tensed. I looked around searching for a place to hide. It was either the secret passageway or the desk. I'd take my chances. "Quick!"

"You cannot be serious." Matthew crossed his arms. "I am not crawling into another cramped space."

Footsteps echoed closer.

"Oh, yes you are." Gripping his arm, I tugged him underneath the desk and tucked myself beside him.

"Ow!"

"Stop squirming," I hissed. "And get your elbow out of my stomach."

"There's nowhere else to put it, since you're sitting on my coattails."

"Oh, your poor coattails. They're the real victims, even though your whole limb is *disappearing into my ribcage.*"

"And deuces, mind you don't break it off while you're at it!"

Two pairs of footsteps twisted into the room, cutting off my retort. "I don't understand all the sudden attention." It was Graham's voice. "It's not as if anything has changed."

"People only wish to pay their respects." Henry. I had to strain my ears to hear the quiet and cautious words. "They are friendlier because they know I shall ship away soon."

"No." Glass clinked. Liquid poured. A hollow, corking sound, then, "No, it's that Wycliffe fellow. It's because he paid you his respects while shunning me, plague take him. What did I ever do to the man?"

Leather creaked as someone sat. "Not what you did to him, but to Alicia."

"And why should he care what happens to her?" Graham grunted, and it echoed like he held a cup to his lips. "Alicia. Anyone can see she marries him for his money."

Pressure built on my hand. I looked down at it, compressing under Matthew's tense grasp. When had he taken it? The dim light made it difficult to read his face.

"Don't talk about her like that."

Thuds shook the floorboards until Graham's pumps came into view, inches away from my thigh. Matthew went still and scowled at the shoes. "Like what?" Graham said.

"With so much contempt. Like she has wronged you somehow. Money is the only reason you cared for her in the first place. You cannot imagine her having a different motive, because you judge her by your own standard."

Silence. I held my breath, able to clearly picture the death glare Graham must have on his face. I shuddered. Graham's voice was slathered in mockery when he said, "And money is the reason you *cannot* care for her."

Henry apparently didn't have anything to say to that. Graham continued. "Have a care, Henry. Attention from Mr. Wycliffe or not, her family will not look kindly upon an imposter trying to infiltrate their ranks. Since Father's money is mine, your real downfall is that you still haven't a penny to your name."

Shrinking into a smaller ball, I gripped the paper in my hand tighter—the paper that would give Henry the fortune he needed. Graham's feet moved away and left the room. After a moment, leather creaked again as Henry stood. His steps were slow as he too, left the den.

We waited another minute, making sure they weren't planning on returning soon, before Matthew and I crept out from under the desk. After examining the state of my dirt-smudged dress, Matthew said, "Wait here," and vanished. A few minutes later, he reappeared with my cloak and gloves draped over his arm. I was too grateful for his foresight to wonder how he'd managed to retrieve my things.

As I slipped them on, he sighed, grimacing at the painting. "Well. That was every bit as painful as I feared it would be."

I couldn't help but smile. Trying to shake off my lingering, jittery nerves, I said, "We should do it again very soon."

"What part of 'painful' do you not understand?"

"Oh, it wasn't so bad. Even with the dark and everything else." I tucked the paper into an inside pocket in my cloak. "Though I daresay your fears were warranted. You almost kissed me after all!" I chuckled just imagining it.

I only said it to tease him and bring some levity to the tense situation we had just escaped from, but Matthew got a strange look on his face—all frustrated confusion. "I did not." But he hesitated as he said the words, making my laugh fizzle in my throat.

How strange Matthew was. Most times, he was painfully honest; brutal with the truth, even when it came at his own expense. And yet, at other times . . . other times, I would swear he was lying.

He had blustery attitudes and an unapproachable exterior, but for the most part, he seemed to be an open book. He didn't encourage others to flip through his pages, but neither did he stop them. And then, when one flipped to the last page, the page containing the key to his story, one found it to be missing. Ripped with care and hidden from view.

What did that key unlock, I wonder?

"I've already informed your aunt that you wish to leave," he said. "Your carriage should be drawn by now."

I stared at him, stunned. But of course—Aunt Beth must've

been the one to fetch my things. Matthew had had the foresight to know that I would need to leave quietly, and had made all the arrangements. He was so thoughtful, it almost made me like him.

Before I could ask him any of the questions buzzing on my tongue, Matthew bowed and said, "Goodnight, Lady Alicia," before spinning on his heel.

Watching him disappear through the doorway, I smiled. "Goodbye, Mr. Wycliffe."

THE CARRIAGE WAS WAITING FOR ME, JUST AS MATTHEW HAD predicted. A footman helped me mount inside. While I settled into the cushions, I did my best to ignore Aunt Beth, face hidden in the shadows. I could already feel her disapproval from three feet away. I didn't need to look at it.

We jerked forward then relaxed into a steady rhythm. Several minutes passed in excruciating silence, before Aunt Beth finally said, "Where did you disappear to? I looked for you for the better part of an hour, only to have Mr. Wycliffe turn up and ask me to fetch your cloak."

"Nowhere."

She leaned forward and fingered a smudge of dirt on my dress. "You are an atrocious liar."

I seized my dress from her grasp. "Only when I choose to be, as I choose to be now. I make no attempts to hide the truth from you, aunt—for I know you will discover it without my help—but you gave me two weeks to act as recklessly as I will. And if you suddenly expect me to treat you like a confidant, then you will be sorely disappointed. You have always belittled me and have done nothing to earn my trust. You are not my friend. I *have* no friends."

I swallowed my tongue. The words came from nowhere, and they hurt worse than I expected, reviving a stinging in my chest I'd long thought dead. Aunt Beth didn't immediately recoil, instead appraising me with an evaluating eye. She sat back and continued to stare at me. Thinking.

I turned my attention to the window, ignoring her. And as we jumbled along the midnight blue road, sudden clarity struck me.

I'd been lying to myself. The reason I had to keep Henry here was less because I loved him, and more because I had no one else.

He was the only one on my side, who listened to me, who let me cling to him when I needed it. The only one who saved me from the dark. As much as I dreaded the thought of him leaving, I hated the idea of facing this cruel world alone more.

Was that selfish of me?

Through some miracle, both of Henry's reservations toward marrying me had been resolved tonight. Tomorrow I would give him the will and perhaps he would propose, giving me what I had always wanted. I thought about him, and seashells on the beach. I thought about books, and papers. Candles. Young boys. Soothing voices in the dark.

The rest of the ride passed in silence, and even when we dismounted and ascended to our quarters together, Aunt Beth still didn't speak a word. After undressing, I fell into bed, physically and emotionally spent, thoughts heavy. And I slept.

But it was not Henry's face I saw in my dreams. The man in my dreams didn't have a face at all.

He was a shadow that whispered calming words and smelled like pine trees—whose only distinguishable feature was a warm hand, strong and sure. A hand that cradled my head on his chest. A hand that led me through the darkness, and eventually, into the morning sun.

CHAPTER 14

THE NOTE WAS GONE.

I spread my cloak out on my canopied bed, decorated with the blinding light coming from my east-facing window. The will—the more important piece of paper—rested safely underneath my mattress, ready to be given to Henry when I met him this morning. But the note containing the information about the third Crawley son was missing. With frenzied hands, I searched all three cloak pockets again, wondering where I could've dropped it.

Tossing the cloak in frustration, I dashed downstairs and outside to the stables. The room smelled like oil and sun-warmed hay. I veered left, away from the whickering horses and stepped into the coach house. After finding the carriage Aunt Beth and I had used the night before, I swung the door open and checked the cushions and floor, running my fingers through the creases. Nothing.

I put my hands on my hips and puffed a lock of hair away from my face.

There were any number of places it could be. In the tunnel, under the desk, in the castle hallways. I thought back, trying to remember if I'd had both papers when Matthew fetched my cloak. But it had been so dark—and even darker in the tunnel.

Perhaps I *had* only tucked one paper into my cloak. At the time, it had felt rather thin. That would mean I'd either dropped the note in the den or somewhere in the passageway. The passageway was more likely, given the lack of light and the distance we traveled.

Oh, bother. Yes, I must've lost it somewhere between Matthew taking my hand and pulling the lever open. Heaven knows I'd been rather distracted. My cheeks warmed at the memory, and I immediately shook my head to dislodge it.

It didn't matter, I suppose. It's not as if I needed the note. Not yet, anyway. If it had been dropped in the passageway, then it wasn't going anywhere. If I dared brave the tunnel a second time, I could find it again.

I marched out of the stables, giving instructions to one of the stable boys as I went to have Cressida saddled within the hour. As I ascended the steps of the house, my thoughts turned to the contents of the note.

The least I could do was find out more about Lenny. Did he have a home? Was he taken care of? Did I alone know of his existence and importance? An overpowering sense of responsibility to him gripped me, making me stop in my tracks. Though I didn't know what it was like to be abandoned completely, I did know what it felt like to be a burden to those around you. In many ways, he and I were the same.

His family—his *real* family—had chosen to be blind to him, never giving him a chance to earn their love. Even if they still rejected him, he deserved that chance. And I wanted to give it to him.

I still didn't know if I should say anything to Henry, but I would decide on that later. First, I needed information. I hurried to my room and rang for Nancy. A few minutes later, she materialized.

Bobbing a curtsy, she said, "My lady?"

I settled in front of my desk and pulled out my stationary. "I believe you mentioned once, Nancy, that you are acquainted with a vicar in Cornwall?"

Her eyes widened. "Yes, my lady. The old widower married my sister a few years back. It was quite the condescension—not everyone viewed the marriage kindly."

I carved the nib of my quill to a flat point and brushed the shavings aside. "I do hate to impose upon you, but might you ask him for a favor on my behalf? I shall make it worth his while."

She gaped at me like a fish. "But of course, my lady! Anything you want, I shall ask him."

"Thank you."

The sound of little scratches filled the air as I composed a letter to Nancy's brother-in-law, asking him to search his parish records and perhaps make inquiries into boys named Lenny, or Leonard, born in the Cornwall region with questionable heritage, aged anywhere from five to twenty. I made sure to leave out anything that might link the case to the Crawleys, in case nothing came of it.

I sealed the letter and handed it to Nancy. "See that he gets this."

She curtsied again and said, "Right away, ma'am."

Just before she scurried out of the room, I had the idea that perhaps Father could take the letter as far as Southampton for me and called after her. Nancy turned back. "Have you seen my father?"

Her features pulled tight, like she didn't want to answer me. She was accustomed to me asking her that question, and every time, she gave the same answer. This time was no different. "He's not at home, my lady. Left last night."

My frame deflated a little. Aunt Beth called him a recluse, but that implied that he preferred being at home, like Matthew did; Father was only ever at Lawry Park long enough to shower me in a scolding. It was far more accurate to say he didn't mind where he was, so long as he was alone. Away from me.

I swallowed the familiar bite and forced a smile. "Thank you, Nancy."

Once she left, I rang for another servant and removed my riding habit from my wardrobe, flinging it on the bed. It was horrid manners to be late to one's own proposal.

I INHALED THE SALTY WIND AND SPURRED MY MOUNT FASTER, angling her toward the cliffs until we were parallel with them. Yellow horned poppies trampled under her hooves as we rode into the sunrise. Blond strands escaped my braid, flapping at my face every time I turned my head. To my right, far below, waves crashed against a shingled beach.

The memory of my dreams—dreams filled with shadows and pine trees and blue eyes that burned orange in the candlelight—called to me, but I gripped the reins tighter and pushed it away. I melded into the saddle, and we became one. We were the ground, the sky, the air beneath our feet. We were free. I drank it in, wishing I could steal away like this every morning.

Spotting the little trail hidden by stone fern, I reined Cressida to a stop. The untrained eye would've glossed over the beginning of the path, but I had walked it so many times in my childhood that its location was forever imprinted in my memory.

After dismounting, I clutched her bridle and led her down the narrow trail to the beach. Stones the size of eggs crunched underfoot as we journeyed along the shore. In the opposite direction, far up the beach near Brighton, the specks of bathing machines rolled into the water to dump their occupants in the sea. The wooden, carriage-like contraptions afforded privacy to change clothing and swim, and since the ocean at Brighton was famous for its healing properties, it was common to see dozens of them this time of year.

As I went, rocks exchanged themselves for sand and large boulders, sharply contrasted against the chalky cliff wall. Up ahead, sand dug into the cliff face, carving out a private corner. A figure leaned against the wall, his horse shaking its mane a few feet away. Henry turned and saw me approaching. He broke into a smile. "I was beginning to think you'd lost your way."

Tying Cressida's reins to a protruding limb on a log, I said, "How could I lose my way to the place I remember most as a child?"

Henry glanced around. "It's been over a year since we've been back. Still looks the same, though."

A spray of saltwater flicked my skin as I turned full circle, soaking in the nostalgia. I stopped when I spotted the corner Henry and I had spent hours in one afternoon, digging holes in the cliff face.

Cubbyholes the size of hat boxes pocked the wall in random places, all of them within reach of nine-year-old children. They were deep enough to hold books, but they'd for years acted as shelves for our various trinkets. I neared and saw that no one had moved them. They sat dormant in the cliff and I took them all in, my heart warming in recognition of my old friends. My smile widened when I saw Henry's cufflinks from last night, resting on their own shelf.

Pins, ribbons, buckles, spoons. Each one was tied to a memory and a wager. My eye caught on one cubby with a long, spiraling shell resting on its shelf. Lines twisted around its exterior like gold strands, making it unique among England's mostly white and gray seashells. I bent and picked it up, turning it over in my hands, smiling.

"Do you remember the day I found that?" Henry's voice came above my shoulder.

"You thought it was pretty and tried to give it to me as a birthday gift." I turned around to face him.

Henry pried it from my hands, chuckling. "And you didn't find it pretty at all—so you hurled it into the sea, saying you didn't like gifts and it was a useless one anyway."

"Oh, do not remind me!" I cupped my cheek. His hand covered

my own, pulling it away from my face. I couldn't help but note how different it felt from Matthew's touch; cooler, and less certain.

Stop thinking about Matthew.

Henry's laugh softened into a smile. "And *I* said that a thing being pretty does not make it useless." His eyes roamed my face, a double meaning behind them. A blush heated my neck.

"So I set out to retrieve it," he went on, quieter, his words dampened by the breeze, "but you wagered I could not find it. I was certain the sea would give it back to me, and made you promise that if I managed to place it in your hands again, you would cherish it forever."

"And so I have," I murmured.

"Luckily for me, you didn't know how to throw very far."

That brought another smile to my face.

I could still picture the memory clearly. Yellow rays glinting off the water, then Henry breaking the surface, gulping in a breath, water dripping off his chin as he pumped his fist into the air, clutching the seashell. He slogged back to the beach and closed my hand around the shell, reverently. And looking at me with those gray eyes of his, said, *Happy birthday, Alicia.*

After that day we'd made all kinds of silly wagers, the cliff acting as a shelf for our trophies. But it held more than just trophies. It held the threads of our laughter and joys, weaving them together to form one hopeful, hesitant dream.

I turned my focus out to sea. The ocean looked just as it had that day, all those years ago, churning in the golden sun. So beautiful. The waves ebbed and flowed, swirling around until they formed a certain pair of blue eyes, vivid and glowing and deep enough to drown in . . .

"What are you frowning about?"

I turned to find Henry analyzing me in confusion.

"Nothing, I—" I bit my lip then sighed. "I only wish I didn't have to pretend to be engaged to Mr. Wycliffe. It is turning out to be excruciating." Even in my thoughts, the man wouldn't leave me alone.

A serious expression overtook Henry's features. He seemed to hesitate, but then finally said, slowly, "Because you love him?"

I blinked at Henry. It was a full three seconds before I could respond with a scoff. "*Love* him? Never! Hardly! How could I? I find Mr. Wycliffe most arrogant and rude. And though I am those things too, I daresay I am not half as bad as he is."

Henry's face relaxed.

"And another thing," I went on, "he dominates every discussion so I can barely get a word in. How he loves to hear himself speak! And as for the content of his conversation, his wit is so sharp, I wonder he has not impaled himself on it."

A dam broke, unleashing the flood of frustration that had been building inside me all morning—anger because after last night, the attraction I felt toward him was no longer only physical. "He's no fun at all. Digging in his heels left and right. And since he is *all-knowing*, anyone with a contrary opinion is a nuisance to be cast aside. He does not say it outright, but I can see it in his eyes. He loathes me. He loathes me with such a passion, I am surprised he has not snapped. Such hate would surely break a weaker man. And I *hope* it breaks him. I hope he crumbles into little pieces at my feet, so I may dance upon his ruin for years on end." I folded my arms, jaw working as I scowled at the sand.

After a minute of stewing, I looked up to find Henry watching me quietly, carefully.

I flushed. That was a bit more revealing than I'd intended it to be. I'd only wanted to assuage Henry's fears, but I'd given him a rant instead and ruined our tender moment in the process.

"So you see . . ." I said slower, straightening up as I attempted to steer the conversation back, "if ever I loved Matthew Wycliffe, it would only be because I know it would make him miserable."

We sat in silence for several minutes, and through it all, Henry never lost the worried gleam in his eye. The quiet was crushing me, but I knew he was mulling over something, weighing its importance, so I said nothing.

At last, he asked, "Why did you ask to meet me here, Alicia?"

Ah yes, the will. "I have something for you." I rummaged through my saddle bag until I found the document, then turned and held it out to him.

He set the shell back in the cubbyhole and took it. "What's this?" After unfolding the paper, he read. Lines etched his brow, furrowing deeper the longer he stared at the paper. "It cannot be . . ." His eyes snapped up. "Where did you find this?"

I clutched one arm behind my back. "I didn't forge it, if you're worried—"

"No of course not, but—" He shook the paper. "Th-This is my father's signature. Right here."

"Yes!"

"And the money. He hasn't left it to Graham after all, he's left it to—"

"You," I finished for him.

He glanced back at me again. "To me." Slowly, his flustered expression cleared. But his eyes remained wide as one corner of his lips turned up. "To me," he said again.

Words, long unspoken, pulsed in the air between us. The fortune that had for so long eluded him was now in his hands. His smile bloomed, and that hesitant dream sprang to life.

"Alicia, I—I cannot believe it. As silly as it sounds, I never wanted a fortune for the money, but for what it meant for my future. For *our* future. I never thought—never dared *hope* for the possibility—"

"Yes?" I said, hands wringing and slipping inside their gloves.

"Now that this will is found, I should have no more reservations about asking you—well, if your engagement is really a charade, like you claim—about asking you if—"

"Oh, that is good news indeed!"

Hand flying to my heart and barely restraining a frightened

scream, I spun around to find Lord Hawthorne dismounting a prancing black Friesian only a few paces away. Henry and I had been so wrapped up in the moment, neither of us had noticed his approach.

After tying his mount near ours, Lord Hawthorne beamed and said, "I am so glad to hear that your engagement is a charade, Lady Alicia. Heaven knows I was on the cusp of despairing! I could not think to do anything but pick a bouquet of your favorite flowers and deliver them to you this morning, with the express purpose of changing your mind." He neared, kicking sand onto my boots when he stopped. "Of course, when I arrived at Lawry Park, your aunt informed me you'd gone riding. But then on my journey home, I saw you riding near the cliffs and simply had to know where you were going. Oh, but what luck I was able to find you!"

What luck indeed.

Henry stepped back a proper distance, and the frustration coiling my stomach wound tighter. He'd been on the verge of proposing—and now, not only was the moment ruined, but Hawthorne knew the truth and would continue in his efforts for my hand.

"I see that I need not change your mind after all—and can also deliver your flowers in person!" Lord Hawthorne produced a bundle of blooms he'd been hiding behind his back and held them out to me. "Daisies," he said reverently, like it was the secret to eternal youth.

I grimaced. Clearing my throat, I said, "They are . . . quite beautiful. But you see, Mr. Crawley and I were having a private conversation just now, and would like to continue—"

Hawthorne's eyes widened. "Yes, private indeed! I should think so. Very sensitive information, your being secretly unattached, my lady. And might I say, I am overjoyed to hear it!" He leaned in, voice lowering. "Though, I'm sure your marital status will change very, *very* soon." His wink was so obvious, I would've noticed it halfway down the beach. Turning to Henry he added, "I didn't quite know what to make of the rumors last night, but in light of this new information, it all makes sense now."

I frowned. "What rumors?" Had the knowledge of mine and Matthew's "entanglement" been brought to light?

Hawthorne looked between us, dumbfounded. "But have you not heard them? They were making the rounds at the ball last night. That your and Mr. Wycliffe's union is not a love match."

Drat, this didn't bode well. It must've happened while Matthew and I were searching for the will. *If you cannot be convincing, Alicia . . . if rumors start to circulate that you are not attached to Mr. Wycliffe out of love . . . you will have broken our deal.* If people were beginning to speculate, it was only a matter of time before they reached the right conclusion.

"Did either my father or my aunt mention these rumors when you visited my estate this morning?"

"I can't say that they did. But surely it is only a matter of time before the gossip reaches their ears."

I shared a glance with Henry, who only looked confused. He didn't know my father and I had an understanding—and that if I broke it, I would also be breaking my chance to be his wife. More than just fortune and standing stood in the way of our marriage now. All my efforts would be for naught if I didn't quell this gossip and hold up my end of the bargain. I needed a plan.

With my eyes, I tried to tell Henry I was sorry. But what I said was, "If you will excuse me, there is something I must do." I marched across the sand and untied Cressida's reins from the log.

"Alicia . . ." The word was so soft, I almost missed it in the wind.

I turned back to see Henry staring at me with an open expression. He didn't want me to leave. He wanted to finish our moment.

I did too. There was nothing I wanted more.

"But my lady!" Hawthorne protested, waving the bouquet in a white blur. "The daisies! I had hoped—"

Using the log to mount my horse, I settled into the saddle. "I am sorry, my lord—but everyone knows I prefer kingcups to daisies. And as I'm certain you cannot produce any of those this time of year, I really must be on my way." I tipped my head. "Good day, sirs." Leaning in, I kicked Cressida into a gallop, leaving a cloudy trail of sand in our wake.

If the rumors continued, Father would order me to cut to the chase and marry Hawthorne. Henry would be taken out of the running altogether.

Which meant that, at least for the time being, I needed to remain engaged. I needed to swoon and admire and make cow's eyes at Matthew until all of society laughed at anyone who said I was less than infatuated with the man. So that I could marry Henry.

Botheration.

CHAPTER 15

To my astonishment, Matthew—not his butler—answered the door, opening it enough to reveal his frame and not an inch wider. Upon seeing me, a look of relief flashed across his features, before he seemed to think better of it and scowled. "What are you doing here?"

I clutched my amber studded reticule. This wasn't going to be easy, convincing Matthew to keep on with the charade—but I had to, to quash the rumors and my father's threat along with them. "I am here to meet your sister. Naturally." I attempted to push the door open, but he blocked it with his foot.

He leaned against the door. "Oh, naturally—except we are no longer engaged."

Bother. I hope he hadn't already told his family. "Yes, we are."

"No, we are not—"

"A gentleman, Mr. Wycliffe, would never engage a lady and then toss her aside. It simply isn't done. And if you were to secede from the match before I've officially released you, your respectability—as well as your title of *gentleman*—would be abolished."

His head craned out the opening, voice lowering. "But you did release me. We found the will, after all."

I leaned in too. "I did no such thing. And there's been a minor setback."

"How surprising."

I huffed and crossed my arms. "Perhaps I would discuss the matter further with you, if you were to invite me inside."

He shook his head. "And let you beguile more of my family into adoring you? No, thank you. It is sickening enough to have Peter and Lily singing your praises. Let's not make it a choir."

I held up my hand in a pledge. "If you let me in, I promise to be on my best behavior and only beguile *you*."

He eyed my hand with a look of annoyed boredom. "I do not find that humorous."

"I shall start now, then!" Sighing, I stepped forward and smoothed the lapels of his suit coat before cupping his cheek. "How handsome you look today, Mr. Wycliffe. Even with that scowl darkening your features." I tapped his brow, making him wrinkle it further, before I turned away and twirled my reticule. "Oh, how it sets my heart aflutter! I am the luckiest of women to have secured your affections—paltry, though they are—and you shall not see them wasted on me. Only give me an afternoon with your family, and I shall reward you with that kiss you so desperately desired in the tunnel!"

Matthew kept silent the whole time, a long-suffering edge to his glare. As if I did this routinely, and the only reason he humored me was to get it over with quicker. "I am looking forward to it," he said like he definitely was not. "But what a conundrum—for I have determined to hole myself up in this house for a fortnight. And I know for a fact you shall not be stepping one foot inside it."

He backed away to close the door, but I was faster. I wedged my foot in the opening, allowing a rectangle just large enough to see the surprise on Matthew's face. He pushed on the door again, but my foot held fast.

"Well, look at that," I said, pulling out my most alluring smile, "one foot indeed. Come now, darling, let us drop pretenses. You are glad to see me, and I dare you to deny it."

Matthew opened his mouth. But to my surprise, the retort never came. His eyebrows came together and he faltered, looking me up and down. And as the moments passed, my smile widened.

Matthew was nothing if not painfully honest. If he could not deny it, then it was as good as true. Was he glad to see me because he'd been worried about me after last night, or because he was coming to enjoy my company in general? Either one I would take, for they both gave me a warm feeling.

He was saved from replying by a muffled cry beyond the door. "Alicia!" The handle jiggled like someone was trying to open it from the inside. I stepped back.

Matthew turned to the intruder, struggling to keep the door in place. "No—stop it."

Another muffled reply. Another yank on the door. A feminine hand swiped at him.

He elbowed her back. "I said no—deuces, Eliza, leave off! No!"

The door swung open to reveal the flushed, victorious smile of Lady Eliza Bentley, dark tendrils of hair escaping their bind. I blinked at her, struck by the surrealistic sight of the only person who had treated me with kindness during my first Season, standing in Matthew Wycliffe's house.

"Alicia!" she exclaimed again.

". . . Eliza?"

Matthew frowned, glancing between us. "'Eliza'?"

She threw herself across the threshold and into my arms. I met Matthew's eye above the embrace. He looked from me to Lady Bentley, then back to me, lips angling down.

Eliza pulled back and held me at arm's length, studying me head to toe. "Oh Alicia, how I have missed you! It has been far too long—especially since I couldn't find you at my garden party. What a shame it took something like your engagement to my brother to actually bring us together."

My jaw dropped. Now it was my turn to stare, eyes swinging between them.

Eliza . . . was Matthew's sister?

Seeing them side by side, the resemblance was unmistakable. They had the same cheekbones and coloring. Matthew had been at Lady Bentley's garden party because Lady Bentley was his sister. An enthusiastic sister who no doubt forced a recluse like him to attend.

"You are already acquainted?" Matthew asked.

Eliza spun around. "But of course! Didn't I tell you? The late duchess was William's distant relation. Alicia was in Town for her first Season when I was recovering from Charlotte's birth, and she kept me sane, those first few months. Even took the baby for a night so the nurse could get a rest! She's a complete angel!"

My entire frame curled inward under Eliza's praise. Though I may have had good intentions in the past, that was far from the case now. None of the Wycliffes knew I intended to sever the engagement in a matter of days. Even Matthew was unaware of the fact that—regardless of whether he helped me—a marriage to me wasn't in his future. I was using them all to meet my own ends, and the knowledge made my stomach twinge.

Matthew regarded his sister like she was speaking a different language. Then he turned to me and gave me the same look he'd given me in the gardens after I'd fallen into him. A look that said, *Perhaps I don't have you figured out, after all.* If nothing else, I should be satisfied that I'd managed to surprise him.

Eliza put an arm around my shoulder. "Who knew you, of all women, would be the one to capture my brother's heart?"

My eyes flicked to Matthew. "Indeed! And I do believe I've captured it quite well."

"Quite," he said dryly.

"Come." Eliza gave my shoulders a squeeze before pushing me past her brother and into the house. "I missed you at my garden party, and we have so much to catch up on. Let us leave the men to their boring conquests."

I chuckled as we ambled down the rosewood hallway past the library. "Unfortunately, I shall have to take *Mr. Wycliffe's* boring conquest with me."

I was referring to myself, of course, and the way Matthew was always able to predict me. I glanced over my shoulder to see if he caught the joke. For the smallest moment, I thought I saw the barest of smiles on one corner of Matthew's lips—so slight it didn't even curve up or press a fold in his cheek. So small, it hardly altered his face at all.

But I would've sworn on my life that it was there.

THOUGH MATTHEW'S HOUSE WAS SMALL, IT WAS ATTACHED TO one hundred and fifty acres of land—and it was beautiful. Like the front of the house, everything was manicured and groomed to perfection, down to every blade of grass. Roses, hedges, sweeping willows and towering foxglove greeted me as I walked arm in arm with Eliza, toward Lady Wycliffe sitting on a stone bench down the path.

Across the lawn near a glistening lake, a few children played peek-a-boo with the fronds of a willow tree while a governess looked on—a boy, four or five years old, and two toddling little girls. Their infectious giggles carried on the lukewarm breeze, making me smile.

"Is that one your daughter, Charlotte?" I asked Eliza, pointing to the darker haired little girl.

Eliza's eyes sparkled with love. "Yes. Though she often gets mistaken for her cousin."

I nodded and smiled. Even from a distance, I could tell they resembled each other. "She is so grown up since I last saw her." The boy and the other little girl must belong to Lord and Lady Wycliffe.

As Eliza and I approached Lady Wycliffe, the young boy ran up and threw himself into her arms. "Mama, did you see that? Diana and Charlotte think I am funny." He reared back to flash his mother a wrinkled-nose smile.

Lady Wycliffe smiled and squished her son's cheeks. "And so you are."

"But Mama, now they'll never leave me alone." He threw himself backwards over her lap and huffed like he was out of breath. "Why must I be so funny?"

After laughing, Lady Wycliffe ruffled his hair. "I'm sure I shall never know." Her pale blue eyes looked up at us and rolled, before she mouthed, *Just like his father*.

The boy put a wrist over his eyes to shield them from the sun. "Such a curse!"

"You poor thing."

He shot up. "Best get back, before they realize I've gone." He spun around but stopped short when he saw me. I gave him a little wave. Backing away, he smiled shyly before waving back and dashing off.

Lady Wycliffe watched her son, sighing. "So much energy, that one. So unlike his pensive little sister." The children resumed their game, this time attempting to include the governess by peeking out of the fronds and scaring her. She humored them by pretending to gasp in horror, making them giggle harder.

I watched the little boy play for a moment. "What is your son's name, Lady Wycliffe?" I asked.

"Please, we are almost sisters. You must call me Lily."

I glanced at her, again surprised to find kindness in her face, an eagerness to be friends. The sight of it made me relax. Growing up without female companionship, I had little knowledge of how to act around my own sex, least of all in a positive way. But both Lily and Eliza's manners put me at ease. Though I was still sure to make a mistake, with them, I wasn't so afraid of making it.

I smiled and amended, "Lily."

She untied her bonnet and set it on the bench, turning in her son's direction. "Matthew Ashley Wycliffe, baron of Sunderly. Though we call him Ashley to avoid confusion."

I cocked my head. They'd named him after Matthew? I glanced at the boy who was blowing willow leaves into his cousin's face, seeing him with new eyes. He was a handsome little chap who looked like his father—and his uncle, by extension. Dark hair, high cheekbones, bright blue eyes.

"Forgive me for asking, but . . . why is he named after his uncle and not his father?" It was not unheard of, but passing names from father to son was much more common.

Lily and Eliza shared a look, before chuckling. "It is a long story," Lily said, "but suffice it to say, when I first came to Ambleside, I was pretending to be someone I was not and Matthew helped me a great deal. After all he'd done for me, he made me promise to name my firstborn son after him. So I did."

I chuckled at the joke, but it puttered out upon seeing Lily's amused but steady expression. "You are in earnest?"

Of all the conceited things.

Lily laughed too. "Matthew said it in jest, but I did not take his kindness so lightly. Without him, I wouldn't have married Peter and gained him as a brother. Though not always readily apparent, Matthew has many redeeming qualities. He is the noblest man I know. I probably would have named my son after him without his suggestion."

Involuntarily, my mind drifted to last night. My hand and the back of my head began to tingle with the memory of his touch. I remembered his soft, soothing words. His tightening fist. His defense of me in front of Graham. *You are a brave man indeed, to insult her in my presence.*

There was some truth to Lily's words. Matthew was rough around the edges—perhaps the roughest I'd ever seen—but after last night, some instinct of mine knew that underneath his dark, coarse exterior had to be the largest diamond known to man. The only question was whether he'd crack open enough to let anyone see it.

What would it take, I wonder? To crack him open?

And why on earth did I suddenly want to know?

"Come," Lily said, standing and joining me and Eliza. "Let us walk along the lake's edge."

A mostly-shaded gravel path bordered the lake, decorated with sprinkles of sunlight. We walked along the pathway, content in the silence for a moment. The wind rippled the lake to look like wrinkles on a palm, driving the water southward.

"So. You and Matthew are in love."

My steps stuttered, but I recovered by whipping my head over to smile at Lily. "To be sure, we are desperately in love."

Eliza turned, walking sideways as she said, "I didn't believe it when I first heard the news. Matthew—not only in love, but engaged? How could he keep it from me?" She heaved an exasperated sigh. "But I suppose I shouldn't be surprised. One can never tell anything, with him."

"Peter came home the day of Eliza's party and announced it quite suddenly! He didn't appear to be shocked by the news." Lily squinted. "Peter must've had some inkling before then, but I find it odd he never said as much."

"And to think it was you who finally caught his eye!" Eliza added.

I stifled a laugh. Caught his sleeve, more like. My muscles relaxed in the knowledge that our efforts in convincing everyone hadn't fallen completely flat.

Plucking a leaf from a branch hanging over the path, I said, "Did Sir William know as well?"

Eliza barked a laugh. "If Peter and Matthew were keeping a secret, you can bet your life my husband knew it. I'm sure he threatened to expose them and was paid off for his silence."

Lily swung her bonnet at her side and looked over at me. "May I ask how you came to love him?"

I ripped the leaf and made a vague gesture with my hand, trying to act nonchalant. "He swept me off my feet!"

Literally.

Even figuratively, it wasn't exactly a lie. From the moment we met, I'd had a difficult time getting Matthew out of my head. And since last night, I'd thought about him almost obsessively. His hands. His soft voice. The rise of his chest. The smell of his clothes. His burning eyes in the candlelight.

Oh gracious me, it needed to stop.

"How?" Eliza asked, eyes twinkling with love for her brother.

"Well," I said, tossing the tattered pieces of the leaf away and struggling to find any words. I detested the idea of lying any more than I had to, but what did one say about a man you loathed?

"He is very tall," I said at last.

Eliza giggled. "Is that all it took for you to fall in love with him? Notice his height?"

"No!" I grinned. "Though it certainly helped me notice him in the first place." That drew more laughter from the pair of women. Thinking of Hawthorne, I said, "Matthew is very knowledgeable, and though it is inconvenient whenever I wish to win an argument, I much prefer that to a man who doesn't know anything at all." Oh bother, what a halfhearted confession that must seem. I tried again.

"He is an intriguing person—just when I think I understand him, he surprises me, proves me wrong, flusters me. In many ways, I feel like I don't know a thing about him. But one thing I do admire is how deeply he loves his family." Expressing love was something I struggled with in my own family. And it was encouraging to think that if someone as hardened as Matthew could do it, then I could learn, too. "Once he stakes his claim on a person, he refuses to let them go."

As we are engaged, you are mine now, too.

Mine.

My pulse picked up speed, and I inhaled a long breath to settle it back down. Matthew didn't mean anything by saying that—or by defending me in the first place.

"For that reason," I went on, "I've seen him exhibit not only thoughtfulness and a tenderness of feeling, but loyalty fierce enough to inspire my own."

As soon as the words left my lips, I flushed. That was a bit more revealing than I'd intended it to be. And where had it come from? Considering my rant to Henry this morning, I was surprised I had anything good to say about Matthew; but here I was, babbling on like I was actually infatuated with the man, when I wasn't.

I wasn't.

Eliza and Lily both smiled softly, as if they knew exactly what I meant. And I was glad of it, because I wasn't sure that I did. Lily nudged me in a meaningful way. "I am so glad your admiration for him is sincere."

"Yes." I swallowed the lump in my throat. "Sincere."

Perhaps in a different world, with a different beginning, I could've come to love Matthew. Perhaps he had those gleaming qualities, hiding behind a rigid façade. Perhaps we were more similar than I'd ever realized. But none of that really mattered when you compared our dispositions, our families, and our varying motivations.

Even if it *did* matter, loving him still wouldn't be possible—because I was going to marry Henry. And if not him, then Hawthorne.

Lily and Eliza were romantics, and they wanted to see Matthew happy. So, surely if they discovered the truth of my situation, they'd see that I was the last woman on earth who would make him so.

"He wasn't always how he is now, you know," Eliza said quietly. After a moment, she looked over at me with a rueful smile. "That is, he was always an annoying little brother, but there was a time when he was sweet, too. Quiet, and shy. Now he is more than vocal about his opinions, but with every year that passes, I watch the *real* him retreat deeper into his shell. I cannot understand it."

We curved around the top of the lake, turning back in the direction of the house. The lulling breeze made the bulrushes sway. Back by the willow tree, the governess gathered up the children and started up the lawn, determining the children had had enough sun for one day.

"Even as a boy, Matthew was brilliant," Eliza continued. "But there was a time when he liked to do other things, besides read. Swimming, bug collecting, even fencing. When my father died, it affected each of us in a different way. For Matthew, that meant turning into a recluse. It was weeks before I managed to get him to come out of the library—weeks where all he did was devour books, mostly studies in medicine. I think some part of him thought he could bring Father back, if he only discovered why he died.

"The bookish side to him became the new normal, and life moved on. Several years passed, and though he had changed, there was still much about him that remained the same." She paused. Then, "The real trial was when Mama died."

Lily and Eliza shared a look. It was obviously an ordeal they had weathered together, but Lily seemed content to let Eliza tell the story.

"I had not thought it possible," Eliza said, slower, "but the cycle repeated itself—and to a much greater extent. We hardly saw him—and when we did, he was never without a book. Never without a shield. I think a whole month passed before I heard the sound of his voice again. And then all he did was voice annoyances, criticisms, noncommittal sentences."

"Why do you think he shut everyone out like that?" I surprised myself by asking. If there was a reason Matthew was the way he was, I wanted to know. And though I doubted I could help the matter, I wanted to know if it was possible. If Matthew could somehow be fixed. If his heart of coal could be cracked open to reveal the diamond inside.

Because if he could be fixed . . . then maybe I could be, too.

"I think . . ." Eliza bit her lip, hesitating. She sighed. "Matthew does not have friends. That isn't to say that he couldn't, if he tried —only that he does not *care* to try. He has Peter and William, but he views them as more of father figures than peers. Through the years, I've tried to be a friend for him, someone he can talk to, but he never seemed interested. Worse, he didn't appear to need it. And it is worse because I know he *does* need someone to talk to—even if he will never admit it."

Lily nodded in agreement. "He's been terribly lonely. I've seen it in his eyes."

Matthew Wycliffe . . . lonely with his clouds of admirers? The idea was almost laughable.

But then, I must seem like a girl with an abundance of friends, too, with all my suitors hanging about. And I did have many prestigious connections—but an unknowing observer couldn't know that my connections hadn't blossomed into any real friendships.

In Matthew's case, it made sense that he was too different to fit in with anyone. We were alike, in that way. Because of his difference —his intelligence and sharp wit—he'd risen so high, and so fast, he'd put himself in a class above the rest; a class completely on its own. And though to others he might appear to live like an emperor, now that I thought about it, it didn't seem that way at all.

It seemed to me that Matthew Wycliffe must get awfully lonely indeed, up there at the top. And he would always be alone unless someone rose to his level and met him head on.

Eliza linked her arm through mine. "I think ultimately," she said, "Matthew has refused to grow close to anyone out of fear of losing them. Grief and loss are the only things that, even with his big, knowledgeable brain, he cannot explain. They are the only unknowns he cannot bear to face. The only way to prevent them is to not care about anyone in the first place. So he tries not to."

The thought was sobering, rubbing me in a way that made me squirm—because in many ways, I was the same way. It was easier to withhold love than to hurt when it was rejected. Hearing Eliza say it made it obvious how wrong it was to shut yourself off from everyone. It was selfish. It hurt those around you as much as it kept your wounds from ever healing.

But how did one learn to love someone? How did one find the courage? The idea didn't just feel daunting—it felt impossible.

Eliza turned to me with a sudden, teasing smile, clearing away the serious mood. "Except me, of course. Matthew always had a soft spot for me."

Lily nudged Eliza with her shoulder. "And me! Though he would never admit it."

"Oh, no," Eliza agreed. "I'm convinced you could dangle Matthew from a cliff, demanding a confession, and still he would cross his arms and say something like—" She contorted her face into a dramatic scowl, pitching her voice lower in an almost believable imitation. "—'Love is a weakness. And since we both know I don't possess any weaknesses, well then, by devil, we can assume I don't possess any love either.'"

I giggled, and Lily joined me. Though I knew Matthew viewed love as a strength, it *did* sound like something he would say.

Eliza continued, bolstered by our laughter. "'Or at least *I* can assume that—it is questionable whether you're astute enough to. Now I'd rather not be here all day, so kindly refrain from asking stupid questions—but of course you can't help it, so best keep your mouth shut. Deuces, that grip of yours on my ankle hurts—and by all England, will you put me back on solid ground already!'"

"Stop!" I managed through my laughter, wiping tears from my eyes. "Or I am sure I shall burst!"

Lily linked my other arm through hers. "Yes, they will hear us from the house at this rate!"

We laughed once more before heading back to join the men.

Every window in the house was open, allowing a refreshing draft to diffuse the humidity gathering inside. I passed a mirror on the way to the library and stopped in my tracks. Lily and Eliza continued on while I studied myself, barely recognizing my reflection.

I didn't know why. They were the same green eyes, heart-shaped lips, and soft blond curls that had followed me all my life. But somehow, the girl in the mirror seemed different than she had a week ago. Flushed cheeks and a hopeful sparkle were new additions, but there was something else, too.

She seemed . . . happier. Excited about something.

But when I blinked, she was gone. I analyzed my reflection for another few moments before catching up to Lily and Eliza just as they slipped into the library.

"Still at it, then?" Lily came to a halt and sighed, putting her hands to her hips.

Near the enormous window, Matthew and his brother hunched over a game of chess. Or rather, Lord Wycliffe was hunched— Matthew slouched back in his chair, hands knitted over his stomach. Sir William Bentley perused a newspaper near the cold fireplace. I remembered Sir William from my first Season. Though I'd spent a large amount of time with Eliza, I'd only interacted with her husband on a handful of occasions. What I had seen of the man I had decidedly liked—but that may have been due to his witty charm.

He bowed his head to me in greeting before folding his newspaper down and saying with a smile, "What else would they be doing?" Eliza joined him and gave him a peck on the lips before dropping onto the sofa.

The gesture surprised me, making me re-evaluate the occupants of the room. Displays of affection—even between husband and wife —were rarely seen. Even if I weren't present and there were only close family members to observe it, it would still be a bit shocking. Something in my heart stirred. It made me even more curious about the Wycliffes. What would it be like to belong to a family who was so open with their affections?

Without looking over, Lord Wycliffe called to his wife, "I shall never give up until I've beat him just *once*."

Lily gave me a conspiratorial smile. Under her breath, she said, "Then we shall be here for the rest of our lives."

Lord Wycliffe's eyes snapped up. "What was that?"

Lily blinked innocently. "Nothing."

His mouth pinched in shrewd amusement. It was the look of someone who knew the other so well, he practically heard her thoughts. Then he turned back to the game, grazed his lower lip with his thumb, and finally, hesitantly, moved one of his pieces.

The moment Lord Wycliffe let go, Matthew sat forward and slid his queen into place in one fluid movement. "Checkmate."

"Blast." Lord Wycliffe flicked his king down onto the board. "I don't know how you do that. I thought for sure I had you on the ropes that time." He stood and stalked to the window, ruffling the back of his head.

Matthew shrugged and turned away, looking bored. "What about you, William? Fancy a game of chess?"

"Mm, no thank you." Sir William took a swig of his drink, before setting his paper aside and flashing a smile. "You know I never play a game unless I know I will win it."

"Smart man." Matthew returned the pieces to their rightful positions on the board.

"What about you, Alicia?" Eliza asked from the sofa. "Why don't you challenge Matthew? None of us have ever come close to beating him, and I would very much like to see him thrashed."

Matthew's head rolled over to look at me dubiously. "You play chess?"

I suppressed a smile.

Did I play chess.

My father was a strategy enthusiast. He could sputter all he wanted about proper behavior for a young lady and acceptable pastimes, but when it came to thinking on your feet and learning how to outmaneuver an opponent, he had spared no expense in my tutelage. Maps that staged hypothetical battalions littered his study, and countless afternoons had been taken up by him drilling into me the different terms and strategies of war. He'd even paid for private fencing lessons.

After my mother died, I'd spent the last hour of every evening with him by the fire, playing chess. I was twelve when I first managed to beat him—Father, whom I'd never seen lose to anyone. Four years later, I was able to do it consistently. Now when we played chess (which was rarely), there was hardly a question of my beating him, only on how quickly I could do it. Regardless of the opponent, I could play the game in my *sleep* and still come out the victor.

"Not often," I said with a careless shrug.

Matthew snorted. "What fun can a match be that does not last more than five minutes?"

"Come off it, Matthew," Lily said, face taking on a scolding look as she slung an arm around my shoulders. "Alicia may surprise you. She may last *ten*."

Matthew's gaze blinked over to me. My mind went, as I'm sure his did, to our conversation in this very room. To when he'd said I was the most predictable woman he'd ever met. His boring conquest. His eyebrow twitched. "I highly doubt it."

"Well, I suppose one little game wouldn't hurt!" I marched to the other end of the room and plunked into the chair Lord Wycliffe had just vacated, flashing Matthew an angry smile. As usual, he gave no sign of seeing it. He held out his hand, gesturing that I was to make the first move.

He thought I didn't know white goes first.

Of all the insufferable—!

I tamped down my anger. If I were going to best him, I needed to keep my emotions in check—and I didn't want to hear any excuse in regards to luck or advantage, either. Without disturbing the pieces, I swiveled the board around until the white set lay before Matthew.

His eyebrows lifted, but he moved his pawn. Careful to maintain a neutral expression, I discreetly scanned the set-up, debating possible strategies, trying to anticipate Matthew's thought pattern.

Pawn, then knight, bishop, then queen . . .

I moved my pawn.

"I hear the Regulars are shipping out a week later than usual," Lord Wycliffe said, turning from the window. "The festivities are slated to begin tomorrow."

"Oh no, not that rabble again?" Sir William poured himself another drink before setting the decanter down and leaning against the fireplace. "It is sure to be a dead bore."

"It is sure to be *exciting*," Eliza insisted.

"Only if you go, my dear—but I know how difficult you are to persuade." Sir William smirked at his wife and took a swallow. Eliza shot him a look that said he already knew she was keen on going.

Lily joined Eliza on the sofa. "I look forward to the games Brighton hosts each year, in honor of our soldiers. It's very patriotic. And there's something attractive about a man in uniform." Lily and Eliza exchanged girlish looks before sighing.

Lord Wycliffe ambled toward the others near the fireplace. Bracing his hands on the back of the sofa, he leaned over. "Lucky for you, I don't need a uniform. For I am already so very handsome, am I not?"

Lily laughed. "Peter, you are never going to let me live that down, are you?"

Lord Wycliffe smiled down at her like he wanted to kiss her. "Not so long as I live and breathe."

Eliza rolled her eyes and swatted at Lord Wycliffe's face until he retreated from his wife. "Anyway—at the very least, we must attend the fencing match. It is the most exciting part of all. Henry Crawley has won the last three years in a row—and it is said he will win this year in a landslide."

The crown jewel of the Brighton games was the fencing tournament. More thrilling than archery and less bloody than boxing, it required grace and finesse, as well as strength and speed. They used real but blunted swords—and there was something electrifying about the sound of clanging metal while two masked men dueled in a field.

I still remembered each of Henry's three winning matches, his beaming smile when he tore off his mask, sweat dripping down his forehead. Victorious. Worthy of any girl's heart.

"As previously posited," Matthew said, face tipping toward the ceiling, "what fun can be a match that lasts no more than five minutes? And I imagine it to be even more tiresome to *watch*. More so if it's Mr. Crawley."

After moving one of my pawns, I scoffed, quiet enough that only Matthew heard. He was purposely baiting me.

"No one expects *you* to go, Matthew," Lord Wycliffe said. "We all know you shan't—that you'll be nose-deep in another fascinating philosophy while we enjoy our mindless entertainment. All we ask is that you refrain from mocking us while we do it."

"Check," Matthew said to me as he moved his queen. Then to his brother, "You know as well as I that I never shall."

"But I'm sure Alicia wishes to go." Lily's eyes sparkled with mirth as she glanced between the pair of us. She thought Matthew would be swayed for my sake. "As she is your fiancée, it is your duty to see her there and back safely."

"Then let her find herself another fiancé." Matthew hadn't skipped a beat. He remained ever insensitive and unconcerned. He met my eyes. "One who will cater to her every whim."

He was referring to Henry. There was no mistaking it. He was angry at me for not releasing him from the engagement and leaving him in peace. And he was trying to make me suffer for it.

The flesh under my fingernails turned white from pinching my knight. I shoved the anger down and moved the piece into position. "But how unfortunate, sir. To engage myself to anyone else would be most inconvenient, as I am already madly in love with *you!*" *Only a few more turns*. There were limitless combinations of possible moves, but if I had gambled right . . .

"Yes!" Eliza agreed. "And I am ashamed of you, Matthew. A man in love should be eager to escort his intended."

He clucked his tongue. "As you've never been a man in love, Eliza, I doubt you are any authority on the matter."

I had to hand it to him—Matthew did not let the women in his family order him about.

"Then as an authority on the matter," Lord Wycliffe said, standing straight, "you should know that I agree with Eliza." His tone was light, but carried the slightest hint of warning. Matthew was treading too close to the edge for Lord Wycliffe's comfort, hinting a bit too openly that ours wasn't a love match.

Tongue in cheek, Matthew sat forward. "If Lady Alicia wishes to attend so badly, to watch a bunch of men uselessly flail around with bits of steel to compete for a useless prize—merely for the prospect of seeing the predestined Mr. Crawley emerge the victor yet again —then perhaps . . ." He paused, deliberately, settling his glittering gaze on me. ". . . perhaps she is not the woman I *fell in love* with."

Nor the men in his family, by England.

Yes, he was definitely angry at me. He was *trying* to test the limits to see who would break first—me, or his brother. I pressed my mouth in a line. It certainly wasn't going to be me.

After a tension-filled moment, Matthew moved his queen. "Check," he said blandly, and looked away.

A smug smile, slow and simmering overtook my lips. *Who is predictable now?* I moved my bishop, blocking his line of fire. "Checkmate."

CHAPTER 16

IT WAS NOT A RESOUNDING DECLARATION, YET THE WHOLE ROOM quieted. Peter, Lily, William, and Eliza all turned to me in shock. Silence reigned in the room for several, stifling moments. Matthew blinked over to me. He scoffed. But he did nothing more—didn't even examine the board to see if it were true—because he didn't believe me.

Then, after a long pause, he noticed my smile. A little crease formed between his brows, the smallest hint of doubt. He glanced down and wandered the setup. Another pause, lengthier than the last.

He shot forward, forehead knotting, eyes darting around.

"I don't believe it," Lord Wycliffe murmured.

Matthew shook his head, muttering something inaudible.

From his corner, Sir William grinned. "Could it be that Matthew's met his match at last?"

"At least in one thing you were right, Matthew," Lily said, lips bottling up a laugh. "The game did not last more than five minutes."

"It was ten at least!" Matthew said. His face flushed—the most emotion I'd ever seen on him, besides the moment we'd been caught in the gardens.

My smile widened at the sound of his petty argument; petulant, like a child denied a toy. My blood pumped with exhilaration. Victory over the stoic Matthew Wycliffe tasted even sweeter than I imagined it would. "You were right," I said offhandedly, unable to help myself. "What little fun it was."

Matthew glanced up and glowered at me.

I set my elbows on the table and rested my chin in my hands, smiling sweetly at him. "Care for another match?"

His jaw clenched.

The whole room burst with laughter, reveling and hysterical. Eliza clapped, beaming. And as for me—my heart soared.

"I'd say Lady Alicia's victory calls for some dessert," Lord Wycliffe announced. "Feel free to join us, Matthew, as soon as you've finished sulking." They laughed again before all four of them filed through the door, presumably to call for dessert. Their lingering merriment echoed with their retreat before a blanket of silence fell over the library.

And Matthew . . . Matthew's glare did not let up. My smile eventually faltered in the face of his smoldering eyes. Inside them was an acknowledgment that he had underestimated me; an oath that he wouldn't make the same mistake again.

I hope it breaks you, I thought ruthlessly. *I hope you crumble into pieces at my feet.*

But in his gaze, underneath all that anger, buried deep, was something else. Something that sparked and leapt across the space between us, catching my breath and blazing a trail in my stomach.

Fear. Attraction. Anticipation.

He didn't look away. His gaze tore into me. It seared holes in my skin, diving into my soul . . . deeper . . . and deeper—

I looked away and stood. And as I bit down on nothing, I cursed my own cowardice.

I had just beaten him at his own game—embarrassed him in

front of everyone he cared about. Yet, with one strange look, he made me out to be the loser. The one who didn't dare acknowledge the thing building inside me. Between *us*. The one who couldn't look someone in the eye without breaking.

In the end, *I* had been the one to crumble. Not him.

Confound him, *confound* him.

I stalked to the nearest bookcase and pretended to read the row of spines, determined to stay in the room if only to show him that he hadn't intimidated me. Besides, it provided the perfect opportunity to talk about maintaining our engagement.

He obviously had the same idea, because he jumped right in. "What is this 'minor setback' you claim to be having? You told me all would be well once Henry had his fortune, and we were inordinately lucky to have come across one in the first place."

I slid a finger along one of the shelves and inspected it. No dust. Of course. Why had I expected any? "It would—it was. But you see, just as Henry was about to propose, we were interrupted by reports of alarming proportions. Concerning you and me."

Matthew reclined, putting one hand behind his head and twirling the black queen with the other. "So. You wish to continue the charade until the reports die down."

"Yes."

"To spare your father."

My eyes narrowed. "In a way, yes," I said hesitantly.

He clucked his tongue. "How noble."

Waving my hand to seem flippant, I said, "Call it what you wish, but yes, I rather think so. Just continue pretending we're in love, and it shall be over before you know it."

"What if I refuse to pretend any longer?"

His wording gave me pause. *Pretend*—as if he was only tired of the charade because we were actually in love. But of course, that couldn't be what he meant—and this was not the first time my mind had twisted his words into meaning something more. What was wrong with me?

"If you inform everyone we are no longer engaged," I said slowly, "I shall tell them you jilted me. The *ton* may overlook your crude manners, but I doubt even your reputation could survive a scandal of those proportions."

Matthew puffed out a short burst of air. "And what of our deal? You promised that once I attended a silly ball and gave Mr. Crawley a fortune you'd call off the engagement, yet now you are going back on your word."

"I gave no such promise! I said I would call it off once Henry has *proposed*, and he has not."

Matthew studied my face. After a long, quiet moment, he set the queen down and asked, "And what if he never does?"

My throat swallowed convulsively. Somehow, having Matthew point out the possibility made it all the more real. All the more likely.

But since Matthew didn't know about my deal with Father, I knew what he was really asking. He didn't wish to continue helping me if it would all prove fruitless and he'd have to marry me anyway. So what was in it for him?

I took a deep breath. "*If* Henry leaves for India without proposing . . . then I shall release you from our engagement. Regardless of what happens, I will disappear from your life forever. Agreed?"

Matthew stilled. His jaw cranked back and forth as he deliberated. At last, he said, "You promise to release me?"

"Yes."

He sighed—a sound that was as long and weighty as one of Lady Hawthorne's sermons. "Then, from the bottom of my heart . . . *fine*." He jabbed a finger in my direction. "But you will not keep me in the dark—metaphorically or literally. You will tell me the entirety of every hare-brained plan of yours, sparing nothing. And if they include any more secret passageways, then by devil, I demand to know about them."

A sense of relief washed over me. Truth be told, I hadn't

expected to make it this far. I smiled. "Of course." My eyes brushed along the titles of books, each one as thick as my arm. Had he read all of these? And how did he have room to store them all? "Why do you live in such a small house?" I asked offhandedly.

Then I remembered the strange little book he'd had at the ball, and I wondered . . . Did he always keep it in his tailcoat, or perhaps . . . was it here, somewhere in this vast library? I scanned the books again, this time in search of a little, mint-green spine.

"I am only one person. To live in anything larger would be exorbitant."

Popping onto my tiptoes, I sifted through the shelf above, before moving down the bookcase. "Yes, but you're filthy rich—you can spare the money. You could have any house you wanted."

"I do not want another one. This is the house my father gave me, and so it is the house I shall remain in."

I caught my smile mid-bloom, wiping it away by telling myself that sentimentality was most definitely a negative trait in a man.

Most definitely.

"I could never abide living in such small quarters," I said, turning to him with a one-shouldered shrug. "When I am mistress of a home, I shall require something much grander."

"Then it is fortunate we won't actually marry," Matthew said, cutting me down with a pointed look.

I rested an elbow on the shelf. "But if we *did* marry, naturally we would find something larger."

"We would stay here." He cocked a stubborn brow.

I put my hands on my hips. "But to please your wife, you would move."

"I would remain. My *wife* is welcome to please herself—if she can manage it. I imagine the endeavor to be quite hopeless."

Oh, by all—

I pasted on my sweetest smile. "Come, Matthew—"

"Do not use my Christian name." He set to gathering the chess pieces and storing them in an engraved case. "It sounds tainted when falling from your lips." His eyes flashed to my mouth so briefly I barely caught it.

I smiled slowly. "Oh, but it pleases me—and as you said I am welcome to please myself, I shall call you what I wish." Folding my arms, I leaned against the bookcase. "Now, about the house. Surely you can see that it would not do. In such a small abode, wherever would we put our thirteen children?"

Matthew turned sharply, arm accidentally sweeping the board and scattering chess pieces all over the library floor. The white king rolled to a stop near my feet. I picked him up, pleased at the irony.

Matthew said something under his breath before gripping the edge of the small table. "*Thirteen?*"

"What is the matter, dearest Matthew?"

"Do not call me—" He cut himself off with a growl. He shot forward and busied himself with cleaning up the remaining pieces.

I batted my lashes. "Don't you like children?"

Plunking a few rooks onto the table, he said, "If you wanted thirteen of them, *dearest*, you are a little late getting started."

I puckered my lips in thought. "How true. We haven't a moment to waste. We'd best get started right away."

Matthew jerked up. He knocked into the table, sending it crashing to the ground where it spilled the remaining pieces. "I *beg* your pardon, madam!"

There was that attractive blush again.

To cover a laugh, I emitted a dramatized wistful sigh. "Come, Matthew, let us elope! This very moment! Oh, my love, I am eternally yours, now and forever. I can scarce keep away from you any longer!" I rushed over and grasped his hands, tugging him up. Then I cradled his face, staring adoringly into his panicked eyes. "And once we have thirteen children—in no time at all, really—perhaps I can convince you once and for all that this house is, indeed, too small."

"Leave off about the blasted house, I am *not* moving—and would you keep your hands to yourself!" He shook me off rather forcefully, appearing to be even more undone than he'd been the last time I touched him in his library. Dodging stray pawns, he tracked to the decanter Sir William had abandoned near the fireplace. Using William's glass, he poured himself a drink and downed it in one gulp. I watched his agitated movements in fascination, oddly satisfied that I'd managed to get under his skin again.

Turning back to the bookcase I resumed my search. Surely he didn't *always* keep the little book tucked away in his tailcoat? Perhaps it was in his study somewhere . . . Or his bedroom . . .

The thought sent a strange thrill down my spine, before I reminded myself that I did not want to see inside his bedroom.

Most definitely not.

After several moments, Matthew looked over. "Deuces, woman, why are you still here? Not even a moment's peace. Must you insist on invading every facet of my life?" After dropping into a wingback chair, he crossed his legs in front of him.

It was true that upon entering it, I had made his life considerably more difficult. But his voice wasn't infused with as much annoyance as before, leading me to believe that he didn't mind my company as much as he let on. That perhaps he even wished me to stay.

Somehow gratified at the thought, I leafed through a thick book—something in Italian—before setting it to the side and saying, "Dessert doesn't appeal to me."

"Has it never occurred to you that you could *leave*? And by extension, never come back?"

"But in my absence you'd have no one to disparage—and I know how vital that is to your well-being. So you see, I stay only out of concern for your health."

"I never knew you cared," he said, untying his cravat with one hand.

Noticing a thin book as tall as my hand tucked behind the others, I pulled it out and flipped through it. No handwriting, just type-set words. Drat. I set it back in its place. "But I do, darling! You know I am madly in love with you."

"As I am with you," he fired back. "But you know, I can't help but get the feeling that you're looking for something."

My hand paused on its way to the next book. I turned to him, chuckling nervously. "Looking for something? But whatever for?"

"I haven't the slightest notion. All I know is you're trying to look innocent again—which only proves to me that I'm right."

Trying to look innocent? . . . Again? Had I tried to look innocent before? "But you have nothing I could possibly want," I said.

"I wouldn't say that. Intelligence. Charm. The ability to make a clever remark. And most of all—oh, for heaven's sake, stop touching them like that."

I faltered, at a loss as to what he could mean until I noticed my hand, fingering the line of book spines on the shelf. I looked back at Matthew, who blinked in annoyance.

Aha, another weakness.

A smile stole over my lips. "You mean like *this*?"

He cringed. "No, don't—"

I swiped my hand down the books, pulling one or two of the spines down for extra measure.

"Stop it!" he growled.

"Stop what?" I lifted my eyebrows. I wriggled one of the volumes out from its tight place, holding it out at hip level. "Stop this?" With a smile I stuck it on a lower shelf, thereby ruining the alphabetical and categorical organization of his library.

Matthew shot to his feet, glowering. But what was he going to do? Whatever it was, it would upset him more than it would me. This was payback for the slew of jabs he'd barraged me with from the first moment of our acquaintance—for making me lose after beating him at chess—and he well deserved it.

Matthew took a menacing step as if to charge me. I snatched the only book resting on the highest shelf and held it out in a threat.

He froze. His eyes widened, gaze magnetized to the new book. "Don't."

"Such a funny thing, to care so much about one's library." I turned the book over, flapping its little, threadbare green cover and crushed spine. Odd. Every other book in the room seemed to be in mint condition, or near it. "This one is worthless. See here, it is about to fall to pieces." I waved it around. "One little drop is sure to break the little thing—"

"By all England, Alicia, please don't!"

I stopped, surprised at my Christian name on his lips, at the helplessness spiking his voice. At the word *please*. I lowered the book, inspecting it with a new interest. The title, adorning the cover in embossed cursive, was too faded to read clearly. In a flash of recognition, I realized this was the same little book he'd had at the castle—the one in which he'd scribbled something about Graham. The one I'd been looking for all this time.

"Not that one," he said.

I glanced back at Matthew, noticing his tense shoulders, his worried eyes. What exactly did this book mean to him? Why was it so well-loved compared to the others?

Again . . . what was inside it? Curiosity prickled my senses—an overpowering impulse to peek inside.

During my mental lapse, Matthew lunged forward and snatched it away. Another moment and he'd whisked it into his tailcoat, out of my sight forever.

Drat it all. I'd held it in my hands! Now he was sure to be more mindful of where he kept it, and my chances of catching him off guard were slim.

"What is in it?" I asked, unable to help myself.

"Again—the day you read it, I shall follow through with this blasted scheme and marry you after all. But since we both know that day shall never come, you might as well give up now." He flattened his coat and swept past me.

For the second time, I watched his back as he retreated out of his own library. For the second time, I was left feeling more confused at the man than I'd been before.

And for the second time, I resolved that eventually, one way or another, even if it took me years of waiting and planning and resorting to underhanded methods, I *would* find out what was in that blasted little book of his.

CHAPTER 17

BRIGHTON WAS AN AIRY TOWN WITH BEAUTIFUL WHITE SHOPS
and cobbled streets—but when new recruits were in town, it transformed into a colorful pocket of joviality and fun. Red-coated ranks
marched through the lanes, muskets poised. Women in feathered
hats and glass shoes eyed them from under awnings. Flags flapped
in the wind. And to the east, the open field of the Steine hosted the
games.

Equipment for boxing, archery, target-firing, rope-tugging,
cricket, yacht racing, and bowling littered the field; any sport which
the common man enjoyed daily, but a gentleman might need a special
setting or circumstance to perform. The games were open to any
gentleman who wished to compete, and since dueling was illegal, they
often served as an arena for dealing out justice for past retributions.

On the sidelines, the white peaks of canopies cut into the clear
blue sky, shading refreshment tables and masses of smiling spectators. No breeze blew through the clearing, making the late afternoon heat even more stifling. Though I was shaded by the canopy, I
still held a lacy parasol, open and propped against my collarbone.

"Where is Mr. Wycliffe?" Aunt Beth said beside me. "I thought he would be here by now. Surely he is not planning on missing the games entirely."

"I imagine he would if he could, aunt."

Aunt Beth's lips twitched. She leaned back in her chair. "I find I rather like the man. Maybe we should forget Hawthorne and urge you to marry him instead."

Unsure how to respond—or how to feel about the matter—I remained silent.

In the field, Henry bowled the white and the batsman hit it with a *crack*. Men around the field scrambled to new positions. I didn't know all the rules of cricket, but I liked watching Henry play. Something about the way his shirt billowed in the wind, free of the weight of his jacket, made my heart do a little flip.

With all the time I'd been spending with Matthew, I'd started to get confused; my feelings had been skipping all over the place. Watching Henry now was just what I needed to remind my heart of what it really wanted.

"Why are you smiling like that?"

Without turning to acknowledge her, I said, "Henry looks rather handsome today, does he not?"

Aunt Beth's attention turned to the match. The wicket keeper stretched his legs before hunching back down, and Henry bowled again. "Just because he is handsome does not mean he is fit company."

"What do you have against Henry anyway? He was fit enough when his parents were alive, and I don't see why that ever needed to change."

A servant passed by with a tray of jam-spread crumpets, bringing a sweet, yeasty smell to the air. To my right, further in the canopy, a group of ladies giggled and gestured to the players.

Aunt Beth sighed, short and forceful. "I hold nothing against him, barring his station. It has improved the last few days, but I am certain it will not last. He shall make some inconsequential, modestly-poor woman very happy one day."

My eyes tracked the players in the field, refusing to meet Aunt Beth's eye.

"As for what your father holds against him . . ." She trailed off, and when I could no longer stifle my curiosity, I glanced at her. "Well. I think it is a different matter entirely."

I waited for her to elaborate, but she didn't, and then she was standing and shuffling toward the refreshment table, greeting old friends and leaving me to stew alone. My brow wrinkled. What on earth did that mean? What were all these mysterious objections? I stood, determined to follow her and get some answers.

"Alicia!"

I halted. Eliza dashed through the crowd, eyes bright and a frowning Matthew in tow. The minute they reached me, Matthew extricated his arm from her grip and scowled at the cricket match. Arm now free, Eliza linked it with my own. "There you are," she said with a grin. "You should know that after our discussion yester-day, I thoroughly chastised both my brothers once you left. They confessed everything and are sorry for attempting to keep Lily and me in the dark."

Keep them in the dark? My muscles froze, sweat coating my palms. Did she know we weren't engaged out of love, then? "Oh?"

She gave my arm a squeeze, leaning in to say in a low tone, "And I think it very sweet that you had your eye on him all these years."

My shoulders softened. Oh. So Peter and Matthew had merely invented a story, detailing mine and Matthew's supposed past.

I was so busy digesting this news that I didn't immediately register the actual content of Eliza's revelation. When I did, I raised my brows and said, "Did I," gaze swinging to Matthew who was watching me from the corner of his eye. "And how many years was that?"

"Thirteen," he said evenly. The significance of the number was not lost on me, after the way I'd teased him yesterday. After a moment, the barest hint of a smile pulled at his lips, before he wiped it away with one of his hands.

"Quite a long time for your love to be unrequited," Eliza went on, oblivious. "I know just how that must've felt, Alicia—perhaps better than anyone. And I think it shameful the way gossip is spreading, saying the match was made for money. People simply cannot mind their own business."

Yes, the gossip.

If people were to discover the truth—that the Duke of Cabourne's daughter was engaged because she was caught in a compromising position—it would obliterate Father's standing in parliament. His anti-war effort would be quashed before it had properly begun.

Last night, I had tossed and turned, trying to devise a way to quell the rumors, but after hours of brainstorming and nothing to show for it, I'd finally given up and gone to sleep. It appeared hopeless. If I had any control over what people said, I wouldn't be in this mess to begin with.

Scandals were the bane of my existence. They'd haunted my footsteps since that first ball at my first Season, when that woman . . .

My train of thought lagged as a new one took its place. I turned back to Eliza. "Are you acquainted at all with the Regent's niece?"

The Regent's niece was a fount of gossip, and a staple in the London *ton*. With the reports she'd been all too happy to spread about me, she'd made my first Season—and the subsequent ones—rather difficult. Some of the gossip was true, some wasn't, but it had all contributed to my infamous reputation. Those reports were a significant factor in Father pushing me to marry Hawthorne; so in many ways, if it hadn't been for her, my life might've been a lot different.

Before Eliza had a chance to answer, Matthew, somehow guessing my plan already, frowned and said, "No. Absolutely not."

"Yes, I am acquainted with her," Eliza said, ignoring her brother with a smile. "Quite well, actually."

I took my cue from her. "Do you think she would accept your invitation to the games, if you were to write her? Perhaps host a picnic in her honor?"

Eliza clapped to herself. "Yes, splendid idea! I have not seen her in an age, and heaven knows I could do with less gloomy company." She lightly hit Matthew on the arm.

Matthew shook it off. "It is out of the question."

I snapped my parasol closed. "Why?"

"Because I detest that woman. She pinches my cheeks."

Chuckling at the picture, I said, "Well, that decides it. We shall invite her."

"Please, no." He cast his eyes heavenward. "*Please* do not invite her."

Chaos erupted in the field, a flurry of darting men, cheers from the sidelines. Henry had hit the wicket. "Ah!" Eliza clapped in excitement and turned to watch the commotion.

"Despite being an incurable gossip," I whispered hastily to Matthew, "everyone takes her word as fact. If we can convince *her* we are in love, everyone in her extensive reach will shortly follow. The gossip will work for us instead of against us, and then we may break the engagement. It is a brilliant plan, and you know it."

Matthew shut his eyes and grimaced like he was in pain. "And just when I thought this couldn't get any worse."

"Ah, there is your aunt, Alicia. I should pay my respects," Eliza said. Then, remembering what we'd been discussing, she spun back. "I shall write the Regent's niece at the earliest possible moment." She gave my arm one more squeeze before strolling off.

Alone now, Matthew's gaze rested on me. "Lady Prima will not be easy to convince. Once her mind is set upon something, the woman refuses to alter it."

I bit my lip in contemplation. "You are right. But how might we change her mind?" I tapped my thumbnail against my chin. "Perhaps if she were to see the seriousness of the match," I mused. "But how might we do that?" An idea struck me, and I gasped. "Perhaps if we obtained a special marriage license!"

He groaned. "I am not going to London on a fool's errand."

I circumvented him. "But as the potential groom, you are the one who must do it."

"We are not even getting married!" Matthew glanced around and lowered his voice, saying in a harsh whisper, "I cannot get a license for a marriage that will never take place. Not only is it scandalous and debatably immoral, I'd be a laughingstock."

I grinned. "It's not as if you aren't already."

"I—" His teeth clamped down. "With you for a fiancée, then naturally!"

"Come, sir," I said conspiratorially, "it won't be too difficult to cancel your plans. Your library will understand, I am sure."

Matthew shook his head and looked off into the distance, muttering phrases that sounded like, *Dirty London,* and, *Waste of time.* He heaved a sigh. "Fine! Tomorrow I shall squander an entire day and ride to my friend, the Archbishop, and beg him for a license we shan't use, except in continuing to perpetuate this deranged lie. I shall be tired, saddle-sore, and in a foul mood for the rest of my existence. I hope you are happy."

I couldn't help my smile. Something about Matthew's perpetual grumpy exterior was beginning to grow on me, now that I'd come to understand it was quite often a façade. After a long moment Matthew noticed my look, and it seemed to magically neutralize his frown. Which made me smile wider.

Which made me remember I really shouldn't be smiling at him at all.

The throngs under the canopies dove into vigorous clapping. When I glanced back toward the field, I saw the cause—the game had ended. Henry shook hands with a few players before turning his beaming smile my direction. He must've won.

At that moment, Aunt Beth and Eliza materialized at our side.

"Good afternoon, Mr. Wycliffe," Aunt Beth said. "Would you care for a stroll, by any chance? There are some new shops I have been eager to visit, and your sister has expressed a desire to see them as well."

Matthew inclined his head in acquiescence.

Aunt Beth took the parasol from my hands and fluffed it open. "Let us be off, then." She and Eliza ambled away.

I bit my lip. Matthew noticed my hesitancy, eyes darting between me and Henry. Finally, he proffered his arm, and slowly, I took it.

As we started down the Steine, I cast a regretful glance over my shoulder, asking Henry a silent question. And the way he stopped in his tracks before nodding and giving a little wave seemed to answer me.

I shall see you soon?

Soon.

THE STREETS WERE CROWDED WITH VENDORS AND SHOPPERS, splashes of red coats plaguing my vision everywhere I turned. Arm linked in mine, Matthew steered me down Castle Square, doing an impressive job of not seeming bothered by it. Ahead of us, Aunt Beth had engaged Eliza in a conversation about her travels through Europe.

"If you marry him, you do realize you shall have to move to India?"

I considered pretending Matthew's question had been drowned out in the rumble of carriages and cries of seagulls—as it was one I'd been avoiding asking myself—but instead gave it some thought.

India both terrified and exhilarated me. Though I was planning to marry Henry, the fear of moving away from home was enough to make me hesitate. Could I really do it? Leave everything behind?

But then, what was I actually leaving? I'd always wanted to see the world, and a change of scene might be just what I needed; somewhere where society wouldn't insist that I either conform to its demands, or risk further alienating my family. In India we would be separated by two oceans, but at least I wouldn't let them down any more than I already had.

I turned to Matthew. "You've read hundreds of books. Surely you can tell me something about the place?"

He steered me clear of a passing couple, then gave me a sidelong glance. "Firstly, you are denser than I first assumed if you think my reading experience is limited to the hundreds. Secondly, what exactly do you want to know?"

"Is it exciting? Do they have the tallest trees in the world? Or the strangest foods? What are their skies like, and their rivers? Are the people short? And what about—"

"It is a dangerous place full of dangerous things. That much I know for certain."

My brow wrinkled. "What things?"

He blinked slowly. "Snakes, tigers, monsoons, poisons in every other plant. I daresay you'd fit right in."

I shrugged. It was getting easier and easier to take his jabs in stride. "Hm. Then I suppose I ought to move there even if I don't marry Henry."

Matthew's face pulled tight but wistful, almost like forced carelessness. The look didn't suit him at all. "Perhaps you ought to. Though I should warn you, there are dozens of local legends— people being dragged into the jungle and murdered in horrible ways. Could happen to anyone. Even a British lady."

I sucked in a breath of salty air. "Are you making that up?"

"No," he said. A tad too quickly. "Why would I?"

"You sound as if you are trying to deter me from going."

He snorted. "The very idea! I should be glad if I never laid eyes on you again. And need I remind you, you've not read any books about India. I have. That makes me the expert on the subject."

"You think you are the expert on *any* subject."

He cast me a dubious expression that said, *And what is wrong with that?* "Because I am."

My lips twitched, and I pinched them. Why was he making me want to smile so much today? It was not helpful.

"Good day, Lady Beth!"

After a moment, I spotted the owner of the voice. Down the street, lightly jumping up to see through the crowd was Hawthorne, snaking toward us and waving an impossibly large bouquet of yellow flowers in one hand.

I cringed. "Oh no."

I barely heard his call through the rumble, but there was no mistaking it either, or the victorious grin he wore. "I've found your kingcups, Lady Alicia!" Even from this distance, the sun seemed to reflect off his teeth, blinding me.

"What is i—?" Matthew cut off as I tugged him to the side of the street, away from Aunt Beth and Eliza who were already returning Hawthorne's greeting.

"Ow! Why are you—would you let me go!"

I looked around frantically. "The man's a complete nuisance. Please—you must help me hide." There were no convenient carts or crates to dart behind.

"Why should I?"

Hawthorne reached Aunt Beth. Using the massive bouquet to shield his eyes from the sun, he scanned the crowd for me, a hawk hunting a little field mouse. I clamped my hands around Matthew's arm and pulled him into the nearest establishment, shutting the door behind us.

CHAPTER 18

INSIDE, THE AIR SMELLED LIKE SMOKE AND BUTTERSCOTCH. AFTER letting my eyes adjust to the dimly lit room, I took it in. We appeared to be inside a tavern, of sorts. A somewhat disreputable one, judging by the grime coating walls and the shanty-singing soldiers who splattered half their mugs' contents on the floor. Few heads turned to notice us, and if they did, their gazes didn't linger.

"Can you never hide on your own? Why must you always drag me into it?" Matthew shook off my grip and moved to an empty corner, flattening his coat as he went.

I followed him, squinting in the yellow-orange light, dodging stray chairs and wandering hands. "The real problem stems from the fact that I have things to hide from, whereas you do not."

"That is *your* problem." Having reached the far wall, he turned around and crossed his arms. "And now what? You expect us to hole up in here for how long?"

"Lord Hawthorne was probably too occupied with my aunt and your sister to notice where we'd gone, but he likely saw us slip away. We should remain here for a few minutes, just to be . . ."

At that moment the door opened, and the first thing I saw was an explosion of yellow flowers, followed by a bright smile. I turned my face away and shrank down.

He'd found me. Oh botheration! And now there was nowhere else to hide! Maybe we could slip out without him noticing? But something would have to lure him away from the doorway first, and I wasn't about to be the bait.

Matthew gave a thoughtful grunt. "There he is. You didn't put much thought into this plan, now did you?"

How to get rid of him? How to get rid of him . . .

My thoughts snagged on that moment at the castle, after Hawthorne found out I was engaged. The only time he'd been the least bit discouraged in his pursuit. None of my hints had found their mark, but when he'd believed my affections to be tied up in another man, it had crushed him almost beyond repair.

A slow smile pulled at my lips as I straightened up and turned to Matthew.

He noticed it and frowned. "What."

I said nothing, just smirked at him. His eyes darted between me and Hawthorne a few times, before he snapped up and unfolded his arms. "No. No, I will not."

"Why not?"

Matthew looked like he was about to be sick. "You want me to *flirt* with you. To make him jealous."

"Only until he leaves."

"You cannot be serious! Here? In this filthy hovel? In front of all these people? Even if I *wanted* to humor you, my lady—which I most emphatically do not—it simply isn't done!"

I tilted my head to the side. Matthew followed the movement until his gaze locked onto a couple in the opposite corner. To say the pair were *preoccupied* with each other was an understatement; and while they kissed, no one in the tavern spared them a second glance.

"Simply isn't done, eh?" I said.

His head whipped back. "Simply isn't done by *me*," he hissed. "By *us*."

I would've laughed at his comically disgusted face if I hadn't caught Hawthorne shuffling further inside, a question forming on his face. "Quick." I clutched Matthew's tailcoat and pushed him until we hit a protruding beam that stretched to the ceiling, shielding us for a few more moments.

Matthew grunted at the impact then inhaled through his teeth. "That's twice now you've shoved me against something for your own devices, Lady Alicia. I suggest you refrain from doing so a third time unless you wish me to—one by one—cut off every hair from your golden head—"

"Shh!" The room was crowded enough that no one paid us much attention, but that didn't mean it couldn't change, if Matthew started to make a scene. I patted Matthew's coat down where I'd wrinkled it, while leaning in and saying seductively, "Come now, Mr. Wycliffe. I thought you weren't incapable of anything."

Matthew shook his head. "When this is all over, I want my sanity back."

The throng pressed in. I craned my neck, trying to track Hawthorne's position. Across the room he approached a tall, wooden counter, saying something to the man behind it. "I regret to inform you, Mr. Wycliffe, that is probably not going to happen." I turned back. Then stopped short when I found Matthew staring at me.

He looked me over a long time, something flickering through his features. "Probably not," he murmured at last. My mind flashed to a dark tunnel. To the feel of the rise of his chest against my face.

He inhaled. "I cannot do this. This is a terrible idea."

It very well might be. "Do you have a better one?"

"A host of them. Jump off the cliffs, impale myself on a rusty sword, drink a gallon of poison and die a slow and agonizing death —any one of them is preferable."

The sound of metal clanging and liquid splashing was followed by cries of laughter. A ring of soldiers shoved each other in good humor. From the corner of my eye, the man behind the counter pointed our direction, and Hawthorne swiveled. That decided the matter.

I leaned in, saying with an adoring expression, "How utterly handsome you look today, Mr. Wycliffe. Did you style your hair differently?"

Matthew tensed, bracing for the contact. The silky locks bent beneath my touch, like the flow of ocean waves. I resisted the urge to twirl them in my fingers. They felt just as I remembered them.

Matthew frowned. "I know what you are doing." He clinched my wrist. "You said nothing of touching each other."

I smiled. What did he think 'discouraging Hawthorne' entailed? "Of course I didn't—or you would have protested more adamantly." My other hand pinched his lapel and slid upward. "It is the fastest way, you know. The more we touch, the more discouraged he shall get, the sooner we can stop, the sooner we may leave."

The racket increased as more soldiers filed through the doors, adding to the already stifling press of bodies. Matthew glanced over his shoulder to where Hawthorne was already pushing through the crowd. He turned back. "Fine. But you won't lay another finger on me. Instead, *I* shall touch *you*."

My mouth ran dry. Him touch *me*? No. No, I didn't like that idea at all. But because I was a fool who overvalued my pride, I forced myself to shrug like my insides didn't just turn somersaults. "Fine."

He pushed off the wall and rotated us around. In that brief flash, I saw Hawthorne's face—his big eyes and creased brows, the flowers drooping at his side—and then we'd switched places and Matthew was the one with a view of the room, and all I could see was *him*.

My back pressed into the wood. Something about the way Matthew's eyes swirled and his hand braced the beam next to my ear made my heart bound out of my chest. I was out of my depth, and if I wasn't careful, I was going to drown.

"Do you want me to be convincing, then?"

I swallowed. "If you can manage it."

He looked down, blowing a long breath of air through his nose. The muscle in his jaw jumped. The idea repulsed him. He hated this. He hated me. "Are you certain?"

No.

"Yes," I said, not liking how wheezy I sounded. Hawthorne was watching, and we needed to make the most of it. "Go on, then. Pretend to be enamored of me—I should greatly like to see you attempt it."

He glanced up, letting his ocean eyes settle on me for a long, excruciating moment. At last, he said, "As you say, I've never been incapable of anything." His palm slid forward until his forearm hit the beam, bringing his face nearer. Bringing his lips closer to my own. "But even if I were, Lady Alicia," he tipped my chin up, eyes softening, voice pitching lower, "I still wouldn't have to pretend."

The cacophony of noise drowned in the thudding of my heartbeat. That was . . . a little *too* convincing. If I didn't know any better, I would think he sounded almost . . . sincere. And instead of being hyper aware of my chin, where Matthew touched me, I found myself focusing on everywhere he didn't. My shoulders, my arms, my exposed throat—all of them tingled with electric anticipation.

Matthew's head bent, his warmth crossing the inch separating us, his breath tickling the hair behind my ear. From the tops of his eyes, he looked beyond my shoulder, gaze smoldering. I knew he was looking at Hawthorne, some sort of message passing between them.

Wanting to know what it was, I twisted my head. Matthew turned it back with one finger to my chin. "He is still looking," he murmured.

Was he? "Oh."

"He looks upset."

After inhaling a lungful of Matthew's smell and barely restraining myself from sighing, I said, "Then perhaps you ought to do something to make him feel worse."

His gaze cut to me. "Like what?"

Nothing that wasn't blatantly scandalous came to mind. My cheeks warmed. Why couldn't I think straight?

I didn't have to answer though, because Matthew's hand slipped up my neck to cup my face. As with in the tunnel, his touch was gentle, surprising me yet again. *May I take your hand?*

"Something like this?" He leaned forward, and before I fully realized what he was doing, his lips skimmed along my skin and lingered on my cheek. He held there for an agonizing moment, and I froze with him, eyes wide, heart pounding.

Then, softly, he kissed me. His lips felt cool against my fiery blush. They lowered the smallest fraction down my cheek, and kissed me again. Then another time. Deliberately, reverently, agonizingly, he traveled toward my jaw.

Surrounded by dozens of people in a cramped room, Matthew Wycliffe was kissing my cheek and bringing time to a crunching halt. Everything around me froze except for the slow travel of Matthew's lips. I opened my mouth but couldn't breathe. Couldn't find my voice. Where in the blasted name was it? There wasn't enough air in this room. Matthew was taking up all of it.

Finally, I managed in an airy voice, "I-I think you've kissed my cheek quite enough, Mr. Wycliffe."

Just as slowly as with his kisses, he pulled away to stare down at me, half a breath away. "Shall I move to somewhere else, then?" The words carried a dangerous dare in them.

He would do it. He would kiss me on the lips if only to spite me; to prove the lengths he would go to be rid of me. By asking the question, he wanted me to prove it too—a test, to see if I truly hated him as much as he hated me.

And here I was, tipping over the edge and drowning in those deep eyes of his, with no land in sight. Under their hypnotic spell, I was ashamed to realize I didn't know the answer. This moment—it was just like the moment after the chess game. A challenge of stares, of dangerous emotion, to see which of us would cave first.

This time, it wouldn't be me.

"Is he still looking?" I didn't sound like myself. I sounded strangled and desperate. Desperate for what, I didn't know.

Without taking his eyes off me, Matthew muttered, "Yes."

"How can you be sure?"

Matthew scanned my face, landing on my lips before meeting my eyes again. "Because if I can't look away, then how the devil could he?"

And how the devil could I, for that matter?

I lifted my chin, attempting to break the spell, determined to gain the upper hand. But I still trembled when I said, "Then do it."

For the smallest moment, I thought I saw something flicker in his eyes. Something almost like fear. But I knew I imagined it because his lips set in a determined line. He wouldn't be the one to surrender first, either.

This is what happened when you thrust two people together who liked to hate the world and guarded their pride from showing anything more—they ended up sharing a kiss in a dingy tavern purely out of spite.

Matthew leaned in and I flattened back against the beam, blood rushing through my ears. His hair swept over his forehead, almost reaching his brows. Just like with the kiss on my cheek, he hovered, hesitating like he didn't trust himself.

My breaths came faster, shallower, until they were so thin, I was sure I couldn't be breathing at all. *Just do it.* Anything to make this moment end. *Just do it already.* Anything to get me as far, far away as possible from Matthew Wycliffe. My fingers curled, scraping against the wood at the sight of his lips so near my own.

Slowly, his head tilted and he backed away, voice low when he said, "No, my lady. Rid yourself of your suitors another way. I will not lose my sanity for your sake a second time."

I didn't know if he was referring to kissing my cheek, or pushing him into the tavern, or the general madness that was our false engagement. But I was filled with both relief and disappointment that he'd backed away. And anger, for feeling those things at all when I was supposed to be feeling them with Henry.

What was wrong with me? Why were my emotions swinging like a pendulum, unable to settle on what . . . and *who* . . . I really wanted?

Raising my chin, I said, "Is that the most convincing you can be, Mr. Wycliffe? I'm ashamed to call you my fiancé, for your actions have had no effect on me."

Matthew said nothing, only studied me head to toe. My skin crawled under his inspection, dreading what he would find. Certain he would find too much.

And he did. I know he did.

Clenching my hands behind my back, I swallowed. I was wavering under his challenge and couldn't take any more. Breaking away, I jerked around the corner and checked the crowd for Hawthorne. The spot he'd been standing in was empty, and a thorough search of the rest of the room proved just as fruitless.

I was about to breathe a sigh of relief when I caught sight of a head of blond hair near the entrance. Henry was frozen stiff, eyes glued to me. To Matthew. To the cheek still blushing where he'd kissed me.

I paled, chest seizing. "Henry," I whispered. He had witnessed everything.

He spun on his heel and disappeared out of the tavern.

"He came in just as soon as we switched places."

My focus jumped to Matthew, whose glittering eyes lapsed back into boredom. "You saw him?" A huff of hot air burst out of me. "And you did not tell me?"

"You asked me to flirt with you, my lady, and so I did." His eyebrows rose, a glint of victory gleaming in his gaze.

Victory . . . ?

My muscles went rigid. Now that he had my promise to release him, there was nothing stopping him from sabotaging me at every turn. He'd seen Hawthorne leave, seen Henry enter, and seen the perfect opportunity to beat me at my own game. If only to revel in it. That message in his eyes, when he had turned my chin back—it hadn't been directed at Hawthorne, but Henry. The man I actually wanted to pursue me.

Which meant Matthew's actions were not him accommodating me. They were an act of petty revenge.

My blood rose to a boil. "Why you little—!"

He crossed his arms. "I never wanted to be part of your scheme —to flirt or be engaged to you, to lose myself in secret tunnels or continue with this stupid farce. Not any of it. Next time you dive headfirst into trouble, think twice before pulling me along."

That mouth. That *perfect* mouth that formed the most heartless of words. How I wanted to slap it! Or clamp a hand over it. Or press my own mouth to it—

No. *Not* that.

Gah, he was so *stubborn*!

Before I could do something I'd regret, I growled and stormed to the other side of the taproom. As far away as possible from the most irritating man on earth.

CHAPTER 19

A greasy man on the stool next to me turned and looked me over. His surprise quickly morphed into a leery grin—which disappeared when I shot him my foulest glare. He took his pint and moved several seats away.

The innkeeper bustled behind the counter, wiping down mugs, mopping his forehead, carrying steaming platters of mutton to men at tables, and calling for his hired boy to come help him. Smoke drifted from one corner where elderly gentlemen puffed their pipes.

I huffed and rested my face in my hands. Why was it I could strike fear into the heart of a stranger, but couldn't begin to faze someone like Matthew? It was annoying how much he got under my skin.

Almost mindlessly, I fingered my cheek, still tingling from Matthew's kisses. When I asked him to flirt with me, I certainly hadn't expected . . . *that*. What had I been thinking?

But I know what I had been thinking. I was so certain he would drag his feet, as he usually did. He'd roll his eyes. He'd botch everything and loathe the whole process. But instead, he'd managed to take control of my senses and fluster me in one fell swoop.

All I'd wanted was his participation. If I'd known he would be so believable, I would have tossed away my plan and conjured a different one—one that didn't crush Henry, or leave me short of breath and full of questions.

The man was infuriating.

And Henry. He'd seen it all, then disappeared before I'd had a chance to explain. Even more puzzling was why—though I felt terrible, and devastated on his behalf—I had no desire to run after him. Why was I stewing at a counter instead of flying out the door and tracking him down? At the beginning of these two weeks, I wouldn't have given it a second thought. So what exactly had changed? Why did I feel so heavy and overextended at the thought of Henry at all?

"Boy!" the innkeeper called again. He neared, noticing me. "What can I get for ye, miss?"

"Just tea, please."

He nodded and disappeared through a back door. I drummed my fingers on the counter, wondering what I should do. Being alone in this tavern, surrounded by people—mostly men—was definitely not a wise decision; but I wasn't about to return to Matthew's company. He could sit and brood in a corner until he rotted with guilt, for all I cared.

Though I now had a plan for stopping the rumors, the day as a whole felt useless, as I was still no closer to receiving a proposal. Perhaps even further than I'd started, since Henry might now believe my engagement to be real. I needed to return home and regroup, decide on a different course of action. I still had six days until Henry left for India, and every minute counted.

As soon as I got my drink, I would venture out—without Matthew—and find Henry and explain everything.

A young boy with shaggy blond hair rushed in from a side door. "Uncle Jasper!"

His uncle, the innkeeper, appeared with my tea. "There you are, boy—shirking your duties again—!"

"Honest, I wasn't! Cuthry threw another shoe, so I took him down to Mr. Walsh's to get it fixed. But he's been so bogged with work since the soldiers come, he made me wait the better of an hour!"

Jasper pushed past him. "All right, all right, lad. Just hurry to the kitchen and fetch the meals for that corner table there."

The boy jumped to obey. Jasper set a chipped teacup in front of me and set to wiping down the ale-splotched counter. "That boy," he muttered to no one in particular. "Should never 'ave agreed to raise him."

"Are you his guardian?" I asked.

"Aye," he said, scrubbing at a stubborn stain. "Not his uncle, though. Don't rightly know who his parents were. Just found him on my doorstep one day, with a note asking me to take care of him. The only reason I've kept him around is because I find a se'lement on my doorstep every month to pay for his expenses."

My brow wrinkled. "How odd."

"Indeed, miss." He swiped his mustache with the back of his arm, then muttered darkly, "Though, the amount of the se'lement went down a few years back—don't know why. He's more expensive to feed now than he was as a babe. All I know is, his parents must be important people, whoever they are. No one else around 'ere could spare the money."

The boy rushed back. "All done," he announced, stomping the floor like he'd accomplished a great feat. I glanced at his feet, noting his skin-thin shoes that had such big holes in them they were barely staying on. Through the holes peeked grubby toes, black from soot.

"Go muck the stables, then, Lenny," Jasper said. "After you say hello to the pretty lady."

The boy turned to me and tipped his head back to see through his matted hair, revealing blue eyes. "'ello." He smiled, dimples pressing into his cheeks.

My hold on my mug slackened. It was Henry's smile.

Lenny.

The boy zoomed off without another word. I stared after him, shock coursing through every limb.

Could this boy be Henry's brother? They had similar features. It was possible, but there was no way to be sure.

"Excuse me, sir," I called to Jasper.

He looked back at me, forehead beaded with sweat.

"Can you tell me anything else about the boy? How old he is, when he was put into your care . . . ?"

His gaze narrowed warily. I knew I was being nosy, but I didn't have the patience to be more discreet. In the end, Jasper shrugged.

"Not much help there, miss. Found him as a babe. Been feeding him ten years." Jasper turned back to his clamoring customers, answering their pounding mugs and forks with refills.

My vision lost focus. Ten years.

I couldn't believe it. I'd found him. I'd found Henry's brother—stumbled upon him by pure luck—and he was mucking the stables at an inn at Brighton. The son of a gentlewoman, living in absolute squalor.

Had Nicholas Crawley known of his whereabouts? Had he arranged for the boy to be kept close? Arranged the payments? Who was paying them, now that Lord Crawley was dead?

I didn't know what to do, or what to say, but I knew I needed to talk to Lenny. In some way, I could help him, I could feel it. My stool scooted out as I stood, ready to head for the stables.

"Well, here's a fine-looking lass!" A dark haired soldier with an Irish accent swung his arm around my neck, leaning in until his nose brushed my cheek. "I've always wanted a kiss from a pretty face." His companions laughed and ringed us, trapping me in a circle of red.

I unhooked his arm and jerked away. "Me too, sir," I said, looking him over, "which is why I won't be kissing yours."

The soldiers chortled. A quick glance at the Irishman's shoulder told me he was a corporal, and outranked everyone there. His pupils were dilated and his breath carried the muggy scent of alcohol. "Ya're a little spitfire, aren't ya?" His smile broadened.

"Careful I don't spit on *you*."

Now the soldiers were slapping each other on the back. Two of them swapped coins. They'd bet on this interaction before they came over, which meant they'd been watching me for a while.

"Don't hold back on my account," the Irishman said, tipping my chin up. "I myself enjoy a little spit." He leaned down, his other hand stealing around my waist.

I was quicker. I stomped his foot and drew back with his pistol, stolen from his holster. More coins clinked as they switched hands, obviously unfazed by a woman with a gun. A mistake. I aimed at his neck.

The Irishman put his hands up, chuckling. "What do ya think ya're doing with that, lass? Tisn't even loaded."

He was lying. I could see it in his eyes. Cocking the hammer back, I smiled. "No?"

The chuckling soldiers quieted, ramping up the tension in the air. Now their hands hovered over their own weapons, unsure whether to draw them on a lady. Around the inn, everyone continued in their revelry, spats with soldiers apparently not uncommon.

"Here now," the Irishman said. "We both know ya won't fire it."

"I wouldn't put it past her." The droll voice came from over my shoulder. I clenched the pistol tighter to keep my arm from shaking. Matthew leaned forward. "Put the pistol down," he murmured in my ear.

"If you were on the other end of this barrel," I said out the side of my mouth, "I wouldn't hesitate in firing it."

"And if you asked me to flirt with you again, I would beg you to shoot."

The Irishman looked between us uncomfortably. "What are ya whisperin' about?"

Matthew ignored him. "Trust me."

"*Now* you want me to trust you? After that deceitful display?"

The corporal grew uneasy, saying louder, "I say, what are ya whisperin' about?"

"Put. The pistol. Down."

"No."

The Irishman gave a small hand signal. At once, every soldier in the circle drew their sword. I jumped back, crashing into Matthew, who steadied me. My hand on the trigger held fast.

Stepping forward, the corporal knocked his head at Matthew and said, "Who are ya, man? You don't have any right to interfere. If ya want a go at the lass, ya'll have to wait your turn. And as for you —" He turned back to me. "—that wasn't very nice o' ya, stealing my gun like that. How about we try that again, only this time, I steal something from you?"

I opened my mouth with a retort, but Matthew spoke first. "You'll not touch her, sir."

I'd heard a commanding tone from Matthew's lips before, but not like that. Soft words that carried the ferocity of lions. At the sound of it, a few of the soldiers shrunk back.

The Irishman did not. He unsheathed a knife from his belt. "Is that so?" This wasn't going well.

Matthew's gaze cut to the knife. To the swords held by the other soldiers. He could go into the fight arms swinging, without a care for his safety; and if he were quick, he could take a few of the soldiers down with him. There was no way to emerge from this fight unscathed, but a brave man would not hesitate to do it. A brave man would take a knife to the gut.

A brave man would be an utter fool.

And Matthew was no fool.

He was outmanned and outgunned, so I knew before he spoke that he was going to outsmart them. Gesturing to them, he said, "You've been hard at work with drills and target practice on the Downs. Do not spoil your plans for a deep drink with this petty squabble."

The soldiers looked between themselves, before one of them lowered his sword and asked, "How did you know that?"

"The grass on your boots, the mud at your knees, the residue of gunpowder on your fingers where you grip your swords. Not difficult to infer at all. I would add the smell of sweat to the list of clues, but I think it's safe to say we are all sweating right now."

Matthew put his arm around me, taking on a long-suffering tone. "This woman here is my sister. And she's a bit dicked in the nob, if you know what I mean."

My face pinched. Sister! Dicked in the nob!

"Just last week she told me of a secret passageway, the entrance to which only she knew about."

How low. *Anyone* would sound loony when he phrased it that way!

Matthew waved his hand in the air. "She's been on this hunt for a missing fortune, you see. So she may earn her true love and move to India—a rather frightful place, if you ask me—but she has fanciful notions of living there all the same." Matthew held his hands up. "The point is, this matter is not worth your effort, sirs. Stop now, before you do something you'd regret. Or before your corporal here does something he'd be ashamed of in confession."

The corporal's brow wrinkled. "How did ya know I am Catholic?"

"Your ring." Matthew pointed to the man's hand, making him glance down at it. "The tools and the lily are the symbols of St. Joseph. But even if I hadn't noticed it, your dialect would've given you away. It's unique to hedge schools in Southern Ireland—schools reserved for faith-based outcasts. Primarily Catholics."

My mouth dropped open. Matthew had concocted a flawless

combination of truth and falsehood—weaving them together so seamlessly the soldiers couldn't pick out the lies. In the face of Matthew's steadfast certainty, what could they do but accept the whole of it as fact?

How often had he done that to me? Hidden little gems in his lengthy barrages; white lies so subtle, so seemingly inconsequential, that I never noticed them?

The other soldiers appeared to be placated by Matthew's logic, but the Irishman's lips set in a sneer. "I'm not amused by yer parlor tricks." His boot swiped at my dress.

I hissed and jumped back, muscles tightening. "You sir," I leveled the pistol at him, "will not lay another finger on me unless you wish to meet a swift end."

Instead of heeding my threat, the man sheathed his knife and grinned at me wickedly. He thought I was bluffing. "Is that so, lass?"

Don't make me shoot. "Do not take another step." *Oh please, don't make me shoot.*

The Irishman's smirk deepened and he inched forward.

"Please," Matthew said, coming forward. "For the love of all that is good—let's skip the part where someone dies, shall we?"

The Irishman lunged. Matthew threw a punch. My arm gave a huge jolt.

Boom!

A window shattered. Bodies ducked for the ground. I stared wide-eyed at the smoking pistol in my hand, then at the Irishman's bicorn hat a few feet away which now bore a hole through its center. If Matthew hadn't punched him, I would've killed the man.

My blood chilled, then flashed hot. I'd just shot at a commanding officer in His Royal Highness's army. The corporal patted himself down and looked around, finally surmising he wasn't hurt. His face turned as red as his coat. The soldiers on the floor scrabbled for their swords.

Matthew sighed, like he'd predicted this all along. "I guess not, then." He grabbed my hand and yanked me into a run.

CHAPTER 20

As we fled out the door, I heard the Irishman's voice behind us, yelling, "Get them," followed by the pounding of a dozen pairs of boots.

We dove into the frenzy of the streets, swimming through the throngs of people enjoying the evening festivities. We pushed through a crowded bottleneck and turned right, toward the sea. Every one of my muscles tensed, listening for the racket of soldiers behind us.

My hand squeezed a useless trigger. I looked down, shocked to find I still clutched the pistol. It scalded my skin. I threw it away and it landed in a water barrel, sending up a splash.

"You couldn't just walk away peacefully. No—much too docile for you. You had to be hell-bent on wreaking havoc by shooting a blasted pistol!" Matthew pulled me along, leading us down the front road bordering the ocean. Crowds shopped around carts and stalls, shaded by flapping flags and pillared columns. A few gave us curious looks, but most kept to their own business, exchanging goods for coins. Some vendors were already packing up their carts.

"I hate you," I panted, drilling it with each hammering step. "Oh, I hate you, I hate you."

"Yes well," Matthew said, jogging beside me, "despite your threatening my life on more than one occasion—despite having every reason in the world—I don't return the feeling." We tucked ourselves under the awning of a cobbler shop.

I bent over, too out of breath to chuckle. "No? What a surprise indeed. I could've sworn you did, what with all your rage-filled looks and defeats in chess and the way you flirted with me *just to get revenge*."

Matthew was panting too. He slumped against the building door and held up a finger. "It was one time. You beat me *one* time. And yes, it was revenge flirting—but you're the one who asked me to do it in the first place. I wouldn't have flirted with you otherwise."

"How unthinkable that would be, when I am only your *fiancée*."

He rolled his eyes. "Oh, for all the—"

"And another thing. I didn't need your help with those soldiers. I could've managed it on my own without your show of chivalry."

"Yes, judging by the way you *shot* a man—"

"I missed, didn't I?"

"—you seemed to be handling it quite well. Whatever did you do before I came along? You only seem to have crises when I am there to get you out of them."

"Because you are the cause of most of them," I spat.

He laughed humorlessly. "You would continue to cause calamity without me. But you prefer me to be present so you have someone to split the blame with."

"Ha! So you admit you are at fault."

He shook a finger. "No. This whole dastardly mess is your doing. I wouldn't know the first thing about making colossal mistakes."

"Except when you play me at chess."

"By every corner of England—it was one blasted time!"

At the mouth of the street, a soldier halted. We both turned. The soldier scanned the crowd, stopping when his line of sight landed on the cobbler shop. He'd spotted us.

A groaning whimper escaped my throat.

Matthew glared at me. "I take it back. I do hate you."

The soldier pointed. "They're down here!" More red coats appeared at his side and broke into a run.

Matthew grabbed my wrist and pulled me back into the chase, passing shops with window displays of curtains, lace, snuffboxes, fans, and slippers. Shouts from the soldiers followed close behind. Getting closer, closer.

We whizzed past bushels of apples and painted signs, pushing into a dirtier part of town, where the windows weren't washed and stray cats roamed every other corner. The smell of fish permeated the air. Pulling me down different backstreets, Matthew wove a maze, trying to lose the soldiers.

It wasn't working.

My lungs burned. My legs felt like mush. I couldn't get enough air. I couldn't go on.

Matthew yanked me into an alley obscured by a big shipping crate, and shoved me down behind it. Sitting, the top covered my head by a few inches. Through the slit between the crate and the wall, I could see out onto the main street. Pounding feet echoed louder.

Matthew ducked behind the crate and hunkered down at my side, pressing close.

Very close.

Still breathing heavily, Matthew leaned closer to look through the slat. Trapping me against the crate.

"Must you do that?"

"Shh." He didn't look at me, scanning for red coats. Men's voices drew nearer, one of them an Irish brogue I recognized.

Matthew's pine smell wafted over me, his thudding heart close to my ear. His cravat grazed my cheek. His breath warmed the top of my hair. I gulped. First in the tavern, and now this. I couldn't take it much longer. I'd face those soldiers and a hundred more before I faced this thing building inside me.

I shoved him away, whispering, "Give me some room."

He shoved my arm back. "If I move away any more, they will see me."

"I'll take that chance."

"Would you just be quiet!"

"You cannot make me."

"Can't I?" He cocked one brow.

My eyes widened. Drat, drat, drat. I shouldn't have said that.

He pushed me up against the crate, covering my soft gasp with one hand. My heart leapt into my throat. The soldiers needn't have bothered chasing me down, because as it turned out, all it took to kill me was Matthew Wycliffe ambushing me against a crate with his body. The slow click of boots came to a stop at the opening of the alley. Matthew's eyes shot up. We froze, listening to the sounds of the soldiers searching the area.

". . . can't have just disappeared . . ."

"—thought I saw them—"

"Not down here."

A boot planted further in the alley. I imagined the soldier leaning in with narrowed eyes, scanning for two runaways. Blood rushed through my ears. An eternity passed. Gravel scraped and the footsteps moved away. All sounds of the soldiers grew distant, then disappeared. We were still for another moment.

Then I became acutely aware of Matthew's warm hand still over my lips, his other hand around my back, cupping my waist. I looked up at him again. His breath, still ragged, tickled down my neck. And *my* breath. I had even less of it than I'd had while running.

He really was the handsomest man I'd ever seen. The taut cord woven through Matthew's body loosened. He glanced down. Blinked, surprised to find me staring. And surprisingly, he didn't immediately pull away—didn't even lower his hand.

His lips parted.

I shoved him away.

He fell back, catching himself with his hands. "Deuces, all right! All right." Scooting against the opposite alley wall, he grunted softly and clutched his side, muttering, "By all England, I hate running." He stretched his legs and leaned his head against the brick, looking at the sky.

I looked too. The dimness of evening was coming on fast, muting the colors. Soon everything would turn indigo, and then black. Where had the afternoon gone?

"I need to return home," I murmured.

As if on cue, a few soldiers marched past the alleyway, muskets resting against their collarbones. They didn't spot us, and they didn't look like our pursuers, but who knew why they were in this part of town? Word might have spread through the ranks.

The weight of what I had done—accosted a soldier—began to weigh on me. If the Irishman discovered my identity and made a fuss, then Father, being a duke, would see to it there were no repercussions; but that couldn't prevent word from getting out. I'd caused yet another horrendous scandal, and the knowledge made me sick.

Though it might take a while in a town brimming with red coats, I'd have to wait until no more soldiers passed the alley before sneaking out. If I were lucky, the men would sober up and forget the whole encounter. By then, Aunt Beth was sure to have given up searching for me and assumed I'd returned to Lawry Park with Mr. Wycliffe.

Oh. Just thinking about the long walk home made my feet ache.

Matthew relaxed against the wall, making himself comfortable. "Might as well settle in. We'll have a better chance of slipping out unnoticed when it's dark." He said nothing of the impropriety of the situation, expressed no concern for my reputation. I thought to be offended, but oddly, I wasn't.

Maybe it was because his fingers drummed in agitation while he watched the sunset, but it seemed as if he refrained from mentioning my tattered reputation—not because he didn't care—but because he didn't want me to panic. Dark was approaching, after all.

As if sensing my thoughts, Matthew said, "Why are you so afraid of it?"

I wrapped my arms around my legs, drawing my knees to my chin. Memories resurfaced. The inside of a cupboard. The smell of brandy. Scrapes on my hands. Blood at my feet. A mother on her deathbed.

With great effort, I swallowed the bile rising in my throat. I didn't want to have this conversation—especially not with Matthew. Being vulnerable and letting him see into my heart wasn't a requirement for our sham of an engagement, and only left me open to pain.

But the words slipped out anyway. "Because I hate being stuck in one place. Unable to get out. Unable to see what's about to happen. Where darkness falls, bad things follow."

I thought not only of my mother, but of my father as well. I continued, softer. "The day I first feared the dark was the day my mother died giving birth to my little brother. The day my Father's spirit died along with them. The last day I saw any love in his eyes."

Water trickled down my cheek before I even felt the tear surface. I swiped at it, mortified to be crying in front of Matthew again—and this time, without the cloak of darkness to shield me.

But when I risked a peek at him, I saw that Matthew wasn't wearing his usual expression of boredom or annoyance. He no longer fidgeted. He just . . . looked at me; eyes holding the smallest, softest slant to them.

"That's part of the reason why I fight so hard for Henry. I conjure mad schemes and cause trouble wherever I go, but the only other option is to stand by and do nothing while he leaves, probably forever. And I cannot do nothing. I've lost too many people that way."

Henry was the only one I had left. I couldn't lose him.

The last thing I wanted on this earth was for Matthew to pity me. And he seemed to understand it, because he offered no sympathetic touches or useless apologies. He just looked at me like he understood my every thought, felt my every feeling. Like he'd experienced them, too.

And for the first time, I felt like his equal. Whether I'd risen to his level or he'd humbled himself to mine, I couldn't tell—but for the first time, I felt like a worthy opponent. Perhaps not even an opponent at all.

"Back at the tavern," I said, shoulders slumping, "I may not have agreed with your methods, but you were right. You did not ask for any of this, and I shouldn't have made you flirt with me on top of it. I pulled you along without your consent—not for the first time—and I should like to say that I am sorry." I bit the inside of my lip. "I know I am thoughtless toward others and their feelings, that I can be stubborn, and impossible. I know I like to argue and tease, and can be difficult to get along with. In fact, now that I think on it, I don't know why I should've ever expected Henry to propose in the first place." I gave a sad-sounding chuckle that wasn't really a chuckle at all. "I do not possess enough good qualities to attract a man as good as him."

Matthew worked his mouth, thoughtfully. At length he said, "If Henry does not yet love you . . . he soon will."

I swiped at another rebellious tear. "How can you be so sure?"

"Because you are Alicia Kendall. You are smart, and clever. Vivacious and daring. Loyal and compassionate, though you try to hide it. You have a temper, I will grant you, but it is easily mollified with the right words and a simple touch. Which means that hidden behind all your barricades beats a soft heart—and these are all virtues as rare as they are priceless. Knowing all that, the real question is how could he *not* love you?" Matthew played with his hands resting on his propped knees. He looked down, adding quietly, "How couldn't any man?"

My lips parted. Again, Matthew saw through me clearly. He pinned me with attributes I wasn't sure I owned—but most surprising was that he saw those things at all. I tucked my hands behind me, feeling the grainy brick dig into my skin. A few more men in red uniform blurred past, accompanied by commonly dressed folk.

Something like sadness glimmered in his eyes. His voice was impossibly soft when he said, "Henry loves you because there's no one else on earth like you, Alicia. Not anyone."

My heart stuttered to a stop. I chuckled lightly, nervously, scraping my foot into his boot. "Is that a compliment?"

But Matthew did not smile back. He swallowed, eyes darting between the ground and my face, before ultimately looking away. "Something like that," he murmured.

Silence engulfed us for a minute. A pink sunset painted the sky in broad strokes. Somewhere in the distance, boisterous voices sang a song I didn't know. My mind invariably went to something he'd said in his library, something I'd been curious about ever since.

Feeling like he owed me an honest, soul-revealing answer in exchange for mine, I dared voice it. "Why don't you wish to marry?" His gaze flicked to me, and he stared at me so long, I feared he wouldn't answer. I rushed on. "I only wonder at it because, from what I understand from Eliza, your parents had a happy marriage. Why should you not want the same thing for yourself?"

"And what if a happy marriage is not possible for me?" He didn't say anything more for a moment. "I know you shan't believe me when I say this," he muttered at last, shaking his head, "but . . . I hate it that I'm right all the time. Truly. You say you despise not being able to see what will happen, but let me tell you, it is worse to see. To *know* your outcome, and have no way of changing it. No matter that you would go the lengths of the earth for the smallest chance at a different path. No. All you can do is watch it all play out and accept your defeat."

I took in the slump to his shoulders, the way he pinched and rubbed one of his thumbs. He was talking of his parents, of the way they'd died. Of how terrified he was of getting close to anyone else because of it. He did not wish to marry, because that would mean opening his heart to the potential pain of losing her forever.

"If ever I were to marry," he continued with a far-off look in his eye, "it would be to someone I never saw coming. Someone whom I couldn't predict, who surprised me in every way. The path we'd take would be full of twists and turns, and maybe it would be headed toward that dreadful, blasted outcome after all—but the important thing is, I wouldn't know it. It wouldn't matter. In the end, all that would matter was the journey we had getting there."

I blinked at him, surprised at the tender words passing his lips. If Matthew were searching for someone he couldn't predict, that automatically ruled out most women. In fact, it ruled me out most of all—the one actually engaged to him.

"That book you're so blasted curious about . . ." Matthew inhaled and sighed, breath catching a little. ". . . my mother gave it to me. And I take it with me wherever I go because when she was alive, she always encouraged me to be social. I hated it. I hate it still. But I cannot bring myself to stop completely, because I know my efforts would make her happy, wherever she is."

The last golden light of sunset filtered out of the sky. Matthew said nothing more. He didn't have to. It explained why he always had the book, why it was so well-loved. He clung to it because it was a piece of his mother that was his alone.

Matthew Wycliffe—the indifferent, unfeeling man from the balcony—was sharing pieces of his heart with me, something that according to Eliza he didn't do with anyone. And I wondered why. I wondered why *me*.

Eliza's words drifted through my memory: *The real trial was when Mama died. I think a whole month passed before I heard the sound of his voice again. The only way to prevent grief and loss is to not care about anyone in the first place. So he tries not to.*

But after defending me in front of Graham, after rescuing me from the secret tunnel, and after punching that Irishman and running for our lives through the streets of Brighton, it didn't seem like Matthew didn't care. Sitting here in the grime of an alley . . . it seemed like he cared more than anyone ever had.

Perhaps he'd been telling the truth. Perhaps he really didn't hate me. The thought warmed my core, melting my insides until they lay in a puddle at my feet. I wondered at it—why I would feel pleased, or even care. But then the quiet answer came.

Perhaps I'd been lying to myself. Perhaps I didn't really hate him either.

I pinched my lips together, trying to hold back my warming smile. "I will find out what is in it, you know," I said, meaning his book.

His eyebrows lifted, gloomy mood replaced with a characteristic haughtiness. "I sincerely hope you do not."

I pulled out my best play-acting expression. "If we're ever going to marry, you must stop keeping secrets from me. You know I am madly in love with you."

His eyes glinted in amusement. "As I am with you."

"Well then, I ask that you let me see inside it—as a test of your love."

"Shouldn't you be testing Mr. Crawley's love?"

"Sir! Any man who professes to love me must prove it—either by sword, or by letting me see inside his most secretive green book. It is the same test I give to everyone. Utterly impartial of me, I know. And since you've never held a sword in your life, well—" I tossed my hands in comical helplessness, "—the book is your only option, I'm afraid. Come! I know you have it on your person. Retrieve it from your bottomless pockets, or I shall be forced to dive for it myself."

Matthew's lips took on a bland slant. "You could try."

"And I would—but the scene would look most scandalous. Us tangled together like a pair of scabs." A grin split my face, until I was chuckling. "I am your *sister*, after all. One that is dicked in the nob, too! Oh, I shudder to think how people shall view me, then."

Matthew looked down. And then, to my utter astonishment . . . he smiled.

At the sheer shock of seeing it, my laugh died in my throat.

His face transformed. It was brilliant. Breathtaking. His white teeth peeked through, his lips pressed into his cheeks, the corners of his eyes crinkled ever so slightly. Muscles that probably hadn't been used in years—and I, I was the one privileged to witness them in action.

After a moment, his gaze lifted and locked onto mine—and if I thought his smile was breathtaking before, now it was blinding.

My heart stopped for three whole beats. Then it spasmed into a gallop, bounding around in my chest while the rest of me froze. I could stare at him for hours. Days. Memorize every crease, every sparkle in his eye.

Heaven help me, Matthew . . . Heaven help me.

For goodness' sake, why didn't he smile more often? If the merest flash of it left me this flustered, I couldn't imagine how incapacitated I'd be if he were to *laugh*.

He looked me up and down, smile fading. "What is the matter?"

I wanted to reach across and shake his shoulders—demand that he smile again, only this time, be prepared for it, ready to appreciate it for all it was worth. To, this time, fortify my heart against the uncontrollable, fluttery havoc it was wreaking in my stomach.

"Nothing," I squeaked. I shrunk back against the brick and cleared my throat. "Absolutely nothing." Blast, why did I sound so breathless? I cleared my throat again, glancing at the street. "It should be dark enough now to slip away."

"Yes." Matthew stood and brushed himself off, blessedly unconcerned with or unaware of the blush creeping up my neck. He helped me stand. Tentatively, we stuck our heads out of the alley and looked around. When the coast was clear Matthew stepped onto the street, and I followed suit.

To my surprise, a warmth closed around my hand and gently tugged me forward.

This time, he had not asked me first.

Up ahead, a group of soldiers came into view. One of them I recognized, making my pulse pump in alarm.

"Keep your head down," Matthew murmured, giving my hand a squeeze and forcing me to slow my pace. I obeyed, huddling closer to Matthew. The soldiers passed without incident and I breathed a sigh of relief. Though the danger had abated, I didn't move away, and neither did Matthew prod me to.

We wove through the city, keeping to busier streets and pressing closer to each other. Bright candlelight from windows illuminated our way. Dozens of people spilled through doorways, everyone eager for a drink and a dance on this warm summer night. Laughter and fiddling carried us to an inn door, where Matthew arranged a carriage.

When we were safely riding through the countryside, I stole peeks at Matthew's long frame in the moonlight, lying across the seat opposite mine, one arm slung over his eyes. He was exhausted —and so was I, but my thoughts wouldn't let me relax even for a moment.

This tall, condescending man was never part of the deal. Not his arrogance, apathy, or brusque attitude. Our association was a business transaction where we both had something to gain. Nothing more. It was simple, straightforward, and in the plan.

But I had not planned on Matthew's brilliant mind. Or his soft heart, brimming with hidden compassion. Or that rare, blinding smile that could light the whole world. There was something so infuriatingly annoying about him, and yet somehow, it had only endeared him to me more.

I studied his full lips, his perfectly shaped nose, his angular jaw. Guilt pricked my conscience, making me inhale a shaky breath. All this time, I'd been lying to make him believe that unless he helped me, we'd be forced into marriage, when that wasn't the case at all.

I'd been manipulating him for my own gain. I hadn't cared before, but after the way he'd bared his heart to me, suddenly I did.

He's been terribly lonely, Lily had said. *I've seen it in his eyes.*

I was under no illusion that he loved me. But pretending like a marriage between us might take place had allowed us to share a common purpose; even form a sort of friendship. He had defended me, fought for me, braved castles and tunnels and alleys alike. If he were to discover the truth—how I'd set out from the beginning to squeeze him for every drop of usefulness and then cast him aside— what would he think of me then?

He'd never smile at me again. Perhaps never *smile*.

And even if he never discovered the truth, in a matter of days, I would sever all ties and ruin every tender thing that had ever blossomed between us.

I rubbed my forehead, watching the shadows move around the carriage, pulling me into their whirlpool. Maybe I'd been wrong earlier, in the alley. Maybe he despised me. Maybe he fought off the soldiers and everything else—not because he cared and wanted to keep me close—but because eventually, it would grant him his freedom from me.

If only to relieve the guilt-ridden pain stinging in my chest, I would choose to believe it.

When I looked toward the day when this charade had to end, I was not filled with the happiness I thought I'd be. The prospect of never seeing Matthew again frightened me. Even . . . *hurt* to think about.

No, I didn't hate him. In fact, I hated him so little I was in danger of falling hopelessly in love.

CHAPTER 21

As I slipped inside the servant's entrance, every muscle in my arms and legs ached. Great wads of blond ringlets which had long escaped their pins hung about my face. My back throbbed from being hunched in the alley for so long. Two floors above, I heard my soft bed calling to me, beckoning me to drown in its covers. But a sliver of light caught my eye and I stopped in my tracks.

It was disconcerting enough to see Father's study door open in the middle of the night, but the flickering beam of candlelight shining through made it even more ominous. Not only was he returned from London, but he was awake. I looked back the way I'd come. Unless I wanted to track back through the kitchen and enter through the main door, I'd have to slip past unnoticed.

I decided to risk it. Going onto my tiptoes, I made careful progress. When I reached the threshold, I paused and peeked around the corner.

Father sat behind his desk wearing his spectacles, the knuckles of one hand propping his head up. His clothes were crumpled from travelling, and his face was drawn and haggard. "Stop sneaking about and come in already."

My mouth ran dry. Not only was he awake, but he'd been waiting up for me. I took one regretful look at my stained, torn dress, before slipping in.

As I neared, Father took in my shoddy appearance with a grim line to his mouth, but he didn't seem surprised. He plinked his quill pen into the inkpot and hefted the open ledger before him closed before turning his full attention to me. Threading his hands together, he said, "Are you aware of the hour, Alicia?"

The silky calmness in his voice made my toes curl inside my slippers. I glanced at the clock on the mantelpiece. "It is almost midnight, sir."

"And your aunt last saw you at what time?"

"At . . ." I thought back. "At half past six."

"And when she searched for you in the street, she found you missing. Five hours. I return from London to find that you've been missing for *five hours*, Alicia, and no one had any knowledge of your whereabouts. The only thing that prevented me from calling the authorities was for fear that word would get out. I couldn't risk the collapse of my maneuvering—my entire political career—because you were *merely* up to some mischief again." His face was cooler than I thought it would be—and for that reason, it scared me. He took his spectacles off and set them aside. In a gravelly voice, he asked, "Were you up to mischief?"

I longed to say no. I didn't want to be the constant failure he'd come to expect in me—but lying would only make things worse. The word stuck in my throat, but I forced it out. "Yes."

"You were with Henry, weren't you?"

It took me a moment to process the accusation. In the face of it, I crossed my arms. "And if I was?"

He stood, slapping his desk with an open palm. "Alicia, you are engaged! You cannot dally with a man—and unchaperoned! Do you know what might have happened to you? What a scandal like this could do to my anti-war efforts? If the legislation is not passed, it will deny soldiers in the territory much-needed aid. Your actions do not only affect you! Why, oh why, must I have such a daughter?"

Why indeed.

"I promised you two weeks, but this goes beyond every other foolish choice you've made. Alone with a man? After *dark*?"

Telling Father the truth was sure to change his opinion of Matthew. Yet, even though none of what had transpired had been Matthew's fault, I couldn't stand here and let Henry take all the blame.

"I was with Mr. Wycliffe," I said quietly.

Father blinked. Slowly, he sunk back into his chair. He pounded his desk with a few soft thuds from his fist. Then, to my surprise, he stopped and said, "At least I may take some comfort in that knowledge."

My hands dropped to my sides. Comfort? *Comfort*? My nostrils flared. "So if I am with Henry, a man who has loved and taken care of me all my life, he is not to be trusted. But if Mr. Wycliffe—a man you have known only a week—is my companion, then he is to be praised?"

"I never said praised—"

"It is what you do not say! You act like Matthew is my champion, my rescuer. But in the same circumstances, Henry is viewed as the perpetrator, the bad influence. You have different standards for them, Father. And I cannot understand why, despite Henry's every effort to seek your good opinion, you refuse to give it!"

"I have—"

"You refuse to give your blessing for my marriage to a man who is good, and honorable, and yes, poor—but now that he has his fortune, it is still not enough! Always you must be stern, withholding everything I want merely because I want it—if you're even here to withhold it at all!"

"Watch your tone with me, girl!"

The shout was a slap in the face, stealing away my courage and resolve. I fell back a step and swallowed. I would not cry.

Father sighed. "I see now all my efforts have been in vain. If you do not see the folly of dallying with a man after dark—whether he is a virtuous one like Mr. Wycliffe or not—then you are no daughter of mine. Every day, you drive me another inch closer to madness—see how far I will bend before I reach the breaking point. Not this day, Alicia. This day, you have truly broken me."

I let the words sink in, knives slowly twisting into my chest. The weight of his disappointment settled on my shoulders, so heavily that my knees buckled and I gripped the back of the chair in front of me to keep upright.

"But you have not had to live your life breaking under someone's expectations, Father," I whispered, the words falling from my lips before I even thought them. I looked up, his form blurring beyond recognition from the mass of unshed tears. "Fracturing, bit by bit until your unrecognizable pieces are scattered in the wind, crushing all hope of ever gathering yourself again. You did not grow up locked in the darkness without a mother. You never had to wonder why your aunt stayed for years but never offered a loving touch. Or why your father never smiled, except when he *wasn't* looking at you.

"I am broken, Father, because I don't know how to change, and I don't know how to love—because no one has ever shown me how. Though I have tried, I don't know how to please you, or Aunt Beth, or find my purpose in life. I don't know *anything*."

Inhaling a quivering breath, I clenched one fist at my side. "But the thing I don't know most of all . . ." My lower lip trembled, and a single tear trailed down my cheek. ". . . is why you would pretend to care now, when you never have before."

Father said nothing. Only shook his head and hung it.

I lingered, wanting him to speak, to explain. If he would only tell me his reasons for pushing me away, I would forgive him in an instant. I'd wipe away the years of hurt so we could start anew. If he would only tell me he loved me . . . I would love him, too.

But the silence only grew heavier, and when it was heavier than my heart, I sighed and went to bed.

Dressed in my nightgown with my hair tumbling free, I hugged my knees to my chest, watching the moonlight creep across my bed. Tears soaked my cheeks, hair, and gown, but I let them fall freely.

Father was disappointed in me—I'd always known that. But even worse, I was disappointed in myself. I didn't want to be the girl who caused scandal. I didn't want to ruin Father's standing, or be the center of everyone's attention. It was all I had done the past three years, and I wanted to be *different*. Be *better*.

I wanted to be loved. By my father. By Aunt Beth. By Henry. By Matthew.

By anyone.

And I wanted to love them in return.

I swept my hair out of my face and climbed under the covers, my movements almost reverent—like if I moved too quickly it would rip the hole in my heart even wider.

Sometimes it felt as if I'd been given a finite amount of love, at birth. It was mine to give away, but once it was gone, it was gone forever. There was no way to create more. And sometimes it felt as if, even though I'd used it sparingly throughout my life, it had all ended up with Henry.

If he left, he would take *all* my love with him. I'd be left utterly alone, even more callous and despicable than I already was. Aunt Beth would ignore me completely. Father would never look me in the eye again. And I would spend the rest of my days pining away— not for a man, but for the chance to feel something again.

Even if Father and I were miraculously able to bridge the divide between us, perhaps I had no love left to give. I was a husk, long robbed of the fruit that had made me valuable in the first place.

And since Father had already spent the amount I'd given him, it was better that Henry held the rest; safer. Painless.

The only way to prevent grief and loss was to not care about anyone in the first place. So I'd tried not to.

Perhaps Matthew and I were the same after all.

CHAPTER 22

THE NEXT DAY I SCRAWLED A HASTY LETTER TO NANCY'S brother-in-law, updating him with the news of the boy at the inn. The vicar's confirmation was only a formality—I knew in my bones the boy I'd seen was *the* Lenny—but I wanted to be as thorough as possible before I made the shocking revelation to Henry. I was planning on informing him as soon as I had the physical proof.

After seeing the letter posted, I summoned a carriage and made a quick stop at the cobbler's before instructing the driver to deliver me to a far less respectable establishment.

Standing outside the inn, I bit my lip as snippets of yesterday flashed through my mind: the taunting jeers from the soldiers, the corporal's wicked smile, a smoking pistol, the hole in his hat. I hugged the package I held to my chest. I was here for a purpose, and wouldn't be deterred by the possibility of an angry Irishman waiting for me behind the doors.

I took a deep breath before pushing the doors open and plunging inside.

The tavern was just as dirty and rambunctious as it had been yesterday, but it looked even worse in the light of morning. Alcohol residue stained the floor; a pile of rags rotted in one corner; the walls and ceiling bowed inward from water damage, threatening to collapse at any moment. My eyes stung in the smoke-riddled air, making it difficult to breathe.

How could a young boy live in such conditions? Pity washed over me.

A figure hunched over the bar, his dress too well-tailored to blend in among the crowd. When he turned to the side, recognition struck me like a bolt of lightning, making me dart behind one of the beams supporting the ceiling. I'd been afraid of encountering a certain soldier here, but I hadn't considered encountering an enemy of a different sort.

Graham downed the last contents of his pint before planting the mug on the counter. He said something to Jasper—nothing very civil, if his scowl was any indication—before tugging on his topper and striding out the door, never once glancing my way.

I breathed easier once he was gone, but had gained even more questions.

Jasper may not know who'd been delivering the settlements for Lenny's care, but now it was obvious. Graham's presence in the tavern couldn't be mere coincidence. And, if Graham was the one keeping up the payments, it would explain why they had mysteriously decreased a few years ago. Graham may not know the significance of the boy, but he doubtless wanted to keep as much money to himself as was legally possible.

The only question was, how had Nicholas Crawley gotten him to do it? Was there some sort of contract between them? And why had he entrusted Graham with the care of his wife's son, when he hadn't even trusted him with his will?

I shook my head to dislodge the thoughts. I could think on all that later—for now, I needed to talk to Jasper.

I marched forward, setting my package on the counter. It was several minutes before Jasper was available, having to help several customers who were there before me. When he finally turned to me, his face blanked, obviously surprised to see me a second time.

"Good morning, sir," I said.

He frowned, his eyes already narrowing in suspicion.

I cleared my throat. "I was in the area doing some charity work, and since I couldn't help but notice the condition of your young ward's wardrobe, I took it upon myself to buy him some new shoes." I nudged the package forward. Noting the innkeepers darkening features, I added hastily, "I hope you do not think me too forward—"

"I don't normally accept charity—leastwise from a *woman*—but since you blew a hole in my window, I won't think twice about taking anything from you, miss."

Ah. Yes. The pistol.

"I am terribly sorry about that, sir—I'd be more than happy to compensate you—"

He grunted loudly and snatched the package away before storming off. My hopes deflated a little. I'd wanted to probe him more about Lenny, but considering his mood, I doubted I'd get more out of him today.

When he returned a few minutes later and found me lingering at the counter, he started ordering me to leave in heated tones, saying something about not wanting me to cause any more trouble.

"Of course, I will be happy to leave," I said evenly. "I was only wondering if I might talk with your ward for a few moments, perhaps ask him some questions—"

"He's not 'ere! I've sent him over to the next county to place an order for a new window." He scanned me in disgust. "And if you come back looking for him, just see if I don't send him away again!"

"I understand." I licked my lips, disappointment making the movement feel heavy. "Thank you for your time." I spun around and left the tavern, grateful to be rid of the stifling air, but wishing I'd had better luck.

CHAPTER 23

I WASN'T CERTAIN HOSTING A PICNIC WOULD TEMPER THE rumors, but it was my only chance. I smoothed my pink day dress, attempting to smother my butterflies with the movement. The sun beat down, promising a scorching afternoon. Down the lawn, servants unfolded blankets in the shade of a large oak. A mountain of refreshments piled two tables near the trunk, and that mountain only grew as more trays filed out of the house in preparation for the party.

"Do we really need all this food?" I asked Eliza at my side.

"Trust me," she said, consulting the list she held in her hand, "you have not met the Regent's niece."

Unbeknownst to Eliza, I actually had met the woman, but I opted to not correct her.

Aunt Beth had introduced me to Lady Prima at a ball in London. She'd seemed harmless enough at the time, but the way she gossiped about me when my back was turned was anything but harmless. Her wagging tongue had prompted three different scoldings from Father in the span of a week, which had prompted me to make a handful of rude remarks in her presence. Not the least of which had been concerning her ubiquitous laughter.

It was safe to say she didn't much like me—which made this meeting even more nerve racking. I needed to make a good impression.

Eliza directed one of the servants where to put the almond tartlets and spun-sugar diadems. Then she turned to me and said offhandedly, "I am still so pleased you're the one marrying my brother, Alicia. I long for you to be my sister, and you are so perfect for Matthew."

"Yes, I—I am glad to be marrying him, too." I scratched my arm then my neck, wriggling in my own skin. If the Wycliffes knew I had entered into the engagement with the intention of breaking it off, they would see me in a completely different light. Only the worst creature used people in such a way.

But I'd made a deal. As such, my choices were set before me, and Matthew wasn't one of them.

Distant laughter of the strangest sort rang out, bringing our conversation to a standstill. It sounded like a chaffinch's call and a babbling baby's coos mixed together; long and high, accompanied by comical inflection.

Lady Prima had arrived.

She strolled round the corner of the house, arm linked in Sir William's. "Bentley, how you tease me. My cheeks are no rosier than last you saw them! Though to be sure, they were rather pale then— as I am always pale—so I shall take you at your word. But you are a scoundrel! Oh, it has been far too long, sir!" Her short, portly frame bobbed with enthusiasm, making a few of her tight brown ringlets bounce on her shoulders.

"Dear 'Liza," Sir William called, holding up his free hand in greeting. "Look what I found in the drive."

Lady Prima slapped the brim of her bonnet. "Oh, Miss Wy—that is, Lady Bentley!" She waved and rushed over. "You would not believe how positively thrilled I was to receive your invitation. A picnic, and then the Brighton games! I have heard of their renown, but have yet to witness them for myself. One would think Uncle Prinny would have invited me, but he must've had some mischievous reason for keeping me away. Men competing in their undershirts, muscles straining, sweat dripping from foreheads—oh! There is nothing, absolutely nothing which gives me more pleasure!" She covered her mouth and giggled.

With a knowing smile, Eliza said, "I know all too well, Lady Prima." She turned to me. "Might I introduce Lady Alicia Kendall."

Lady Prima's wrinkled eyes widened when they landed on me. "But Lady Alicia and I have already met. And not under the best of circumstances, I might add—"

"Do forgive me, Lady Prima," I said, before she had a chance to mention "The Hedgehog Incident." "I was such a child then. Surely you can forgive a foolish girl."

She frowned. "A foolish girl I may forgive—but I mayn't forgive your engagement to Mr. Wycliffe. Word of this attachment has reached my ears, and might I say I am most distressed by it! Mr. Wycliffe, the man with the most sigh-inducing face of all—besides you, dear Bentley—is to be married? And to a woman who does not love him? No! No, it cannot be so!"

She clutched the lacy fabric at her collarbone. "Why, it took me *years* to forgive Miss Wycliffe for stealing Bentley out from under my nose so suddenly—and then only because she was one of my dearest friends! Now she is Lady Bentley and all is well, but it is not the same, you see. And now Mr. Wycliffe is to be taken too?" Her lip trembled, hand flapping under her chin. "The mere thought of it puts me in such a state as I cannot go on."

Sir William's lips twitched in an effort to hold back a smile. "I say, Lady Prima," he said, "you have this all wrong. Lady Alicia and my brother-in-law are deeply in love. Someone has wronged them by spreading malicious rumors about their union. You wouldn't happen to know who it was, would you?"

Lady Prima stopped her blubbering almost immediately. "Well .

. . I can't say as I do. Whoever it was must have great social reach and an outstanding impact on society. Impeccable sources. And she likely only wanted to ensure that Mr. Wycliffe's fiancée deserved him in every possible way. But you see, no one can, so I think her reasons were justified. Whoever she is."

My brow crinkled. *Lady Prima* had propagated the rumors?

Sir William waved a finger at her. "Now Lady Prima, you know I normally couldn't care less if you slander people into infamy. But when it comes to my family—"

Her eyes widened innocently. "Slander?" Her hand cupped one rosy cheek then fiddled with the golden feather adorning her bonnet. "Goodness me! I would never slander anyone! But I don't know why you should be cross with me, Bentley. If indeed Mr. Wycliffe and Lady Alicia are in love, I have yet to see any evidence of it!"

"Well, today you shall," I said, drawing everyone's eyes.

Sir William grinned. "And we are all looking forward to it."

Lady Prima suddenly giggled. "Dear Lady Alicia, do not look so serious! I am open to being proven wrong, I assure you. Though, as a matchmaker, I feel I ought to warn you that I have a rather high standard."

A chance was all I needed.

Sir William steered Lady Prima toward the oak tree, leaving me alone in Eliza's company once more.

Eliza nudged my shoulder with her own. "If she intimidates you so, you could plead a headache. It is not too late to change your mind."

But it was. It was far, far too late.

"Where is he?" I said.

Eliza shrugged. "The last I saw of Matthew, he was in the wisteria tunnel with Charlotte." She pointed in the opposite direction, before following Sir William and Lady Prima.

Picking up my skirts, I went in search of Matthew.

THE WISTERIA TUNNEL WAS QUITE LARGE, EASILY TWELVE FEET wide and spanning half the length of the house. Purple flowers hung down from the metal framework like ribbons, giving the bright tunnel a soft, other-worldly glow.

I could hear his voice from within. A deep baritone, lightened by the lilting way he spoke. Almost musical in its effortlessness. I peeked inside.

Book in hand, Matthew Wycliffe sat on a stone bench. Charlotte, Eliza's daughter, perched on his lap, swiping her black curls out of her eyes with a chubby hand. He bent close to her, pointing at the pictures.

". . . but the peasant girl did not want the trolls to eat her, you see, because peasant girls aren't very nutritious. And also because she didn't particularly like the idea of having her bones crushed into flour."

I grinned at Matthew's interpretation of the story, knowing he was almost certainly embellishing what was written on the page.

Charlotte's eyes bulged up at her uncle. "I don't have bones!"

"Don't be silly, of course you do. 'Help me!' the girl cried, running from the castle in search of her loyal servant. Unbeknownst to her, the trolls had already caught him and eaten him for supper. Poor man. But then he was an ignoramus in the first place, so we shouldn't feel too sorry for him."

"A ig-more-anus!" Charlotte said happily.

"Yes, and don't tell your mama I taught you that word. Now, the peasant girl couldn't find her servant, so she fled to the forest, thinking to lose the trolls in the trees."

I stepped inside, saying, "But of course she couldn't." Charlotte jerked up and Matthew glanced over—but he didn't seem surprised. Would I ever manage to take him unawares? Moseying closer, I continued. "Trolls are very fast, after all."

"Indeed," Matthew said, not the least bit fazed. "And they have tempers as hot as boiling kettles."

Under his steady gaze, memories from the night in the tavern resurfaced, making my heart flutter nervously. I turned to Charlotte to smooth over the sudden awkwardness I felt. "But the trolls wouldn't have been irked at all, had the peasant girl not taken a shot at their king, blowing a hole through his favorite hat."

Matthew's brows rose, catching on to what I was doing— twisting the tale so it followed the events of the night at the tavern.

Charlotte beamed. "I have a favorite hat!"

"And can you imagine how angry you'd be if someone ruined it?" There was just enough room on the bench for me to sit next to Matthew, so I did. Our legs brushed.

His eyes darted down at the touch, lingering just a beat too long before turning back to Charlotte. "That is how the trolls felt. Not to mention that the girl also broke their window."

I rolled my eyes. "It is not as if she meant to. And then she was forced to run for her life."

Matthew's gaze softened, and he was no longer hovering over Charlotte, telling the story to her. He was telling it to me. "And her loyal servant turned out to be alive, because he suddenly appeared at her side, showing her the way through the magical forest and helping her elude the trolls by hiding behind a large tree. She was an ungrateful little minx, as usual. But, the trolls passed by without incident, never suspecting for one moment they had been outfoxed."

I chuckled. "She *was* rather ungrateful—but I am sure she was grateful in her heart. And while the girl and the servant hid, keeping quiet behind the tree, they discovered something. The most wonderful secret of all . . ."

I trailed off, suddenly without any words. Matthew blinked at me, waiting for me to finish the story; *our* story. But I wasn't sure I wanted to know how it ended, because I didn't see how it could end happily.

"What secret?" Charlotte asked, hopping up and down in Matthew's lap.

Matthew glanced down at his niece. When I still didn't say anything, he answered for me. "That the peasant girl was no peasant after all. She was a princess." His gaze locked with mine. "She always had been."

The tight grip around my heart that had been there since my fight with Father, loosened. Warm tingles traveled down my legs, heightening where they touched Matthew.

A floating sensation covered my limbs when one corner of his lips curved ever so slightly up. Something tender passed between us, my heart beating so fast I feared my ribs would break. The smile was the barest hint of what I'd seen in the alleyway, and yet it said something completely . . . *more.*

He snapped the book shut, and the moment was gone. "But then the trolls found her, and tossed her into a pit where she starved to death and died alone."

I sank back to the bench and suppressed a smile. "And the loyal servant was still an ignoramus."

"The end." He helped Charlotte off his lap and handed her the book.

She dashed away, calling, "Thank you, Uncle Matthew!" over her shoulder.

The moment she reached the mouth of the wisteria tunnel, I stood and ran my hand along the velvety, hanging petals. "You are a wonderful storyteller, sir."

He grunted. "If so, then Charlotte is the only one who appreciates my talents."

Letting the scene replay in my mind, I smiled, then wiped it away. I needed to hate him. It was easier that way. I needed to squeeze some consistency from my feelings and use it to enact my plan and marry Henry. I squared my shoulders. "Were you successful yesterday in obtaining the license?"

"Yes. Unfortunately for me, the Archbishop likes me a great deal."

All Matthew had to do was frown at someone, and they would like him. It was an inexplicable phenomenon. I nodded, relieved that if our acting couldn't convince Lady Prima, we had a piece of paper that might. "Well, Mr. Wycliffe, the whole afternoon stretches before us. Are you ready to pretend to be in love with me?"

Matthew's answer didn't immediately come, and when it did, it sounded strained. "As I'll ever be."

"Is that mere reluctance I hear, sir? I did not know you had grown so fond of me!" After inhaling the sweet, musky scent, I plucked a petal and spun back, surprised to find that Matthew was neither grimacing nor glaring. His expression was carefully neutral, mouth set in a solemn line.

"Do not mistake me. The sooner this madness ends, the better."

I blinked, and my heart fell. Of course I shouldn't mistake him. Just because he had smiled didn't mean he liked the situation any better—or liked me better, for that matter. It would be foolish to hope for anything beyond tolerance from Matthew. So utterly, fathomlessly, mind-blowingly foolish. I pinched the petal between my fingers until it rolled into a scroll.

I didn't have the best record when it came to not doing foolish things.

To my right, Lady Prima's chocolate eyes peered inside the tunnel, and she gave a cry of delight. "There you are, Mr. Wycliffe!" She shimmied toward us, fluttering her handkerchief in greeting. When she stopped, she hit Matthew's arm with it. "I have been searching high and low for your handsome face. Wherever have you been?"

Matthew frowned at her. "Hiding from you."

She giggled, and its pitch scaled so high, I barely restrained myself from covering my ears. "You tease me, sir! Such a sullen one you are, so entertaining with your withering words—but I know you do not mean them." She leaned in, and with one hand, squished his cheeks, her short arm only able to reach them because Matthew was sitting. "You are still just as enamored of me as the day we first met." She wiggled his head back and forth.

Cheeks still pinched, Matthew turned his scowl on me instead of his assaulter, his eyes saying, *I told you not to invite her*. Then he yanked his head away and glowered at her. "In that assumption, madam, you are one hundred percent correct."

A breathy laugh passed my lips.

Lady Prima, taking it as a compliment, tittered again. "I must say, I am all agog at the news of your engagement. I was under the impression that no woman could win your heart! When is the wedding to take place?"

I said, "October," just as Matthew said, "September."

We shared a hasty look before I added, "That is, we haven't exactly decided on the day yet, Lady Prima. Though, I am sure Mr. Wycliffe will see reason. October is cooler and a better time of year."

Lady Prima nodded and opened her mouth to say something, but Matthew cut her off. "I *always* see reason, my lady, which is why I know September to be the better month. And I assumed that is why you sent me scampering to London to fetch a special license— so that we may be married sooner."

Lady Prima gasped. "You obtained a special license, sir? Why, that bespeaks true devotion!"

I barely had time to celebrate that my plan to impress Lady Prima had worked before Matthew waved her off, turning back to me. "Yes, yes. And as we are so hopelessly in love, and as I obtained it *at your request*, I am sure you will agree to September."

I didn't know why something as silly as the date of our pretend marriage was sparking such debate. It was a pointless argument. Yet, the challenge of it—the challenge of *winning* it—was suddenly the only thing on my mind. And judging by the stubborn gleam in Matthew's eye, it was the only thing on his mind, too.

"I thank you for retrieving the license, Mr. Wycliffe. Yes, we are hopelessly in love, and *as such*, I would expect you to be more lenient." I rose one brow.

"It is because I love you that I am not," he said with a straight face.

Botheration. "But to please your future wife, you would consent to having the ceremony in October. As well as moving to a new house, afterwards."

Matthew's lips compressed. "For the very, very last time, stop trying to drive me out of my house. It is bad enough that you've driven me out of my mind."

A smile pulled at my mouth, but it faltered when I noticed Lady Prima's gaze volleying between us, a thoughtful look on her face.

Oh dear. She saw through us. She knew we were pretending, and now we were done for. "Lady Prima, you mustn't think—"

"I see Sir William was right, Lady Alicia," she announced. "And I never would have thought it possible, had I not seen it for myself."

I pinched my arm to keep myself from squirming. "Seen what?"

"Why, that you and Mr. Wycliffe are madly in love, of course! How could anyone doubt it, the way you both carry on? I've never seen him frown so little at anyone. And then there is the longing way you glance at him when he isn't looking. Believe me, I know the feeling, Lady Alicia—though I can't say as I've done it as intensely as you do."

My cheeks flamed red. I had not glanced at him with longing!

. . . Had I?

She threw up her arms. "You have been deeply wronged by these mongrels spreading falsehoods. Such villains! Such an atrocity! Well, I cannot stand by and see my friends slandered by ill-meaning blackguards. I shall compose several letters—however many it takes —to see to it that all of England knows of your devotion."

Face still hot, I finally managed, "Thank you, Lady Prima. We are in your debt."

"Indeed, you are." She sighed wistfully, patting one of Matthew's cheeks. "It is a sad day when another handsome face falls prey to love's clutches—and in Mr. Wycliffe's case, I never dreamed the day would come! But no matter. I shall quickly forgive you when you invite me to the ceremony. I do love a good wedding!" After grasping her hands to her breast, she spun around. "La! Now I must find some of that feast Lady Bentley promised before I starve. Do not tarry here too long else one might think you do far more than talking." She turned back to waggle her eyebrows at us and emit another giggle before disappearing out of the tunnel.

Matthew stood and rubbed his cheek with his shoulder, wiping away Lady Prima's touch. He glanced down at me, looking nauseated. "We are *not* inviting her to our wedding."

I laughed.

CHAPTER 24

As it turned out, Lady Prima wasn't the only influential person invited to the picnic. One by one, a dozen different people with high social clout arrived in their bedecked bonnets and shiny toppers, and I wondered how Eliza had managed to plan such an elaborate event in only two days.

Around the lawn, the exalted guests lounged on blankets and nibbled on buttery pastries, chortling and giggling so loudly, I was sure they could hear us all the way from London. Eliza and Sir William didn't take much part in the conversation, appearing too amused by the spectacle to be impressed or disgusted by it.

For Lady Prima's benefit, I kept near Matthew's side, though it was difficult to do when he perpetually wandered off to corners and reclined against tree trunks. Though, I was grateful for it when it allowed me to dodge Hawthorne and his numerous attempts to question me about what he'd seen at the inn. Peter and Lily arrived, bringing with them a host of new topics to keep Lady Prima's ever-flapping mouth occupied.

I tucked my feet under my legs, trying to focus on anything but Lady Prima's third recounting of her fateful meeting in Hyde Park last Tuesday—a recounting which had drastically changed with each telling.

A familiar figure wandered near, and I perked up. I didn't know Eliza had invited Henry. The last he saw of me had been at the tavern when Matthew kissed me, and I squirmed at the sudden impulse thumping through my veins to pull him aside and explain the truth. I'd hesitated to go after him that day, but I knew my feelings now—and had already ordered them back into the box I built for them long ago. Perhaps I could even find a moment to tell him about Lenny.

"Yoo-hoo, Mr. Crawley!" Lady Prima called, waving her biscuit in the air.

Henry, who had been heading toward the back of the group, halted, obviously surprised at being acknowledged by the prominent Lady Prima. She'd likely only noticed him at all because news of Matthew's attention to him had spread. Now that Lady Prima accepted him, that news was only going to gain momentum. He approached, stopping at the edge of our enormous cotton blanket. He dipped into a bow. "Lady Prima."

"I am told you are good friends with Lady Alicia, are you not?"

He seemed to hesitate. Why was he hesitating? "Yes."

"Then you must know of her dashingly romantic engagement— how she and Mr. Wycliffe are smitten with each other!"

My chest tightened. *Oh, Henry.* I clenched my hands in my lap.

Slowly, his gaze flicked to me and to Matthew at my side, before darting back to Lady Prima. He clasped his hands behind his back. "Yes. I know of it."

She clapped. "Good! Then perhaps you may be beneficial in rectifying the horrible reports which are being spread. Some person —who I shan't name, as I am not one to gossip—has been claiming Lady Alicia marries him only for his money. But it is not so, as you can plainly see."

"Yes," he said, only he wasn't looking at Lady Prima. When I could no longer bear staring into his sloped eyes, I leaned forward to say something—but he went on before I could. "I shall do all I can before I leave in three days, Lady Prima."

She tottered to her feet, fluffing her voluminous skirts. "Excellent news! Now Lady Bentley, what is this I hear about wild blackberry bushes in the woods nearby? We must form a party and hunt them down! Mr. Crawley, you shall accompany me. Oh, and Mr. Wycliffe, I wouldn't dream of letting you stay behind—" She pulled on Matthew's arm to raise him up from the blanket.

Knowing Matthew, he was making himself slouch with dead weight—so it was even more impressive when she managed to heave him halfway to standing. Matthew finally gave in and locked his legs. Sighing and straightening his cravat, he said, "Wonderful."

Servants fetched baskets and distributed them before setting to clean up the delicacies. Now armed with receptacles, everyone hiked toward the tree line: Lord Wycliffe with Lily, Sir William with Eliza, Lady Prima with Henry and Matthew, and everyone else with their various groups.

When I saw Hawthorne notice me and pivot, I scurried into the trees, feeling like the peasant girl trying to evade the trolls in Matthew's story. Only this time, my servant wasn't around to aid me. It somehow managed to work, though, because soon I found myself alone, branched away from the other berry-hunters, but still visible as we picked our way through the undergrowth.

Patches of sunlight dappled the ferns and long grass of the forest floor. Muted bits of commentary from Lady Prima drifted to my ears, but I ignored it, taking deep breaths of air that smelled like bark and sap. Birds twittered in the trees, echoing each other's songs. I hiked my skirts up and stepped over a slick, mossy log.

"Careful," Henry warned.

I glanced up to find he'd hung back, and now extended his hand in assistance. He was always so thoughtful.

I took it, murmuring, "Thank you."

He offered a little smile, but it didn't reach his eyes.

We pushed deeper into the forest, Henry now at my side. When the silence grew unbearable, I said, "What you saw at the tavern . . . it wasn't what it looked like. We were putting on a show—it meant nothing."

Henry didn't say anything for a long while, making me wring my hands.

He didn't understand. I was being forced to juggle unwanted feelings, a monumental secret, my bargain with Father, a meddling aunt, a pestering suitor, an irritable fiancé—and now the man I actually loved doubted my affection, because truth be told, I wasn't doing a good job of it. My plans for Henry and myself had been consistently interrupted or thwarted, and now the delay had driven a wedge between us.

Henry was who I wanted. It had always been as simple as that. I needed to convince him of it or he would never propose and would drift out of reach forever.

"I believe you," he said at last, making me sigh in relief. "But, though it may have been nothing to you, Alicia . . . I do not think it was nothing to Mr. Wycliffe."

My feet came to a stop. A balmy cloud lifted my stomach up until it was spinning and weightless. "What makes you say that?"

"Just—" He stared down at his boots as they crushed grass and snapped twigs. "A feeling. A certain way he looked at you."

I thought of the message Matthew had sent over my shoulder in the tavern, when he'd turned my chin back. Had Henry noticed it? Is that what he meant? It couldn't have been anything else— certainly not anything involving Matthew looking at *me*.

"Here!" Henry called back to me, pointing at a patch of brambles. "I've found some."

Similar exultant cries echoed to my left where Lady Prima and her party stumbled upon some bushes, their bottom halves hidden by vegetation. Henry hunched and popped a berry in his mouth, cheeks squeezing as he savored the taste. "Still a bit early, but not bad."

I stooped and picked a handful of berries before placing them in my basket.

"I am glad, you know," Henry said, making my hand freeze on its way to the next berry. "That it was all a show in the tavern." He gave me a half smile. "I don't know what I would do if your affection for Mr. Wycliffe was real."

Ducked down like this, none of the rest of the group could see us. We were completely alone. And the way Henry stared at me made me eternally grateful for that fact. He pulled my hand away from the bush, sandwiching it in his warm grip and bringing it to his lips. His eyes closed. "Alicia . . ." he whispered.

He was going to propose.

"What a relief!"

Henry and I both spun to find Hawthorne tromping through the brush behind us. Teeth clamping down, I stood, and a heartbeat later Henry joined me. That was *twice* now Hawthorne had interrupted Henry's proposal. Would the man ever leave me alone?

Hawthorne shook off the grass and bits of vegetation clinging to his tailcoat, beaming like he'd just been given the world. "You and Mr. Wycliffe were being entirely too intimate the other day at Brighton—though I am sure you didn't know I was a spectator, Lady Alicia. I was devastated! Not only that, but Mother would've been scandalized at the spectacle. But now you say it was all for show. I cannot believe I did not think of it myself—for truly, that is the only possible explanation there could be." He laughed and slapped his forehead.

It was just my luck for Hawthorne to overhear our conversation. Now he was sure to redouble his efforts and make it a point to never leave me alone in Henry's company. I heaved an exasperated sigh.

"I did find your kingcups, my lady—but they're sad, droopy fellows now, I'm afraid. Perhaps you would like some more?"

My eyes widened. "No! That is, you shouldn't trouble yourself, my lord. My favorite flower has changed yet again. Quite suddenly, you see."

"Pray tell me what it is, and I will fetch it for you." His eyes lit up with eagerness, and with each step he took toward me, I fell back one. "Wild roses? Honeysuckle? I believe I saw some honeysuckle over the ridge there. Or perhaps I shall bring every flower I can find—so you may choose between them. One of them *has* to catch your fancy."

I opened my mouth to bluntly tell Lord Hawthorne I had no wish to marry him, but then Henry, seeing my need for a rescue, jumped in with a new topic. "Do you plan to attend the tournament tomorrow?" His purple fingers reached for another branch, his basket already halfway full of berries.

"Yes, I—"

"I've been meaning to ask you, Lady Alicia, if you would like to attend the tournament with me." Hawthorne shook off a clinging blackberry branch, freeing up his broad smile.

Henry set his basket down. "Excuse me, my lord, but I believe I asked her first."

Hawthorne plucked a few thistles burrowed in his palm and tossed them over his shoulder. "Here now, Crawley, it's not as if she's engaged to *you*—"

"She *might've* been." Henry flushed, uncomfortable with the turn of conversation, but not backing down. His newfound wealth and status emboldened him, and it was an attractive look. Content to see how far it would take him, I sat back and crossed my arms. From the corner of my eye, Matthew plucked the leaf of a fern and sauntered within earshot.

Hawthorne exclaimed something that sounded like 'Bah.' "Rather audacious assumption, sir! Anyone will tell you that if it weren't for Lady Alicia's engagement to Mr. Wycliffe, she would be engaged to me. Just ask her father."

"Has *she* told you this?"

Hawthorne sputtered. "No, but—it is one of those matters

where it does not need to be said!" He turned to me in supplication, eyes wide. "The kingcups, my lady. The *kingcups*."

"Flowers aren't the way to win Alicia's hand," Henry muttered quietly.

But Hawthorne seemed to hear him. "No? Then I challenge you, sir! If Lady Alicia cannot decide between us, let the decision be made by the sword. Tomorrow, while everyone looks on, the man who wins the tournament shall win her hand."

I dropped my basket, and the blackberries tumbled to the forest floor.

I opened my mouth to protest, but Henry cut me off. "I accept." He turned to me. "That is . . . if Lady Alicia does."

My eyes bulged as they waited for my answer. They could not be serious. This was madness! Letting men compete for my hand in marriage, as though I were some trophy? Leaving my future up to chance? Fate? After everything I'd done? Everything I'd worked for?

Minutes ago, Henry had been moments away from proposing. Why pointlessly risk everything, when he was sure to try again?

Then again . . . I was running out of time. Only three days stood in the way of Henry's departure, and if his proposal had been interrupted twice before, who was to say it wouldn't happen a third time? What if the clock ran out and Henry left, having never confessed, never resolved our feelings?

I'd never seen Hawthorne fence before, but I didn't need to. I knew he couldn't beat Henry. Henry had won *three* years in a row. And, according to the Wycliffes, his competition for this year was dismal as well. He was the obvious champion and everyone knew it.

What, then, would I really be risking? I'd have the certainty of Henry's proposal—as soon as tomorrow—and wasn't that what I wanted?

When I came to this conclusion, I tried to keep my focus on Henry, on what he and Hawthorne were proposing and nothing else. But before I could stop myself, my eyes darted to Matthew, reclining against the trunk of a tree a few paces away. At first glance, he was as bored as usual, head knocked back as he chewed a stalk of wild wheat, staring out at the berry pickers. But as I looked closer, a muscle in his neck ticked.

Hawthorne held out my basket, bringing me out of my study. When had he picked it up? "You *are* in agreement, Lady Alicia?"

"Yes!" I said, before I lost the nerve. "I am in agreement. Whoever wins the tournament tomorrow shall win my hand in marriage."

"And if neither of us wins?" Henry asked.

I stared at him, sending a double message when I softly said, "Then I can only give my hand to someone who proposes."

A hint of a smile touched Henry's lips.

Hawthorne beamed. "Excellent news. My lady, I regret to say I haven't the time to find your bouquets at the moment—I must go practice my swordplay. It's been an age since I last fenced, and I need to freshen my skills. Oh, but I am looking forward to tomorrow. And what a funny thing that Wycliffe—the man *actually* engaged to Lady Alicia—won't be competing at all!"

Hawthorne burst out laughing and Henry cracked a grin. But I didn't, and I didn't know why. Two weeks ago, I would've laughed at the irony until I was beside myself with giddiness. Now, that reaction felt wrong. Too flippant. Too painful.

Hawthorne's laughter still ringing, Matthew flicked his stalk into the bushes and tracked past us, face unreadable. A sick feeling sank into my stomach.

"I shall see you both tomorrow, then," I said with a curtsy. Then before either of them could persuade me to stay, I plunged into the foliage after Matthew. I didn't catch up until we were emerging from the forest.

"Are you angry with me?" I asked, panting to keep up with him.

"No." He strode across the lawn and angled away from the house, toward the wisteria tunnel.

"You are even fouler than usual."

"I could say the same to you."

Me? In a foul mood? When I was so close to getting everything I'd ever wanted? Absurd. "Are you not curious? How Henry and Hawthorne know our engagement is a farce?"

"No."

"Because you already know the answer?"

He halted and turned on me, face calm but eyes hard. "Because I don't care."

I reared back like I'd been slapped, more offended by his words than I had any right to be. From the day we first met, he'd made his feelings about me perfectly clear, sparing nothing, softening nothing. So why did I expect him to now? Why did I expect him to protest until he was red in the face and demand that I not go?

The words shouldn't have hurt.

But they did.

I lifted my chin. "Why are you not launching into a tirade about how foolish I am being, how you don't want any part of it?" Without answering me, he dove into the wisteria tunnel. I huffed and trailed at his heels, determined to get some answers. "Smaller things have set you off, and I don't see why this should be an exception—"

Gravel crunched as he whirled around. "Because you are already aware of your foolhardiness; you just don't care. And because this time, my lady, no matter what you do—push me, pull me, coax me or threaten—I *already* won't be taking any part in it. Not if you offered me the world. Not if you held a pistol to my skull. Even if you managed to drag me down there and bring me to my knees in front of a sea of onlookers, I still *won't*. Do you understand? Not this time."

I blinked, taken aback at the sudden passion spiking his voice. At the anger boiling under his calm exterior, only visible because his façade was cracking.

His fiery eyes blinked away and he sat on the bench. After whisking out a hidden book, he opened it and began reading, not even bothering to flip through the pages or find his place. Apparently any spot would do. He was trying desperately hard to remain composed, but judging by his thinned lips and tight grip on the spine, he wasn't succeeding.

I crossed my arms and let silence echo in the tunnel. Matthew persisted in reading, doing a magnificent job of ignoring me, standing before him. Eliza's words rang in my ears. *We hardly saw him—and when we did, he was never without a book. Never without a shield.*

"What are you hiding?" I said quietly, eyes narrowing. "What is behind those books of yours?"

His gaze stumbled over something on the page, before continuing to scan. "Nothing."

"Really? Because I am half convinced, Matthew, that the reason you do not give an answer is because you do not know it."

He scoffed. "Perhaps you are right. Perhaps I do not. But when I do not know an answer, I make one up, because I am the one supposed to *have* all the answers. That is what people expect of me." He flipped a page in his book, muttering darkly, "It is what I expect of myself." He continued reading, but now it was entirely for show. His eyes skimmed the pages much too quickly for him to be reading in earnest.

When he said nothing more I raised my chin, a surge of contradicting emotions pulling me both toward him and away—and keeping me perfectly balanced right where I was. He may not know what he was hiding behind all those books, but I did.

A heart.

Why did he try to rid himself of the tender thing, treating it like a nuisance, a vice, a thing to be ashamed of? Over the years, he'd tried so hard to harden it, but hadn't quite been successful. And now his heart was something strange and in-between. Not hard enough to hate, and not soft enough to love. It merely beat, never knowing who it should beat *for*. It was the diamond beneath his unfeeling front, and what a fool he was for wanting to bury it away.

"You are the smartest man I know." The words slipped off my tongue and I breathed an empty laugh. "You defend those who cannot defend themselves, and show tenderness at the strangest times. I once believed you to be arrogant and unfeeling, but you've stripped me of that notion with every earnest glance. Every touch. By all accounts you are the perfect man—you know everything about everything. And yet, when it comes to trust, and love, the only things that really matter . . . it would seem you know nothing."

Matthew blew a puff of air. "You speak nonsense."

"Do I? Well, I am sure you are right, as you do know *everything*, Matthew." I thought I'd managed to have the last word, but just as I twisted around, Matthew slammed his book shut and stood.

"You accuse me of pretending to know more than I do, but what an ironic thing, Alicia—when you do the same." He came around me, forcing me to look into his sparking eyes. Warning bells pealed in the back of my mind.

Using his book to point down the tunnel, he said, "I will readily admit I am not an expert when it comes to handling relationships— but you are a hypocrite to stand there and pretend that you *are*. Begrudging though they may be, at least I can speak two words of love toward my family. Whereas you cannot even look your father in the eye."

His words embedded into my chest like arrows loosed from a bow, made more violent by his closeness. I wasn't prepared for this line of attack. "Stop this," I whispered through gritted teeth.

Matthew ignored me. "Everything you do, you do to get his attention. All the lies, the scandals. You think there is no other way to get it, too afraid that if you simply asked for it, he would reject you. This entire scheme—winning Henry back—it's not about Henry at all. It's about your father. When Henry is around, he pays attention to you and acts like he cares—and so you cannot abide to lose Henry, because that would mean losing your father as well."

"I said stop this!" All my defenses crumbled away into oblivion at his blows. How *dare* he use that stupid perceptiveness of his to shred my heart into little pieces. "I am not some spoiled child acting out to get attention. And for the very last time, I am in *love*!"

Matthew looked me up and down like he didn't believe me, at last murmuring, "Of course you are."

Angered at that, I decided to turn it back on him. "You live in your house to keep your father's memory, and attend balls you despise because it was your mother's wish. You hide your hurt over the past, your reluctance for the future—anything that would make you appear human. But you cannot let anyone know that. No. Far better to push them away and then insist they are beneath your notice."

I stepped forward, digging a finger into his chest. "You give *such* a show of knowing everything about everyone—their innermost desires and feelings—when you barely even know those things about yourself!"

His nostrils flared and he swatted my hand away. "I know I do not want a wife. I know I never have."

"Is that so."

"I enjoy being alone."

"A lie."

"Especially when yours is the only company open to me."

"Another lie."

"Oh, by all England, of course it's a lie!" He slammed the book onto the bench. The powerful *thud* made me flinch. "My parents had as happy a marriage as any. My brother and sister are happily married as well—but you see, in their spouses, they each found their equal. They found someone who complements them in every way. There is no such person for me. And if I cannot marry my equal, then I truly have no wish to marry."

I folded my arms. "You do my sex a great injustice. There are many women who are your equal, Matthew."

"Name *one*."

"Me."

I regretted the word the moment it left my lips. Not because it wasn't true, but because for the first time, I knew that it was.

And contrary to what I expected, Matthew did not deny it either. The sudden silence rang in my ears and the moment stretched into an eternity, on and on until it was a lifetime of its own. He relaxed, brows furrowing as he glanced between my eyes. His Adam's apple bobbed. At last, he murmured, "But tomorrow Henry shall win the tournament . . . and then you will marry him instead."

My blinking stuttered, unsure which word to focus on in that one loaded sentence. *But, will, Henry . . . instead.*

I shrugged, trying to show that I didn't feel helpless and hopeless and impossibly small. "Which is what we both want," I said quietly.

"Yes." Matthew turned away, but not before I saw something flash in his eyes. "What we both want." He strode out of the tunnel, never once looking back.

CHAPTER 25

I WAS ON THE CLIFFS AGAIN, ENSCONCED IN AN ALMOST-TANGIBLE *dimness. In the distance, my mother stood on a craggy outcropping, speaking a farewell with her eyes. Blackness slithered around her, eating at her ankles, knees, waist, neck . . . until it had consumed her completely.*

"Mother!" I cried, hand shooting out, tears in my eyes. "No! Do not leave me!"

As if the shadows heard me, they froze, then turned my way. They inched toward me, drawing the life out of everything between us. My heart beat faster—each beat a punch to the chest.

"I would never leave you," Matthew murmured beside me.

But when I turned toward the voice, it was Henry I saw. His cool grey eyes wrapped around me, a safe harbor in the dimness. I flung into his arms, sobbing, clinging to his jacket. He had saved me. He would always save me.

He held stiff, not returning the embrace. "Alicia," he said with a strangled voice—his voice.

I pulled back. Then gasped in horror when I saw the blackness curl around his ankles like eagle's talons. Henry looked up, and I expected his face to mirror my terror—but it didn't. His expression held calm, a resigned gleam in his eye. As if he always knew this would happen.

No. No, no, Henry, it cannot take you too!

The cliff wall beneath him crumbled. He reached for me, but his hand slipped down my arm, ripping off my glove.

"Henry!" *I screamed.*

He fell backward. I screamed again. And the last thing I saw before the darkness consumed him, was a wad of white fabric, stark against the shadows, still clutched in his grasp.

My left glove.

CHAPTER 26

I TOOK A DEEP BREATH AS THE CARRIAGE ROLLED TO A STOP.

The footman swung the door open, but I didn't move to get out, letting the cool sea air permeate the carriage. My stomach was a pit of nerves, winding tighter and tighter until I had to pinch my abdomen to get a moment's reprieve. Images of my terror-filled dream flashed through my mind, casting an ominous veil over the events about to unfold.

What if Henry didn't win? What if my dream came true and I watched him tumble out of my sight forever?

When I agreed to marry the winner of the tournament, it had seemed like an obvious course of action. But after a full night of wondering and agonizing and reliving every moment of the past two weeks, it had begun to feel like a foolish choice.

A foolish, irrevocable choice.

My shaky hands curled into fists. I couldn't let Henry slip through my fingers. Not again. I would chase after him until I couldn't stand, until I couldn't breathe, and I would do anything —*anything*—to ensure my ugly dream from last night didn't become reality.

The footman, no doubt wondering why his mistress was taking so long to disembark, snapped to attention when I appeared at the carriage door. I stepped onto the wild grass and released a wobbly breath, before pushing toward the white tents down the field. To my side, other carriages had pulled off the main road, like dinghies towed ashore to avoid the pull of a river.

Aunt Beth had come down with a chill last night and was unable to accompany me today. It was improper for me to be here without a chaperone, but I wasn't about to stay home and wait for word about my future. I would see it happen with my own eyes. I would've preferred Aunt Beth's presence to being alone, even if she *did* spend the whole time berating my choices.

Misery loved company. And I was certainly miserable.

Drifts of sea lavender swayed atop the fields. Dark storm clouds crackled in the distance, blocking the sun and sending a cool breeze over the chalky cliffs. Far below, the sea coated the rocky beach in a frothy, moth-eaten dress. I gulped, uncomfortable with the similarities the setting shared with my dream.

Along the jutting ridge, canvas tents formed three walls of several rings, the cliff acting as the fourth. Multiple matches would be taking place at once, so the winners could rise through the ranks more quickly. Twenty-four competitors in all. A staked-in wooden sign bearing roughly-painted tokens of each competitor's crests stood at the center; a scoreboard for all to see. Only a hundred yards from the sign sat the little trail that wound down to mine and Henry's spot. I took it as a good omen. The only one I'd managed to find so far.

I neared the throng, scanning it for a familiar face.

"You came."

I spun to find Henry directly behind me. He wore the loose undershirt and black breeches that all the contestants wore, his fencing helmet hooked under one arm. His blond hair ruffled in the breeze above his soft smile.

I returned it. "Yes." Then, because I feared I would burst into tears if he said something serious, I said, "I wanted to be here when you win, of course."

He chuckled. "You have a lot of faith in my ability."

I didn't add that I had little choice but to have faith in it. An announcer called for the first match to begin and Henry spun toward the sound before turning back. "I need to fetch my sword." His hand found mine, giving it a squeeze. "When this is all over . . . come find me."

Not trusting myself to speak, I merely nodded and watched him depart. A flurry of activity buzzed around me—women standing on tiptoes, men shaking hands and slapping backs, children chasing each other through the maze of adults with wooden swords. I put a hand to one of the tent poles for stability.

"How well you look, Lady Alicia." Hawthorne appeared at my side, his smile stretching wider than the gaping hole in my gut. I was sure I looked the exact opposite of well. "My first competition is scheduled after this one. Have you come to witness me win your hand?" He gave his sword a few test swipes, sending a few women yelping and scattering back. He didn't seem to notice, though, grin still permanently in place.

"You know me so well, my lord," I said in a bland tone that sounded like Matthew.

I cringed. I didn't want to think of Matthew right now. In fact, I wanted to think of anything else. I'd rather imagine myself as Lady Hawthorne, Duchess of Cabourne, than imagine what he was doing right now. What he was thinking. What he *wasn't* thinking.

Hawthorne hopped from foot to foot, stretching his arms. "Never fear, my lady! I was up all last night practicing, and didn't get a wink of sleep!"

The news should've been relieving—for if he'd been up all night, he was sure to tip over in his first match—but it did little to settle my nerves. And I didn't know why. If the fight wasn't between Henry and Hawthorne, then who was it between?

The circle surrounding the ring tightened, more bodies pressing in to witness the beginning of the match. Wind whipped my hair, sending blond tendrils across my face—but I didn't tuck them away. I was too riveted by the two figures poised in the center, ready to begin, heads completely covered by their masks; I was watching my future hang in the balance, knowing it would tip with every strike of the sword.

My stomach turned over. I wasn't ready for this. *Oh Henry, please win. For me, you must win.*

The officiator blew a conch shell, announcing the start of the tournament.

♞

THERE WERE TWO WAYS TO WIN A MATCH: EITHER SCORE THE most points with nicks and disarming maneuvers within the time constraints, or manage to poise your sword in a killing blow—near the neck or chest.

The ringing of striking metal mingled with the distant thunder, too far away to be a threat but still ominous. Sprinkled clapping erupted down the field when a round finished, only to be replaced with more ringing steel. Somewhere in the distance, a recognizable giggle squealed, accompanied by fits of laughter.

Though I didn't care to be alone, I also didn't care to be in Lady Prima's company at the moment. She would only question me about my engagement and force me to pretend like I loved Matthew, when I didn't.

I *didn't.*

I squeezed my midsection against another onslaught of anxiety.

On and on it went. Match after match, narrowing down the contestants to eighteen, then sixteen . . . twelve . . . then six. I breathed a sigh of relief every time a round ended and Henry was still standing. Hawthorne had managed to survive this far, too—thanks to several of his opponents stumbling on rocks or getting their feet caught in a patch of mud.

During the next round though, Hawthorne was eliminated, and a spark of hope lit in my belly, melting my knot of nerves. He walked off the field with his head hung low, his face devoid of a smile, for once.

The worst of it was over. From here, Henry had a clear path to victory.

The winners dwindled to five, four, three, until finally, there was only one more opponent Henry had to face before he'd be crowned champion. I bounced in eagerness, my toes curling inside my shoes.

With no other matches taking place, everyone who'd been spread out along the cliffs gathered near to watch the final fight, forming a tight wall of bodies fifteen people deep.

The officiator walked to the center, announcing the tokens of the final contestants and eliciting another round of uproarious applause. The wind picked up, shooting down the field in strong, short gusts, making the two remaining contestants' shirts flatten against their torsos. Raising their swords, they held steady, poised to begin.

With their heads completely covered, it was difficult to tell which figure was Henry. They were both equally tall, but I finally settled on the one with slightly broader shoulders. When the conch shell sounded and they jumped to action, I knew I'd guessed right. Henry's skill was evident in the way he moved, with confidence and grace. Like the sword was an extension of him.

Because this was the final match, it had no time limits. If someone won the tournament, it would be through a potential killing blow.

Jab for jab, parry for parry, they continued, equally matched in both strength and speed. Henry managed to nick his opponent on the arm, but he was losing ground. Slowly, he inched backward, toward the cliffs. My dream flashed before my eyes, and panic clawed up my throat.

A man pushed his way forward, blocking my view of the fight. I nearly grabbed his red coat and yanked him out of the way—but stopped myself when I saw his bicorn hat and the little bullet hole in its center.

Now panic coursed through my blood for a completely different reason. He turned back and noticed me. I ducked my head and covered it with my hand for extra measure.

"Can ya see all right, lass?" he asked, Irish brogue heavy.

I gulped and squeaked out, "Yes. Fine." He hadn't recognized me yet.

Somehow, he managed to hear me through the cacophony, because he laughed. "Well not with yer eyes covered like tha'." He grabbed my hand and attempted to pull it away from my face. I struggled to conceal myself, wishing I'd had the sense to run when I still could.

Oh bother, oh *bother*! It was now or never.

He grunted as I shoved him away and dove into the crowd, using the sway of startled onlookers as a cover. A few people cried out in protest, but I didn't look back until I'd circled around to the other side of the ring, where I could watch him from a distance.

What was I to do? I didn't know if the corporal had recognized me or not. I didn't want to risk him spotting me again, necessitating another chase, but I couldn't leave the fight without knowing how it ended. To my luck, someone had abandoned their shawl a few paces to my left. Not caring whose it was, I pushed through the crowd and snatched it up before wrapping it over my hair, ready to cover my face if the Irishman happened to look my way.

The cheers around me rose to a feverish pitch, so loud it made my ears ring. My eyes snapped to the field, where Henry and his opponent were blocking and swiping and dodging so quickly their limbs blurred. It took me a long moment to identify Henry. They were both so swift, so skilled.

Sweat clung to their shirts, but they pushed through, neck and neck, neither willing to surrender. Lightning flashed in the distance, glinting off their steel.

His opponent saw an opening and lunged.

A fatal mistake.

Henry feinted right and knocked him away, sending his sword tumbling to the grass. His opponent rushed to reclaim his sword, but just as he turned back to strike, Henry knocked it back out of his hand and pushed him onto his knees, levelling his own sword at his neck. The crowd bellowed and clapped even louder, women screamed and fainted. Handkerchiefs and flags waved in the air.

Henry had won.

The conch shell blew three times and the crowd surged, rushing to congratulate the contenders. I watched as Henry immediately backed away and slipped through the crowd. When I watched another moment longer, I saw why. He darted toward the edge of the cliff and disappeared down the little path, unnoticed by his adoring throng.

Come find me.

He knew I was watching, knew I'd follow him to somewhere more private. Our little corner on the beach was the perfect place, and he was leading me there.

Abandoning the shawl, I picked up my skirts and followed after him. When I finally made it to the top of the hidden trail, he was already on the beach, heading toward the cubbyholes. I half-ran down the trail, hopping over bushes and almost slipping on loose pebbles.

I chased after him, but he was fast, his long legs maintaining the distance between us. "Henry!" He didn't turn around. I cupped a hand to my mouth. *"Henry!"*

He halted and twisted around.

I lifted my skirts again and ran down the sand, stopping when I was nearly ten paces from him. Out of breath, I smiled. "Are you not going to let anyone congratulate you?"

He didn't say anything, just stood stock still, mask still in place. Was he suddenly shy at what his victory meant?

The thought made me smile wider. "Are you not going to let *me* congratulate you?"

Henry lifted a hand to his mask.

I flung into his arms just as he took it off. And then I kissed him, full on the mouth. I combed my fingers through his hair, pouring all my heart into him, imagining our future together, telling him I loved him in a way that no words could.

I needed this. A perfect release of all the confusing, pent-up emotions that had been swirling inside me for two weeks. A release of the painful angst that had hardened in my chest, ever since I'd agreed to marry the winner of the tournament.

He'd won. For me. Because he loved me, and wished to marry me.

The kiss was glorious. Golden. Full of setting suns and quiet forests. His lips slid against mine so tenderly, so pleadingly, I ached inside. Deeper, deeper . . . more . . . more . . . His hands pushed into my hair.

But, in the middle of kissing him, I realized something felt wrong. No—not *wrong*. Strange.

These lips were fuller than Henry's. I caught a whiff of pine, and some dark hair in my periphery. Recognition jolted through me, and I broke the kiss and reared back. My heart dropped into my stomach, and then into my feet.

For the very first time in our acquaintance, Matthew Wycliffe stood completely at a loss for words. He blinked at me. I blinked at him.

"What . . ." he said softly, ". . . the devil . . . was that."

CHAPTER 27

ALL THE BLOOD THAT HAD DRAINED FROM MY FACE CAME rushing back tenfold. I had just kissed Matthew Wycliffe. Not Henry. *Matthew*. My nemesis. And it wasn't terrible.

No, it was *magnificent*.

Oh, this was very bad.

I stared at his lips—*Matthew's* lips—trying to imagine how they could be the cause of a kiss like that. They were pink, slightly swollen, and looking more inviting than they should. My stomach tightened and I jolted back to reality.

I shook my head. No. No, this couldn't be happening. How had Matthew won the tournament? He'd never fenced in his life! My eyes flew to his sleeve, slightly torn and bloodied where Henry had nicked him. But Matthew had been the one to win, I was sure of it —I'd watched him go from holding a sword to Henry's neck, to wading through the crowd and slipping away.

It was that Irishman. If I hadn't been distracted by him, I would've realized Henry had lost. I wouldn't have followed Matthew down here and—and—

Had he cheated somehow? Had he really competed against all

those men and won? How had he managed to defeat Henry? And why on *earth* had he entered in the first place?

Matthew scowled and threw his fencing mask to the sand. Hard. "I did not ask to be kissed!"

It took me a few moments to formulate any words, and when I did, all that came out was, "W-Why are you angry?"

"Why shouldn't I be? I have just been assaulted in the most brutal manner!"

My senses returned, one by one. I put my hands on my hips. "Oh, I am sorry," I said with forced sarcasm. "How repulsive it must've been for you. I shall remember to spare you my accidental affections in the future."

"I am not angry because it was repulsive," Matthew snapped, "I am angry because it wasn't." A pause, then his eyes went wide. So did mine. His jaw clenched. "By all England. Alicia, you make me say the *stupidest* things!" He spun on his heel and stormed down the beach.

Mouth ajar, I huffed and sputtered for a moment.

I followed after him, tromping across the beach while the wind whistled against the bluffs. Clambering over the line of boulders blocking the path, I said, "Matthew, we need to talk about this!" When he didn't respond, I quickened my pace and caught up, kicking at the sand seeping into my slippers. "So you liked it. What a pleasant surprise!"

He growled something unintelligible.

I couldn't resist teasing him a little. "I must say, I am all astonishment. But I do have nice lips, so I suppose it is not a total shock. To think we could've been kissing all this time! Oh, but what a lot of fun we could have had."

"Go away."

"But you must find me attractive then, contrary to your numerous disavowals on the subject—"

He spun back, bringing me to an abrupt halt before him. We were at mine and Henry's spot, the cubbyholes in the cliffs to my right. Black storm clouds rumbled on the ocean's turbulent horizon.

"Is that what you want me to say?" he spat. "You want me to admit it for all the world to hear?"

He stepped back, flung his arms out, and spun in an agitated circle. "Yes! I admit it. I find you attractive. I find you *disturbingly* attractive, so much so that it drives me mad. How shall I describe it? Ah yes, like a spear in my side, or a boulder in my shoe. Like I am the road on which Spanish bulls run—but instead of it occurring only once a year, it is every hour of every day, without a pause, without reprieve—every moment since that blasted night on the balcony.

"And how am I to rid myself of it? This dreadful, torturous attraction? I've no idea! Despite my best efforts, I have been unable to—and for that reason alone I loathe it. I loathe it with such passion I will do anything in the world to make it stop."

My mouth dropped open. "*What?*"

In the silence that followed, Matthew's face relaxed out of its scowl. His lips parted, as if the words that had flown from them surprised him just as much as they surprised me. He fidgeted, licking his lips and stalking to the left, then the right. It made me nervous. I'd never seen him so unsure of himself. So utterly misplaced.

At last I said, "How did you win?"

"I . . ." He halted. "Fencing is a—a hobby of mine."

I folded my arms and put on a dubious expression.

"Fine," he said. "I fence a *great deal*. What of it?"

I studied his figure again, spotting the toned muscle that I had never noticed before now. A moment from the tunnel drifted into my mind, the one where I'd held that rusty sword.

"You are surprisingly adept with that."

"Adept enough to run you through."

He scoffed. "I should like to see that."

"Does your family know?" I asked.

"No—no one knows. I've learnt in secret with a private tutor."

"How long?"

"Six years."

My eyebrows came together. "Right after your mother died?"

He huffed. "Deuces—yes, if you must know. Now will you cease the interrogation?"

I ignored him. "Why have you not competed before? They hold the tournament here every year, and you thrashed Henry, the best swordsman I know. You could've been easily winning all this time."

"I don't care for adulation."

I shook my head. Then why compete now? I didn't understand it. Henry had been about to win, and once he did, he would propose. This whole nightmare had been about to be over, and wasn't that what Matthew wanted?

Matthew's mouth snapped shut. He looked away, unwilling to say anything more.

Slowly, an explanation dawned on me, but it was so outlandish it took me several more moments to voice it.

"You . . . you did not *want* . . . me to marry Henry. That's why you did this."

His eyes darted to me, once, before returning to the ground.

"That's it, isn't it."

He kept silent, holding completely still.

I put my hands on my hips. "*Isn't* it."

"I did not want you to kiss me either," he muttered.

That was as good as a confession.

I snatched his mask from the sand and shook it in his face. "So you decided to crush my only chance at happiness? With this? In some misguided effort to repair your pride? I was so close!"

"Oh, for all the—!" He gripped his hair. "It is true I may have ruined everything, Alicia, but by all England, so have you."

"I?" I tossed the mask away. "What have I ruined?"

"You *kissed* me."

"And what is wrong with that?" I meant, of course, besides literally everything. I was supposed to be in love with Henry, not kissing Matthew or constantly thinking about how thoughtful and gentle he was; about how safe I'd felt in his arms. But Matthew's objection made no sense. At most, he should've been indifferent, or disgusted —emotions I had come to expect from him whenever it concerned me. But angry?

"Because," he said softly through his teeth, eyes sparking, "I've been doing my utmost to ignore this attraction, and now with that stupid kiss, you've made it ten times bloody worse."

The world around me spun in a circle. I scoffed—a sound half chuckle, half disbelief. Then the full force of what he was admitting to hit me, and everything clicked together.

That moment in the tavern when Matthew didn't want to flirt with me. How he always tensed when I touched him. All the insults, the steely eyes, the frowns of disdain and looks of disgust— they were never directed at me at all, but at his own feelings. He was attracted to me, and desperately wished that he wasn't.

He could barely keep it in check.

I may have thought I was kissing Henry—but Matthew knew it was me the moment I threw my arms around him. For all his accusations and angry words, he hadn't tried to stop me. He had melted into the embrace.

And he had kissed me right back.

A slow smile pulled at my lips. I couldn't help it. The stoic Matthew Wycliffe—so besotted with me he thought about me day and night? The woman he hated above all others? No wonder he glared at me so. It must have been absolutely maddening. And when I got through with teasing him for it, that glare of his was going to burn holes in my skin.

He watched me quietly as I approached him. But instead of frowning like he always did, he looked almost . . . worried. "Please don't . . ." He trailed off, blinking rapidly.

All his dignity and condescension crumbled as the distance between us shrank, until it lay in a heap at his feet. When we came toe to toe, I crunched it underfoot. He gulped, alarm lighting in his eyes. I cocked my head and smirked. "Only *ten* times worse?" I slid my hands up his arms and across his shoulders, interlocking them behind his bare neck.

A misting of sweat from the tournament covered his forehead, making his hair damp at the temples. He stopped breathing, and I thought I felt him shudder underneath my touch. He swallowed again. "Twelve at the most."

"Fifteen."

"Thirteen. And not a jot more."

I pulled on his neck to bring his lips closer. He resisted by putting his hands on my waist. But it was a half-hearted attempt, and I managed to shrink the distance a few more inches.

"Interesting number," I murmured with a smile, twirling the hair at the nape of his neck. "The same amount as our children." My fingers crept up into his hair until they were buried deep at the back of his head. It was so thick, so glorious. I thought I saw his eyes roll back before he shut them.

"Please stop, Alicia." The words were airy.

I drew his head down to nuzzle his nose with mine. His lips were so close. "Stop what?"

"Stop—" He inhaled a shaky breath. "—Stop touching me."

"That's right. I forgot you do not like it."

His eyes snapped open, pupils so large they looked like two black moons. "I don't like when anyone touches me. *Except* you. And that is why I wish you wouldn't."

But he didn't pull back or nudge me away. He held perfectly still. Minute twitches of his features showcased the inner battle he was waging. One little prod from me could tip the scales. And I wasn't certain why I wanted to tip the scales—only that it made my head swim and my blood heat, and I doubted I would ever tire of the feeling. I doubted I would ever catch him off guard and figuratively bring him to his knees like this again.

"But darling, you *know* I am madly in love with you."

That made Matthew freeze. Slowly, his eyes locked onto mine, and what I saw there made my smile slacken.

Fear.

He swallowed, gaze dropping until his lashes splayed against his cheeks. "As . . . as I am with you," he murmured.

The scene around me tipped, sloshing the waves and the beach around until they circled a single thought. Something in the way he said it shifted everything. Shifted it from our normal playacting, into something . . . real.

But it couldn't be real. Every one of Matthew's actions was born out of anger or resignation. That must be the case here, too. He was toying with me. He was toying with me and I would toy with him back. I made my voice sound light. Unconcerned. "That . . . That would be a very foolish thing to do, Mr. Wycliffe. To fall in love with me."

He kept his eyes lowered, like he was ashamed of something. His mouth moved, soundlessly, before he finally whispered, "I know."

"We argue incessantly."

"I know."

"You could not find a more ill-suited pair."

"I *know*."

"And of course there's Henry. I love him more than I love you, you know."

His lashes raised with his eyes. His gaze deepened, something flickering inside it.

Attraction.

"Do you?" He leaned in closer, stealing my breath away. A lock of hair fell onto his forehead, his pine scent washing over me.

Oh heaven help me. Could I say I loved Henry? Not in this moment. How *could* I, when all I could think about was how close Matthew was? About how it had felt to wrap my arms around him and feel his heated lips on mine?

"Well then, my lady, I'm liable to be overwrought with jealousy.

And then I might do something reckless, like steal the kiss intended for him. You are, after all, still *my* fiancée."

Anticipation.

It hit me with a flurry of wings in my stomach, with a rush of longing in my mouth. I held my breath, frightened at the realization that I wanted Matthew to kiss me. Desperately. I didn't know why, or when that had changed, but remembering what he tasted like—like a deep forest, like books and mysteries, like gentleness and glory wrapped in one—made me realize I wanted to do it again. To do it *knowing* who it was this time.

"Only until Henry proposes."

More playacting. *It is pretend, it is pretend.* I knew that same attraction was glowing in my eyes too, burning and building and flooding my senses.

"Then we don't have much time, do we?" he muttered. And before I knew what was happening, Matthew had backed me up against the cliff and was standing over me with a desperate look in his eye.

His hands—those warm, tender hands of his—lifted and slowly skimmed along my cheeks until they cradled my head. Like he was afraid to break me. His thumbs slid under my jaw, prodding my head up ever so slightly. Tipping my lips up toward his.

Wind tousled his hair and made his billowy undershirt flap at the collar, exposing his collarbone.

He was so tall. So fiercely handsome. So close.

My heart pounded in my ears, drowning out the sound of the waves crashing on the shore. This was the same challenge as in the tavern, and after the chess game, where we both refused to back down. Prodding each other toward the edge, seeing which of us would lose their balance and plummet to their deaths. We'd walk any dangerous line before admitting what we really thought. What we really felt. But unlike the other times, this moment was somehow softer and more intense at the same time. More momentous, more irreversible.

I was frightened of it, of what it meant. But what frightened me most of all was the uncertainty woven through Matthew's features. He was never unsure of himself. Never did he not know exactly what to say, exactly what to do. Exactly what he wanted.

I didn't know what I wanted either—all I knew was that Matthew felt like something out of a secret dream, wild and different and totally unexpected. I remembered his words from the alley. *If ever I were to marry, it would be to someone I never saw coming . . .* I knew now exactly what he'd meant. But then—

You, my lady, are the most predictable woman I have ever met.

That one sentence plagued the caverns of my mind, its echoes wrapping my heart in a firm grip and squeezing out all the drops of hope that had accumulated there. I couldn't breathe.

Matthew . . .

I couldn't do this. I had to know. "Did you see this coming, too?" My voice was soft but tight; strained as I tried to keep my longing in check.

Ever so slightly, Matthew shuffled closer, his eyes deepening into something almost celestial; the stars and the moon were envious of his gaze. Thumb brushing over my lower lip, he whispered, "This is all I have seen for a long time."

I flattened my hands against the cliff. One of them met air, before wrapping around a hard object. Smooth ridges with a blunt, spiraling point. Without looking, I knew what it was. The shell.

Happy birthday, Alicia.

Images flooded my mind. A dark closet. Yearning glances. Seashells. White gloves. A crumbling cliff and a man slipping out of reach forever.

Henry.

Matthew's head descended. Closer . . . closer . . .

Whatever game Matthew was playing was just that—a game. How childish I must seem to him; just a girl so frantic for love that she'd kiss the wrong man under a stormy sky.

Women tend to value love above all else. When it is offered, compro-

mised, or taken away, it evokes patterns of behavior that are, in a word, predictable. If Matthew foresaw this moment, as he'd foreseen everything else about me, then he didn't love me—*couldn't*, as he'd so thoroughly explained.

Whereas Henry . . .

Henry did.

"No," I ground the word out, forcing my senses to return. I couldn't do it. I couldn't kiss him again when he didn't love me.

Matthew froze. Behind me, I gripped the shell so tightly my arm shook, and I was sure I'd broken skin. He let go of my face and backed away, blinking out of a daze.

"I am in love with Henry." I said it more for my benefit than his, solidifying my resolve and clinging to it with desperation.

Matthew's Adam's apple bobbed. "Of course you are." He turned away and put his head in his hand, before smoothing it back through his hair. "Of *course* you are," he said quieter.

What on earth was that supposed to mean?

"Yes," I said, "of course I am. He's only the whole reason we did all this in the first place. I never would have enlisted your help if I wasn't certain of my feelings for him."

"Yes. Wonderful." Matthew's face shuttered closed, lapsing into his usual annoyed look. There was an edge to it I'd never seen. Something sharp and almost spiteful.

But I didn't want to think on that—or on the way my heart suddenly felt like lead. This was my path, and I wouldn't be deterred from it.

I put the shell back on the cliff shelf. "We still have time before Henry ships away. I'm sure sometime in the next two days he'll find an opportunity to propose. In the meantime, you and I shall have to continue keeping up appearances—"

"No."

I pushed off the cliff, straightening. The word wasn't loud, but it echoed with finality.

Matthew shook his head, grimacing like he tasted something

bitter. "No. No, I cannot do this anymore. Release me from the engagement."

My lips parted, my leaden heart falling to the sand. "But . . . But Henry has not yet proposed—"

"He will. A *blind* man can see that he will. You have been stalling the inevitable because you are afraid of accepting it. And as I can no longer stomach being a front row spectator, for heaven's sake, release me and go and be happy together."

I blinked at him, not knowing what to say.

When I didn't say anything, Matthew prompted, "I've fulfilled my end of the bargain three times over. As a gentleman, I cannot walk away from the commitment unless you release me."

I licked my lips. "We still have a few days left—"

"We both know they won't make a jot of difference."

I glanced around the shore, at the jutting rocks that looked like obsidian knives, feeling like I'd just been skewered by one.

"*Release* me."

I opened my mouth. No words came. None that Matthew wanted to hear. Why was this so difficult? Why couldn't I let him go? Matthew's right hand fidgeted at his side.

I hesitated, biting my lip, feeling smaller than the grains of sand beneath my feet. "But . . . why . . . ?"

His hands fisted. "Blast it all, Alicia, just do it!"

That revived my fire. "If you hadn't sabotaged my efforts, I would be spouting it from the rooftops!"

He kicked a puff of sand. "Don't you dare pin this on me. You have dragged me around on one mad scheme after another. I roamed a dark tunnel, rescued you from soldiers—deuces, I *flirted* with you—all because you wished it, and in exchange you made me a promise. All I ask is that you fulfill it."

My head shook in such small motions I feared it would vibrate off my neck. I didn't understand. Why was he asking this of me when I was so close to achieving my goal? But that thought was quickly trailed by an ugly explanation—one that, to my horror, made my eyes prickle with rising tears.

Matthew may have been attracted to me, but that didn't mean he hated me any less. In fact, it probably made him hate me more. So much so that he would compete in a tournament just to take revenge.

If ever I were to marry, it would be to someone I never saw coming.

I was too stubborn, too brazen. Too infuriating. Ultimately, far too predictable. It was because, even though I'd managed to attract and affect him, I was still not his equal, nor the person who surprised him in every way. And I never could be.

Tremulous emotions, strong and foreign crept up my throat. I didn't know where they came from, or why they surfaced—but they made me hate Matthew with such a passion I could barely breathe. Barely see. Brighter and hotter than ever before.

My hands punched the air at my sides. "If it hadn't been for you, I'd be in Henry's arms right now. I'd be—!"

He stepped forward. "Spare me the details, I can imagine the scene well enough. And if you love him so much, then go! Console him on his loss and kiss him to your heart's content! I won't care a whit."

I stepped toward him. "I never asked you to care in the first place."

"A good thing too—because I don't take orders from you anyway."

"As if you'd bother taking the time to listen!"

His nostrils flared. "As if I need to hear it from your lips to know what you will say!"

I stomped my foot. "Ugh! You are absolutely insufferable!"

"The best compliment you've ever given me."

"How remiss of me," I spat. "I can do much better. Matthew Wycliffe, you are the most horrid, excruciating, hateful man I've ever had the misfortune to meet. And if you *ever* dare kiss me again, I vow I shall slap your irritating face!"

"No need. I'd spare you the trouble and slap it for you—because kissing you would be the absolute stupidest thing I'd ever done. And if I didn't die from my own blow, I would surely die of self-loathing."

"If *I* didn't die of repulsion first!"

"Finally something on which we agree—death is preferable to sharing another kiss."

I bared my teeth. "Fine."

"Fine."

"Fine!"

"Deuces, fine!"

Our chests heaved, our eyes burned with anger. But after a few moments passed, I noticed we only stood half a breath away. So close, that if I leaned just slightly in, our lips would meet again.

I froze.

Matthew seemed to realize it at the same moment, because slowly, his face relaxed out of its rage. His blinking stuttered, flashing down my face then up.

From the first day, he'd been trying to rid himself of me, telling me over and over to leave him alone; but I'd been too desperate to be loved to listen.

A hundred memories flashed through my mind. Whispers in a dark castle. Brushing shoulders in an alleyway. Warm hands. Soft eyes. A golden smile gracing his face when I pretended to be his sister—a smile so rare and blinding that I would do anything in the world to see it again. With these memories came a heartache stronger than any other I'd felt.

And as horrifying as this was, the realization that came with the tear slipping down my cheek was even worse.

I loved him.

Not Hawthorne. Not Henry. *Matthew.* The tall, condescending man who was not part of the bargain. A man who could never be my husband because my hand was already promised. A man who wanted nothing to do with me. This was a chase between Henry and Hawthorne—but somewhere in all the mess, I'd started chasing after someone else entirely. I'd pretended to love Matthew so convincingly that I'd even convinced myself.

If you do not take care, Aunt Beth had said, *you will lose your heart before the end—regardless of which man you marry.*

Matthew was everything I knew him to be from our first meeting on the balcony—dismissive, assuming, rude. But he was so much more than that. He was brilliant. Compassionate. Wonderfully different. Unexpectedly soft.

And now, knowing what a predictable girl I was, knowing I would never see it coming, he'd made me fall in love with him. Out of anger or spite or whatever it was—it didn't matter. All I knew was that I'd been lost to him from the beginning.

In both anger and pain, in both attraction and hurt, Matthew had managed to make me feel more than Henry ever had. And now that we would cut ties . . . Now I would never feel anything again.

My eyes filled up with tears, and this time, I let them fall. Matthew was right. I had ruined everything.

His eyes traced one of them as it fell down the same cheek he'd kissed. Something unnameable crept into his gaze. His brows pulled together ever so slightly, his lashes fluttered, his lips parted, he inhaled like he wanted to say something.

"I release you from our engagement," I whispered.

That snapped Matthew out of his stupor. He blinked at me for a moment, then swallowed. He straightened up. "Thank you," he said. But he didn't look relieved. He looked somehow . . . disappointed. Accusatory, even. He took a step back, then another, and finally turned and stalked away, leaving me to stare after him until he disappeared down the beach.

More liquid dripped onto my dress, onto the sand, staining it dark, raising the ocean level until I was fighting against the tide to stay afloat. I swiped at my face with my arm. I didn't want to cry. I certainly didn't want to cry over *him.* But the tears kept coming and my heart kept aching and soon I couldn't hold myself up anymore.

Collapsing onto a boulder, I hugged my knees to my chest, letting myself drown.

♞

I DIDN'T KNOW HOW MUCH TIME PASSED BEFORE HENRY FOUND me, huddled in a ball and my tears dry, but the sky was darkening.

"There you are. I've been searching all over for you."

I stared at his shiny black boots, not possessing the strength to even lift my head and meet his eyes.

"I should've known you'd come here." His boots shifted in the sand, burrowing deeper and sending a few grains over his toes. The lightning and thunder in the distance had stopped, leaving a gloomy cloud cover to follow in its wake.

"I wasn't thinking straight after losing the tournament," Henry went on. "I still don't know who the man was, but he was incredible. Had to push myself harder and faster until I'd fairly reached the breaking point. And yet with every move he made, I got the sense that he was barely even trying. That the only reason the match went on as long as it did was because he let it. I've never fenced anyone like him. You don't happen to know who he was, do you?"

I tried to swallow, but it hit a lump.

Henry settled beside me on the boulder, sparing me from an answer. "At least it wasn't Hawthorne. That much is for certain."

He didn't seem to notice my puffy eyes, or the way I turned away to hide my face. Though I was grateful for it, I couldn't help but wonder why. Why he didn't notice. Why he'd fought in the tournament for me. Why he'd stayed by my side all these years. Why he was choosing to leave.

Why he loved me, when there wasn't anything to love.

". . . Alicia? Are you well?"

"I am fine." I inhaled a shaky breath and stood, brushing off my dress.

"You are not disappointed? That I lost?"

I twisted back and finally met his gaze. A worried crease darkened his forehead, his blinking rapid. *Oh, Henry.* He was always so good. So thoughtful.

"No. No, of course not."

"It doesn't matter, anyway. Who won." He stood and took my hands in his. "All that matters is that it wasn't Hawthorne. And now finally . . . *finally* . . . we are alone."

My frame sagged, suddenly exhausted from standing. My vision flickered. "Yes."

He tucked my hands against his chest, brushing a kiss along my knuckles and staring deeply into my eyes. "Will you marry me, Alicia?"

The air rushed out of my lungs, and my knees buckled. Henry scooped his arm around and caught me, but not before I'd taken a step back. Not before I felt my ankle hit something solid in the sand. I glanced down at it and blinked.

I would never leave you.

Henry's grip around my waist tightened. He pulled me closer . . . closer . . .

Images flooded my mind. A shadowy castle. Longing glances. Books. Pine trees. A hand cradling my head and soothing me in the dark.

Matthew.

There, on the beach, where Matthew must've somehow dropped it, was his little green book, fallen right at my feet. My heart pounded in my ears as I stared at it, hardly believing my eyes.

"Alicia?" Henry's hesitant voice catapulted me back to the present.

I snuffed the memories. What a fool I was. What a stupid, useless fool I was to open my heart and believe I could love someone. I didn't know how to love, let alone *who* to love. That much was evident in my aching, empty heart, bleeding out onto the beach.

Matthew wasn't here. Matthew didn't *want* me.

Voice quiet but determined, I said, "Yes. I will marry you."

Henry breathed a smile, a smile that grew wider the longer it sat on his face. He took me in his arms. "Oh Alicia, you've made me so happy. Now we can finally be together."

I felt stiff as I tried to return Henry's embrace. "Together."

He nuzzled into my hair, smiling against my skin. "It's what we've both wanted for so long."

My eyes darted to the little book at my feet, to the set of footprints in the sand, disappearing the way Matthew had gone. "Yes. What we both want."

CHAPTER 28

THAT NIGHT FATHER HADN'T WAITED UP FOR ME, SO I WASN'T surprised when he summoned me to his study the next morning. I paused out in the hallway to take a fortifying breath before turning the corner and stepping inside. The room smelled like sea salt and clary sage—the smells of my father, my childhood.

He sat behind his desk, not preoccupied with anything even though his desk was piled high with papers to sign and ledgers to look over. In his hand he held a soldier figurine, a mirror image of him. The stern, war-hardened hero. When I entered he didn't look up, still studying the toy soldier.

"You are to be married, then." The words were an admission of defeat, but they also carried an unexpected note of sadness. Though I hadn't told another soul, word had already reached his ears. It didn't matter how or when he'd found out; it was always going to happen, and as such, this was a conversation I'd been dreading.

I didn't know what to say, so I decided the truth would be best. "Yes. Henry has proposed and I have accepted him."

"And when is your marriage to take place?"

I swallowed. This was something Henry and I had discussed on our way home yesterday, but in the light of day, our plan sounded positively reckless. "Th-the day after tomorrow. After we cross the Channel."

I waited for Father to glance at me with a spark of rage, to stand in protest, to demand I delay until the banns could be posted and an appropriate amount of time had passed. Marrying in France was only something unsavory characters who had something to hide did. But he merely nodded. Either he understood that it would be seemlier for me to embark on the journey to India as a married woman than for me to wait, banns or no, or he simply took it in stride. I'd acted irresponsibly so many times before, he was no longer surprised by it.

"Am I to be there?"

It took me a moment to realize what he meant, and my lips parted when I finally did. He was asking if I wanted him at my wedding. "Of course," I said, wondering why he'd think my answer could be any different. "You and Aunt Beth. If you wish to be."

The soldier clinked as he set it on his desk. His deep green eyes flicked up to me, and the anguish I saw in them made my throat clog with sudden emotion.

I stared down at my shoes, at my hands wringing in front of me. He disapproved of my choice, and my actions, and I feared that if I looked him in the eye any longer I would discover that I disapproved of them as well. My shoulders went stiff and I added, "That is, if you will finally give Henry your blessing."

Silence met my ears, and it wasn't until I glanced back up that I saw why. Father sat back in his chair, his Adam's apple bobbing, his lower lip trembling. I hadn't seen him like this since those long months after my mother had died.

"Forgive me, Alicia, I . . . I have wronged you."

A blind, childish hope flickered to life inside me upon hearing the words, and I waited with bated breath, bracing my heart against whatever the next ones would be.

"When your mother died—" His voice broke, forcing him to

start again. The fingers of one hand rubbed together on his desk, pinching and digging in nervousness. "You look just like her, you know. Act like her, too. So spirited and full of life. Through the years it has hurt to see her come alive in you, more and more every day, because every day, she only fades further and further from my reach.

"I cannot look at you too long, or I find myself thinking things are as they used to be . . . that she is still alive. And when reality sets back in, as it always does, I endure the heartache of losing her all over again."

I thought of my dreams—really the nightmares—I'd had since I was a child, and I knew what that pain felt like.

"So I've pushed you away," he went on. "I gave the responsibility of raising you to your governess and my sister, when instead I should have held you close. Cherished you for all that you are to me." A tear slipped down Father's cheek, completely at odds with his stony exterior.

I didn't know when I'd started crying but my cheeks were wet, too.

His voice grew quieter. "And because of this unconscious decision I'd made, I've watched helplessly as you slipped further away, just like she did. Each foot you drifted from me pulled you closer to Henry, until you no longer came to me with your troubles or your sorrows, but to him."

He blinked, lips tightening. "I'm trying to tell you, Alicia, that my dislike of Henry is not indicative of his worth, but my own. I don't despise Henry. I despise myself, for driving you to him. This whole business—it has plagued me with guilt, jealousy, and an unadulterated fear that, just as with your mother, it is already too late. Now you are to leave tomorrow, and I shall never see you again."

I shook my head. I was leaving for India, but it wouldn't be a permanent goodbye. Regardless of our quarrelling and disagreements, I could never leave my family for good. We were a damaged lot, but our souls were still tied together, and until those ties were severed completely I'd never stop trying to shore them up.

With slow movements, Father stood, letting out a low, thin sigh that sounded like it caused him pain. "You say no one has ever shown you how to love, Alicia—and that is my fault. Because I don't know how to, either." There was a pause before Father's face crumpled, a choked sob escaping his lips as he braced a hand against the desk. He looked broken; like he'd just walked out of my mother's bedroom with the knowledge that she was gone.

All the years of suppressed grief and hurt surfaced in a torrent, strangling me, squeezing me, pounding inside me until I was sure I would break, too. And perhaps I did, a little. But in this moment, with my father opening up to me in a way he'd never done before, I wasn't so frightened of being broken anymore.

Being broken isn't such a bad thing, if you have someone to be broken with.

A breathy chuckle fractured my crying. My feet moved, and suddenly Father was before me and crushing me to him and I was burying my face in his jacket, clinging to him like I'd never get the chance to again.

"It wasn't your fault, Papa. I always understood why you did it—and you are not the only one to blame. I've been so foolish, so utterly thoughtless at every turn. I wanted your attention—even your anger was better than your avoidance. But it was wrong of me. I hope you can forgive me." I was babbling uncontrollably, but I couldn't stop. "I'll return soon. Before you know it. And you and Aunt Beth can come visit me in India, and it doesn't have to be too late. It is *not* too late."

He squeezed me tighter, making my tears spill over onto his waistcoat. His voice was soft when he said. "I love you, Alicia. And so did she."

The quiet of the room, of that moment, drowned out the sound of my sniffles, bringing with it a peace I hadn't felt in years. A soothing, comforting knowledge that I was cherished.

But even though the years had seen Father neglecting me and lashing out, and Aunt Beth had perpetually smiled but kept me at a distance, and I never got the chance to say goodbye to my mother all those years ago, Father still hadn't needed to say the words aloud. Because deep down, underneath all the pain and selfish understanding, under all the blaming and regret and blind conviction that I had been wronged . . .

I already knew he loved me.

It just took me breaking a little to finally see it.

♞

AN HOUR LATER, MY EYES WERE STILL SWOLLEN FROM ALL MY crying, but so was my heart. For the first time in a long time, I felt at peace in this house, in this family. I marched down the hall, on my way to change to go riding, when a green lump on the entryway table caught my eye and made me halt in my tracks. A needle pricked the happy bubble surrounding me, making the air fizzle out.

Matthew's book. A simple, threadbare intruder among the gold-varnished décor.

All the way home from the beach and all last night, only sheer stubbornness had stopped me from opening it and discovering its contents right away. I wouldn't subject myself to pointless heartaches and wonderings by making *yet another* decision that was both foolish and wrong.

Then again . . . it's not as if I stole it, or even meant for it to come into my possession. And I was leaving tomorrow anyway, so what would it hurt to peek at it? Nothing I found would alter my decision. And for once, Matthew wasn't here to stop me.

I stared at it, debating what to do, hating that it was suddenly in arm's reach and plaguing me with a curiosity bordering on obsession.

Before I could change my mind, I whisked the book off the

table and strode to an inset window seat under one of the large, arched hall windows. I flopped across the plush cushions, leaned my back against the wall, and creaked the book open.

On the inside flap was an inscription.

To my little Matthew. Do not live so much inside your head.
-Mother

I turned the page.

Gold sunlight streamed through the latticed window, illuminating neat handwriting that covered the page in broad strokes. The left-hand side bore a small column of dates, and underneath them, names.

January the 5th, 1811

Mother:
    Too worried about how I spend my time, and where I live and other nonsense. Jolly good of her to give me this journal, though. Now I can make an account of all the lies people tell me, starting with her. Her eyes narrowed and twitched when she read the inscription on this book to me. Won't admit it, but she needs spectacles.

I stopped reading, face scrunching. An account of lies? Underneath the first paragraph, in script not quite as faded, were two more words.

She's sick.

I gulped. Maybe I shouldn't be reading this after all. Quickly, I scanned the rest of the page. It appeared to be a journal—only instead of it focusing on Matthew, it was his observations about other people. A sort of catalogue, characterizing everyone he'd ever met. A record of secrets he'd unearthed and predictions he'd made about them, before they ever came to pass.

I continued to read, picking out a few sentences about each person before moving on to the next.

Peter:

Says he wants to come home more often, but his hand won't stop fingering father's signet ring. He's still deep in mourning. Deuces, but I wish someone would make him fall in love and bring him out of it.

Eliza:

The most annoying creature on earth. And ironically, the only one who doesn't lie to me.

~~Mary Raynsford. Julia?~~ Lillian Markley:

She is not who she pretends to be, although I'd venture to guess she is far better. A contradiction. Appears to have good breeding, but possesses characteristics of a servant. Loves Peter. Promised to name her firstborn son after me, but she's just the sort of person to have only girls.

Sir William Bentley:

Difficult man to read. Carries an invisible weight on his shoulders—a past riddled with regret. Self-centered. Treats Eliza and Mama with a softness exclusive to them. Stupid man can't even see that he loves my sister. Better he marry her before my eyes roll out of my head.

Lady Prima:

Obscene. Senseless. Her fingers always smell of chocolate—a fact which I'd be all too happy to forget but can't, since she pinches my cheeks at every opportunity. Horrid, cloying woman.

My gaze darted down the page, heart rate spurring faster by the sentence. Words leapt out at me. *Stodgy. Pathetic. Insipid. Cunning.*

People lying and hiding things, and Matthew seeing right through them.

One description bled into five, then ten, then twenty. Some lasted for pages, and others were only a few short sentences, but all carried Matthew's signature sarcastic tone. My eyes froze when they landed on a description that mentioned me, followed by a few more.

The Duke of Cabourne:
Military type—perhaps even served, at one point. Loves his daughter to a fault. Would do better to keep her on a leash.

Lord Hawthorne:
Jovial and over-eager to please. Tiring enthusiasm. Much too certain of Lady Alicia's affection for him.

Lord Graham Crawley:
Repulsive man with little character. Resents Lady Alicia for some reason—and yet is envious of anyone in her presence. I suspect a former attachment. Will use any means necessary to achieve his own ends. See his treatment of his brother.

Henry Crawley:
Nice fellow, albeit somewhat timid. Unassuming and a bit too genuine. A lucky man indeed. One can only hope he drowns on his passage to India.

My heart was thumping uncontrollably now, making blood rush through my ears. With fumbling fingers, I turned the page and—

I stiffened. It was blank.

I flipped to the next page. Blank again.

No, no, no.

Where was my name? What had Matthew written about me? I was desperate now, flipping through the pages like a madwoman. Blank, blank, blank.

I slammed the book shut and sat up, swinging my legs until my feet met the floor. Even without his knowledge, Matthew managed to annoy me. My thoughts ground to a halt.

What if . . . what if he *knew* I'd find his book? What if he'd purposely refrained from penning my description because he knew, one way or another, I'd see it? That it would drive me mad if it wasn't there? What if he'd left it on the beach, knowing I'd find it and look inside like the villain I was, demonstrating once again that he held all the cards and knew what I'd play next? What if—

I pressed my fingers into my temples. Oh, he was inside my head! He couldn't have planned it. What reason would he have for toying with me, when he knew I was leaving tomorrow?

Short of revenge, that is.

I glared at the book in my lap. As if he wrote nothing! He'd spent the last two weeks glued to my side, and I didn't even merit one little sentence? A wave of anger surged to the surface, but it was quickly stifled by something deeper and more painful, before evaporating completely. In its wake it left only emptiness. Resignation.

Why *would* he write about me? I was so obvious, so beneath his notice that my name wasn't even worth the page space. The book had proven to be a wild goose chase—one that didn't even give me the satisfaction of reading how much Matthew hated me. He'd told me often enough, so why would he bother writing it down?

And yet . . .

This book offered no new insight, no clues or juicy surprises Matthew might be hiding. Nothing secretive, nothing embarrassing or revealing. Nothing extraordinary at all.

So why had he been so adamant I not read it in the first place?

A footman appeared and cleared his throat, snapping me out of my musings. He extended a piece of paper to me with a gloved hand. "An urgent letter for you, my lady."

After setting the book aside, I took it from him. "Thank you." He bowed and plodded down the hall. I studied the scrawled script adorning the letter's surface—totally opposite of Matthew's—and frowned when I recognized it.

Urgent?

I broke the seal and unfolded the paper. The short sentences swam into view and immediately my blood chilled. I sucked in a quiet breath. My fingers shook, loosening until the letter fluttered to the floor, hitting my slipper.

I know you know about Lenny. Meet my demands or he will suffer the consequences.

CHAPTER 29

CRAWLEY CASTLE WAS OVER 500 YEARS OLD, BUT SEVERAL additional wings had been added through the years, tucked safely behind the inner curtain wall. It was built on the only hill within miles, so I was able to see the intimidating structure from far away and watch as it loomed closer. The location had likely been a strategic choice meant to inspire fear in the hearts of the Crawleys' enemies, and as evidenced by my rapid heartbeat, that tradition had continued down through the ages. I glanced at my reticule resting on the seat next to me, hoping it contained enough funds.

We turned down the path and soon the crunch of gravel changed to the hollow sound of wood as we rattled across the bridge and under the portcullis. After the footman helped me down, I marched up to the big wooden door and pounded on it with one shaking fist, the urgent letter I'd received clutched in the other.

Shortly, the door groaned open, and Thatcher, the Crawleys' butler, poked his head out. His face formed a question, obviously surprised to see me. "My lady? Mr. Crawley has gone to visit Lawry

Park—you've only missed him by a few minutes. Perhaps you might want to—"

"I am here to see *Lord* Crawley," I said, pushing past him. The cold, mossy smell of stone assaulted my nose. I spun back. "And I would appreciate it if Mr. Crawley never discovered I was here."

He nodded slowly. "Of course, my lady. Lord Crawley is with a business associate at the moment. Would you like to wait in the library?"

I tensed, stomach sinking. Who knew how long their meeting would last? It could be another few hours—and at this rate, I wouldn't last another fifteen minutes before I exploded with both anxiety and anger. But I forced a polite smile and said, "That will be fine."

Thatcher bowed and dismissed himself, already knowing I didn't wish for his escort and would see myself there. I turned the corner and scurried toward the west wing, the most modern addition to the castle.

Hiking up my skirts and grasping the shiny mahogany bannister, I ascended the stairs that led to the library, but only made it halfway up before the muffled sound of something crashing echoed through the castle. Tingles traveled down my spine.

"That's not good enough! I am to give away my biggest bargaining chip merely on your *word*?" The shout sounded distant, like it was coming through the open doorway of Graham's study down the hall.

"Unlike you, Lord Crawley, I actually keep my word."

The new voice halted me in my tracks. I would know that voice anywhere. Soft, deep, and thoroughly disinterested. I knew I shouldn't listen in on whatever this conversation was, but my feet were lead, the rest of me ice, unable to cover my ears, unable to move.

"You are in no position to negotiate." Graham again. "I hold all the cards."

"It is true you have something I desire. But let me make one thing unmistakably clear: I am not your servant waiting on your beck and call. I am not some lovesick hound content to perform a trick for a pat on the back, kept on a leash and loosed only when you have use for me. I am a man. And there are levels to which I will not degrade myself."

"Not even for that wretched Alicia?"

My pulse stopped. I strained my ears to hear his answer, but Matthew was silent. I could picture his glare perfectly. Severe. Deadly.

"That *is* why you are here, is it not?"

"You make a wild assumption. I have come in my own self-interest."

Graham scoffed. "You pretend to be so high and mighty, Mr. Wycliffe, when in reality you and I are not so different. You gambled and lost. Just as I did."

Matthew was quieter when he said, "I never gamble."

"Don't you?" Graham laughed, so loud and forced that the echoes were still ringing in my ears when he went on. "Isn't that what all of this has been? One big gamble? How uncanny, watching you repeat my own past right before my eyes. Forced to keep up appearances. Brushed aside in lieu of my brother. And just like me, you shall hate the miserable woman until your dying breath."

My fingernails dug into the wood of the bannister as another wave of anger washed over me. This time I embraced it. It was better than the pain.

Matthew's response didn't come for a long moment. And when it did, it was so quiet, so bordering on uncontrollable rage that I first mistook it for Graham's. "I would never marry Lady Alicia. But if you dare utter one more disparaging comment about her in my presence, sir, I will not hesitate in calling you out."

The air around me froze. A duel?

"Is that a threat?"

Matthew's voice raised several pitches. "You have the audacity to write me with the sole purpose of preying upon my interests, and expect me to act a gentleman? I have done my best to remain honorable. But not even for that enviable title will I stand here and let you insult her name. You know absolutely nothing about her, about the hardships she has suffered and her strength despite them. You persistently mock her, and belittle her, and act as if she has wronged you when it is the opposite!"

Another pause, then Matthew continued, slower.

"Though my intent was worlds apart from your own, I have wronged her too. I take no pride in admitting it. But you see, that is where the similarities between us end, making your comparison not only wildly offensive but deeply flawed. Forced to keep up appearances? How could I, when none of my actions have been insincere? Brushed aside? That implies I presented myself as an option to her, when I never did, and I never shall, and heaven help the man who does. And as for hating her . . ."

An eternity passed as I waited for his answer, so riveted to his words that in my mind's eye I was in the room with them, watching Matthew's face contort, watching his eyes spark and set Graham afire with the loathing burning inside them.

"As for hating her," he repeated in a low, harsh tone. ". . . A man like you could not hope to understand the depth of my feeling, so do *not* patronize me, sir, by attempting an air of comradery. I am not your friend. And I am *nothing* like you."

I willed my feet to move, to ascend to the library and wait to be summoned, but instead I locked my knees and listened for Graham's response. It never came.

"As for your proposition, my word still stands. I will return within the hour. And you had best live up to your end of the agreement, my lord, or you will find my sword is even sharper than my tongue."

Something thudded—like a hand coming down on a desk, before footsteps echoed in the hall, growing louder by the second. I thawed and jerked around just as the top of Matthew's hair passed the railing and headed for the door.

Words leapt to my tongue, but they died at the sight of his retreating figure. Tall and proud. I was always seeing the back of him, it seemed. Soon, he was out the door and Thatcher appeared at the bottom of the stairs. "His lordship will see you now."

My grip on the blackmail letter tightened as I remembered why I was here. I glided back down the stairs and strode into Graham's den, where he was waiting for me behind his desk. The room was just as littered as the day Matthew and I had snuck into it. Papers, dust, cobwebs, ink spills.

Graham's hair was disheveled and he wore a leftover glower from Matthew's visit. Without a word, he made a hand gesture to Thatcher, who immediately shut the door.

My nerves jumped. There were no windows in Graham's den, and Henry was gone. It was just me and Graham behind a closed door in the heart of his castle. The warning bells jangling at the back of my mind rose to a deafening pitch, not helped at all by the way Graham's glare morphed into a smirk.

"I knew you'd come running."

None of the responses I could give would mollify him, so instead I held up his note. "What is this?"

"Sweet revenge." His arm swept out. "A gift from fate."

"How dare you blackmail me. Use an innocent person as leverage—just to satisfy your own ends!"

The words, though foreign on my tongue, sounded familiar. Then I remembered Matthew's book, where he'd written almost the exact same thing about Graham, noticing it upon their first meeting.

Graham lit his pipe and puffed, shaking out the match. He wasn't ruffled by my outburst, nor by the immorality of the situation. Smoke filled my nostrils. "A third Crawley son," he mused, ignoring me. "You can't imagine my disgust when I found out, nor my relief when I discovered who 'Lenny' actually was. Never liked the boy anyway."

Remembering his unkempt appearance in the tavern, his bare,

scabbed feet and threadbare clothes, a swell of protective anger washed over me when I said, "You don't even know him."

Graham shrugged. "Perhaps not much—but better than you think I do."

"How did you know to threaten *me*?"

Graham smiled, smugly, tapping his pipe on an ashtray before steepling his fingers. "When I'd retired to my den after the ball, I found the most curious thing. A note addressed to my dead father, at the foot of my desk. Only the funny thing is, it wasn't there an hour before. Someone had been nosing around in my study."

My mouth ran dry, and involuntarily my eyes darted to the large painting behind him, concealing the entrance to the passageway.

Graham stood and came around his desk. "The next day, Henry came home with the will in his hands, given to him by none other than you. And I couldn't help but ask myself: how could Alicia Kendall, a duke's daughter who isn't remotely related to my family, have obtained this will, when I've searched for it for months—*years*—to no success? It couldn't have appeared out of thin air. Either you'd had it all along, or you'd found it. Recently."

His head cocked as he placed one foot in front of another, steadily approaching me. "None of it made any sense until I remembered the night of the ball. How you had mysteriously disappeared for half the night. You *and* Mr. Wycliffe."

I gulped. I hadn't thought anyone had noticed our disappearance. If Graham had, that meant he'd been watching me very, *very* closely.

"Though it baffles me," he went on, "you managed to find some secret compartment I hadn't noticed before, containing all of my father's secret documents. And then, in your haste, dropped one of them on your way out. Ironic, that by finding the will and stealing my wealth, you gave me the tool I needed to orchestrate your downfall."

My hands fisted, angry that he was dragging an innocent a boy into his petty games. "How did you know I care about what happens to Lenny?"

"Lenny! How charming." Graham chuckled, a disturbing, menacing sound. "How could you not care for him? You've always had a soft spot for broken things. And if I produce the note which discloses his parentage—his illegitimacy—everyone will talk. It will spoil his life and demolish his future, as well as any prospects he might have had. As your fates are intertwined, I think you will do anything in your power to prevent that."

I did strangely feel connected to the boy, like I was watching myself in another life and whatever misfortune befell him would befall me too. Maybe there was a reason Nicholas Crawley had kept the truth hidden from his sons. The truth, in the hands of someone like Graham, could be deadly, and it was my fault he'd discovered it in the first place. This was yet another consequence of my rash decisions, and I couldn't let Lenny bear the brunt of it. At any cost, I would make this right.

"The note says I must meet your demands. Well, what are they?"

His face neared my own, until I could smell his breath, reeking of tobacco and brandy. "There is a lot I could require." His eyes flicked over me. "A lot I once desired from you."

"Step away from me," I muttered.

"You are not afraid, are you, Alicia?" His hand nudged my shoulder, forcing me to flinch back. A look entered his eye, crazed with power. "Henry isn't here to save you now, is he?" He pushed me back again.

Suddenly, the only thing I was aware of was the way Graham towered over me, how his fingers dug into my collarbone, how his eyes smoldered with hatred, how the door was closed and only Thatcher would hear me if I were to scream.

"There are many things I could ask of you. *Many* that leap to mind." He pushed me a third time, making me stumble backward into the bookcase. I gritted my teeth, every part of me tensing as he took one step closer . . . then another. He was proposing again, shoving me into a corner, backhanding me across the face when I refused him.

"Now I have you alone, and if only to save your precious boy, you would give me anything I asked for. This time, you daren't refuse."

My body shook but I bared my teeth. "What do you *want?*"

"Thirty thousand pounds. That is my price. It is only right you should pay a fortune, since you stole mine out from under me. Twice. First when you refused me, and then when you found that plagued will."

My hands gripped the shelf of the bookcase behind me. "I don't have that kind of money!"

"Your dowry alone is larger than that."

"A dowry I have no access to. And when we marry the day after tomorrow, it shall be Henry's!"

He shook his head. "What a great many things you give my undeserving brother. The will, your fortune . . . yourself. All things that should have been mine." After a pause, he backed away, his pupils shrinking as his senses seemed to return. His nose wrinkled in disgust. "But they are things I no longer desire."

He turned away, moving around his desk. "Perhaps you are right. The prospect of my brother taking you halfway around the world should be more than enough compensation. Give me whatever money is in your purse and be gone."

I didn't ask how he knew I'd brought a large sum along. Five hundred pounds had been set aside for my wedding, to be spent on decorations, a new trousseau, and an extravagant wedding breakfast. With my wedding being so rushed, there hadn't been time to organize any of those things; so earlier in his study, Father had gifted me the money as a present, saying I might need it on my passage to India.

Now, it struck me as suspicious that Graham would settle for a fraction of what he'd originally asked for. Why the sudden change of mind? He didn't possess a merciful bone in his body. "In exchange for this money, you will give me the letter?"

Graham said nothing, only slumped into his chair and held up a piece of paper, eyebrows raising in agreement. When I neared, he flipped it around, preventing me from inspecting it closer. "Money first."

I glared at him. "You're despicable."

"But you've always known that, haven't you?"

I snapped my reticule open, aware of the hungry way Graham watched my movements, eyes riveting to the bank notes when I slammed them on his desk. He fingered them, mouth pulling into a twisted smile before tossing the letter at my feet.

I snatched it up and looked it over, relieved when I recognized it to be the one Matthew and I had found. After securing it in my reticule, I turned back to Graham, no longer intimidated now that I had what I came for.

"That day you proposed to me—is it any wonder I refused you?" I knew I was shaking, but I couldn't stop. "After years of treating me the way you did, it is more surprising you thought you had any chance at all. Only the blind would be fooled by the way you pretend to love Henry. And if you cannot love him, then how could you love anyone? He has only ever shown patience and thoughtfulness while you persistently belittled him, though he is your moral better, though he is your *brother*."

Graham emitted a soft scoff. "He is no brother of mine."

I shook my head. "You are miserable. And I pity you because you do not see it. You will blame your misery on everyone else until you're rotting in a cold grave, with only the worms to listen to your mewling complaints. Well, if that is the case then you deserve your torment."

I spun on my heel and stormed out of the den, not waiting for Graham's angry rebuttal. He shouted something after me, but I was too angry to hear it. I walked down the hall past stern paintings and gloomy tapestries and turned the corner, the front door now in sight.

When it groaned open, I stopped short. My mind went to the secret passageway when we'd hunted for the will. A gold sunset haloed Matthew's form for a moment before the door shut behind him and he strode forward at a brisk pace, his hair bouncing with each step, a piece of paper clutched in his hand.

Seeing me, Matthew halted only a few paces away. I waited to witness that disgust I'd pictured so clearly earlier enter his eyes, but he only stared at me, a blank expression on his face that bordered on soft. Almost as if, just as on the beach, he wanted to say something but didn't know if he could manage the words.

Wanting him to speak, to stop staring at me in his intense way, I blurted, "Why are you here?"

He looked away to his right. "Graham wishes to sell the castle, and I am here to purchase it."

My forehead wrinkled, remembering the conversation I'd overheard. Negotiating a transaction would explain Matthew's presence, but . . . "I thought you said you would never move."

"Just because I own something doesn't mean I have to live in it."

Graham had mentioned a bargaining chip, and had insinuated I was the reason Matthew had come willing to buy. But Graham would never sell this castle, his birthright. He'd gloated to Henry all growing up that it would one day belong to him, the firstborn son. Why would he suddenly change his mind now?

And indeed, even if Graham did wish to sell it, that didn't explain why Matthew was interested. Short of buying it as a secondary home—one he had no need of, since he refused to live in any other house—there was no reason why Matthew would make the purchase. Even as an investment, it made little sense. Matthew did not make senseless investments.

In the end, though, I was leaving for France tomorrow, so it didn't matter what Matthew did with his money, or why. What mattered was how we were going to part ways, what things would be left unsaid. Though I didn't relish the task, there was a certain matter I had to set straight.

"I have something I must confess."

Matthew said nothing, only waited.

I took a deep breath. "Before we became engaged . . . I made an agreement with my aunt, and father, that if I could not secure a proposal from Henry, I would marry Hawthorne. Two weeks were given to me to seal my fate, and when you entered the picture I realized having you as an ally would be convenient. So I made you believe our engagement was real—made you do things you despised. I duped you. I used you. And I want to say that I am sorry."

His eyes darted to the floor, unwilling to look up.

I had to finish. "You see, all this time, the question was never between you or Henry. You were never even an option. From the beginning, there was never a possible scenario where we would marry."

"I know all this," he said quietly.

I sucked in a quiet breath, shock pulsing through my veins. What? But how could he?

"I have always known." His eyes locked onto mine, and the intensity there, the fierce hopelessness, cut a pit in my stomach and drove me to remember his words from the alleyway.

It is worse to see.

To know your outcome, and have no way of changing it. No matter that you would go the lengths of the earth for the smallest chance at a different path. No.

All you can do is watch it all play out and accept your defeat.

He'd known this whole time, then. That our engagement was a sham and that I was going to leave him in the end, no matter what happened. And because of it, he'd kept his distance, he'd kept his attraction in check and had cause to hate me from the beginning.

"But," I said, so stunned I could barely form the words, ". . . how? When?"

"Your aunt told me of your deal moments after we became engaged."

I thought back to the way Aunt Beth had come upon me and Lord Wycliffe in the gardens after Matthew had gone. How had I not suspected anything?

"It is not a gamble when you know how it ends," Matthew muttered, brushing past me, reiterating what he'd said to Graham earlier.

My feet froze to the floor as a new realization entered my mind, strong and confusing and bewildering all at once. As much as Henry said he loved me—and I believed he did—from the outset, he had already given up. He said a lack of fortune and social recognition were obstacles that separated us, but never once had he tried to tear them down. He'd made no attempt to win my hand, or a future where we could be together.

Whereas Matthew, for all his glaring and grumbling, had made *every* effort toward that future. At first, I believed it was because he dreaded the thought of being tied to me himself. But, if he'd really known the truth the whole time—that I'd release him in the end, regardless—then why help me at all? Why would he care about a future that wasn't even his?

I spun around, heart pounding, needing to glimpse the back of his head one last time, but he had turned at the end of the hall, facing me with a sorry look in his eye.

"Goodbye, Alicia," he said, tone ringing with finality. He didn't just mean for a week or a month or a year—he meant forever.

My breath caught at the soft way he said my name. Like I was a friend; someone he had come to cherish.

As for hating her, a man like you could not hope to understand the depth of my feeling. "Goodbye, Matthew."

But he didn't turn the corner and disappear. He just stood there, staring at me, one hand fidgeting as if he were waiting for me to do something. For *himself* to do something. And I got the sense that even if I remained transfixed in this hallway for a whole lifetime, he would linger just as long, staring me down, waiting for that *something*, waiting . . .

Unable to bear it any longer, I tore my gaze away, just as I had done every other time he'd issued me a quiet challenge. Like the predictable girl I was; the coward.

Then I headed for the door and didn't glance back, too afraid that he already knew I wanted to.

CHAPTER 30

THAT NIGHT, NO NIGHTMARES CAME, BUT NEITHER DID SLEEP.

THE MORNING PASSED IN A BLUR OF GOODBYES TO WELL-WISHERS who spontaneously dropped by, and rushing to complete tasks before the ship cast off at eleven. Both mentally and physically exhausted, I trudged upstairs to help Nancy finish packing the wardrobe which would accompany me to India.

"Have you heard from my brother-in-law, miss?" Nancy asked, extricating dresses from the closet and laying them out on the bed.

"No." Graham's blackmail letter had nullified the importance of having the vicar investigate the case. I'd already found the third Crawley boy at an inn at Brighton; now that I knew it was him, I didn't need someone else to verify those facts. "No, I have not. But it hardly matters now, does it?"

I'd dropped off more supplies for Lenny after leaving the castle yesterday: clothes, food, and simple books and school things in case he ever wanted to read. It wasn't much, but it was all I could think to do. Jasper had been cool toward me, but far less hostile than during my last visit; I'd taken it as a good sign.

With the whirlwind of the last few days, there hadn't been a good opportunity to tell Henry of his brother, but I had resolved to mention it to him as soon as possible. I was sure once things settled down we could find a way to help Lenny more permanently. Maybe he could even come live with us in India.

"Ready to go, then?" Aunt Beth swept into my bedroom smelling of rose perfume. "Both Henry and your father are waiting in the carriages, ready to depart."

I turned back to my task, saying, "Nearly there." It struck me as odd that I was spending my last moments as an unmarried woman on English soil by packing shoes and stays, instead of weaving flowers through my hair or skipping from cloud to cloud in a daydream. I didn't feel at all how I thought I'd feel the day before my wedding. After using a few handkerchiefs to individually wrap my necklaces, I stored them in a case and set it in the gaping trunk, now halfway full of my belongings.

"What a disappointment. You lost your chance with Mr. Wycliffe, and now you're running off to India."

I glanced at Aunt Beth, noting the shawl wrapped about her shoulders covering the cream muslin she would wear to my wedding. I looked away. Shaking my head, I said, "I am not running."

"Aren't you?"

I dismissed Nancy and set to folding up my dresses without her, needing a task to keep my hands busy. To keep my mind from wandering places it shouldn't. Nancy curtsied and left the room. "If indeed I am running, it is toward what I want. Toward what I have *always* wanted." I stuffed a dress into my trunk, my movements growing quicker and more agitated.

"That is the problem, isn't it? It's what you have always wanted, but it is not what you want now." Her intelligent eyes bored into me.

"You can't know that." I shoved the last dress inside. The lace at the hem caught on a wood splinter, ripping a hole as wide as my hand. Growling, I pulled at it, but it only ripped it further. I tugged at it, harder and harder, until I had shredded the dress just as thoroughly as I had my heart, then threw it inside where it would always stay for all I cared, rips and all, ugly and battered.

"Don't take your anger out on your dress, Alicia. The poor thing's done nothing to you."

I slammed the trunk shut and whirled on her. "You told him of our bargain." I didn't specify Matthew, but by the way her features blanked and calmed, she already knew who I meant. "You let me forge ahead—bumbling and stumbling and dragging him along—knowing the entire time I was lost to him from the beginning. Knowing he could never, *never* love me back. You watched me and mocked me—just so I could, what? Learn my lesson? Learn to be as callous as you? Learn what it means to feel heartache so potent I can barely breathe? Well you have got your wish!

"Matthew hates me for what I've done to him. He will never forgive me. And why should he? I'm a stupid, senseless girl—and so says my aunt!"

Too drained to stand, I caved in on myself and sunk onto the bed, hitting the mattress but still falling, falling. "I am going to marry Henry," I said quietly. "But, though I love him—though I always have—it is not in the same way. It does not even compare."

I buried my face in my hands. As the tears slipped onto my palms, my aunt said nothing. After several quiet moments, a weight settled on the bed next to me, Aunt Beth's words coming slowly, haltingly, as if they had to be forced out.

"I never had any children of my own, and so have always been averse to coddling. It never made sense to me, and you of all people know this. But after Henry's ball, I realized that I'd gone too far. I should have been . . . more like a mother to you. My stay here was only ever temporary, but then your uncle died, and . . . well, I didn't want to grow too attached. I was afraid to spoil you and treat you like the daughter I'd always wanted."

Her words washed over me. I couldn't remember a time when Aunt Beth had talked to me like this; side by side, with both understanding and vulnerability in her eyes.

"I am not your mother, I know that. I am not your friend—I know that, too. But I *am* your aunt, and perhaps the only person who can beat some sense into that thick skull of yours."

She pinched my chin, forcing my face to hers until all I could see were her piercing brown eyes. "Let Henry go," she murmured in the soft, commanding tone of a parent. "You cling to him—not out of love, but because you are afraid to lose him."

"Yes," I whispered. The word hurt, but the moment it left my lips, I felt a release of pressure in my chest. A floodgate of tears dropped down my cheeks as I thought of my childhood. Of the pounding of the doctor's footsteps down the stairs, and the echoes of my father weeping. "Yes, I am. Because once Henry is gone, who will I have left?"

"You have your father and me. You may not think so, but we have always been on your side."

Hands on my upper arms, she angled me toward her. For once, her gaze didn't look shrewd and cutting, but serious and wise. Almost desperate in her effort to get me to see something.

"Do not cling to Henry. Do not cling to your memories. Do not even cling to your mother. Because as beautiful as each of these things are, they are not worthy of your obsession. They are flawed. And so, my dear, are you. But while the past will always remain untouchable, you have the priceless freedom to *change* your flaws, whenever you wish to. To love in the way you have always wanted.

"You can give someone else the love we failed to give you; for you have that strength within you, Alicia." Something like pride shone in her eyes, something I'd never seen her looking at me with. "The ability to catch a vision and make it your reality. Do not throw that away simply because you are afraid. Chase after that vision—

do not let it out of your sight—or the only reality you shall live is one like mine. Full of heartache and regret."

I processed her words, letting the truth of them settle inside me. "What about the deal?" I hugged myself, rubbing one arm. "Hawthorne or Henry—those are my options."

"The bargain was that you must secure a proposal from Henry. Well, you have got it. Now what are you going to do?"

"Matthew does not *want* me."

"Oh, foolhardy girl." She scoffed. "You don't honestly believe that, do you? He's beside himself with desperation to keep you— he's just too proud to admit it. You'll have to pry it out of him, that one."

My eyebrows pulled together, a spark of hope lighting in my chest. ". . . You think he loves me?"

"Of course he does." She said it like I was being unaccountably stupid, and her patience was wearing thin.

It didn't really feel like an answer. Something as simple as my aunt's hunch wasn't enough of a reason to throw an entire life away —or to break Henry's heart. It was too risky, too foolish, too like everything else I'd done to get me into this mess.

As for hating her, a man like you could not hope to understand the depth of my feeling.

Henry was a good man. My best friend. Unless I found evidence that my aunt's claims were true, I would marry him.

And no evidence existed.

Aunt Beth straightened her shawl and stood. "There is still time to change your mind." With that, she swept out of the room to join Father in the carriage.

Servants entered a minute later and carted my trunk out. I stared around my room which now felt empty, and let out a long, slow sigh. I stood, gathered my bonnet, cloak, and gloves, and slipped down the stairs.

Halfway down them, I was met by a figure emerging from my Father's study, the last man on earth I'd expected to see.

"Lady Alicia!" Lord Hawthorne beamed up at me, coming to the foot of the stairs.

I repressed an exasperated sigh. Twice he'd interrupted Henry's proposal, and now he was going to make me late to the boat, and by extension, my own wedding. I nodded in greeting, summoning every last shred of patience I possessed. At least I wouldn't have to put up with him much longer. "Lord Hawthorne."

He slapped the bannister. "After all that's happened, I've come to invite you to a ball at my estate tonight, as a gesture of goodwill. Only it had somehow slipped my mind you were leaving the country!" He slapped his forehead. He was always slapping things. "What a dashed shame, as the company is sure to be splendorous."

"I'm sure it will be, Lord Hawthorne."

"Mr. Wycliffe shall be there tonight—I made him promise he would come."

I bristled inside at the mention of Matthew, but I didn't let it show as I put my gloves on. "How ever did you manage that?"

"He didn't want to, believe me—but just yesterday I did him an enormous favor, you see. And he made me promise not to breathe a word of it to anyone."

"I see." I descended the remaining steps and attempted to brush past him, but he caught my arm and walked with me to the doorway, not seeming the least bit inclined to keep his promise.

"It had to do with his shares. I've been overeager to invest a substantial amount in the tobacco trade, you see, but Mr. Wycliffe wasn't willing to part with any of his assets. Yesterday, he stopped me on my way to town, wanting to know if my previous offer still stood. Naturally, I jumped at the chance. I paid a pretty penny for them, though, and for the inconvenience of rushing through the exchange, Mr. Wycliffe promised to attend tonight as a favor to me. People have still been raving about seeing him at my last ball three weeks ago. How amazed they shall be when he attends *two* of my balls in such a short span of time!"

My hands clenched. I had no desire to hear about Hawthorne's investments, and even less of a desire to hear about Matthew. I was on my way to be *married*.

"You are a lucky man, my lord. Now if you'll excuse me—"

"I can hardly believe he asked for thirty thousand pounds, as the shares are worth well more than that! I count myself lucky indeed!"

I halted in my tracks. My vision lost focus, every muscle going rigid. *Thirty thousand pounds.* Hawthorne continued to prattle about something, but I didn't hear him, too distracted by an extraordinary, outlandish possibility.

No. No, it couldn't be.

Slowly, I swiveled to look at Hawthorne, and he stopped talking. I stared at him in such shock, such confused suspicion that after a moment, his smile dropped and he started to squirm.

"Thirty thousand pounds?" I put my hand on his arm, clutching the fabric of his jacket in my fist. "Are you sure that was the amount? The *exact* amount?"

His eyes went wide. "Of course! I should know—I paid for it, after all."

I let go and turned away. No. No, it was a stupid explanation, conjured only because I was desperate, because Aunt Beth had revived my hope. I was mad! Utterly mad!

I shook my head to clear the absurd thought away. "Thank you for the invitation, Lord Hawthorne, but as you have stated, I am leaving the country tonight. I don't think we shall see each other again."

His face pulled into a pout, so childlike in its disappointment. From behind his back he withdrew a pop of color. "But surely you have time to receive this bouquet—"

I rushed past him and out the door, calling over my shoulder, "No! No time, my lord," more grateful than ever that I had a wedding to get to. With each step, I grabbed one of my swirling questions and locked it away, not daring to stop and listen to any of them.

But as I fled down the long, curving steps of the manor, a

different voice called out to me—one I'd never heard before. I slowed and glanced back. Coming from the opposite stairs, face frantic, was a man I didn't recognize. He waved his hat over a graying crown of hair. "Lady Alicia! I have news for you!"

"I beg your pardon, sir, but I don't know who you are, and I am dreadfully late—"

"I am a vicar from Cornwall. Nancy's brother-in-law. We've been exchanging letters." He reached me, out of breath, wadding his cap in one hand. "I've discovered the truth about that matter you wrote me. But then, yesterday, I was informed you were leaving the country. No time for a letter, you see. So I've come in person to tell you what I learned, before you left. Please—I've been travelling all night."

I took in his disheveled state, his sweat-slicked forehead and rumpled clothes. "I apologize for your trouble, sir, but I already know who Lenny is—a boy living in Brighton. I fear your journey has been in vain."

His eyes widened. "No, no it hasn't! Lenny isn't a boy at Brighton. He's not a boy at all, in fact."

What nonsense. Of course he was. Graham had known it too, and blackmailed me.

My gaze darted between the vicar and the carriage, knowing my talk with Aunt Beth and my run-in with Hawthorne had set us back a good half hour. Henry and I would miss our boat if I didn't hurry.

"Excuse me, sir, but Mr. Crawley and I have somewhere to be." I hiked up my skirts and wove down the steps, the vicar at my heels.

"That is precisely why I am here, my lady—Mr. Crawley. The person you've been searching for *is* Mr. Crawley—christened Leonard Henry Crawley."

For the second time, I stopped in my tracks.

The vicar held out a few pieces of paper. Proof. "Besides his name on the church records, someone in my congregation was harboring correspondence between Mr. Crawley's blood father and

Nicholas Crawley—and they were kind enough to disclose it to me. Apparently, Lady Rachel Crawley had an affair one summer in Cornwall and returned to her castle with a son. A *second* son, not a third. The truth of Mr. Crawley's parentage wasn't discovered until a few years later, upon Rachel's confession to her husband—and by that time, Nicholas held great affection for the boy. Instead of disowning him, he chose to continue the charade. Never told another soul. That I stumbled upon the letters at all is a miracle."

He is no brother of mine.

Air rushed out of my lungs, and a full five seconds passed before I managed to replace it.

The claim that Henry was conceived because of an affair was absurd on its face, and yet every part of me believed it. It explained everything—the letters, the secrecy, Graham's hatred. There was no third Crawley son. It was Henry. It had been Henry this entire time.

I couldn't care less if he was illegitimate—it was not his decision, or his fault. But the implications if this were true were earth-shattering.

In a blur, I descended the remaining steps, not knowing how I did or how long it took me. My foot collided with the gravel drive and suddenly Henry was at my side, smiling and saying we needed to hurry. Vaguely, I registered that the vicar hung back while Henry pulled me forward, gently leading me toward the carriage, toward our wedding, toward our future.

And then time slowed and a stream of realizations hit me, each one a blow to the temple, the key to the entire, elaborate puzzle clicking into place.

Graham knew about Henry's birth. He thought I knew as well, and that's why he blackmailed me. *If I disclose his parentage, it will demolish his future. And as your fates are intertwined, I think you will do anything in your power to prevent that.*

If the news of Henry's illegitimacy got out, it would obliterate both his standing and marriageability, as no one would marry someone who was born out of wedlock. Graham hadn't been threat-ening to take away the future of a small boy from the village, he'd been threatening to ruin *my* future. By telling the *ton* of Henry's parentage.

And if Graham had held my entire future in his hands, he *never* would've settled for a measly five hundred pounds. He would've squeezed me for every penny I was worth. Which meant he'd either spread the truth anyway, or someone had paid him off. *Someone must've paid him* . . .

Thirty thousand pounds.

Matthew hadn't been there yesterday to purchase a castle, he'd been there to purchase a future. *My* future. With Henry.

Even after everything, after knowing how I'd cheated him and used him and chosen Henry time and time again, Matthew had gone out of his way to guarantee my marriage would happen.

And as the carriage loomed before me and Henry took my hand to help me clamber inside, the only question left, was . . . why?

Why?

It burned bright and hot, unable to be satisfied, stifled, or ignored.

"Alicia?"

My gaze snapped to Henry who was watching me with slanted brows.

"We must leave now if we are to make the boat."

But I couldn't leave. Not yet. Not until I knew for certain.

"One moment." I dropped his hand and picked up my skirts. "Just wait for me one moment!"

Then I ran as fast as my legs could carry me, as fast as I did when soldiers had been chasing me, leaping up the stairs and passing through the hewn stone entrance. There was no sign of the vicar or Hawthorne, but I wasn't looking for them. I dashed through the foyer and angled toward the study, throwing the door open so hard it crashed against the far wall.

My gaze landed immediately on what I had come for.

I stared at it a moment, chest heaving. The little green spine was snug between the other books, right where I left it before venturing to Graham's castle yesterday. I shot forward and pulled it out, the pressure in my chest building and building, silly hope making my hands shake.

I flipped and flipped, scanning the pages, searching for my name, growing more frantic by the second. It had to be here. It *had* to be here. The pages dwindled, further and further until I turned to the last page and my eyes snagged on something. I gasped, softly. After a sea of blank pages, Matthew had finally written something. Something he'd obviously wished to hide.

There, on the very last page, by itself, was a date—the day of Hawthorne's ball, the night Matthew and I had met. Underneath it, written in bold, black ink, was my name. Where others had entire pages of descriptions and observations devoted to them, Matthew Wycliffe had penned only a single word for me. The word, under-lined three times, indented into the paper, like it had been agonized over. Traced and re-traced by both pencil and quill a thousand times.

One word that held a thousand meanings.

Lady Alicia Kendall:
Unpredictable.

CHAPTER 31

You, Lady Alicia, are the most predictable woman I have ever met.

Unpredictable.

If ever I were to marry, it would be to someone I never saw coming.

Unpredictable.

Someone whom I couldn't predict. Who surprised me in every way.

Unpredictable.

And the day you read this book, I vow I shall follow through with this blasted scheme and marry you after all.

"That little liar," I whispered, happiness and anger warring inside me until it was blazing out my fingertips, making them curl around the book. "That stupid, egotistical, wonderful little liar."

"Alicia!" The call was distant, but grew louder until Henry stood in the doorway, wearing a frantic, confused expression. "Why did you run off? We need to leave."

I closed the book and turned to Henry, the newfound knowledge of what I needed to do weighing heavily on my shoulders. I shook my head. "I can't."

A whole minute passed and Henry's face didn't change a fraction as he looked between me and the book in my hands. Slowly, it cleared; like he always knew this was going to happen. "I kept thinking these past few weeks were a dream too good to be true. I suppose I was right."

"Oh Henry, I'm sorry. I'm so, so sorry." I crossed the distance between us and clung to him.

He returned the embrace, whispering into my hair, "It was a good dream." We stayed there for several minutes, both of us too afraid to let go. When we finally pulled back, tears glimmered in his eyes. His hand cradled the side of my face. "I've always loved you, Alicia. But I've also always known you were never meant for me to love."

Slowly, he reached down and tugged my glove off, placed a reverent kiss on my palm, and slipped a simple wooden ring on my finger—the one that would've bound us together for the rest of our lives. He backed away out of reach. At the doorway he halted and saluted me with my limp glove. "I will cherish this. Our last trophy. A reminder that for a time, though brief, I once held the hand that filled it."

I offered him a wan smile, trying to keep myself from breaking down. Then he left, toward the military, and India. I rushed to the doorway and watched him pass Father and Aunt Beth on their way in as he exited the house, imprinting the sight of the back of his head into my memory.

"Alicia!" Father said. "We're devilish late as it is! If we don't—"

Aunt Beth saw my face and put a hand to Father's shoulder to silence him.

I had thought that all my love lived in Henry alone, and that if I ever lost him, I'd be left destitute. But as I watched him walk on the path that steered away from me, I discovered that I'd been wrong.

Love didn't work like that—in finite sums, differences, and dividends. Love only ever *multiplied*. It was not a thing you collected in a basket and gave to others at your leisure, one by one until the basket was empty. It was something you planted in the earth and grew with purpose: watering, weeding, and tending with care. And once it had risen into a great tree, its seeds would drop and spread in the wind, scattering to those around you, bearing fruit and bringing more *life* into their lives.

My love was not finite, after all. And though neither was it endless, it certainly could be. If I chose to make it so. If I planted it and refused to see it wither. If I only had the courage to open my heart and act on it.

Love. You grew it through adventures and smiles, eye rolls and sarcasm, through running from soldiers and listening to each other's heartbeats. Love was something I could choose.

And whatever the hardship, whatever the circumstance, whatever the thing I was chasing . . . I was going to choose it for the rest of my life.

Starting now.

Taking a deep breath, I squared my shoulders and turned to my aunt. "Aunt Beth, will you please chaperone me? I have a ball to attend."

CHAPTER 32

BRIGHT CANDLELIGHT ILLUMINATED EVERY CORNER OF THE LARGE
ballroom. Unlike the last ball Hawthorne had hosted, this one
wasn't dull, stifling, and boisterous. Or perhaps it was those things,
but unlike then, I didn't mind it.

"Lady Beth." Lord Wycliffe appeared in front of me and Aunt
Beth, a question in his eyes. He bowed. "Lady Alicia, I was under
the impression you'd left the country."

"Did your brother tell you that?"

"Indeed."

"Where is he?"

Instead of asking how I'd known Matthew would be here, Peter
tipped his head toward the balcony. "Where else?"

My eyes travelled upward. There he was, reading a book, just as
he had been the night we'd met.

Aunt Beth's eyes cast me a meaningful look, ready to witness the
spectacle that was about to unfold. "Will you be long?"

"Yes," I said, already walking away and leaving Aunt Beth to
converse with Lord Wycliffe. "Yes, I will."

1

"Good evening, Matthew."

He didn't turn, but he stiffened, letting me know he recognized my voice. I smiled.

"I know you heard me, so it is no use trying to ignore me this time."

He snapped his book shut and straightened, still looking forward, blinking rapidly.

I neared until we were almost touching, then folded my arms and reclined against the coiled cast-iron railing, relishing the way his eyes darted toward me once, before immediately snapping away. Twice. Now that I knew he got nervous around me, it was easy to spot. How had I never noticed it before? It was evident in every taut muscle, every contour of his expression.

"Are you surprised to see me?"

"No," he said, a little too quickly. He cleared his throat. "No, naturally I knew you would come."

My grin widened, tone turning taunting when I said, "*Did* you?"

His gaze cut to me, a spark of alarm in it. His lips parted and moved infinitesimally, as if sifting through his responses in search of one he approved of. At last, he settled on, "Where is your husband?"

I glanced down at Henry's ring on my finger, realizing I'd forgotten to take it off, and Matthew had noticed it. Of course he would—he noticed everything. But maybe it wouldn't hurt to tease him, a little. He had *lied* to me, after all.

I shrugged. "He's decided against India, and is at home waiting for me. Let him wait. But I am glad to see you, Matthew. How I have missed you since yesterday." I leaned forward and thumbed over his cravat, tied in a meticulous, orderly way. Just like him. He swallowed, inching back at the contact. "Oh, and I plan to drop by your house in the future," I went on. "Every day, in fact, since I am actually in love with you. Bother, why did I even marry Mr. Crawley in the first place?"

"Please stop, Alicia," Matthew said quietly, looking me dead in the eyes.

"Stop what?"

"Stop getting so close to me. Stop blathering things you do not mean. Stop showing up everywhere I turn and making me question everything I know."

The soft, serious way he was staring at me made me falter and lower my hands.

"Why are you here?"

I knocked my chin up. "I'm here for a dance. That is, after all, what people do at balls, Mr. Wycliffe. They don't read or sit gloomily in a corner—they dance."

"I'm not in a corner." Matthew's mouth shut firmly, realizing a beat too late that he should've protested the "gloomy" bit instead. Which meant he *was* miserable.

How utterly wonderful.

"I came up here to inquire if *you'd* like to dance with me."

His eyes slanted up and roamed my face. He wanted to say yes. But he backed away and said, "No," before walking down the balcony.

Well, he wasn't getting away that easy. I spurted after him, catching up in a few moments. "You paid Graham off."

Matthew halted, frame going rigid.

I halted too. "Graham blackmailed me and you paid him *thirty thousand* pounds."

When he swiveled back, his expression was carefully blank.

"You didn't tell another soul—made Graham promise he would demand only a small sum from me so I would believe he was satisfied, while you handed him a fortune in secret."

Matthew didn't say anything, but I could tell by the muscle that jumped in his jaw that I had hit the mark. The little white lies he was so fond of only hid so much. Faced with a direct accusation, he was defenseless. If what I claimed had been false, he would've scoffed and put his quick tongue to action, but instead he stayed silent, unable to deny it and unwilling to acknowledge the truth.

"You made Graham promise to give me the letter. Swore him to secrecy. Wanted me to leave for India never knowing what you'd done—"

"Yes," Matthew said, surprising me. "Yes, I did. What of it?"

What of it? That's what he had to say for himself? He was acting like I'd just accused him of playing cards with the man, and not of paying him an *enormous* amount of blackmail money. *My* blackmail money. "If Henry's birth was brought to society's attention, he would be barred from marrying me. And you knew it. I used you terribly, yet you still chose to help me."

"Deuces, yes. Now go be with him already."

"Why did you do it?"

"I was feeling generous."

"No—why?"

"So you would finally leave me alone—though that plan seems to be failing."

"*Why?*"

"Oh, by all England, I don't have to sit here and listen to this tripe!" He stormed away.

I trailed close behind, undeterred. Tonight, even if it meant kissing him in the middle of the ballroom floor, I would get the truth—the *whole* truth—out of Matthew Wycliffe. I would make him say it if it killed him.

"I will not be put off," I said, tromping down the stairs behind him.

He turned to the side but didn't glance back. When he reached the landing, a thick group of ball-goers passed in front of him, forcing him to stay in place a moment. I halted on the step above him, studying the back of his head, then leaned forward and whispered in his ear. "I have your book."

He spun around so quickly he lost his footing and knocked into me, sending us both plummeting to the stairway. I sucked in a breath. Sharp edges dug into my back, promises of future bruises. But they weren't what I focused on. I focused on the sudden closeness of Matthew's face, his worried eyes as he assessed whether I was hurt.

He must've decided I was unharmed because he shortly scowled, remembering why he'd lost his balance in the first place. "You larcenous vixen. You—!" Noting the people who turned toward us at the outburst, he jumped to his feet and lowered his voice to a shouting whisper. "You stole my book? Deuces, I've been hunting all over for it. I should've *known* you had it—"

I accepted his proffered hand and stood, brushing out my skirts. "Don't go pinning it all on me—you're the one who dropped it on the beach! But if you ever want it back, you will have to dance with me, Mr. Wycliffe."

His eyes narrowed. "Again you are blackmailing me into serving your ends?"

"Indeed." I lifted my chin higher. "And might I say, you're terrible at meeting my demands, considering how much practice you've had."

He growled. "Fine! Fine, if that is all you want, blast it all, I will dance with you. And then you will return my book and *never* visit my house again. Understood?"

"Fine," I said innocently, sidling up to him and taking his arm.

His stare magnetized to my hand, already looking like he regretted his decision. The climax and applause of a finished set distracted him long enough for me to steer him toward the middle of the ballroom floor.

As we waited for the music, he avoided making eye contact like I was some kind of demon. He looked every bit like sheer dignity was the only thing keeping him from bolting from the room. That, and his fierce hatred of running.

Other couples lined up next to us, trapping us. A flute played the intro as the line of men bowed and the women curtsied.

Neither Matthew nor I moved. As one, we stepped forward and met in the middle. We didn't touch, but I felt that familiar energy spark between us—half attraction, half challenge.

"I can't believe you took my book," he said at last. "You're always stealing things from me, it seems. My book, my sanity, my will to go on . . ."

"For the last time, I did not steal it! It had fallen in the sand and I merely retrieved it. You are most welcome." I didn't add that I *would've* stolen it, if given the chance. "But it hardly matters. Because I saw what you wrote."

His mouth dropped open. Actually dropped. A delicious blush crept over his cheeks, growing redder by the second. "You . . . You mean to say you've *read* it?"

"Cover to cover—to *back* cover, I might add—and," my voice lowered to an intense whisper, punctuating every word, "what a cold-shouldered, two-faced liar you are." Partners clapped off each other's palms and spun around. I followed suit, pushing Matthew much harder than necessary. "I'm predictable? Ha! You could scarce keep up with me, and that scared the life out of you. So much so that in order to slow me down, to make me second-guess myself, to cover the fact that you were frightened and flustered and completely at my mercy, you told me I was predictable?" I gave up all pretense of dancing and put my hands on my hips. "Ohhh, how *rich*!"

"Fine!" Released from the dance, he gripped his hair. "Since you wish me to say it, then yes! I lied to you. You scared the life out of me. And a pity it didn't kill me, because upon my word, death would've been less torturous."

A few stares wandered over to us, the only couple not in motion, but I ignored them, poking Matthew in the chest. "That day I came to your house, when I asked you for a fortune, you told me no man was worth thirty thousand pounds. Yet you give it to a terrorizing cad like Graham? Now you are a liar on two counts!"

"I never lied."

"Yes, you did! You are a cold-shouldered, two-faced liar!" The couples nearest to us halted, heads turning toward the scandal-ridden lady who was yelling at the most influential man in the *ton*. Whispers circulated around the room, accompanying the music like its own vicious song.

Matthew took my shoulders and gave them a little shake. "By all England, Alicia, I did say that—but I never lied. On my honor, I didn't. Not about that."

I folded my arms, waiting for his explanation. More heads turned our way, more ears listened in on our conversation—but it didn't matter.

Matthew sighed, softly, casting his head down. "No man is worth thirty thousand pounds," he went on, quieter. "But . . . a woman can be." He swallowed and looked up, a defeated gleam in his eyes. "A certain woman *is*."

There it was. The full truth, so long eluded, laid bare in front of me. Warm tingles travelled down my spine and spread to my toes, to the tips of my fingers, wrapping me in a cocoon of happiness.

He let go of me and backed away. One step, two. "Do you have any idea what it's like to help the person you're in love with become engaged to someone else? To have them at your fingertips, but know it's all a sham? For even a moment, can you fathom it?"

He blinked, gaze hard, lips tight. "I gave Graham the money, because even though I saw this ruinous end coming, I couldn't help but fall in love with you anyway. I did it, because from the first moment I saw you, I knew you'd wreak chaos in my life and I'm a stupid fool who craves that. I did it, because even though ensuring you married Henry meant being stripped of my heart's desire . . . it is enough to know that at least you have yours."

Oh, Matthew.

"There," he muttered, all of the pride that had held him upright missing from his frame, from his usually commanding voice. Unable to meet my eye any longer, he cast his head down again, looking like he hadn't a hope in the world; like he'd bury himself in his library and never come out again. "You have the truth, stolen from my lips like the pathetic sap that I am. Now please—by the devil, woman —" he shook his head, "—*please* leave me in peace. You have tormented me long enough, and heaven knows you will continue to do so long after you've gone."

Violins squeaked and stuttered to a stop, finally giving up all pretense of playing. The whispers rose to a low murmur and the last of the couples slowed until the entire room stood still, holding its breath to see what scandal I would cause next.

"My heart's desire . . ." I took on a confused, thoughtful expression, enjoying Matthew's agony but deciding to put him out of it. "But Mr. Wycliffe. How odd that you think it is Henry, when I have not married him. I broke off our engagement this morning."

Time seemed to pluck Matthew out of this moment, rendering him immobile while people all around us shifted and craned their necks to get a better view. At last, slowly, without moving his head, Matthew raised his eyes.

"And how could you ever doubt I would, sir?" I sauntered forward until we were toe to toe and I had to crane my neck to look up at him. "You *know* I am madly in love with you."

He blinked at me, serious. Then, a tiny half-smile pulled on one corner of his lips. The tiniest sliver of hope. ". . . As I am with you," he whispered.

Slipping my arms around his neck, I pulled him closer. This time—for the first time—he didn't resist. "You vowed the day I knew the contents of your book, you would marry me. Well, Mr. Wycliffe? Are you a man of your word, or aren't you?"

He took a deep breath and it lodged inside him as he glanced between my eyes. Then it rushed out all at once and his hands wrapped around my waist before sliding up to my hair and bringing my lips to his. When they met, I was whisked back to our kiss on the beach, perfect in its uniqueness, magical in its rightness, feeling every horror we'd gone through with every movement of his lips, feeling the power that came with overcoming them. Together.

I suppose that meant yes.

Because I was breathless when we broke apart, I first mistook the gasps of shock rippling around the room as my own. A ring of spectators surrounded us with dropped jaws and wide eyes.

After glancing around, I smiled up at Matthew, content to stay in his arms. "Matthew Wycliffe, that was the absolute stupidest thing you've ever done."

He chuckled—actually chuckled, blinding me with his wonderful, glorious smile. "I know," he said. He leaned in closer, touching his nose to mine. "And I am going to do it again."

Our lips met again, and the first kiss was nothing compared to this one.

Then Matthew swept me up into his arms, eliciting another round of outbursts from the onlookers. Fans either beat in a nervous frenzy or clattered to the floor. The only people who weren't conveying complete astonishment were Aunt Beth, who smirked at me from the refreshment table, and Lord Wycliffe, who sighed and shook his head even as the corner of his lips curved up.

I threw my head back and laughed as Matthew carried me out of the ballroom, into his dark carriage, down a moonlit country road, and then up to the pastor's door, banging on it until the man woke up.

What great scandal we had caused. What rumors and looks of shock. What a long time it would be before people stopped wagging their tongues with looks of disdain upon their faces, relaying to their children, their parents, their distant relations and acquaintances just how utterly brazen and eccentric the pair of us were, kissing in the middle of the ballroom floor. How mortified all of society would be when they woke the next morning to find us married.

And for the first time—how little I cared.

EPILOGUE

"It is your move."

"Shhh."

I puffed a lock of hair away from my face, annoyed that Matthew could take ten whole minutes to move a single piece. He wouldn't admit it, but he was being more careful than usual with his decisions, trying to ensure I wouldn't beat him a second time.

Morning light bathed the library, transforming it into a fairy-tale haven. With his rumpled hair, rosy cheeks, and loose shirt, Matthew looked the opposite of a prince, but I didn't mind. In fact, I thought his casual dress made him even handsomer, as impossible as that seemed. It made it easier to see who he was underneath. And I was looking forward to seeing him like that for the rest of my life.

"Perhaps we should set a time limit," I suggested.

"Shhh."

My lips trumpeted. "This is no fun at all. Maybe we should try something more exciting—like exploring a secret passageway. Or perhaps we can convince some soldiers to let us shoot at them."

"It is only ten in the morning," Matthew said, as though the hour were the only objectionable thing about either of those pastimes. He studied the board closer, muttering, "Perhaps I should use my pawn . . ."

"I've been telling you all this time that you should, but you never listen to me."

"Just as you don't listen to me."

I inspected my fingernails. "Rather rude of us both. Now that we're married, it won't do at all for us to go around not listening to each other."

"Unless I am reading—in which case it is rude for you to expect to be listened to." Matthew's fingers hovered over one of his bishops, before deciding against it and retreating.

I cocked one brow. "Afraid I shall defeat you again?"

One corner of Matthew's lips lifted, an acknowledgement that though he didn't think I'd win, he wouldn't mind all that terribly if I did. The sound of the front door opening was followed by the clamor of shouting and joyous cries and shrieking children.

Matthew's mouth curved further up. "It appears my family has finally heard the news."

Eliza's offended voice grew louder, saying something about how she was going to kill Matthew for getting married without her. Sir William's voice chuckled behind her, while Lily and Peter offered clever commentary and guesses as to where we were and what we were doing.

And I laughed. It felt good to have found my place in my family, to have my father and aunt stand as witnesses for my wedding even though it had occurred in the middle of the night. And just when I thought I couldn't be happier, I realized that I now had *two* families I belonged to. I wasn't just a Kendall anymore.

I was a Wycliffe.

We only had a few moments before they burst into the library and ate up the rest of our solitude for the day, and probably the rest of our lives. Somehow, I didn't mind. At last, Matthew moved his queen.

"You know," I said, giving Matthew my most thoughtful look, "now that we are married and I am your wife, I am not afraid to tell you . . ." My grin broke out as I plunked my knight into a checkmate position. I glanced up. "I do believe this house is too small."

Matthew's almost-smile dropped, and he blinked into a glare. "Deuces, woman."

THE END

AUTHOR'S NOTE

While true that military maneuvers were popular on the Old Steine and the Downs at Brighton during the summer, *and* that it was thrilling entertainment for local residents, I never found any research to support that there were organized tournaments, much less that they were held annually. "The Brighton Games" was something I invented as a way to forward the plot and develop the characters.

ACKNOWLEDGMENTS

You'd think by the third book I would've gotten used to this whole "writing" thing, but nope. NOOOOOPE. I don't know how I survived writing this book. Lot of bubblegum. Lot of Pringles. Someone please hook me up to a ventilator.

Alicia was such a challenging POV character to write. It took me a long time to figure her out, and even longer to soften her up a little. I admit, I was worried about how this book would be received, since it's more "out there" than my others—intentionally so. But, in the end, I decided that my job as an author is chiefly to *entertain*, so why change the story to be less entertaining?

As with the others, I've learned so many new things while writing this book. And there are so many people I want to thank.

First, I want to thank God. He knows what for.

I want to thank Matthew Wycliffe for being a consistent, soft-hearted jerk. Unlike *all* my other protagonists, I never had to rethink his character. I always knew what he would say/do in any given situation, and that's made writing him a dream come true.

Next, I want to thank all my die-hard fans out there. (How are there so many of you? I'm still blown away.) You guys have been the

BEST cheerleaders, and I hope this book was everything you dreamed it would be. I'm so thankful to all of you for following me on this journey. It's been a great one. I hope you'll follow me on the next one!

Thank you to all my beta readers. I'd like to specifically mention Mary-Celeste Lewis, Camille Peters, and of course, the one and only Chrissy Cornwell (thebomb.com). You guys made this story really shine.

Thank you to my always-enthusiastic brainstorming partner, Alayna. How the heck are you so good at it? I need your brain. Actually no, because then we would have no reason to come up with *brilliant* ideas like bigfoot, bathtubs, big ben, and statues. See you soon, in a slanted London. ;)

I also want to thank my sisters here. They've been so supportive from the beginning. Karen, Michele, Angela, Stephanie, Shannon, Kjerstin, Allison, Sydney, and Kacey. I love each one of you.

And last but not least . . . we come, yet again, to Daniel.

Oh, Daniel. Daniel, Daniel, Daniel.

So. You've finally read one of my books, eh? You read *A Lily in Disguise*, did you? To the very *end*? Well it certainly TOOK YOU LONG ENOUGH. Why did you put it off? Why aren't you screaming your love for it from the rooftops? Why am I pretending to be offended right now? All mysteries.

As a reward for finishing my series (if you ever make it this far, which part of me affectionately doubts), I want you to go and check my pink box. You know the one. There's a surprise waiting for you. Even if it takes you a hundred years, it will still be there. I hope you find it. I hope you love it.

You're the main reason I believe in love. In friendship. These books will always be written on my heart, but you were there first. Thanks, Danny, for scooting over and making room.

ABOUT THE AUTHOR

Jessica Scarlett grew up in rural Utah, where lots of wide-open space served as a blank canvas for her rampant imagination. Along with being an author, she is a songwriter and a huge Broadway fan, so don't be surprised if she hears the people sing or defies gravity on a regular basis.

Being mother to three crazy-eyed kiddos, she has been forced to develop a deep appreciation for humor—which is probably why she laughs so much at her own jokes. Though Jessica currently writes regency romance, she loves dashing heroes from all eras in history, and hopes to one day branch out.

Connect with Jessica on social media!

Printed in Great Britain
by Amazon

38181797R00189